# Disorderly Notions

# *Disorderly* Notions

## Tom Darby

**IGUANA**

Copyright © 2011 Tom Darby
Published by Iguana Books
720 Bathurst Street, Suite 303
Toronto, Ontario, Canada
M5V 2R4

All rights reserved. No part of this publication may be reproduced, stored in a retrieval system or transmitted, in any form or by any means, electronic, mechanical, recording or otherwise (except brief passages for purposes of review) without the prior permission of the author or a licence from The Canadian Copyright Licensing Agency (Access Copyright). For an Access Copyright licence, visit www.accesscopyright.ca or call toll free to 1-800-893-5777.

Publisher: Greg Ioannou
Editors: Meghan Behse; Greg Ioannou
Front cover image: Patrick Darby
Front cover design: Lea Kaplan
Book layout design: Sharlene Hopwood, Meghan Behse
Author photo: Chris Wightman

Library and Archives Canada Cataloguing in Publication

Darby, Tom
    Disorderly notions / Tom Darby.

Also issued in electronic format.
ISBN 978-0-9878267-7-0

    I. Title.

PS8607.A67D58 2011        C813'.6        C2011-908043-5

This is the second print edition of *Disorderly Notions*.

# Praise for *Disorderly Notions*

"Disorderly Notions' backstories, tributaries of individual and collective history, flow together across time and space to create a crescendo of significance.... You cannot help but be caught up in a cataract of characters, circumstances, events and ideas. You suddenly find yourself swept into a new sea of meaning, surprised and delighted at the new horizons and new perspectives Darby's tale has provided. I found myself comparing Disorderly Notions to magic-realist novels like Gabriel Garcia Marquez's masterpiece One Hundred Years of Solitude, or Jorge Luis Borges' short story The Garden of Forking Paths, with their shifting time frames and non-linear stories.... Darby's book is earthy, funny, violent and, occasionally, both profane and politically incorrect.... [The novel's tragedy] provides the book's theme: Our need to confront our pasts, to follow the rivers of our lives to their source, if we are to achieve any redemption in this life. Such a theme gives Hamilton's final revelations a resonance that will reverberate with the reader for a long time."

– Robert Sibley, *Ottawa Citizen*

"'Progress' is the buzzword of our time, which suggests our society reflects the kind of ideas explained by philosophers such as Kant, Hegel and Nietzsche. Anyone wondering what 'progress' entails, but does not wish to wade through these thinkers, will benefit from Tom Darby's very funny novel, *Disorderly Notions*."

– John von Heyking, *Cardus*

"*Disorderly Notions* is provocative, enlightening, sad, funny, and most of all philosophical. It is both the Odyssey and Don Quixote wrapped up and served together as one. I urge you treat yourself to this brilliant saga novel."

– Joseph Khoury, Department of English, St. Francis Xavier University

# Acknowledgements and Declarations

Most of the places that serve as the stages for the surface narrative I visited during the nineteen eighties, thus giving me first-hand familiarity with what these countries were like during that decade. This part of the book is a weave of threads from my actual notes, memories and imagination. The one exception is Tibet, which I did not visit. For this part of that fabric I am indebted to Heinrich Harrer's classic, *Seven Years in Tibet*; "Tibet's Hidden Kingdom," a video documentary produced by *National Geographic* in 2008; and, wouldn't you know it, the Internet. All of it, like the rest, is pure fiction, except, of course, historical characters such as Judah P. Benjamin, and these have been subjected to distortion wrought by my imagination. I should add that "Dikshit" really is an old and noble Brahman name. If any of these characters resemble any actual person or people, it is by the rarest of accidents and would be altogether unknown to me.

Many of the places pertaining to the internal narrative I visited much more recently than the nineteen eighties. I have been to Belize twice to investigate the Confederate colony that once existed there. Were he still alive, I would make sure that Mister C.S. Mason read this acknowledgment. I met him, quite by accident, at his house across the road from the cemetery of the Confederate colony of "Forest Home," located in a jungle clearing near the town of Punta Gorda, Belize. Mister Mason provided me with all the historic records relating to the colony, and these records are what gave birth to my internal story.

When my father, William Thomas Darby, Esq. died, among his many files was one pertaining to a particularly gruesome ax murder case he tried in Toombs County, Georgia, during the late nineteen thirties when he was a young criminal lawyer in Vidalia, Georgia. This murder, unlike the one in this novel, was committed by a white man whose victim was also a white man. Here I am grateful to these serendipitous ways of fortune that allowed me to attain these facts so as to distort them in the service of fiction.

I am also indebted to the National Archives in Washington, D.C., for access to the correspondence of Judah P. Benjamin. And I acknowledge two biographies: Robert D. Meade's *Judah P. Benjamin: Confederate Statesman*, published in 1943, and Pierce Butler's *Judah P. Benjamin*, published in 1906, both of which were invaluable to me, especially the latter one. Because this older book was closer in real-time to the events in the biography, the idiom in which it was written rang true to my ears and I did my best to capture it. I am also grateful for the reported true story of Benjamin's escape from America, and while I borrowed liberally from this book, I also distorted liberally. Most of this part of the story is grounded in the "facts" associated with these events, but practically none of the following two chapters are remotely associated with known events pertaining to Benjamin's real history. Despite the title of the third narrative, this is neither history nor biography. It is fiction; pure and simple. But because this story is about Benjamin's "secret history," well, who knows? It could have happened an infinite number of ways.

I would like to state that Kobu Abe's novel, *Box Man*, set fire to my imagination. Also, I have made much use of Alexander Bogdanov's science fiction: "Red Star," "Engineer Menni" and "A Martian Stranded on Earth," which I read under the single cover of *Red Star: The First Bolshevik Utopia*, edited by Loren Graham and Richard Stites, translated by Charles Rougle and published by the University of Indiana Press, Bloomington, Indiana, in 1984. I also am indebted to the essay written by Professor Loren Graham, entitled "Bogdanov's Inner Message," published under the same cover.

I hereby declare that I am aware that what is now the main and historic campus of Mercer University did not appear in Macon, Georgia, until it was moved there in 1871. Also, I know that the École Boulle – Lycée Technique in Paris was established in 1886, well after the date that it appears as a prop "borrowed from the future" and placed on the stage, thereby allowing the concocted dramatic action to occur. I am aware that the two court cases tried by Mister Benjamin that influenced the evolution of the political, legal and cultural future of Canada took place a short time after they appeared in this book. In all these instances, I have granted myself poetic license.

I am grateful to Greg Ioannou for his long-lasting and resolute encouragement, and to my skillful, insightful, energetic and dauntless editor, Meghan Behse. I also should thank my copy editors, Lisa Sparks and Stacy Plowright, whose keen eyes have well served this book. And I thank Sharlene Hopwood for formatting the edited manuscript.

It is imperative that I recognize Francis Itani, my mentor. I doubt that this book would be published were it not for what Francis has taught me. I thank my family, especially my son Patrick, a photographer by vocation and profession, who just happened to have the right image on hand to serve as the cover of this book. Special thanks also to my wife, Kay Darby, who has endured and continues to endure my unending stream of curses directed at my computer.

Finally, I wish to pay homage to circumstance and coincidence – specifically my own circumstances of being a son of the True South and to the coincidence of my having become a man of the True North. Whatever truth there may be, so it seems to me, is about this relation – the limits of circumstance and the possibilities of coincidence.

Tom Darby,

Ottawa, November, 2011

# Map of Altamaha

- OCONEE
- OCMULGEE
- SWAMP
- MACON ROAD
- EAST PARK (NIGGER TOWN)
- BENJAMIN ESTATES
- KIM STILL
- SAW MILL & MAX'S
- TOBACCO WHSES
- DEPOT
- HOTEL
- SOUTH SEA BOARD ST.
- COOT'S STORE
- BUD'S THEATRE
- MALACHAI ST.
- PIGGLY WIGGLY
- BENJAMIN BANK
- COURTHOUSE
- FAIR GROUNDS
- FARMERS MUTUAL EXCHANGE
- BENJAMIN HOUSE
- PINE BLUFF CEMETERY † † †
- N.F.W.
- SAVANNAH ROAD
- ALTAMAHA R.
- AFRICAN BAPTIST CHURCH
- SCOUT HKT
- BRUNSWICK

# Genealogy of the Benjamin Family
## Beginning with Jospeh M. Benjamin

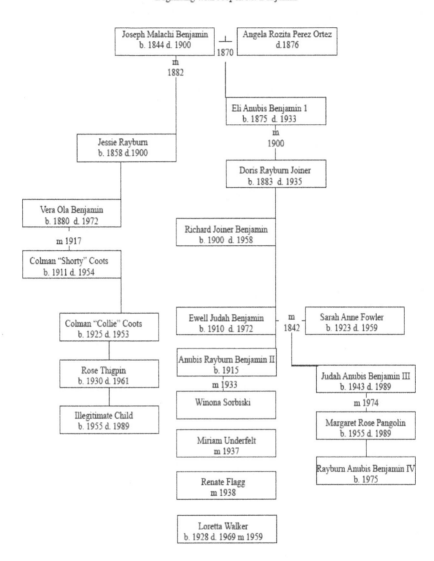

# Genealogy of the Benjamin Family Cont'd
Beginning with Judah P. Benjamin

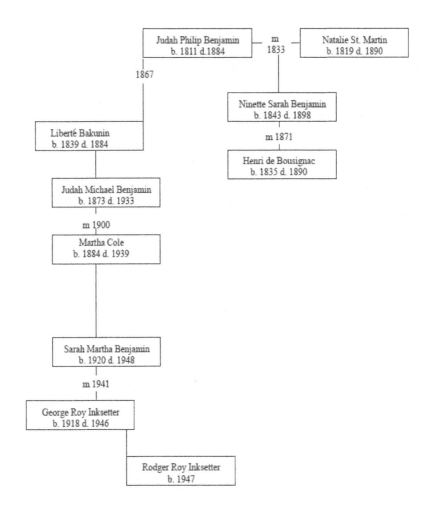

To Kay

as promised

"A world of disorderly notions pick'd
out of his books ..."

DON QUIXOTE

OFFICE OF THE DEAN OF ARTS
(416) 723-1232  FAX (416) 723-9434
FAX TRANSMITTAL RECORD 8776     (PRIVATE AND CONFIDENTIAL)
DATE: Sept.11, 1989
TO: Philip Goodman, Chair, Philosophy
FROM: I.B. Bland, Dean, Faculty of Arts
RE: The West problem

MESSAGE:
   As indicated on the telephone, your 'humane scheme' has backfired. I am sending over the evidence and when you read it, you will see for yourself. Fair enough, you assured me Professor West would meet our requirement and produce something if we granted him the early sabbatical and provided him with the $6,500 for his expenses. About this much, you were correct. But what he has produced is this scurrilous document, detailing how he has spent his time and our money. He is his own main character and refers to himself in the third person. Only the mad and God do that! Frankly, I am not surprised by anything I have read in the manuscript. West has incriminated himself!
   This morning I spent an hour talking to the owner of the janitorial service that cleans the campus at night, then another hour talking to their lawyers who are suing us. Yes, it is true, West actually was living in his office, and now I have learned that the night cleaning staff he invited to his 'party' and got inebriated are mentally challenged.
   Along with West's damning manuscript, I have included the following items that I catalogued after we spoke yesterday:
   1) the correspondence concerning complaints from colleagues about West's unprofessional behavior and also those letters that document what he said and did at that conference;
   2) protests from both the Soviet and American embassies;
   3) the correspondence concerning the sexual harassment charge against West and letters of protest from the Women's Center about his comments in class;
   4) statements documenting that West was behind the 'chicken incident';
   5) photocopies of three insulting postcards; and
   6) the correspondence between us concerning <u>Hamilton West</u>, which provides ample evidence that, from the beginning, I was opposed to your so-called 'humane scheme'.
   I hereby give you notice that I have begun negotiations for West's dismissal and that he will be hearing from our attorney. Since classes begin tomorrow, I have signed a one-year contract with Mr. Ringer to do his lectures.

And by the way, yes, I too have read in the papers about this other person who has come up with this 'end of history' idea - some American with a Japanese name, I think - but this does not make West look anymore sane. All of this is nonsense. Do you know the latest news? Hungary is in revolt. There is an exodus going on and the Russians are just standing by and doing nothing.

You will find West's manuscript in the same old metal box as we received it. As we have no need for the box, or the original manuscript, perhaps you will have better luck contacting him and will see that he receives this. The address is:

   c/o Mr. Durden Fowler, Esq.
   Attorney at Law
   Box 09 Altamaha, Georgia, 30317
   U.S.A.

SIGNATURE:


Fax 8776 - 09 - 89 followed by official letters to Chair, Philosophy; V.P. Academic; the Chancellor; Chair, Board of Governors

## *DEPARTURE*

*West* (1989)

As the train pulled into the station, Hamilton was awakened by a dream – the dream that always woke him. He and Jud were duck hunting on the beach at sun-up, and there they saw the dead Indian baby being picked over by buzzards. Hamilton rose from the bench, pulled up his sleeve and looked at his watch. It was an old but good one. Once it had belonged to his father. And then he remembered his father lying on his back in the muck behind the barn – his eyes looking into the blue of the prairie sky. Hamilton had wondered how it would be for your heart to burst. The watch was round – a throwback to a time when people lived by the rhythms of the seasons or by the cycles of nature: birth, life, and death. The hands had stopped. Hamilton took the watch from his wrist, wound and shook it. Then he placed it to his ear. Yes, it had stopped. Dead.

"Come on, Hambone. Get on the train," the old man shouted.

Hamilton snapped from his reverie and, with his blue bag, charged up the steps and into the car. The train jerked. Hamilton stepped, stumbled and fell, muttering "Damn!" as he plopped down on the seat inside the compartment. The train jerked again, moved a few feet and stopped.

"Gotta step back before you leap. That's what ole Nietzsche says."

"Leap my ass! That was a stagger if ever I saw one. And I oughta know, 'cause I've staggered plenty in my day. Remember who you with and quit quoting fascists. Don't want anybody to think I share any of your reactionary opinions, Hambone."

The name Hambone was short for Hamilton – Hamilton Fowler West. His mother had always called him Hammy and his father's name for him had been Ham. Years ago, when he played goalie for the University of Toronto Varsity Blues, he had been known as Red Rider. The adjective was a reference not to his politics, but to his rusty hair. He kept this name, but only for what lately had become one of the less reliable parts of his anatomy.

"Names, names," Hamilton West always said. "To name it is to master it. With names worlds are created."

To some he was known as Dr. H.F. West, Professor of Philosophy, though some would prefer that "erstwhile" go before his title. But the nickname

Disorderly Notions

"Hambone" Hamilton had happily accepted during one of the many summers when he took the train with his mother from Cumberland House, Saskatchewan, to Altamaha, a small town in southern Georgia and the home of his mother's family, the Fowlers. It had been his cousin by marriage, Jud Benjamin, who, with boyhood affection, had anointed him with what he called Hamilton's Georgia name. Despite the disparate and often curious personal histories of Hamilton West and Jud Benjamin, their lives – time and again – meandered together like the waters of two converging streams running into the sea, only to eventually return back to the place from which they began so they can converge once again.

As far as Hamilton West was concerned, people could call him what they damn well pleased. He knew who he was, where he had come from and where he was going. To himself, he was just Hamilton West, who, like his cousin Jud, had originated from a little place in the hinterland of the American Empire. Af-ter a twenty-year stopover in Toronto, he was off to Asia. Hamilton looked at his reflection in the window, took the ends of his mustache between his fingers and gave them a twirl.

The man who was sitting across from Hamilton was Jud Benjamin's uncle, and although Hamilton bore no blood relation to him, he often addressed the older man as did his cousin: "Uncle Andy." This just seemed right. Hamilton's memory of the man went back to a time he will never forget. It was a night in 1954, when Hamilton was six; a night when Uncle Andy and his actual blood-related uncle, Durden Fowler, had taken him and Jud to a baseball game. Most people referred to Uncle Andy as Andy Ray, or just Andy – both names being short for his real name, Anubis Rayburn or, in full, Anubis Rayburn Benjamin II. Andy at one time was as tall as Hamilton, but with the settling of his old bones he was shrinking. Yet he remained large, if a bit on the thin side. Andy was not eating as he should, preferring drink instead, and still many remarked on his stamina and resiliency. As Andy said about himself, in his long stagger through life, he had "seen everything but the air and been everywhere 'cept the 'lectric chair." Well, everywhere except the electric chair and Asia. Andy made Hamilton think of a scruffy old rooster.

On the other side of his reflection, Hamilton looked at the dark morning. There was a light over the sign locating the station as "Rye," a medieval town on the southeast coast of England once famous for seafaring, pirates and smugglers. At the dim edge of the light were Jud and Rodger Inksetter, a distant relative of Jud and Andy's. Jud and Rodger both were leaning on Rodger's green Rover – Jud's eyes smiling and Rodger, as usual, grinning. They both waved. Hamilton held up two fingers, making the "V" for "victory" sign, and then he stuck up his middle finger and shot them a "bird," at least that was what he and Jud had always called the rude sign when they were boys.

"You know, Hambone, they think we're nuts."

"Yeah, I know. But they secretly like it because it's different ... different for two guys like us to be wandering off to the Orient. You won't be sorry you decided to come. Hell of a lot more fun than boring old England. Nothing happening here."

"And I just gotta tell you this, Hambone. You ain't like you used to be. Don't know why, but you acting as happy as a dog with two dicks. Don't know what's gotten into you, boy. Why, I wouldn'a gone to the outhouse with you before. Nope, don't know what's got into you, but whatever it is, hope it don't go away."

Hamilton turned away from the window and grinned. Then he slumped in his chair and closed his eyes. His tongue tasted as if it had been soaking in Scotch. Well, it was the day after Christmas. He thought about the night before. My God, that was only three hours ago! He tried to doze, but Rodger's words came back to him.

"You blokes, you're daffy! Bet me knickers you won't make it 'til spring. And, I'll put fifty quid on that," Rodger said.

"Well, I'll put two hundred Yankee bucks on it. I'll bet you'll be back before the first rose blooms!" Jud quipped.

Then Andy wandered into Hamilton's dozy memory, craning his skinny neck, pushing his glasses up on his nose, looking over at Hamilton and winking. And Hamilton heard himself say, "You're on, Jud. We'll go two hundred. It's a bet." And the four of them raised and clinked their glasses, sealing the bet as to whether Hamilton Fowler West and Anubis Rayburn Benjamin II would actually make it to Asia and not return until spring.

This is how it had been mere hours before, when Hamilton and Andy sat with Jud in Rodger Inksetter's house polishing off their second bottle of Johnnie Walker Black Label: Rodger had been leaning against the edge of an old dining table stacked high with finished and unfinished canvases. Andy and Hamilton were engulfed in green wingback chairs on either side of the gas fireplace, Jud's tall frame etched by flickers of the flame, his arm resting on the mantel, his slight backside warming. The first dead soldier of Johnnie Walker was sitting at his elbow.

The studio, as usual, was chaos: painted and half-painted canvas, squeezed and twisted paint tubes, books, newspapers, bottles, glasses and cups. In the clutter, only three furnishings stood out. First there was a great hoot owl, stuffed and preserved under a glass bell jar. It sat alone on the marble top of a side table of Eastlake Style. On the wall behind it, hanging in a gilded frame, was a scarlet silk map of the eastern half of North America. Both of these things – the owl and the map – had been inherited from ancestors. The third item distinguishable among the clutter was a painting hanging above the mantel – a large canvas with a mere strip of dark molding around its stretcher. In the foreground of the painting one could see a nude with her back to the room. Waves of dark, silky hair spilled to her elbow, partially covering her arm and her hand cradling her head. Although her face was not visible, one could tell that she was looking into the background at a painter busy at his easel. In one hand the painter held his palette and a cluster of brushes, and with the other he applied paint to his canvas, which was turned just enough so that the viewer could tell that he was painting the reverse of what was seen by both his subject and the viewer of the painting. The painter wore bloomer-like breeches, tights and a tunic – the fashion in the Netherlands during the seventeenth century. Under a floppy, black velvet hat, the face, framed by a bobbed haircut, belonged to Rodger – a younger Rodger grinning mischievously at his reclining model.

Unsteadily, Jud shifted his weight, removed his elbow from the mantel and faced Hamilton.

"Listen, Hambone. A message from Anubis – Anubis III: 'You went to the verge, you say, and came back safely? / Some have not been so fortunate – some have fallen.'"

"That yours?" Andy asks Jud.

"Nah. How I wish. Stole it from Conrad Aiken," Jud told him, tossing down the last swallow of Scotch from his glass.

"So, Hambone," Jud said to Hamilton, "since you and Uncle Andy insist on buggering off to Asia, Rodger and I have something for you ... to take along."

"Indeed," Rodger laughed, "we come from the West bearing gifts."

"And may your house be blessed, oh Magi," Jud added.

"You two are full of it!" Andy scoffed, laughing.

"Here," Rodger said, producing two boxes of the same size, both wrapped in slightly wrinkled gold, green and red paper depicting, over and over, a nativity scene. "Open mine now."

And they did open them and found inside pairs of red-and-white Reebok running shoes.

"Thanks, Rodger the Dodger," Hamilton said, grabbing his cousin and squeezing him in a head lock. Then he plopping back into his chair and started to put on his new shoes.

"Ah, my favorite color!" Andy announced, adding, "Oh, how touching. But how did you know? Rodger, you limey chicken fucker."

Andy had already placed the shoes back into the box. He got up and splashed Scotch into his glass.

"Okay, here are my gifts," said Jud, "but you must agree not to open them until the New Year."

"Okay, but why?" Hamilton asked as he took the heavy package from Jud. It too was wrapped in some old paper Rodger had dug up from somewhere. The striped box was about the size and thickness of a big-city telephone book and, when Hamilton shook it, it clunked. Andy's package was about the same size, but when he shook it, it sloshed and clinked. The box was wrapped in old birthday paper: a rabbit conversing with a kangaroo, a blond boy scolding a bear with his paw in a pot of honey, with a donkey and a pig dancing around a maypole.

"Well, Andy," Rodger laughed, "you'll like Jud's gift so much that it'll soon be gone, and then you'll look down at your red shoes and you'll thank ole Rodger. Aren't you going to see if they fit?"

"They're red. They have to fit," Hamilton said and they all laughed. Andy was the oldest living member of the American Trotsky Party, or so he claimed. But then, at the end of 1988, there couldn't have been many members left.

"So, we drink to the house of our ancestor," Jud said in mock solemnity. And everyone raised a glass except Andy, who muttered, "Necrophilia! Bullshit, if you ask me."

And, indeed, they were in the house of an ancestor, for Rodger Inksetter had inherited the seventeenth-century gray stucco house. It had been constructed for a Dutch shipbuilder, built during the days when Rye was one of the Cinque Ports; the center for exporting to the colonies the wool produced from the sheep that grazed around the Romney Marsh, and a port of call for spices arriving aboard ships of the East India Company.

The house sat next to the road that led to Winchelsea, directly across from a yacht basin that once had been the yard where ships were crafted to sail the waters of the New World. The house had come into Rodger's family in the 1870s when his ancestor, Judah Phillips Benjamin, purchased it along with the rotting shipyard and a crumbling Martello Tower, from the descendants of the Dutch shipbuilder.

Judah P. Benjamin had been the Secretary of State for the Confederate States of America and, with a large price on his head, had fled to England when his country was defeated in 1865. Benjamin's brother, after a decade of exile in British Honduras, returned to his vanquished land and founded a town in southern Georgia, naming it Altamaha. And it was in this town that both Jud and his uncle had been born, as had several generations of Fowlers, Hamilton's mother's family. Thus, Judah P. Benjamin was the common ancestor of Rodger, Jud and Andy. Jud was so fascinated with this ancestor that, for the previous three years, he had been trying to write something about him – a biography of sorts, he said, but he admitted to having difficulties with the genre of biography. Both by training and by inclination, Jud was a poet.

Andy first visited Rye and Benjamin House during the Second World War, when he was stationed in England. Jud visited for the first time almost three decades later, where he met Rodger. Soon after, Jud brought Hamilton along. Their lives – because of both blood and circumstance – were like the tributaries of a stream that flowed together. And that morning, when the train rolled out of Rye, part of that stream flowed eastward.

As the train jerked to a start, Hamilton looked again at his reflection in the window. His new red mustache reminded him of the horns of a bull. Yes, he liked to think of it that way. He once told Jud that had it been possible, he would have grown the horn on his head. Jud had laughed his ass off. The mustache also made him think of a picture he once had seen – a depiction of the Virgin standing on one of those crescent-shaped, or horned, moons. In all her glory, she stood between heaven and earth, her presence joining the two. Behind her was the sun with its bursting rays making a halo around her head. All of this was supported by that horned moon she stood on, so if you were to snatch the moon out from under her, the whole firmament would just tumble down – all of it except perhaps the sun.

Hamilton smiled at the thought, and at the tattoo that he knew to be resting under the skin over his left shoulder blade. This tattoo he recently acquired from a body-art shop down off College and Spadina in Toronto. The Jamaican tattooist nearly had a bird when Hamilton presented him with El Greco's version of the virgin standing on the moon. The artist protested tattooing what he called "holy pictures." And until Hamilton persuaded him that he had been commanded by a vision to have the Mother of God placed beneath his skin, the man had been altogether persistent. It was the day after Hamilton had acquired the Queen of Heaven as his eternal passenger that he stood at the bathroom sink and shaved his head. And it was that very day that Hamilton decided to grow his horn.

But alas, what Hamilton had told the Jamaican about the vision was not altogether a lie. Yes, Hamilton had had a vision of sorts – a revelation, or a discovery, really. Hamilton discovered that history had died. Whatever happened now were just combinations and permutations of whatever had gone before. Everything and everybody, everywhere, were becoming alike: "alike," as he had put it, "like nice, white, American women." Anyway, this is the kind of thing he had gone around saying to anyone who would listen. Now that history was, in principle, becoming universalized and homogenized over the whole planet, Hamilton had decided – with the help of Hegel and Nietzsche – that this had been the whole point of history in the first place and that, in principle, it already had been realized. What was left to do was elaborate this principle so as to make it actual, that is, real, for the whole planet. So, for Hamilton, the horn-like bar of rusty whiskers between his mouth and nose, together with his tattoo and shaved head, were ciphers, but most importantly, they were monuments marking the death of history.

Across from Hamilton, Andy was already snoring. He gasped at the air, snorting it out in irregular bursts: the fitful night-breathing of age. Hamilton faced Andy and listened to his noise. He looked at Andy's red running shoes. Andy had tied the laces into double bows, something he had learned back – yes, way back – in school. He's a good ole guy, Hamilton thought.

Hamilton leaned back against the side of the compartment and looked into the dark. With his seat facing the direction of the town, Hamilton was moving backwards and he swiftly saw Rye disappear in the gloom. By the time they had crossed Romney Marsh and then the Rother River, even the tower of St. Mary's had eclipsed into the darkness of the past.

As they entered Victoria station, Hamilton glanced up at the clock hanging from an arching steel girder. It was nearly ten.

"Hey, wake up you ole rooster. We're in London. A little over four hours 'til our flight leaves. We can get breakfast at Heathrow."

Hamilton helped Andy with his tan trench coat and tried to take his bag, but Andy protested: "Can take my own goddamn bag, thank you."

They entered the Underground, and in less than an hour they were in Heathrow. Because most of the shops were full of people – being the day after Christmas,

Boxing Day – Hamilton and Andy ordered their coffee and sausage biscuit from an obliging vending machine; then they made their way to the British Airways section. British Airways handled the business for Aeroflot. Yes, they were flying with the Soviet airline to Moscow for a four hour stopover and a change of planes, and then, on from there to New Delhi. A little detour, you might say.

Hamilton had insisted on this route. When he returned to Rye from London, where he had bought the tickets from the Aeroflot office near Oxford Circus, Hamilton announced that he had chosen Aeroflot because he knew that it would be safe, referring to the incident of four days before when the Pan Am 747 had been bombed out of the sky over Lockerby, Scotland. And, of course, Andy might just appreciate patronizing the Soviet airline and, yes, the tickets were cheap. But Jud knew there was more to the decision than this, and he told Andy and Rodger that Hamilton did it because the Soviets would not give him a visa and that he just wanted to go through Moscow for the hell of it. And Hamilton admitted that this was true.

Several months before, Hamilton had been accepted as an exchange scholar with the University of Moscow. But at the last minute, for some reason never explained, the Soviets refused to issue him a visa. It was then that his dean, along with others who were anxious that Hamilton spend the year abroad, made the arrangements for him to do research in London. Hamilton was writing a second book on the Russian thinker and polymath, Alexander Bogdanov. Unbeknownst to the authorities at the university, Bogdanov had been part of Hamilton's discovery about the demise of history. But after three months in London, Hamilton decided he needed to do some field research, as he had put it, and he would take the money from the grant they had given him and make better use of it in Asia. Well, so he claimed.

"Hell," Jud had laughed, "do you blame the Russians for not letting you in? Do you blame them after what you wrote? What was it that you called the Russians? What was it? 'Poor Americans'?"

Jud was referring to Hamilton's article entitled "The End of History and the Russo-American Way of Life." It was published in the scholarly journal *The National Interest* and had infuriated both the Soviets and the Americans. This resulted in letters of protest written to the chancellor of the university from the embassies of both the U.S.A. and the U.S.S.R. Oddly enough, the language of both formal complaints had been similar: something to the effect that Hamilton's article was an irresponsible tissue of wild imaginings and gross insults to their people. Although Hamilton's article was just one thing among many that Hamilton had done lately to embarrass most of his colleagues and all of his superiors at the university, this little essay had brought matters to a head, for it made public Hamilton's discovery that history was dead.

Before Hamilton made this discovery, his colleagues had looked upon him as a moderate, conservative, even stuffy man and a competent, if not a particularly gifted, scholar. But then, after coming to the conclusion that history was over, Hamilton became determined to change and to live as he thought a man ought to live at the end of history. And this, of course, was when he grew his horn, did away with the hair on his head and acquired the icon on his shoulder blade. Hamilton also became more outspoken, began using the Nautilus equipment at the gym and became intimately acquainted with a beautiful redheaded graduate student with a diamond stud beside her right nostril. And it was then that many of Hamilton's colleagues came to the conclusion that a man in his forties should not have so many gifts. Yes, they were just a bunch of jealous prigs who were so set in their ways that they were incapable of understanding what it meant to live dangerously, Hamilton told himself.

And why did Hamilton choose to take the grant money and bugger off? And why to Asia, of all places? His answer was that history first began in the Orient and ended in the West, and now that it was all over that ragged, old, worn-out world called the West had become an endless facsimile of itself. Well, this is how the theory goes, but then maybe it's wrong. Like all theories, it needed to be tested. Hamilton figured that he just might find something different – really different – in the East. Jud and Rodger had tried to talk Hamilton out of it and almost had, but then Andy blew in and, when he learned about Hamilton's travel plans, he decided that he would go along for the ride. Yes, Andy thought he had nothing to lose and he also decided that he had been altogether wrong about Hamilton. Hamilton had changed. Hamilton was a real blast.

For the last two decades Andy had lived on an AA farm at a place called Seven Bridges near Macon, Georgia, but he just recently had a falling-out with his comrades there and left in a huff, announcing that he was never coming back. The truth was that Andy had no place to go, so for Andy any place was about as good as the next. Besides, Andy had never been to Asia.

They checked in at the counter and a red-faced man with a Yorkshire accent looked at them askance as he processed their tickets, stamped various documents and gave them each a boarding pass. They found some seats and waited for the announcement telling them it was time to board, but soon there was an announcement informing them that the flight had been delayed. They both became resigned to the situation and snoozed.

For whatever reason, Hamilton dreamed of the old brick house he and his wife had bought in a downtown Toronto neighborhood called the Annex. But then that had been almost twenty years before and the marriage had not lasted two years. In fact, Jud, Rodger and Andy had also been married. Rodger's wife, Marti, died in a car crash on Winchelsea Road in 1979. Jud's wife, Meg, left him in 1978. Andy had been married four times and he didn't even know whether the first two were dead or alive, but he knew that he had outlived the last two.

Of the four, Lotty was the only one of Andy's wives that Hamilton had never met. Lotty was a black woman Andy had met in what once had been called

British Honduras. She died during a drunken fight with Andy in the Fort George Hotel in Belize City. But Hamilton dreamed neither of her nor of Rodger's dead wife, nor, for that matter, of Jud's ex-wife, whom he also had never known. He only dreamed of how empty the house had been when his own wife had left.

They awakened to a buzz of activity. People were everywhere. A few wore turbans and some were in saris. Most had several suitcases, boxes or bundles, some of which were tied up with rope, and others had black, plastic garbage bags sealed together with silver duct tape. Some talked and others appeared to be arguing. A few just sat, their brown faces blank as if they were deep in meditation. The place smelled of curry.

As they were riding in the contraption that was taking them to the airplane, a woman plopped down into the seat beside Hamilton. He could hear her sigh as she landed. He glanced at her from the side of his eye. She was clad in jeans, boots and what looked like an expensive blue sweater. She had long legs, was tanned – even looked athletic – and her dark hair was done in one of those sculptured haircuts – cut close on the sides, but not exactly clipped, with a strip of longer hair down the middle. A Mohawk, Hamilton thought. She looked tired.

"Excuse me," he said, as she pulled the edge of Hamilton's parka from under her thigh.

"It's okay," she replied, not looking at him.

American, Hamilton thought. He could not guess her age. She smelled of soap.

"So, what takes you to Moscow?" Hamilton asked when he had screwed up enough nerve.

"Oh, I'm just passing through."

"Really? Going to Delhi, I bet."

"No. Singapore."

"Singapore. Holiday?"

"No. I live there."

It was clear. She did not want to talk.

As the passengers filed out of the vehicle and walked across the tarmac to the airplane, Hamilton noticed the logo on the fuselage just under the cockpit: "Aeroflot" in the Byzantine-looking Cyrillic letters and bird's wings with straight intricate lines and detailed curves. In the center where the wings joined was the curve of a sickle crossed with the straight handle and square head of a hammer. Under it was a waning moon-shaped wreath and a red star. Squaring the circle, Hamilton thought. That's what it's all about. He was tired.

At the top of the stairs they were met by a solidly built flight attendant whose orange hair was done up in a beehive-like coiffure. Inside the plane was a chaos of swarming bodies and the aisles were jammed with people pushing and shoving, attempting to claim seats. Many were trying to stuff bundles, boxes and suitcases into the overhead baggage compartments. Hamilton glanced down at the number on his boarding pass, turned around, looked at Andy and, with a motion of his head, signaled him to follow. Through the moving bodies they eventually arrived at the seats that had numbers appearing to correspond to their boarding passes. But there was a woman in one of the seats. Hamilton could see rolls of brown flesh protruding from the wrap of her pink and yellow sari. In the maelstrom, she appeared calm.

"Sorry, Madam, but you are in my seat," Hamilton said, producing the boarding pass for her to see. She glanced at the pass and casually looked up at him.

"No," she said.

"Look lady, I'm sorry, but you have to move to your own seat."

"No," she replied without looking at Hamilton.

"That purple spot between your eyes looks like a bullet hole," he told her.

"You white devil," the woman replied calmly.

Hamilton made his way to the front to find the flight attendant. "There's a woman in my seat and she refuses to move. Here's my boarding pass and seat assignment."

"Ha! We have no seat assignment. This is Soviet airplane. All is equal here," she said shooing him back into the swarm.

"Fucking Stalinists! Told you, Hambone," Andy said.

Finally, they did get seats. The engines roared and they were in the air. It was dark outside and the lights of London and England's little island passed under them. Hamilton marveled that such a tiny island had once ruled an empire so vast that at any moment in time some part of its territory had never been dark. Through the crack between two of the three seats in front of them, Hamilton noticed the woman who had been sitting beside him in the loading vehicle. She had raised the armrest and was asleep across all three seats. Suddenly, there appeared an old brown man wrapped in layers of coats. He smiled and looked at the reclining figure through spectacles as thick as slices from a crystal ball. Behind him was the flight attendant.

"You must move. There is one seat only for every persons. You must move."

"Sorry," the reclining woman replied. She was groggy and sounded confused. "I haven't slept for two days."

"You must move and let them seat!"

A second man was behind the flight attendant. She took two black garbage bags and a tied-up box from him, opened the overhead compartment and jammed them inside. After several tries, she latched the door. Hamilton could see the tired woman gathering her things – a sweater, jacket and bag – move to the inside seat and close her eyes. The two men crawled in and sat, and the attendant left. Andy was snoring again. When the attendant came around with a cart of drinks, Hamilton ordered two little bottles of vodka, but then decided not to wake Andy and ended up drinking them both. Then he dozed. He dreamed of himself and Jud sitting on the rocks at the island on the Ottawa River. It was Jud's island where he has a cottage in which he's lived for the past three years. Jud looked at him: "... some have fallen," he said. Jud wore an orange turban. Hamilton's dream faded and he slept deeply.

He was awakened when the attendant came by with a cart of food, but Hamilton was not hungry and Andy was still asleep. They could eat in Moscow.

"No thanks," he told her and, without even a glance, she went on.

Hamilton thought of the first time he was in Rye. It was during the seventies when he and Jud were together at Oxford. Marti, Rodger's wife, was in France and Rodger joined her after one day, giving Hamilton and Jud the run of the place. With them were two girls who lived near Oxford. They borrowed Rodger's old Morris, threw back the top and rambled through the Romney Marsh. They went to the castle at Salt, and they took the road that leads into the downs and through the wood to Canterbury. They cycled the public paths around the town and, on one day, walked across the meadow behind Benjamin House, went up the hill to Winchelsea and swam in the sea. On the way back, they made love in waist-high wheat, each couple laughing at hearing the other lying a few feet away. That night they took a ladder and crawled to the top of the Martello Tower near the house and, over bottles of wine, pretended to be fierce smugglers slipping contraband into Rye; pirates preparing to sail to the Indies; and Royal Marines standing on the tower and looking out over the marsh, the rivers and the Channel in an attempt to sight Napoleon's invading ships. Those days were gone now, and with them the magic.

Hamilton's attention turned to a commotion in front of him.

"Bathroom! Please, you must let me out. BATHROOM!"

It was the woman with the Mohawk haircut. "RESTROOM!" she repeated desperately, but the men on either side of her did not understand. Hamilton could see the old man with the thick glasses looking and smiling at her. "Never mind," she said, and like a cat she was up above the seats, one foot on the armrest between the two men and the other dangling in the air. Her hand was on the outside of the overhead baggage compartment, steadying her. She was about to leap, but the latch to the compartment sprang open and, with two bundles bound in black garbage bags and a tied-up box, she fell. She landed astride the lap of the old man, knocking off his glasses. Hamilton could hear the two men laughing. It was surprised, embarrassed laughter. Then, like a frightened bird released from a cage, she disappeared down the aisle.

Hamilton looked over at Andy. Although he could not hear because of the drone of the engines, he knew Andy was snoring. He could feel the vibrating air. He looked out the window. In the distance he could see streaks of rose, crimson and orange. The sun was rising. Just as he closed his eyes again, the woman was back and the flight attendant was behind her. The woman wore silver loops in her ears, her nose was prominent but not too large and, despite her dark hair, her eyes were sky blue. But they were bloodshot, as she had been crying and, as she had informed everyone, had not slept for two days.

"Please. My sweater, jacket and bag." She pointed to her things and looked at the old man.

"Sweater. SWEATER!" she pleaded, reaching as the man finally understood and handed them across to her. She took her things and with a blank, tired expression, turned and followed the flight attendant down the aisle. Hamilton wondered where she had gone.

It was getting light outside. Hamilton looked down and could see water and land. They passed over the Baltic and then there was the frozen coast of Finland. Hamilton could not go back to sleep, but dozed. Some time later, he was pleased to see the flight attendant come by with a cart of coffee, tea, juice and buns. The inside of the airplane was beginning to stir. There was a soft buzz of conversation and people were lined up to use the toilet. Andy stretched, raised his head and looked around as if trying to figure out just where he was.

"Andy, we're over Russia. Here, coffee. We should be landing any minute now. What time does your watch say?"

"Hell, I haven't known the time since 1968. I'll take that coffee."

Andy lit a cigarette and drew deeply. They were descending, circling. The flight attendant came down the aisle to make sure everyone was buckled in. Andy did not like it when she made him extinguish his cigarette. Suddenly, they left the blue sky and were in the thick clumps of white clouds that had been under them. Hamilton's ears popped. He looked across and saw the flaps on the wings lower and the red light on the wing tip flashing on and off – white, white everywhere. Then they were through the cloud, descending fast and, like a great bird of prey, the airplane swooped down, bumped twice and taxied toward the box-like terminal. Moscow. Yes, they had been in a snowstorm.

When the airplane stopped, people crowded in the aisles, reached for their baggage and pushed toward the door. Hamilton and Andy decided to sit and wait for the throng to leave. Finally, they gathered up their bags and moved down the empty aisle. When they were standing near the door, Hamilton noticed a floral, plastic curtain covering an entranceway. He stepped back and looked through a crack between the two panels. There she was, reclining across three seats. The side of her head rested in her hand, propping herself up on an elbow. She stared blankly. With thumb and index finger Hamilton opened wider the two panels of the greasy plastic curtain. She at first continued to stare blankly, but then tightly focused on him. Hamilton smiled and, with his other hand, waved. Hamilton could feel the current of her glare. It was then that she raised her middle finger and jabbed it up into some imaginary space. "Fuck off," she hissed. "Fuck off, you creep!"

They sat at the bar in the Moscow airport. It was a holding pen really, a temporary stopover just for passengers who were destined elsewhere. Hamilton reached into his pocket and pulled out his slip of paper that each of them had been issued upon being admitted to the terminal. He studied it. It read: "Food

Ticket for Transfer Passengers. One Feeding Only" and "1400 hrs" was written in pen. He glanced up at the clock on the wall. "Feeding time should be soon," he said, adding that he had to go to the gift shop and that he would return shortly and then they would eat.

"Okay. That gives me time for just one more quick drink," Andy replied. "And Ham, while you're there, get me some Winstons."

"Sure, Unc. You just sit tight. Just want to see about a couple of postcards and maybe even buy a watch."

"Ha! I know what you're really gonna do. You're gonna look for her."

"Her? Who's her?"

"Now don't give me any of that bullshit, boy. You know. The one what gave you the finger."

"Sure. After all, that was an invitation, Unc."

"Before you go ... What's the Russian word for Scotch?"

"Scotch, Unc. Just say 'Scotch.'"

Hamilton found a shop that sold souvenirs: little painted wooden eggs, babushka dolls, plastic busts of Lenin, vodka in fancy bottles with tassels on the tops and glasses with pictures of Marx, Lenin and their newest guy, the one with the raspberry on his forehead. "God, they must be broke. They'll do anything for a buck," Hamilton told himself. He saw postcards on a plastic rack. He studied the pictures carefully until he found just what he wanted. Finally, he chose two. On one – a picture of the wedding-cake skyscraper that is Moscow University – he wrote: "Canada is fabulous! Wish you were here!" He signed it and addressed it to the dean at his university. Then he selected two identical cards with pictures of troops, tanks, missiles and lots of red flags – a parade down Red Square. Hamilton scratched out the words "May Day" and "Moscow" and wrote English words under the picture that read: "4th of July parade in Washington." Then he printed carefully: "Wish you were here." He signed the cards and addressed them to the Soviet and American embassies in Ottawa. Hamilton smiled to himself, turned to the counter and, after he was satisfied that the old woman understood that the cards were to be mailed to Canada, he paid her in pounds and received a wad of red bills in change. She stamped the cards and dropped them into a slot behind her. Not once did she smile.

Just as he was leaving the shop, Hamilton remembered the watch and Andy's cigarettes. When he returned to the counter he noticed some watches under the glass near the cash register and chose a black, plastic digital one. Its blue numbers flashed "BLIP BLIP," and when he strapped it to his wrist it was so light he could hardly tell it was there. They had only Russian cigarettes, but Hamilton thought that was fine, for he wanted to see Andy smoke one.

Soon Hamilton and Andy were walking up and down the brown-carpeted corridors looking for the restaurant where they were supposed to eat. They saw a large room with many tables and chairs. They entered, but found the room practically empty. Hamilton went to the nearest table and put his blue parka over the back of a chair. Before they could sit, a woman in a black uniform with white cuffs and a white hat rushed over to them.

"Food ticket for transfer," she demanded with her palm open. They looked at her and surrendered the tickets. The woman looked at them, then extended her arm and tapped her watch. It was 14:11. They were late. Casually, Hamilton glanced at his new Russian watch blipping on his wrist. The uniformed woman shook her head in disapproval, saying: "You come!" She motioned for them to follow.

The tables had white cloths, a vase and a red plastic flower. She took them to a table where four people were sitting and then she left.

"We have been ordered to sit with you," Hamilton announced, smiling.

"Well, we are glad to see that you are doing as you are told. Do sit down, gentlemen."

The man had smooth, nutmeg-colored skin, a shiny head and he wore a blue pinstriped suit with a polka-dotted bow tie. He spoke schooled English of the Indian variety.

"My name is Dikshit. Yes, I know how it sounds to English ears, but it is an ancient family name – a Brahman name – and I could not bring myself to change it. But do call me Dicky. Everybody does. I'm from Brighton and so is my missus. This is Jerilyn."

He motioned toward the woman sitting across from him. She had blonde hair – real blonde hair – and, although her nose was rather large and slightly humped, she was attractive – even pretty – Hamilton thought. She was about half her husband's age.

"Call me Jeri," she smiled.

"I am afraid that neither of these gentleman can speak our language, nor we theirs," the older man who called himself Dicky said, referring to the other two sitting at the table. "If I am not mistaken, they are from Afghanistan."

Both men wore suit coats and white shirts buttoned at the top with no ties. They had thick, silky black hair and stubble on their faces. They ate silently and acted as if everyone were invisible.

"Come, come. Sit," the man called Dicky said.

The waitress brought a plate of sardines, olives, bread and a bottle of wine.

"The wine's quite good, actually," the brown man announced. "It must come from the Crimea. It is a bit sweet, but good. These men do not drink, so it seems," he smiled, amused at their good fortune, for the third bottle of wine had just appeared on the table. Hamilton could feel the woman's eyes on him. "Help yourself, Mister...."

"West, Hamilton West. And this is Andy, Andy Benjamin. He's my red ... ah ... redneck uncle."

"Ham, you bas ..."

"Oh, I see. As I was saying, we are from Brighton."

"Brighton? We were just through there today, weren't we Unc? Do you know Rye? It's not far from ..."

"Rye, oh yes, near Winchelsea. Yes, near Hastings."

"Then you must know the Benjamin House? It's now a B&B. Well, sometimes it is. There's a sign. It's on Winchelsea Road?" Hamilton asked.

"Oh, Jerilyn, that is the old shipbuilder's house, the one across from the old dry docks. The house is next to the Martello Tower. It is the one with the tunnels."

"Oh, that's the one," she replied, clearly not interested.

"Tunnel? Never heard anything about any tunnel and I've been going there for years. Owner's a relative," Andy chimed in, dismissing what had been said with a sweep of his arm.

"The tunnels were once used for smuggling. They are probably not there anymore. You are American, but from ...?"

"Damn right I'm American. But Hamilton here is one of them who's always pretending he ain't an American."

"What my uncle means is that I'm Canadian," Hamilton winked, adding that they were on their way to India.

"Oh, how exciting! I'll bet you are an anthropologist or an archaeologist or something. You just look like one," Jeri said to Hamilton.

"No, sorry. A professor on sabbatical, sort of. But my uncle here ..."

"Well, well, I'm an academic myself. I am recently retired. Developmental Historian, the University of Sussex. And you?" asked Dicky.

"From Toronto. My field is philosophy. I'm interested in the Russian thinker, Bogdanov. Ever heard of him? Had planned to come to Russia to find Bogdanov's assistant who is still alive, but the authorities wouldn't let me in."

"Sorry."

"Well, what the hell. So, here we are in Moscow. I've made it this far. And I should tell you, I've spent a bit of time in England myself," Hamilton said, now feeling the effects of the wine. "Took my degree at Oxford. But Andy has spent a lot of time in cell meetings in Manchester and Sheffield."

"Damned lie. But it could've been true. That, I don't deny. Actually, was over here fighting the Huns. Hamilton, here, likes to joke around. Little snip, he wasn't even born yet."

"He does like to joke," Jeri laughed.

"Yes, I was stationed in England. During the war. Been going back ever since. Just as I said, relatives," Andy added.

"Well, well, good for you both. I went to Cambridge myself, but I spent many years in America. That is where I met my Jerilyn, at the University of California in Los Angeles."

"Really?" Hamilton said. She was looking at him again.

They ate their sardines and drank from what had become a large supply of free wine. Whenever they could, Hamilton and Andy merely nodded while the old professor nattered on. His talk reminded Hamilton of a ribbon flapping without aim or effort in a soft breeze.

"You know that Rye has always been popular with literary types?"

Hamilton looked up, politely grunting.

"Henry James. There is a plaque to him on a garden wall. He used to write in there. Most of it was destroyed by an air raid in 1942. And there was Lowry. He used to frequent the pubs. He is buried over in a little churchyard in the nearby town of Ripe. Remember, Ducky?" he said, nodding toward his wife.

"I guess. If you say so, Dicky," she replied, smiling at Hamilton.

"Look, I'd better tell you right now," Andy interrupted, "Lowry and I were great, long-time friends. I know all about Lowry. We got drunk in Cuernavaca and in Acapulco. Knew his second wife, an old party worker. He was a good comrade."

"Really?"

"You' damn right."

"Hmm." Hamilton was trying to turn his full attention to the beefsteak in mushroom sauce that had just been put before him.

"Now I remember, that tunnel of yours was built, let's see, after the time of King Charles. No, it was about a century later, about 1750. It would have been about the time of the excise on alcohol, tea and coffee. That is right, once I even ran across a map of that tunnel of yours. It was quite by accident, mind you."

Hamilton had heard enough. He swallowed a big chunk of beef, washed it down with wine and broke in: "And where did you say you are going?"

"Singapore. I am retired, as I said. It is so much cheaper than wintering in Spain. If you do it right, that is. But it is easy, you see. You do not even need a visa for Singapore. Everything is easy there."

"Yes, and they have such wonderful birds there," the woman added.

"So, you'll fly to there from here?"

"Oh, heavens no," the brown man chuckled. "It is much too far. We will stop in Kabul, but only for fuel."

"Kabul!" Andy was excited by the idea.

"Yeah, the Russians had the stew beat out of them," Hamilton said after washing down another mouth full of beef. "Now they're high-tailing it out of there. You'd think they'd learn to mind their own business. But then they never ..."

"The Stalinist bastards!" Andy interrupted, slapping his hand on the table in order to make his point understood. And it was at this moment that Hamilton felt Jeri's foot resting on the top of his shoe. He moved his foot slightly, took a sip of wine and tried to ignore it. Without thinking, he wiped his mouth and then uncomfortably twirled his whiskers. He looked across at her. She was smiling at him. Her eyes were green.

"We must go Jerilyn dear. A good trip Mister ... er ..."

The absent-minded professor had forgotten his name, which, of course, allowed Hamilton to take advantage and give Andy another jab:

"West. Hamilton West, and this, of course, is my communist uncle, Andy Benjamin. And bon voyage."

"Oh, you speak French. I just love French," Jeri laughed.

"Ducky, the man is Canadian!" the man called Dicky muttered under his breath. He rose, extended his hand and said: "Yes, we wish you a good and safe trip," adding, "and who knows, perhaps we will see you again. Next month we will be in India for a conference. But you will probably be gone by then," the old professor chuckled.

"Do be careful, Mister West," Jeri whispered. s

She waved and they walked away.

As they descended over the Himalayas, Hamilton awoke and looked out his window. The sun was rising and the soaring plane shone pink in its glow. "From this height you have access to all things," he said to himself. He moved to another rung of wakefulness and, reflecting on the excessiveness of his own imagination, was amused. Andy was still snoring. He made Hamilton think of a badly tuned outboard motor – the kind of motor Jud had on the boat at his cottage. He thought of Jud and something he had said during their last night in Rye. He had quoted Kipling: "East is East and West is West and ne'r the twain shall meet ..." Jud's full of shit and so was Kipling, he thought.

Hamilton looked out his window again. Below the dark mountains was a green strip. He could tell that it followed a river. The Indus, he guessed, but then he had no idea where they were in relation to the hundreds of mountains below – except up. Soon they were low enough to distinguish towns and villages, but with no particular details yet. Then he could see the tan rivers and blue reservoirs that turn the brown land around them green. There was another river. It grew wider and darker as it cut along the base of the mountains and across the plain before it opened its fingers to the sea. It must be the Ganges, he thought, thrilled. The holy waters bearing ashes representing another turn of the eternal wheel. They began to circle.

"Well, we're here," Hamilton said to Andy, gently touching his shoulder.

"Coffee, Hambone?"

"Okay, ole Unc. I'll see what I can do." Hamilton slid past Andy and the old Indian in whose lap the pretty, rude woman had fallen. When he was in the aisle, the flight attendant came toward him. She was not the woman with the beehive, but she was just as solidly built.

"You! Back to seat. We land. Make belt," she said.

Hamilton did not argue. The descent was long, wide and gradual. Finally they streamed over roof tops, roads and motorized vehicles, bullock carts, bicycles and pedestrians. Then they were in a wide arc, circling, preparing to land.

At the end of the runway were three airplanes. Each was painted a black, tan and green camouflage. The planes had plastic bubbles encasing .50 caliber machine guns at the tails, tops and under the noses. Hamilton recognized the planes as Canadian Dash 8s, designed for hops to nearby cities or for sorties to close enemies. Then he saw the soldiers lined up along the runway. They were standing at rest, their legs apart and their rifles tipped with shiny bayonets.

The engines bumped and reversed their thrust, and, with a rolling burst, the flaps extended and the aircraft landed. The soldiers marched toward the plane. They moved fast in close order, and then split two abreast, forming columns along the sides of a long, red carpet. The soldiers wore brown, British-looking tunics and trousers, red berets and black jump boots. What a welcome.

Everyone scrambled for luggage and rushed for the door, but none were allowed to exit. The band struck up a tune. It was familiar, but Hamilton could not place it. Some stairs were pushed up to the plane and a woman and six men descended, stopping before a man who stood at the end of the red carpet between the columns of soldiers. His light-green Nehru suit was severely pressed. With his praying hands under his chin, he bowed. Then the people who had gone down the stairs returned his gesture and everyone clapped. At that moment, two women in green and orange saris came from behind with garlands of marigolds and the band began to play again. It was the same tune.

"Ah, the 'International,'" Andy said. He began to hum along.

The old commie, thought Hamilton.

The garlanded party was whisked off in two black Hindustani limousines that were both lead by and followed by two jeeps with machine guns mounted on their backs. The soldiers marched away and so did the band. Once the red carpet was rolled up, the door was finally opened and they were all permitted to descend.

The passengers were driven to the terminal in a bus without sides. When it stopped, they stepped down and walked across the tarmac to a corrugated metal building with an opening extending across its entire front. There, under the peeling, gray-painted roof were three signs: "INDIAN," "COMMONWEALTH" and "OTHER." Under each sign was a line of people. Hamilton stood under the sign marked "COMMONWEALTH"; it was a one-man line.

"Commonwealth?" Hamilton asked himself. These signs had probably been there for forty years, he thought, oddly uneasy to be standing there alone. Andy hobbled to the end of the line marked "OTHER" because he was an American and because the United States is not a member of the British Commonwealth. Hamilton, who was finished in no time, stood in the shade of a ratty palm tree and waited for Andy, who was wiping the sweat from his face with his balled-up trench coat. Finally, Andy put his passport on the desk and Hamilton watched as a dark man in a brown wool uniform snapped it up. He peered at Andy and then closed one eye, squinted and looked at Andy's picture. The man had a great hooked nose.

"Visa?" the officer asked sternly.

"Visa? I don't need a visa. I'm from America. You can see, it's written right there on my passport! Right there: U.S.A."

"It is the law."

"There's some mistake ..."

"No. No mistake. It is the law."

"Okay. So I don't have a visa, now what?"

"You must leave," the officer said without looking up.

"Leave? I ... I just got here! That's the craziest fuc ..."

Hamilton, who could not hear all that was being said, figured that something bad was going on. He pushed his way through the crowd and over to where Andy stood before the officer.

"What's the trouble here?" he interrupted.

"Who are you?"

"I'm Hamilton West and this man here is my uncle. What's this about a visa?"

"He must have a visa. It is the law."

"Now you just wait a minute. You can't do that."

"You go with him," the officer said, nodding toward a subordinate with an AK-47. "Corporal, take them to the Aeroflot airplane. Tarmac four. I am telephoning the tower."

"You can't do that," Andy protested, "I'm an American!"

"Yes, mister, and so is the C.I.A.," the officer barked while hardly looking up.

"What do you fascist bastards do with noses like that? Open cans or catch bugs?" Andy shouted at the officer.

Their bags lay next to the wall of the aircraft they had arrived in. It seemed the Indians were forcing the Russians to take Hamilton and Andy back aboard. The officer had shouted to the protesting pilot that because Hamilton and Andy had arrived on that airline, they had to leave on it. The officer referred to them as "security risks" and "suspected U.S. government agents." In the end, he and the international airline regulations won.

"Where are you taking us?" Andy asked the pilot.

"Singapore," was the Russian's curt reply.

The flight took a little less than six hours. Although the time zone had changed, Hamilton could tell by his watch how long they had been on the plane. They landed, picked up their bags, said nothing to anyone and walked down the portable ramp. In the terminal, the blue carpet was new and the yellow walls were freshly painted. The corridor opened into an area with tropical plants and columns of water shooting from fountains into the air. It was there that they heard someone calling, "Mister West. Mister Benjamin. Your passports!"

"Jesus H. Christ!" Hamilton said under his breath. "How could we forget? The Russians took our passports!"

The man calling to Hamilton and Andy was Russian. He wore a brown suit and a red tie, was about Hamilton's age, but was heavier and, some would think, more handsome. He smiled and held out their passports, which they took.

"Thanks," Andy grunted.

The Russian smiled again and then replied, "You are very welcome." His expression turned grave. "Mister Benjamin, you and Mister West each owe us five hundred American dollars."

"Owe you? Owe you for what?" Hamilton growled.

"For the air tickets from New Delhi to Singapore, of course," he replied, looking surprised and hurt. It was only then that the Russian mother tongue broke through his carefully spoken English words.

"But we have no tickets," Andy said.

"Yes. I know, but that is no problem. We will make for you a ticket."

"Save yourself the trouble, Ivan. We don't want one," Hamilton said sternly, holding back laughter.

"But you must ..."

"But we must do what? Look, we know that you people are hard up for cash. You should get the Indians to pay. They're the ones who stopped your goddamned airplane and made you bring us to the asshole of Asia!"

The Russian was taken aback by Hamilton's sudden burst of rage and vulgarity. Bewildered, he shook his head. Then his expression changed and he said, "I think that there is a way. Please, Mister West, you and Mister Benjamin wait here. I will not be long."

They thought about leaving, but in no time the Russian was back with another man, perhaps his superior. This man was dressed just as he was.

"This is Comrade Shevtsov."

"Hi, Shev," Andy said, getting into the spirit of the moment.

"You pay us five hundred American dollars altogether. Then you can get visa and we fly you back to India."

"No thanks," Hamilton replied, smiling. "Now that we've had this free trip, we think we'll just stay a while."

"Yeah. We hear that Singapore is a good place to do some bird watching," Andy laughed, as he pushed his glasses up on his nose and blew smoke into the Russians' faces.

"You cannot do that! They put you in jail!" the Russian named Shevtsov said with a look of horror.

"Jail? For looking at birds?" Hamilton asked, laughing.

"No. No. Not that. Jail because you have no visa, no visa for Singapore," he replied, astonished.

"Don't need one. Singapore is a free port." Hamilton smiled. He knew that they had won. The Russians knew it too and immediately warmed toward them.

"The Indians should not have done that to you. They are very unpredictable. We must do business with them all the time and this is very unpleasant."

"Yes. Yes." The other Russian agreed.

"In my country, business is now very important. Tell us, Mister West and Mister Benjamin, what do you think of Aeroflot?"

Hamilton slid a finger down one side of the new crop of hair under his nose, thought for a moment and replied, "Well, it's alright for the money." He and Andy looked at each other, nodded and walked away.

# *BOTTOM OF THE WORLD*

Hamilton woke to the smell of ginger and the sound of birds. Bars of light streamed through the partially opened slats of his shuttered window. Hamilton rolled over on his back, covered his eyes with his hand and listened to Andy snore in the next bed. Through his fingers he saw the empty Scotch bottle on the table. He tried to put together the events of the past two days, but they folded into his dreams. After drifting in and out of sleep, he swung his feet to the floor, sat up and rubbed his eyes. The floor was tiled. Cool. So this is Singapore?

Soon he was outside in his shorts, Toronto Blue Jays T-shirt and the red running shoes Rodger had given him. The sky was a dull yellow and the streets were damp from dew. Already it was hot. Some men were unloading trucks and the old man who had checked them into the hotel was sweeping the sidewalk out front. He stood there and looked around. Surrounding him were building cranes. They looked like long-necked birds, but yes, of course, that's why they are called cranes, Hamilton thought.

There were more buildings under construction than those already completed and the completed ones were of great variety. Some looked like buildings one may find in a tropical metropolis in the West. Pastel colors made the new skyline dazzle like jungle flowers. On the tops of these tall, twenty-story buildings were fantastic decorations: bright-green, tile, pagoda-style roofs decorated with rich, gold-leaf inlay. And then there was the building with one of those Indian-looking tops like the bulbous arch of the Taj Mahal.

There were buildings that made you think of Malaysia and others of Thailand. This scattering of lower buildings, Hamilton concluded, had been built when the boom had started some years before, during those early years of Kim's urban-renewal projects. These buildings reflected the cultural diversity of Singapore in a self-conscience and comical way, and they were in stark contrast to the towering steel-and-glass buildings that dwarfed them. First, Singapore had shed its old colonial skin, replaced by its inward-looking multicultural facade, only to be again replaced and overwhelmed by a shining, overarching cosmopolitan.

There was water everywhere, and everywhere was spanned by bridges, both old and new. Wooden, barge-like boats with bent and rounded wood-frame tops were covered with soiled canvas. They looked as if they had plied the waters of Singapore's rivers and canals forever.

Hamilton hefted a leg up the side of one of the stone pillars that supported the arches over the sidewalk and stretched his tendons and muscles. When he finished stretching, he stepped into the street, threw an arm over his head and kicked high into the air. Then with the other leg, he reversed this procedure.

Hamilton trotted along the side of the narrow streets and, increasing his stride, felt life come into his muscles. He looked around, dodging people and vehicles as he ran. Well, this was different. There were no renovated nineteenth-century brick houses, no maples and no driveways with Volvos. Not his neighborhood. He turned left on Mountbatten Road. Yesterday seemed a world away.

Along the way there were billboards advertising things in many languages. One of the signs made him stop, run in place and look up. A young woman with shiny black hair hanging coyly over an Oriental eye looked down at him from the advertisement. Although her skin was a light brown, her look was that of the Occident. On her slim hips hung two ivory-handled Colt .45s and on her feet she wore hand-tooled snake-skin cowboy boots. Behind her arched back were the words: "Come West with me and my wonder bra." Just past the billboard Hamilton could see the golden domes of a mosque. The rising sun made them glow and a loudspeaker cracked and called the faithful to prayer.

When Hamilton returned to their room, he found Andy still asleep and chose not to bother him. He pulled off his clothes and entered the shower stall. He expected the water cascading off the mildewed walls to wake Andy, but when he stepped from the stall, he saw that Andy had not stirred and, for a moment, the thought crossed his mind that Andy might be dead. But then Andy grunted and Hamilton sighed in relief. Not bothering to be quiet, Hamilton dressed in the lightest things he had and went to the desk and asked the manager where they might find a clothing store, for even the lightest clothes that they had brought would be far too hot. After receiving directions, he returned to the room.

"Hey, Andy, get up. We're on the bottom of the world. Get up and let's have some coffee. We have to look for some cooler clothes. Come on, you ole redneck, time to get up."

Hamilton had to go downstairs and bring back coffee in order to entice Andy out of bed. Finally, after two cups and two Russian cigarettes, Andy was awake enough to move.

After losing their way several times, Hamilton and Andy found what they were looking for: a men's clothing store. It was located in a place called Lucky

Plaza on Orchard Road. The building was a four-story affair with Lucky Plaza, emblazoned in red and green lights bright enough to be discerned in the early day, in English, Mandarin, Urdu, Thai and Malaysian. It was new looking and had a grand hall in the center with a food market where most anything a human may or may not consume was sold, ranging from the mundane to the extremely exotic. There was the Chinese fare: live octopus, shellfish and golden carp, legs and roasts of dogs, ducks on a spit, live snakes and birds, along with common dried food and fresh vegetables and fruit, a great many of which were unrecognizable to Hamilton and Andy.

In keeping with the multicultural Asian population, the Indians had their fair share of spices and tandoori chicken and such, and, again, an array of exotic items that were beyond the North American range of recognition. This pattern persisted with the Thai and Malaysian goods. Around the top of the gallery were three additional rows of galleries with shops, little cafés of all ethnic types, and sweet stalls for ice cream and the juice of every drinkable fruit in South Asia. Flowers were sold and bulk staples such as flour, rice, tofu, beer, rice wines, familiar western liquors and local knock-off ones, too. There were automobile, scooter and bike parts, tobacco shops, pots and pans, small kitchen appliances, herbalists, dentists, acupuncturists, jewelry shops and many clothing and tailor shops.

Hamilton bought a pair of shorts, two pairs of khakis and three white, short-sleeved shirts. Andy chose two white knit shirts, and after trying on a pair of shorts, took two pairs of polyester pants instead. Then the smiling clerk talked Andy into buying a short-sleeved safari jacket with matching trousers and lots of flaps, buttons and pockets. Andy was told that it must be altered and that it would be ready at five the next afternoon. Hamilton almost commented that Andy's bush outfit was a style of clothing inspired by erstwhile imperial masters, but he didn't. Why spoil Andy's fun? So, after a failed attempt to get Hamilton to buy a yellow silk suit, the clerk gave up. Hamilton and Andy put their old clothes in plastic bags and, dressed in their new tropical garb, left the shop feeling much more comfortable than when they had arrived.

When they were on the sidewalk, Hamilton reminded Andy that they had had nothing to eat since they wolfed down the dry sausage and stale Aeroflot bread chased by vodka, so they started to look for a restaurant. For a while, they walked down Orchard Road. The shops directly around Lucky Plaza sold mostly expensive things: clothes by Ralph Lauren, perfume, jewels and furs. But soon the buildings became smaller. They passed a sporting-goods shop and another selling exotic birds, lizards and snakes. They stopped and looked into the window. Andy wanted to go inside, but Hamilton said that he was too hungry.

Down a side street there were older buildings; the kind with the arched sidewalks that had been constructed during colonial times and similar to the covered sidewalks around their hotel.

Spilling from the sidewalks and into the street was a great throng of people. As Hamilton and Andy moved closer, they saw that many in the crowd were squatting, yet others were standing on tiptoe, all eyes fixed upon a Chinese-looking man with a blue bandanna tied around his head. With a long cigar stuck between his teeth, the man shouted through the side of his mouth. He appeared to be challenging the crowd, teasing them and directing their eyes upward to an odd looking thing he held in the air. Was it a fruit, a vegetable – perhaps a nut? Hamilton had no idea. The tan-green thing was about the size of a football and was covered with sharp spikes. As the man moved to the center of the throng, people scattered, making room for him as he held the thing up over his head as if presenting it as an offering to the blazing sun.

Suddenly the man hurled the thing into the air and, producing a machete seemingly from nowhere, lunged as the thing fell, bringing the blade through it. WHACK! The man caught one of the pieces as the other bounced along the street and was retrieved by an old woman. The crowd cheered.

The crone held her piece of the bisected thing at arms length, affectionately inspecting it, and then she slowly brought it to her face and sniffed it. Inside, it had four greenish pods – or cods? Yes, they looked like testes, Hamilton thought. She poked her blackened fingernail into the flesh of a pod and then she stuck her finger into her smacking mouth, licked her lips and smiled in approval. Suddenly, she shouted something at the man with the bandanna and the jeering crowd rollicked with laughter. It appeared that somehow she had bested him. Then, cackling as she went, she hobbled down the street like a wounded bird with her prize safely tucked in her bag.

They walked on. At the base of a hill they noticed a low building with a sign painted in blue letters that read: "Bob Chang's Café," with tables along the sidewalk. Through the large open windows, they saw more tables under ceiling fans and cooks preparing food in great cauldrons. The smell of miso and peppers was in the air. They went inside and just as they began to look around for a table, Hamilton heard someone call:

"West! Doctor West."

And there he stood – brown, bald and smiling. It was the man from the airport, the man named Dikshit.

"Dicky here. Moscow? The airport? Sardines and Crimean wine? Remember? What on earth are you doing here? We thought that we would never..."

He was sporting a blue Hawaiian shirt with white-and-black beaches and green swaying palms. His chunky brown legs showed at the knees, the rest of which were covered by white knee-length socks and a pair of loafers.

"Oh, Jeez! Ah ... Dicky, eh? Sorry. You look so different in those clothes," Hamilton replied blinking, trying to shake the disbelief and disorientation from his head.

"Do come sit with us," he said, motioning them toward the table. "Do you remember my missus?"

"Hi. Ah ..."

"Jeri." She smiled and extended her hand first to Hamilton and then, as an afterthought, to Andy.

Hamilton and Andy explained the odd circumstances that had brought them to Singapore and the old professor listened, unable to hide his amusement, while Jeri kept glancing at Hamilton. They all ate hot Malaysian food and drank cold San Miguel beer.

After telling the Dikshits where they were staying and explaining that the accommodations were fine for the short time they were planning on being there, Jeri told them, in grand detail, about their condominium:

"Yes. It's the one we always get. We own it, sort of. Time shared. Not far from the beach. Good, if one likes that sort of thing. Personally, I do. I was raised on the beach in Santa Monica. Best thing about our place is that it's close to Birdland. We're birdwatchers. Are you, by chance, a birder? No, you don't look the type." She was speaking to Hamilton, ignoring Andy.

"You're right, young lady," Andy replied, adding that, "Hamilton, here, he don't know nothing 'bout birds. Don't even notice 'em 'less they cooked. But he does like to shoot 'em. Imagine that! Hamilton here's a duck hunter. But me, I've watched my share of birds. Yeah, I like birds a lot."

Andy was looking straight at Jeri and snorting. He plopped his empty beer bottle on the table for emphasis.

"Oh?" she responded, thinking Andy was making some corny joke.

"Yeah, I even raised 'em. In Georgia. Tropical ones too."

"Well, well, what a nice hobby," Jeri said, turning her glance back to Hamilton.

"Hey, wasn't just some hobby. Got right down scientific about it. Made money on 'em too," Andy replied, visibly hurt by her rebuff.

"So, with all of this interest in birds, we must all go to Birdland," Dicky said, raising his open palms as if having an epiphany.

The sun was almost directly over the tin roof and Hamilton could feel the sweat gathering at the bottom of his back. He moved to the edge of his chair and pulled his shirt from his wet skin, raising it discretely to allow the breeze from the fan to blow down his back. He ordered three more beers and Andy ordered himself what a sign said was Bob Chang's special martini.

Hamilton and Andy told them about seeing the man in the street holding up the spiky thing and how he threw it into the sky and slashed it. They also told them about how the old hag had scooped up part of it and how she had cackled as she made her hobbled dash down the street. Dickey informed them that the fruit, called a durian, was prized in that part of the world for its supposed magical powers and was often called "the love fruit" because it was thought to be an aphrodisiac.

Hamilton looked at his watch. Since it was still set on Moscow time, he reset it by Dicky's. Then he announced, "Well, think we'd better go. We plan to find the Indian Embassy and see about getting Andy's visa for India. Wouldn't happen to know where the place is?"

"Oh yes, I know where it is," said Dicky, "but I am afraid this will do you no good. They are closed for the Thaipusan Festival, which is rather like our New Year's celebration. I wouldn't expect them to open for several days, you see. Speaking of New Year's, there is always a big celebration given at the British High Commission. We always go. It is just like home. You would be welcomed to come as our guests. Will you come? It is tomorrow night."

"Oh, please come," Jeri said to Hamilton.

"We have some presents to open," Hamilton said while looking at Andy. "And maybe a phone call – need to call Rodger and Jud."

"There will be music and dancing, and there are always loads of interesting people. Please," Jeri begged.

"You bet we'll come. Hamilton is just making excuses. He's shy, kinda chicken, you know," Andy said, now winking at Jeri, recovering his lost dignity and popping the kumquat from his finished martini into his mouth.

"We don't have proper clothes," Hamilton grumbled.

"But attire is no problem. Come as you are. Maybe not the shorts, but casual. No one cares. Everybody gets jolly pickled and has a grand ole time. I will write the directions down and draw a map. Come at eight and tell them at the door that you are my guests. I will include our phone number if for any reason you should need to reach us."

Andy entered. Along with his red Reeboks, he wore his new safari suit and an Australian bush hat turned up on one side and fastened with a pin made from a crocodile claw. Hamilton glared at him and then looked at his watch, tapping it with his finger to let Andy know that he was annoyed. They were supposed to have been at the New Year's party at eight and Andy had been gone since before five, when he had left by taxi to pick up his safari clothes at the store in Lucky Plaza. Hamilton had wanted to make sure Andy ate before he started drinking and had been waiting for him in the Chinese restaurant beside their hotel. But it soon became apparent that Andy had already started.

"Hey, Hambone. Yeah, I know I'm a little late. Like my hat?"

"Hat? My royal Canadian arse! I didn't come all the way down here to babysit some crazy ole redneck."

Andy just grinned. Hamilton noticed his white arms hanging exposed from the short sleeves of his bush jacket. On one arm were terrible scars – chaotic waves and webs of flesh once torn and crudely stitched back together. Hamilton had seen the scarred arms before, but he had forgotten. In a flash, for just a moment, he associated the wretched arm with past events, but the memory faded as quickly as the sympathy he was feeling.

"Where have you been?"

"Been all over. Boy, this is quite a town! And I got us a ride to that party."

"What kind of ride?"

"I'm talking 'bout a ride with two guys who own one of those little putt-putt things – one of those little motor-scooter-type cars. Been scouting things out for us and that's why I'm late."

"Scouting around, eh?"

"Yeah. We've been all over. They'll drop us off and wait for us. Then, when we get tired of the party, we'll go out and blow it outta ..."

At that moment a smiling Chinese and a dour Indian entered the restaurant.

"Jesus, Andy! What ..."

"Hey, my friend. How it goes, old chaps?" the one who looked Chinese said, grinning and extending his hand to Hamilton. Although it was dark, he still wore his aviator glasses. When Andy noticed the bewilderment on Hamilton's face, he quipped, "Not as weird as somebody with a superstitious picture tattooed on his butt."

"Back."

"Yeah. Back. That's worse."

They got into the autorickshaw, Hamilton cursing under his breath. He was angry at himself for bringing Andy along, sabotaging his trip. He glanced over at the old man, imagining him as one of the scruffy feral cats that he remembered seeing in the muddy streets of the Negro section of Altamaha, Georgia.

"Me, I'm Starsky and this is my excellent partner, Hutch. Hutch, he does not have our language," the grinning Chinese announced and then started the engine.

"Yeah, Starsky and Hutch. I saw you on TV about twenty years ago," Hamilton shouted over the noise.

The driver nodded in agreement, laughed and shouted back, "In Singapore still on TV. Re-runner. Call me Ski. Everybody does. We are in tourism. In Singapore you can be anything you want. For go it! That's what we say."

When they had pulled past the sentry box beside the parking lot of the British High Commission and the autorickshaw's engine was mercifully turned off, Hamilton growled and said:

"Look Ski, or whatever they call you, we really appreciate the ride, but we're going to be here for quite a while so don't wait around on us. How much do we owe you?"

"Ah, Hampeldon, what friends are for?" he said holding up open palms and looking hurt. "Money? What money is? Later we see you. Go to Bogey Street. We for go it! Okay?"

"Come on Hamilton, I've already taken care of it. Need a drink," Andy laughed and at the same time thumped Hamilton on the shoulder with a long nicotine-stained finger.

They walked around to the front of the stone house, went under a yellow-and-white striped canopy and there, beneath the British Royal Arms, was the door. Before Hamilton could reach the knocker, the door opened and a Chinese maid dressed in black and white looked at them.

"My name is West and this is Mister Benjamin," Hamilton said. Considering his and Andy's attire, he wondered if the maid would order them around to the back door. Before she could continue, a man appeared behind her.

"Oh yes, Doctor West. And this must be Mister Benjamin. Jeri has told us all about you. Please do come in." He extended his hand. "I'm Gerald Orbell. And a happy New Year to the both of you."

"Thanks. Hot outside, eh?" Hamilton replied, taking the man's hand.

"Oh, but not inside. We have air. Cool, just like home." He smiled, showing tobacco-stained teeth.

The man, who Hamilton assumed to be the host, wore a light gray linen suit and a fastidiously elegant, perfectly knotted, pink silk tie that would have passed muster for the Duke of Windsor.

"So, Doctor West, you are from America?"

"No, I'm from Canada. And please call me Hamilton. Mister Ambassador?"

"Yes, some call me that, Hamilton. But you must call me Gerald. Canada. Yes, of course. Sorry about that."

"No problem. Used to it. But Andy here is from the States."

"Good for him! If you gentleman would come on in. Down this way you'll see the bar set up over in this room. Please, have a drink and do have a good time. It's so nice to have guests from America!"

They walked on worn black-and-white tiled squares that looked like a giant chessboard and then entered a room through a large arch. Most of the guests were standing, leaving the velvet and chintz upholstered furniture empty. Hamilton smelled evergreen. On the far side of the room, through the legs of the guests, Hamilton could see a blazing fire. But it was behind glass and the room was chilly. Most talked in a relaxed yet animated way – the English-speaking speaking English.

Hamilton and Andy made their way over to the bar. Andy told the little brown Father Christmas to give him a Scotch and Hamilton a San Miguel beer. The room smelled of a northern forest and of ladies' perfume. The chamber ensemble was playing something light from Gilbert and Sullivan. Hamilton wondered what Jud would have thought of the place.

"There you are! Better late than never!"

It was Jeri who had come from behind, surprising them. She crooked her arm through Hamilton's and looked up at him, smiling.

"Where's the professor?" Hamilton asked.

"Oh, over there somewhere. Giving some lecture or other. I need a drink," she said, gently tugging Hamilton toward the bar.

She wore a silk Oriental chemise and her blonde hair was knotted in a French braid. Hamilton tried not to think it, but she was stunning.

She ordered herself bourbon and, noticing that Andy's glass was empty, got him another Scotch. Hamilton stepped over to a table covered with food, picked up a plate, filled it with hors d'oeuvres and returned to the bar.

"Fine old place; the house, I mean," Hamilton said to Jeri while munching on a stalk of celery.

"Uh huh. Some merchant built it. Somebody who sold cloves, or something like that. Rich, too. Was used by the Japanese for their headquarters. After the war, the British got it for a song, so Dicky says. Oh yes, Andy just told me that you'll go to Birdland with us."

"Birdland, eh?"

"To go see the birds, remember?"

"Well, if Andy says so then I guess it's okay."

Hamilton's plate was empty so they poked back through the crowd to the table with the food and stood there, talking. Andy haunted the bar. The band played a Gershwin tune.

"Dance with me," she said to Hamilton and, reluctantly, he agreed. It had been a long time. Through the whole piece they did not talk. She pressed herself to him. He could have sworn she wore no underclothes.

When the music was over, the band stopped for a break. Hamilton and Jerilyn began making their way back to Andy, who had been watching their approach in the mirror behind the bar. Before a word could be spoken, Doctor Dikshit appeared.

"There! I thought I spied you," Dicky said, extending his hand first to Hamilton and then to Andy. "There is someone I would like all of you to meet." Dicky was looking fine in his blue pinstriped suit and polka-dotted bow tie. "Get yourselves a drink and then come and join us. We are over beside the fire. He is one of your Americans, Andy. You will have a lot to talk about if ever we are able to get Gerald away from him."

Jeri moved to Dicky's side, and Hamilton followed them across the room.

"Be with you in a minute," Andy called after them.

"My dear, meet Mister Jinkens. This is Jerilyn, my wife. And this, Mister Jinkens, is Professor Hamilton West. His uncle, Andy, the American I was telling you about, will be along shortly."

He stood alone before the fire. His head reached halfway past the middle of the constable look-alike hanging above the mantel. Mister Jinkens was not just tall, he was huge. He was in his late thirties, Hamilton guessed, and he wore a blue seersucker suit with a red paisley tie, white cotton shirt and oxblood loafers. The man was as black and as shiny as a coffee bean. When Hamilton took his hand, he was struck by the power. The squeeze was firm yet gentle and suggested that, had he wanted, he could have crushed every bone in Hamilton's hand. He looked down at Hamilton through brown horn-rims. The lenses were thick and his black eyes were flecked with the dancing amber of the fire.

"Mister Jinkens currently is at Oxford, but is originally from Virginia," Dicky announced, again taking charge.

"Well, to be honest, I'm afraid I'm playing hooky. I'm trying to ignore my M. Phil. thesis. Please call me Starman." His speech was mellow and measured with a schooled Tidewater accent.

Andy walked up in his bush hat and Hamilton cut his eye in Andy's direction to let him know that he knew that Andy was drunk. Starman and Andy were introduced and, after Andy revealed that he originally hailed from Altamaha, Georgia, Starman confessed that he had been raised in Opelika, Alabama. After that, they began a long conversation about racial relations in the American South. They became very involved in the topic, ignoring Dicky, who could have cared less and wandered off.

Again Jeri asked Hamilton to dance with her. The electric lights had been exchanged for candles and they danced for two or three numbers and talked little. Hamilton was sure she wore no underclothes. Suddenly the music stopped and someone began to chant: "Mo! We want Mo! We want Mo!" Others joined the chant and some began to clap. "MO! MO! MO!"

"More what? Always thought the English were a bit daffy," Hamilton said, craning his neck to see over the cluster around the piano.

"I'm glad to hear you say it. Sometimes I just miss America so much," Jeri replied dreamingly.

Then someone began to play the piano. It was a jazz tune. Hamilton did not know it and asked Jeri what it was, but she told him that the only music she knew was rock and that she had been away from America for so long that all the music she knew was now old. They rejoined Andy and the great black man, who again insisted they call him Starman. Andy had a fresh Scotch in his hand and was in the midst of reciting Whitman. The last jazz piece ended in a flourish and the crowd, which had become boisterous, clapped, whistled and shouted. It was in that small moment of silence that Andy's voice boomed:

"Victory, union, faith, identity, time / The indissoluble compacts, riches, mystery / Eternal progress, the kosmos ..."

Many were looking at Andy. Someone began a polite applause for his recitation and a few others joined in. Hamilton glanced at Andy, shook his head and smiled, indicating that he thought Andy incorrigible. He then looked back in the direction of the piano. The crowd had cleared and he could see a woman in a dark-blue dress sitting on the bench, talking to several people clustered around her. Her dress was cut to her shoulders, and around her neck she wore a string of pearls. A white, pearl-studded shawl had slipped to the small of her back. Her hair was short and dark.

"Isn't she good?" Starman said. "I especially liked the Allmaude Jamaud tune."

Dicky, who had just returned, answered, "Oh, yes, she is good, but I'm afraid I don't know the music. I'll ask her over."

"So, you know her?" Jeri asked.

"Oh yes, I know her, but I know her former husband better. A damned fine chap, he is. Lives in Hong Kong. Exporter. She's been in Singapore for a long time. Long before we ever came here, Ducky. If I'm not mistaken, she's American."

Dicky walked over to the piano and spoke to several people. Hamilton watched him as he took the woman's hand and led her toward them. The silver loops in her ears flashed in the light of the candles. She smiled and as she talked to Dicky, Hamilton heard her voice.

No. It can't be! Hamilton thought.

Oh, but yes, it was. Hamilton stood there, mouth open and, for a second, time stopped. It was the woman from the airplane – the one who had given him the finger and had called him a creep. Both the woman and Hamilton fumbled through their introductions. Andy, who was probably wondering if he had had so much Scotch that he was seeing things, was looking down at his running shoes and scratching his neck.

As it turned out, Mo was short for Margo, but everyone called her by the shorter name. Although she grew up in Maryland and had spent time in England, she had been living in Singapore for over a decade and was currently the tennis pro at the Raffles Hotel. The socially skilled Dicky managed to establish all of this within the few minutes it took him to acquaint everyone. Then Dicky changed the subject:

"Mo, dear, listen to me. Tomorrow we have planned an outing to the Jurong Bird Sanctuary and we insist you join us. Hamilton, Andy and Starman have all agreed to come. Jerilyn and I will prepare a picnic, and I will arrange for a car. The car may be a bit crowded, but it is not far. Both you and Jerilyn can sit on Hamilton's lap. We'll have a splendid time."

"Well, I ..."

"Now do not say that you have to give tennis lessons. No one plays tennis on New Year's Day. We will meet at half past one at Bob Chang's Café, the one just off Channing Road. You know the one. Good! See you all then. Jerilyn and I must be going. I'm afraid I shan't make it to midnight."

Jeri squeezed Hamilton's arm. "Sorry, I have to go. See you tomorrow." And they left.

Hamilton turned and looked at the woman called Mo. Her eyes were the color of a bright blue sky reflected in pools of deep water. As their eyes locked, she smiled. It was a shy, embarrassed smile. Andy and Starman wandered off toward the bar; Hamilton and Mo were now alone.

"I am afraid that I owe you an apology," Mo said. Her voice was low, almost husky. "I wasn't myself. I guess I thought you were trying to hit on me or something."

"Oh, don't worry about it. It was sort of funny, if you don't mind my saying so."

"Yes, I guess it was. But then it wasn't so funny to me. I was very tired. I hadn't slept for days."

"Yes, I know."

"You heard that, too! I'm so embarrassed. Well, I couldn't make them understand. I had to get out. It was an emergency." She laughed. "I hope you'll forgive me for what I said to you."

"Sure I will. Wasn't the first time someone told me to do that." He paused. "I see you've done away with the Mohawk."

"Mohawk? Oh, that. Yes, it didn't suit me. I guess my getting that haircut was an expression of my state of mind. I actually let the hairdresser in London talk me into it. Oh well, it will grow out."

The haircut had left her hair about two inches at its longest. In the flicker of the fire Hamilton could see a few flecks of gray, and around her eyes were fine crow's feet. She was an aging beauty, but she had spent too much time in the sun, Hamilton thought.

At her invitation, they danced. Her body was firm, almost hard, but then, she was a tennis pro – a piano-playing tennis pro, Hamilton thought. She smelled of soap.

"I hope whatever upset you so badly has finally gone away," Hamilton said, close to her ear.

"It never goes away. Not completely. I have a son in Britain. In school. Every time I go there I get upset. But when I return home everything tends to settle down. Distance gives me perspective, I guess."

"How old is he?"

"He's almost sixteen."

The music stopped and there was commotion around the piano. A man with a saxophone waved at Mo and she waved back, smiling. The sax bleated, charging the room with energy. Hamilton looked at his watch and noted that it was close to midnight, then turned his eyes to Andy, who was across the room sprawled out on a wingback chair. Andy held an empty glass in one hand and, with his bush hat in his other hand, kept time as he continued with the poem:

"Forever and forever – longer than soil is brown and solid – longer / than water ebbs and flows."

"I have to get my uncle a taxi. I won't be long."

Andy protested, promised Hamilton that he would not take another drink and said that he wanted to talk to the big black man whose name he had forgotten, arguing that he needed to finish his story about how he helped free the blacks in Georgia during the civil rights movement. Hamilton told Andy that Starman had probably left, but that he could talk with him tomorrow. Then he tightly clutched Andy's good arm, all but forcing him out of the house and into the parking lot. He put Andy into the back seat of a taxi, gave the driver the hotel business card and paid him extra so as to make sure that Andy got safely to his room. Andy rolled down the window and his body hung partially out. As the taxi pulled onto the road, Hamilton could see Andy slinging his bush hat around for emphasis and shouting words of Walt Whitman into the Singapore night. On his way back inside, Hamilton spotted the autorickshaw. He hurried, trying to pass unnoticed, but they had already seen him.

"Take your time, Hampeldon. No hurry, man! We go to Bogey Street." Hamilton ignored them.

When he re-entered the large room, Hamilton saw an older woman, the ambassador's wife he assumed, standing at the piano. There was a drum roll.

"Two minutes before midnight," the woman announced, placing an alarm clock on the piano.

Hamilton made his way to the bar, but Mo was not there and he guessed that she was in the restroom; after all, she seems fond of them, he thought, chuckling to himself. The crowd grew quiet. They exhibited an attitude of solemn anticipation for in seconds it would be midnight. Yes, the usual thing – a kind of pious investment of silence before an event.

The hands of the clock merged and the alarm rang. It was midnight and the band played the usual tune and, as usual, people sang along, some kissed and embraced, some swore oaths and made promises and others made resolutions, few of which would be kept. Some made propositions, propositions that were likely to be taken as flattery and nothing more.

"Hamilton, you may kiss me. It will prove your forgiveness."

Mo had come up from behind, and when Hamilton turned, he found Mo standing there with her neck arched vulnerably toward him. He nervously twisted the corners of his mustache, looked into her eyes and kissed her lightly on the lips.

"Andy's taken care of. Why don't we go? I have a car, sort of. Let's go somewhere for a drink."

"I don't drink, but fine, that sounds good to me. I could use something to eat."

When Mo saw the autorickshaw, she was amused and unable to suppress her laughter when meeting the two "directors of tourism" who had anointed themselves with the names of characters from the old television show. She grinned as Hamilton was told that Mo was much prettier than his previous date, and she playfully took sides with Ski when he insisted that a café on Bogey Street was the best place for them to go. So they flew out into the Singapore night and Ski shouted, "For go it!" and Hamilton, annoyed, corrected him.

"You mean 'go for it.'"

The four of them – Hamilton, Mo, Ski and Hutch – sat at a table that was set up in the street. Colored lights were strung overhead. Ski explained that he knew the people who owned the restaurant and that they were allowed to put the tables in the street only during festivals and only after midnight. Yes, they sat in the center of Bogey Street. Ski ordered for them a special dish at a special price at a special place.

The special dish arrived along with beer, soup and a Diet Pepsi. It was placed in the center of the table and served on a banana leaf. In the middle of the leaf was a wooden bowl containing a reddish paste. Surrounding the dish, which was accented with orchids and fiery azaleas, were several dozen tear-shaped pods, each about the size of a man's testicle.

"Love fruit. Ignorant people, they say the gods eat it – those who still believe in the gods," Ski said laughing. "Hampeldon, do like me." He picked up a pod, dipped it in the red paste and popped it into his mouth. Hamilton reached for a pod, dipped it and bit. It was fleshy, slightly sweet, but it had an odd, bitter aftertaste.

"Pretty good. What is it?"

"It say it is durian. It big nut. Nut with sharp knife things. Grow on big tree."

"I've tasted one before," Mo said, adding that she didn't care for it. She proceeded to eat her noodle soup and drink the Diet Pepsi.

"So that's what it tastes like," Hamilton said, and he told them about his and Andy's encounter with the man with the machete. They ate, talked and watched the motley throng drift by. When they had finished the beer and all of the pods, and Hutch had scooped the remaining red paste out of the bowl with his finger, Ski said, "We go. It is time. We know special place. Hampeldon, you pay, okay?"

The autorickshaw bumped off the sidewalk and into the road. Ski gunned it and they flew down the street, which turned into a maze of short blocks. When they came to a wide road that ran beside the river, Ski slammed a cassette into the tape player. The music was louder than the putting of the engine, and Ski and Hutch sang along to Stevie Wonder's "I Just Called To Say I Love You," Hamilton put his arm over Mo's shoulders and they turned to each other and laughed. With his free hand he smoothed his mustache.

The autorickshaw turned a corner and went down a road past warehouses behind which Hamilton could see the tops of loading cranes and the masts of ships. Ski stopped the engine and they could hear chanting, gongs, bells and horns.

"We walk," Ski announced.

They walked along in the dark for a block, turned and saw people chanting in firelight. Hundreds of them were carrying paper lanterns lit by candles and flooding into a concrete building.

"There! The car park," Ski pointed, indicating that they were going to follow the crowd inside the building. They hurried to catch up with the chanting crowd and followed them down a ramp into a great room, empty except for an abandoned car. It was an old Cadillac sitting with four flat tires, hood up and fins that looked stupid, like a dead shark. At the far end of the room, the crowd was gathered. A fire blazed under a ventilation grate and before the fire was a platform made of loading flats. The flickering blaze of the fire seemed to keep time with the chanting: "SUB RA! SUB RA! SUB RA ..." Hamilton pulled Mo close to him.

"It's part of the festival, I guess," she shouted. Under him, Hamilton felt a dull thud and a vibration on the souls of his feet. KAPLUNK! KAPLUNK!

"What's that? What's that noise?" Hamilton shouted.

Mo leaned toward him. "Tunneling for a new subway line," she shouted. "It seems they are always tunneling under us."

Suddenly a naked creature covered with ash sprang to the make-shift stage. "SUB RA! SUB RA!" the crowd chanted faster. In the center of the platform was a great black pot and the creature gestured to the crowd and climbed into the pot. "SUB RA! SU BRA!" faster and faster they chanted. A man in a gray cowl jumped to the stage. He looked at the crowd, shouted something unintelligible, pulled the cowl from over his head and placed it over the top of the pot. He stood there naked, said something very quietly to the crowd and they immediately stopped the chant. He reached for the cowl, snatched it off the pot and out jumped the creature now covered from head to toe in gold sequins. "SUB RA! SUB RA!" the crowd resumed their chant. KAPLUNK! KAPLUNK! The gold man was chased around the rickety stage by the naked man. "SUB RA! SUB RA!" The naked man grabbed the gold man by the neck, forced him to his knees and mounted him from behind.

"SUB RA! SUB RA!" KAPLUNK! KAPLUNK! Hamilton felt dizzy and bitter juices from deep inside him were forced into his mouth.

"Mo, I have to go." He covered his mouth and pushed his way through the crowd, staggered up the ramp, out of the smoke and into the thick, dark night. Hamilton fell to his knees, bent over and vomited. The taste of bile was in his mouth, and it felt as if his insides were coming out.

## *BIRDLAND*

Hamilton opened one eye and squinted at the white ceiling. Rolling on his side, he looked blankly at the green and gold wallpaper with its repeated English pastoral pattern – a young straw-hatted shepherd leaning on his staff, watching his sheep, and a young maid in a hoop skirt hiding behind a gnarled oak, watching him. There was a chest of deep red mahogany drawers: a copy of an antique Sheraton. Beside the drawers was an electric keyboard and speakers, a door and a window, a drawn chintz curtain, and beyond that, the blue sky. Because his bed was folded out from a sofa, there was not much room – just enough for him to slide his feet to the floor. He sat up and attempted to stand, but then he felt dizzy, gave in to the inertia of his body and plopped back down. There he, Hamilton Fowler West, sat, just like the day he was born: naked as a jaybird.

At that moment the door opened and there, in red silk pajamas, wearing straw flip flops and holding a stack of folded, freshly washed clothes, was Mo.

"Oh my God!" he muttered, grabbing the sheet in a wad, urgently pressing it into his lap.

"Oh, sorry. Thought you'd still be asleep. You're in my suite at the Raffles Hotel. You were a sick boy last night. You had a high fever. It must have been some kind of allergic reaction. That's what the hotel doctor said. I just called him, again. Said to phone him back if you're not better and he'd come up and have another look."

"What do you mean? Allergic reaction?" he asked, rubbing his head.

"Something you ate, I'd think. But, you're definitely better. I know about these things: I, myself, am allergic. I know from experience that such a reaction can be serious, but not necessarily deadly. Hamilton, do you remember being driven around by those two nationals?"

"Nationals? Oh ... sure. Starsky and the one who never said anything."

"You mean the Indian one called Hutch. And our going to Bogey Street? And eating that durian? And going to that parking garage?"

"Yes, I do remember all of that. Bogey Street and their playing that stupid telephone song – the song by whatever his name is.

"Stevie Wonder, yes. But nothing about any garage?"

"Garage? No. No, garage."

"Just as I thought. It was the durian. You had a violent reaction to it. Get dressed and we'll see how you feel then. The shower is through this door, down the hall past my bedroom. Here's a towel. You'll find a new toothbrush on the sink. Hope you don't mind using my razor. It's on the back of the toilet. Feel free to even use it on your head if ..."

"No, no. Like you, I'm letting it grow out."

"Well, that's good. We're supposed to meet the professor and whatever her name is in two hours, and Starman too, but I have my doubts that he'll show up. If, of course, you feel up to it. If not, I'll call the Dikshits and tell them something. But I'm not going if you don't. What about your uncle? He's probably worried because you never went to your hotel. Shouldn't you call him?"

"No. He's already mad at me for sending him home in the taxi. I'm sure he could care less about where I am. And don't worry, if we do go, you'll see him soon enough because he'll be right there at that café. Andy doesn't like to miss anything."

Soon they were sitting in Mo's tiny kitchen beside a window that overlooked the tennis courts three stories below. When she gave Hamilton his soft boiled egg and toast, he found his stomach to be as empty as a cavern. He asked for more coffee. She asked him if he really was sure that he felt alright, to which he responded that he was fine, except for being embarrassed. She said that it was okay, that he shouldn't feel bad, that he had been poisoned. He drank his coffee and she told him about the strange things that had gone on in the abandoned parking garage, how their two "tour guides" had just disappeared and how a nice taxi driver had helped her get him to the hotel. Hamilton said that he thought that he might remember bits of what had happened, but had she not just told him about it, he might have mistaken it for a dream. Then, embarrassed, he told her that he also has forgotten her last name and she told him that it did not matter, but that her last name was Pangolin.

As discussed and agreed upon – for the purpose of avoiding innuendoes – two blocks from Bob Something's Restaurant, Mo got out of the taxi and walked so they would not appear to have been together. When Hamilton stepped into the restaurant he saw them all sitting at a large table in the back under a whirring ceiling fan. They immediately noticed him. Starman and Dicky stood, but the others remained seated and Andy glared at him from under his bush hat. His left arm was in a sling. Starman extended his hand and then Dicky did the same. Hamilton looked at Andy and asked about the sling.

"Slipped on the goddamned steps. Thanks to you. It's my bad arm too. But it'll be alright. Went to that place near the hotel and they fixed me up. It's just bruised. Where in the hell have you been?"

"You mean you went to that acupuncture place? You must be nuts."

"Quiet, Hambone. When I need your medical opinion, I'll ask for it," Andy grunted, adding that the sling would come off in a week, and then he pushed up his glasses, looked at the others and winked. "It's the arm I hurt in 1954 in Mexico. Was there with my last wife. Tried to impress her by diving off the rocks in Acapulco. It was our honeymoon. Tore the friggin' thing right outta the socket."

Hamilton looked at Andy and shook his head. Starman rose. Mo had arrived. There she stood smiling. Hamilton looked at her tanned legs, her blue shorts and her T-shirt with a great sunburst across her breasts. A beam of light played with her silver earrings.

"Morning everybody," she said. "Guess we're ready to fly away to Birdland."

And it was at that moment, without either reflection or ambiguity, that Hamilton knew he loved her.

"Yes, the car is waiting. I suggest we go. Mister Benjamin here has made all the arrangements for our transportation. You are really getting to know your way around, Andy. I am amazed," Dicky said, his bald head beaming.

When they left the restaurant and walked toward a dark-blue, older-model Toyota van, Hamilton saw Ski's stubble head turn toward them. Ski was looking through his aviator glasses, grinning and waving. Andy had made the arrangements, alright. He must have taken their number off their card and called them.

As Dicky had foretold, the car was crowded, as any car would have been for the six of them. The smaller seat held just two and the larger, three. As it turned out, the joke Dicky had made the night before was only partially right. Someone had to sit in the lap of someone else; by her silence, Jeri showed her displeasure with the arrangement. But Mo was fine with it; Hamilton could tell she was relaxed by the way she sat on his lap – easy and natural.

Neither Hamilton nor Mo had much to say as they darted through the traffic and then glided along a wide boulevard into suburbs toward Jurong Bird Park. Hamilton and Mo paid little attention to Dicky's constant chatter or to the questions Andy fired at Starman, or to the calm and measured answers Starman gave him. But Hamilton, having played university sports, did take note of Starman's admission that he had once played middle linebacker for the University of Alabama Crimson Tide.

"I can't imagine a man like you taking part in such a barbaric game," Jeri said, but Starman had replied that he played because he had won a football scholarship and that the money had been necessary for his going to college. Then he admitted that he had liked it.

"Not much farther," Dicky said. "Who would have thought, with of all these high-rise buildings around, that the best ornithological park in the world would be here? This is all reclaimed land from Singapore's garbage, actually. And by the way, the real name is not Birdland. I think Jeri is responsible for that."

"That's simply not true, Dicky! Everyone calls it that," Jeri snapped.

"Yes, Ducky," Dicky said to her sheepishly, "the name has just caught on."

They got out of the van. Hamilton hoped that Ski and Hutch would stay where they were and that Ski would continue to keep his mouth shut about his carting Mo and himself around the night before. Ski did remain silent and Hamilton wondered if maybe they had slipped something into his drink before they disappeared.

"We wait in car. No hurry," Ski said in a contrite tone.

Hutch grinned and waved, and, aside from Ski's conspiratorial wink, it was as if the previous night had never happened.

Dicky bought tickets for everyone. They entered the gate, walked up a ramp and looked out over the most varied of habitat: savannahs here, stands of bamboo there, clusters of pine woods, deciduous forest, sandy desert and broad-leaf groves as dark and secret as the tropical night. It is as if all of nature had been gathered into one place. A kind of man-made Eden, Hamilton thought, but made for the birds. They stood under a great canopy of clear nylon mesh, hardly visible above the trees, and birds were everywhere. Long-necked cranes stood and nested near ponds and fierce-eyed predators perched on the carcasses of trees. Brightly colored birds could be glimpsed in the jungle.

At the far edge of the park they could see a sign marking the entrance to a tunnel leading to the semi-polar regions, and next to it Hamilton recognized waddling Canadian geese, loons and mallard ducks. It gave Hamilton a tinge of homesickness. Dicky explained that few of the birds were indigenous and that most of them – like the ducks, loons and geese – had been flown in from various parts of the globe.

"That's not true," Jeri interrupted, "some were hatched right here in Birdland." Dicky conceded the point and Jeri read aloud from her handbook: "Coexistence of nature and industrial man will have to be maintained as the world of nature is an integral part of the cosmos ..."

An electric tram rolled along on silent plastic wheels pulling a dozen cars. It stopped under the canopy at a McDonald's restaurant with its brass fixtures, lacy ferns and ceiling fans blowing cool air under the yellow arches. As they stood in line for a seat on the tram, a slim but large-breasted woman with long, dark hair carrying a diaper bag and a sleeping child on her back butted her way in front of Andy. He cursed under his breath, stepped aside, and entered the car behind her; Starman, Mo, Hamilton, Jeri and Dicky sat down with her. The woman wore Birkenstocks, jeans and a T-shirt with a picture of a blue and green Earth taken from space. She wore sunglasses and a baseball cap with her ponytail sticking out the back. The tram jerked, its electric motor whirling, and there was a crack. A message came from a speaker:

"Welcome to Jurong Bird Park, the largest urban bird sanctuary in the world. Here, a great number of the birds on our planet live peacefully together in their man-made, natural environments ..."

They rolled through rain forest and desert, and then along a brown creek with fingers of mangroves grasping muddy banks.

"... *Chrysotrogan caligatus*, or the Long-tailed Green Trogon, lives along the swamps of Central America and the extreme Southeastern United States ..."

"Just around this corner and we'll see the path to the footbridge," Dicky told them. He pressed a button and the tram stopped. They all stepped to the platform, left the woman and sleeping child and started up the path next to a small sign that read "FOOTBRIDGE" in at least a dozen languages. The path wound through a great grove of bamboo shoots and soon they found themselves in mist. They could hear the rush of water. Occasionally, the sun shone through the foliage making the churning droplets sparkle and, looking up, Hamilton noted that, at times, it was impossible to even see the nylon net strung high above. Below there were scores of parrots with blue heads and red breasts and beaks.

"Rainbow Lorikeets," Andy said. "They're from New Zealand."

"Australia," Jeri corrected him. "Says so right here in the book." Giving Andy a smirk, she asked, "Where did you learn so much about birds?"

"I told you already. In Georgia."

Andy's tone indicated this was his final answer.

They had come to the footbridge – a span of thirty feet that stretched across a waterfall and a rushing stream fifty feet below. From the spot where they stood high upon the rocks, from which clung the bridge, they looked out again over the park. Taking charge, Jeri told them all to come and, motioning toward a clearing, indicated to Starman that he was supposed to put the picnic basket down on a white plastic table standing under a twisted pine tree. Jeri opened the basket and with deliberation began to empty its contents: sandwiches, fruit, cheese and a bottle of German wine.

Mo took a can of Diet Pepsi from her bag, placed it on the table and started to sit. She stopped suddenly and, with her hand covering her nose and mouth, said, "Oh! That awful smell!" And at once, they all smelled it.

"It's coming from over here," said Andy as he stood at the edge of the gorge, pointing down. "Look there. There on the rocks next to the creek." And then they saw vultures dining on a pig.

"Oh, God! Let's get out of here!" Mo said, gagging.

Hamilton and Starman – under Jeri's direction – quickly scooped up the picnic, threw it into the basket and they all hurried across the bridge. It was when they were just across that they heard a PING and then another PING and then a SNAP. They all looked in the direction of the noise. Down the hill, at the edge of the bamboo near the mangrove swamp, they saw people scurrying about. One of them was the woman with the baby on her back and the other, who appeared to be a man with a long, blonde ponytail sticking out from behind a baseball cap, held what looked like a pair of wire cutters. They continued to snip the wires supporting the nylon mesh above. The pinging and snapping of the wires continued and Hamilton's group watched in amazement as the nylon mesh dropped, landing limply and draping over the branches of the limbs below. And when a great hole appeared, letting in the open sky, the pinging and snapping stopped and they watched as a single bird darted through the opening, then another and another, and then a flutter of birds escaped.

"Oh, how awful! Look what they've done!" Jeri cried.

They could see the woman with the baby taking the wire cutters and putting them into her diaper bag. There was a hissing noise and the baby began flinging its arms. They could hear its cries. As the man toyed with some sort of canister, from which the hissing came, they watched in wonder as a great, yellow balloon suddenly appeared into existence as if from nowhere. The balloon soared upward through the hole and out into the sky. As the great, yellow orb floated over them they could read the message written on its side: "FRIENDS OF THE BIRDS." Hamilton looked down and watched as the two of them and the screaming baby dashed into the thicket of bamboo.

"They went in there," he pointed.

A loud speaker cracked. An excited voice spoke in Chinese and then said in English: "ATTENTION. ATTENTION. EVERYONE MUST LEAVE PARK. EVERYONE MUST LEAVE IMMEDIATELY!"

Jeri was furious at the people who had ruined their bird watching. She said that they were nature-hating perverts who should be put in prison. Andy laughed, agreeing with Jeri, but then added that the culprits must be anarchists like those who could be found in great numbers in California and who are usually stoned on alfalfa or carrot juice. Jeri retorted that they likely were rednecks escaped from Georgia. Dicky laughed and calmly told everyone that it did not matter who the crazy people were, the day was far from ruined and they should go to the tower across from the park to have a drink.

From the tower they could see the park below, the harbor and sea to the one side and the river, the city and the causeway that connects the island to Malaysia on the other. They took a table beside the window and everyone ordered a beer except Mo, who opened her Diet Pepsi, and Andy, who ordered a double vodka martini with a twist. The waiter brought the drinks and Starman got up, excused himself and asked the waiter the way to the restroom. While he was away, Dicky told Hamilton and Mo that Starman taught English and coached lacrosse and soccer at a private boys' school in Virginia, commenting on Starman's cultivated speech and manner.

"Yeah, the boy speaks like a white judge from Savannah or Charleston," Andy agreed.

"And he's at Oxford. He must have taken advantage of one of those wonderful programs for disadvantaged minorities. Except for his color, you would never guess he was an Afro-American." Jeri added. No one responded except Dicky, who attempted to deflect everyone's attention from Jeri's comment by directing it toward a great bird that had landed on a flag standard protruding from the side of the tower near their window.

"My God, look at the size of him," Mo said, pointing with her Diet Pepsi can.

"Must have escaped," Andy remarked as he put down his martini, pushed his glasses up on his nose and fumbled with his good hand for a cigarette.

"Here it is," Jeri said, "right here in my book: Lammergeier, Lamb's Vulture, or sometimes *Gypaetus barbatus*, Bearded Vulture, because of the feathers that hang from its beak forming a mustache. Found in the high mountains of Asia."

"Don't you think it looks a bit like Hamilton? The whiskers and all," Jeri asked.

At that moment, the bird sprang from its perch, dropped for a second, flapped its wings and then soared off into the sky. Everyone was silent as they watched the great creature until it vanished somewhere between the sea and the horizon.

"Well, I don't know about anyone else, but I'm starved," Jeri said as she placed the picnic basket on the table and began to empty it of its contents.

Dicky was looking at her disapprovingly and shaking his head, indicating that one does not bring one's own meal to a restaurant, but she dismissed him, saying that she had made the picnic herself and they could not let such good food go to waste.

"Ham sandwich anyone?" she asked.

Andy, who had been watching her, was smiling in amusement and at the same time was fumbling with his old World War II Zippo lighter. Finally the lighter produced a flame and Andy, with his eyes still on Jeri, brought the fire toward his long Winston cigarette, only to drop the lighter into his double vodka martini.

"Jeez, Andy!" Hamilton shouted as blue flame burst first from the exploding liquid and then, when the glass spilled out across the table, from the table cloth itself. Everyone pushed away – everyone except Andy, that is, who just sat there, his eyebrows singeing. Hamilton, already up on his feet, grabbed a corner of the blazing table cloth, flung it to the floor and began stomping on it, along with a smashed jar of mango chutney, sandwiches, Stilton cheese, bananas and a broken bottle of Mosel wine.

After returning from the restroom, Starman at once heard the confusion and saw the mess and began running toward the scene. It was then that he collided with a waiter racing along with a fire extinguisher, knocked the waiter down and his glasses off. For a few seconds he felt around for the glasses, but with all the shouting and confusion, his instincts took over and, squinting at the red shape of the fire extinguisher lying at his feet, grabbed it and sprayed a group of terrified Japanese tourists with foam.

When the fire and the Japanese were both extinguished, Andy apologized to the manager and tried to make some joke about having had a barbecue, but the manager did not understand and coolly replied, "No problem, Mister. But we do not like the Barbie doll in Singapore."

Andy laughed and told the man that this was okay, that another double, dry vodka martini with a twist would do just fine. He, too, had never been a fan of Barbie.

"Didn't that just blow your mind?" Jeri asked, as if she just had some mystical experience.

"Ah, but this is Birdland, Ducky," Dicky replied, smiling. "In Singapore, anything is possible."

"So I've been told," Hamilton said as he took Mo's arm, pulled her toward him and whispered in her ear that the two of them were leaving. Soon they were telling everyone that they were going back to town to play tennis. Hamilton didn't even know how to hold a tennis racket, but now he no longer cared what they thought. And neither did Mo. Hamilton was astonished by the intensity of his feelings and the clarity of his thought as he turned around and looked at Mo. Wonder lit his world with sharp-edged clarity. Hamilton was seeing the world from the perspective of a demonic zone and he knew that he was in love.

During the night, when Hamilton returned to his and Andy's hotel, Andy was already snoring. Hamilton was so excited that he had trouble falling asleep, for he had spent the rest of the day and all of the evening with Mo. He felt light – so light he could float away. Yes, he told himself, somehow things were different.

The next morning, Andy tried to make Hamilton feel guilty about his abrupt departure the day before. Andy reminded him that he had even forgotten all about the presents sent along by Jud: the gifts they were supposed to have opened on New Year's Day.

Hamilton humored Andy and finally Andy showed Hamilton the two bottles of Johnnie Walker Jud had sent him. He brought Hamilton his package and, with his room key, Hamilton slit open the paper. The package contained a rusty metal box with a dent across the top. The box was about the size of a big-city telephone book. Jud had taped a brass key to the lid.

"I recognize that box," Andy grumped. "Thing's been in our family for years – generations even. Hoped I'd never see it again. What kinda doggone joke is this?"

Hamilton removed the brass key, inserted it into the lock and opened the box. Inside he found two fat, brown envelopes, a small plastic freezer bag and a used letter-sized white envelope with a return address:

Ira S. Thompson
132 Rosedale Avenue
Toronto, Canada
M4T 1C9

Hamilton pulled the contents from the two brown envelopes and placed them on the bed. The top envelope contained a court transcript of a trial that had taken place in Altamaha in 1954, and in the other was Jud's manuscript about Judah P. Benjamin. Although Hamilton remembered Jud mentioning the court transcript, he had never seen it before. But Andy knew right away what it was. Jud's manuscript – if one could call it that – was a real mess. It consisted of a mixture of notes, typed and hand-written pages of prose and verse, mostly in iambic pentameter and one epic poem about some black guy.

"That damn Jud, he really is nuts," Andy muttered.

Hamilton opened the plastic bag and let its contents spill out on the bed too. There was a silver locket with the initials "R.O.P." and inside, a ringlet of black hair. There were also a couple of old documents and several yellowed letters.

"I've seen all that old stuff. In fact, I'm the one who gave it to Jud. Was over a decade ago. Yep, it was when he came to Seven Bridges to visit me. It was before he moved up to Canada. Just put it back in the friggin' box. I don't even want to look at it," Andy growled.

Finally, Hamilton reached inside the used letter-sized envelope and found a note Jud had written on the old typewriter Hamilton had seen in Rodger's studio at Benjamin House.

Dec. 26, 1988, Rye

Happy New Year, Hambone,

The contents of the plastic bag belong to Andy. Give it to him and tell him I'm sorry I kept it xxxso long. The court transcript is the xxxone you've heard me talk about – the one uncle Durden gave me. It was already in the box and I just xx decided to leave it there for your amusement. Unc won't be interested in any of it. Well, you said you'd help me straighten out my story about Judah P., so, here it is. Have a look. I xxxguess I just don't know what I have to do in order to write this kind of story. I've tried for three years, but this is about the best I can come up with. Perhaps the letters will help. Anyway, you'll enjoy them. Although Rodger and I expect to see you and Unc soon, and for you to lose your bet with us. When you return, I'll be gone, so pay up xxxxto Rodger. Have you found where history began? If it hasn't ended yet, I think it will end soon.

Your cousin, Anubis III (Jud)

"Well, he's right about one thing. I don't want anything to do with this. Jud's crazier'n a piss ant. Why he wants to spend his time writing a book about our reactionary ancestor beats the hell outta me. And that other stuff? That trial ... don't even wanna be reminded of it!" Andy said. His face had turned red.

"Well, you don't have to convince me of that, but you have to appreciate the fact that for some reason the biography means a lot to Jud. I can't understand why he's having so much trouble. But then I promised him, eh? So I have to see if I can help."

"I've known it all along. You both are fucking nuts."

"Look, Andy," Hamilton replied, trying to change the subject, "Mo has tennis lessons to give in the mornings. I'll work on Jud's manuscript then. We're in no hurry to get to India. As it turns out, Mo has a tennis tournament in New Delhi in two or three weeks. We can get your visa and go there then – with her. And there's also that conference in Jaipur that Dicky was talking about; he's been trying to get me to deliver a speech – that might be fun. And Dicky says his organization will pay for all of it."

"Can't believe what I'm hearing."

"Tonight I'm taking Mo to the movies. Want to come?"

"Look here, Hamilton. You realize how you're acting? You're so fucked up; I guess I'd better spell it out for you. You're running around here happier than a dog with two dicks. Boy, you're going too goddamned fast. You don't know the first thing about that girl! There's just something about you ... you trying to jump over your shadow and ... and you're gonna get hurt."

"Well, thanks for caring, Unc. I'm touched. Really, I am. But I'm a big boy. I know what I'm doing."

"Yeah? Big dick maybe. And the shit, it's gonna hit that fan."

For the next two weeks Hamilton was with Mo every afternoon and every night and sometimes he stayed over at her place. As one might surmise, this annoyed Andy. One afternoon Hamilton and Mo saw a ring at Lucky Plaza – a gold ring fashioned in the shape of a durian – and Hamilton bought it for her. It was impractical because of the spikes, but was made less so when filed down. Even when blunted its beauty shone clearly in the light and the lady at the Lucky Plaza had sworn it had magical powers. Mo bought Hamilton an 1861 edition of Don Quixote, printed in Sidney in 1910.

Sometimes Hamilton and Mo took trips in Ski and Hutch's car with Dicky, Jeri, Starman and Andy. They spent several afternoons at the beach and saw everything there was to see on the island. Andy's wing healed and soon his sling came off. They never returned to Birdland. In the end, the entire group agreed to go to India together and to meet up with Mo at the conference in Jaipur after her tournament in New Delhi was over.

During the mornings, Hamilton worked on Jud's book. He decided to let no one see it until he was done and planned to be finished with a rough draft before he and Andy returned to Rye. In order to write it, he decided that he must step backwards – back to those conditions that make Jud's story possible in the first place. And when Jud sees what Hamilton has done, Jud will laugh his ass off.

And yes, Andy had been right about it. Hamilton had flipped for Mo. In fact, he even worked on Jud's story at Mo's place using Mo's Zenith 286 laptop while she gave her tennis lessons. Hamilton was just finishing the first chapter. He stopped for a minute and glanced at his watch. He thought about Mo – about how they would make love when she returned all sweaty from her lessons. He put the last period on the last page, saved and printed. He ripped the paper from the printer and began to read.

# JUD'S STORY
by
Judah Anubis Benjamin III

For the Savages,
because they always get the last laugh.

"The first thing he found was the rough draught of a sonnet ..."
Cervantes, DON QUIXOTE

## CHAPTER I
### ALTAMAHA

On the banks of Altamaha River, across and slightly downstream from where the Ocmulgee and Oconee come together, my great-great-grandfather arrived in 1876. His name was Joseph Malachi Benjamin. Formally, he had been Captain Benjamin of Wayne's Dragoons of the Army of Georgia, but that had been over a decade before and the new world, born out of the war, made no room for such a past. The previous year he had sailed with his wife and infant son from British Honduras, where he had taken refuge in a colony established by veterans of the defeated Confederate States of America. Rozita Ortez Perez, his wife of a mere few months, died of the fever in the Florida Panhandle, and my great-great-grandfather buried her in the sand of a dune overlooking the Gulf of Mexico. That same day he left with his little son, Eli Anubis, for a river he had learned about in a letter written by his brother. Indeed, his brother had been right about the river, for its basin was rich in virgin pines and its waters could be used for transporting logs and timber to the sea. It was there that my great-great-grandfather started a sawmill.

For nearly ten years, in the jungles of Central America, he tried to forget all that had happened in the previous world. He lived among others who wished to do the same, to start life again, and he lived in peace among his former comrades in arms until the colony was later joined, and eventually taken over, by several hundred members of a religious sect. They banished Malachi from their midst – expelling him not only because he was a Jew, but also because his brother was Judah P. Benjamin, the former Secretary of State for the Confederacy. They, among many others, blamed Judah for the loss of the war. So Malachi left the colony and found work in a sawmill in the northern part of the country near the Mexican border.

It was there in a border-town whorehouse that he met Rozita. She became pregnant with his child and Malachi knew that he must take her away. So he wrote his older brother, Judah, who had fled to England and had become a famous barrister there. His brother sent money and wrote that, since Rozita would never be happy in England, they should consider going to southern Georgia. While escaping the Yankees in 1865, Judah had passed through this place on the Altamaha River and remembered thinking that it would be a perfect place for a lumber mill.

In the rolling hills just south of where the city of Atlanta now stands, the Altamaha River begins. Its source is two separate streams that bubble up from what I've heard is a great underground sea. Both these waters bear ancient names of neighboring nations of Indians that, at one time, were great rivals and often were at war. The stream that flows from the northwest is the Ocmulgee, and the one coming from the northeast is the Oconee. The rivers rush and tumble through the clay hills, and just past Macon they slow. It is here that the piedmont stops and the earth flattens into a coastal plain. The rivers become quiet and deliberate, for what they have lost in swiftness they have gained in volume and depth. Sixty miles from where the plain begins, the rivers converge and it is there, at the confluence of the rivers, that the short but great Altamaha River is formed, beginning its hundred-mile journey to the sea. Gradually, the peach-colored clay bluffs give way to white sandbars and the muddy water turns black with tannin. The secret and silent river winds its way through pine barrens, scrub oak dunes and mossy swamps. Finally, engulfed by the Atlantic tide, the water turns brackish and the river spreads its fingers and forms with its caresses the delta and its marshy islands of green savannah land.

The grassy islands are still known by the name of the Indian tribe that once lived there – Guale, or Guale Land. The region upriver the Indians called Tama: the Land of Fortune. There is an old story that after the Battle of Bloody Marsh – fought by the Spanish and British in 1742 – the Spanish buried their gold upstream and hastily departed to Florida, thinking that they'd return for it. The Spanish had their own name for the river. They called it Rio de Talaje, but Hernando De Soto in 1540 referred to it in his chronicles as Al Tama or, again, the Land of Fortune. Even the English, thirty years after the fateful battle, retained the Indian name. This was in 1770 when Oliver Goldsmith, in his poem "The Deserted Village," called the land Altama.

Although this legend was lost by both the Spanish and the English, it was remembered by the Indians who, in the end, had the final word. At some forgotten time, it was they who added the "ha" to the end of the name, thereby giving us Altamaha and the Indians the last laugh.

Thus, it is as if the conditions that make this old story possible were lost in the twists and bends of the river itself: in its secret currents, its flows and eddies, its underground source and its culmination into the eternal formlessness of the sea. Rivers have power because of what is buried in their waters, and the power of old stories lies in the darkness of their origins and the ambiguity of their meaning. It is through what was forgotten that this story, and all stories, acquires magic, mystery and authority.

When Malachi and Eli arrived at the river there were only a few inhabitants. These were the two scores of Indians who were the remnants of a massacre that allegedly had taken place some years before. Their settlement was near the spit of land formed by the confluence of the rivers and it was on that very tip of earth – the site of an ancient burial ground – that my great-great-grandfather found a blue-gray metal box.

In the box he put the certificate of his birth and circumcision, dated 1844, and another stating that he had won the Talmud award in Hebrew school. Both documents were from the Ezra Bessaroth Sephardic Temple in Wilmington, North Carolina. Then there was his diploma for an A.B. degree, taken in classics from Mercer University, donare in urbs Maconus, anno Domini, MDCCCLX (1860). There was a letter from Jefferson Davis commissioning him that same year as an officer in the army of the Confederate States of America, and a silver locket containing a few strands of Rozita's hair. The box was discovered by Eli after his father's death and it was passed down through the family by members of successive generations, each keeping its contents secret. The box came to me from my Uncle Andy, who received it from a family friend and relative by marriage, Durden Fowler Jr. Durden had acquired it from the Altamaha County Courthouse after the box had been submitted as evidence in a murder trial in which he was the public prosecutor in 1954. With the box now in my possession and since all of the Benjamins are dead except Uncle Andy (Anubis Rayburn Benjamin II) and me, Jud (Anubis Judah Benjamin III), and since we live in a time when nothing such as this would even matter, at last the story can be told.

Malachi hired a strapping young Negro, Jack, and a Creek-Negro named Cora, both from the town of Baxton, ten miles upriver on the Oconee. It was said that Jack could pull a fat-lighter stump from the ground with his bare hands, and he helped Malachi fell the pine and clear the land while Cora cared for Eli. With the money his brother sent him, Malachi bought a boiler, a steam engine, belts and a saw blade, and brought them by raft to their new clearing next to the bluffs on the river.

The clearing got larger and the mill grew. People came to cut the pines and float the logs downriver or to slice them into boards to be barged down to Brunswick and taken away by ships. Shacks were built for the wave of timbermen and mill hands, and then they built houses and a store from Benjamin board. The store was owned and operated by a family named Coots, who had been around those parts since General Oglethorpe founded Savannah in 1733. For generations they had thrived on the manufacture and sale of illegal whisky.

On the orders of a stern, green-eyed Baptist preacher, a church was built by a few God-fearing mill hands. He was known as Brother Rayburn, and he just arrived one day on a raft with his daughter, two beds, a table, two chairs, a piano, a spotted dog, six chickens and a sow. It didn't take long for the "hell-fire man," as they sometimes called him, to find a large following, and soon, with his daughter at the piano, he had most of the community singing the hymn "Shall We Gather at the River?" But none from the Coots family ever went to his or any other church, and he and the Coots family became enemies.

Malachi soon fell in love with and married the preacher's cross-eyed daughter. Her name was Jessie and her tongue was like a razor and her vision even sharper. It was Jessie who persuaded Malachi to have bills and receipts made up that read: "Benjamin's Mill, Altamaha, Georgia." She announced: "We have started a town," knowing that their destiny and that of the town were to be one. The practical and stern woman never asked about Malachi's past and he knew better than to tell her. With the help of Cora, she raised Eli as if he were her own and it wasn't long before Jessie swelled in the belly with their first and only child, Vera Ola.

Malachi hired a carpenter from Savannah, and, with two mill hands, the carpenter built Jessie a house. While the house was not grand, it was what they would have called "proper," with its high ceilings and big windows, its porch across the front, down one side and on the second story as well. With hygiene in mind, they sat the house on brick pillars so that air could circulate beneath. The house resided in a clearing at the end of a new road and its white-washed boards glistened against the nearly black tree line that stretched off to nowhere between the earth and the sky. In the house they all lived:

Malachi, Jessie, Eli, Vera Ola and Brother Rayburn. Jack and Cora stayed out back in a little clapboard cabin next to the river.

Following the urges of his wife, Malachi expanded the Benjamin operations to include first a turpentine still and then a small brick kiln. Soon more houses and a school were built with Benjamin boards and Benjamin brick, and "Altamaha Turpentine" became common throughout the South. There were half a dozen new stores all built with Benjamin brick, and the Seaboard Railroad that had extended a trunk line through Altamaha constructed a new, brick terminal with a terra-cotta roof and a hotel that they named the New Altamaha. From the porch of the hotel you could sit and rock and look at the trains as they stopped, took on coal and water, loaded and passed. You could smell the rich, sweet smoke. You could count the train cars and place bets on how many you'd see that weren't those of the Seaboard, the Macon and Savannah, the Louisville and Nashville and the Crescent City Railroad from New Orleans. Money could be won on those cars from far away: the Rock Island, the Santa Fe, the Chesapeake and even more on the Canadian Pacific.

The mill grew and so did the town. The Benjamins, together with the Seaboard Railroad, built a bank. They called it the First Benjamin Seaboard Bank. It was built across from where the Altamaha County Courthouse now stands, and they ordered two granite columns from a quarry north of Atlanta that were so heavy it took two teams of mules to wench them off the flatbed. A pharmacy was also opened. A barber, a blacksmith, a dentist, a doctor and an undertaker came to town. A warehouse was built to store tobacco and onions and, beside it, the Farmers Mutual Exchange built a tin silo for storing grain. The Cootses built a tavern and Brother Rayburn said from his pulpit that the entire town was going to smolder in hell. A lawyer named Fowler became the first mayor and established a city government in the new town hall. Taxes were levied to enlarge the school and to pay the pretty, young schoolteacher who had just moved there from Baxton. And as the town grew, so did the Cootses' graveyard and they gave it the fancy name of Pine Bluff Cemetery. Negroes arrived from all around to do the work the whites did not want. The Coots family built shacks for them and that part of town became known to all as Africaville.

Malachi forgot his past. His new world became Altamaha. But he did correspond with his brother Judah, telling him all that happened in their town beside the dark, red river. On the occasion of his brother's sixtieth birthday, Malachi sent him a gift: a great hoot owl that had raided his chicken yard and that he had shot one night with his Colt Single Action Army revolver. Brother Rayburn, who was skilled in the art of taxidermy, stuffed it for him, perched it on an oak twig and sealed it under a glass bell. Malachi included a note to his brother saying, "This, dear Judah, is Minerva's owl; and owls fly only at dusk," implying that with age comes wisdom.

One Sunday afternoon, Jessie and Malachi were returning by steamboat from their biannual trip to Brunswick where they signed shipping contracts for the next logging season. It was early spring and they were standing on deck watching the jungle, the swamp and the woods pass – she with her parasol and he in new tight shoes. Suddenly, the boiler blew, and Malachi and Jessie were hurled into the swollen eddies and were never found. Eli was twenty-five. The year was 1900.

Just after the Great War, the Navy built a large facility at the mouth of the Altamaha near Brunswick. It was to be called Glencoe Naval Air Station, and the Benjamins were invited to sit on the platform with the other guests who were being honored at the ceremony opening the base. And why were the Benjamins among the honored guests? Because it was of Benjamin lumber and brick that the great hangers for the dirigibles had been built, along with barracks, a chow hall, officer's mess and quarters, an infirmary, a school and a church. The Benjamins had been able to fill all orders and for this it was said that they were true patriots.

Exactly who were these honored patriots there on that platform in 1919? Well, there was dark, wiry and mustachioed Eli with the Mayan blood of his mother and the Sephardic blood of his father. There was Doris Joiner Benjamin, the pretty schoolteacher from Baxton who had become Eli's wife. There was Richard, their eldest son, crippled since birth and just turned nineteen. There was Ewell, my father, who was nine. And then there was their youngest son, Andy Ray, four – his parents' afterthought.

So where were the others? Where was Brother Rayburn? Where was Vera Ola? And where were Cora and Jack? This too must be told, for it is their whereabouts that provides for the conditions that make this story possible.

I will begin with Brother Rayburn who, before his own pulpit, married Doris and Eli in 1901 and then died of a heart attack while raging from that same pulpit one Sunday morning of that same year. The sermon was more directly than indirectly about the Cootses and their "Godless clan of peddlers of liquor and sin." Brother Rayburn never tired of denouncing the Coots family, who he thought was in competition with the Devil for the dominion of hell. But the morning of his death he had been especially angry, for Eli had "taken to drink," and Brother Rayburn blamed this on the Cootses.

Doris had tried to calm the preacher by reminding him that Eli had Indian blood in him. Brother Rayburn raved and ranted, and as he was imploring God, goading the Devil and cursing the Cootses, he fell over the pulpit into the offering plate. Eli had the body put on the train and sent to Milledgeville where, as it had turned out, lay the buried remains of Brother Rayburn's wife, who had succumbed to a Yankee cannonball during the siege of that city in 1864. Eli cried when he remembered Brother Rayburn arriving on that raft decades before, and he swore on the memory of Jessie never to touch liquor again. That, to the benefit of the Cootses, was a vow that soon was broken and then forgotten altogether.

It is a good thing Brother Rayburn died when he did, for in 1910, Vera Ola married a Coots. Like most of the Cootses, his reddish hair was like wire, his pink skin was sprinkled with freckles, his sour breath was hot and dry, but his eyes were bright green like spring grass. His name was Colman Coots and although everyone called him Shorty, he really wasn't that short. Maybe they called him Shorty because he acted the way some short men do, always bragging and pretending to be bigger than they really are.

Vera Ola was not a pretty woman, and when everyone was sure that she would spend her life as a respectable spinster, she was made pregnant by Shorty, the only man who had ever paid her any attention. The baby had been badly formed and lived only a few weeks. They were not to have another for nearly a decade. It was said that Shorty married her and remained with her only because she was a Benjamin and he hoped one day to receive part of the family fortune. But the Benjamins never accepted him, and Eli humiliated him. Shorty got back at them by neglecting his whiny wife, and when he wasn't selling Negro property, cemetery lots or funeral insurance, he was busy with the girls in Baxton or carousing in the bars in Jesup, Brunswick or Savannah. There is no other way of saying it, Shorty was just plain sorry.

Although Altamaha was no different from most small towns, in that gossip was the oil that kept it turning, most of what the Benjamins heard about Shorty's escapades was from their Negro cook, Cora. Now there were reasons for this. First, people were just too embarrassed to talk to the Benjamins about what Shorty was up to, but more importantly, most people were scared to death of the Cootses. The next reason had to do with Cora being privy to information that most people were not. This was due to Cora's extensive contact with other Negroes, and the Negroes loved nothing better than to talk about the misdeeds of white folks. But also, Cora was told things because of her special standing among the community of Africaville. Cora was what was called a root doctor, which means that at an early age Cora had been selected by a practitioner of this ancient craft to be taught the secrets of the animal, vegetable and spiritual worlds. For the Negroes, Cora was the matriarch and for this reason she was told everything.

Cora had been a mere thirteen when she had first come with Jack to care for Eli. But in 1919, Cora was forty-six and already her skin was loose, wrinkled and hung on her like an old brown suit. Much to everyone's surprise, her first and only child was born when she was forty-four and everyone, including Jack, attributed this to her special powers. The boy was born one stormy morning. Cora and Jack had been sitting in the summer kitchen of the Benjamin's house eating biscuits and molasses. There was a clap of thunder and Cora jumped so high that the baby just slid out. She cried, "Lordy, Lord if it ain't a miracle," and she sent Jack out into the storm and down to the river to gather her a few things for the baby: a swamp cabbage, a sassafras root, a Catawba bean and a salamander. When Jack returned she announced to him that the boy's name was Black Strap Jack. Jack did not ask her why she had chosen to name her boy after a brand of molasses. Jack knew she had good reasons for doing it and, besides, he never questioned anything she did.

So in 1919, the boy was two and he spent most of his days on the floor of the summer kitchen while his mother cooked. As if to the rhythm of some far away African or close-by Indian drum, she hummed and sang a tune about marching to Zion.

And what about Jack? Well Jack, who had become a deacon in the First African Baptist Church, became known as Deacon Jack. It was Deacon Jack who was driving the car that very afternoon in 1919 when the Benjamins were returning to Altamaha from the ceremonies at the new airport near Brunswick. As usual, the Deacon was keeping quiet and trying to keep his thoughts clean while Eli ranted and took the Lord's name in vain. Yes, Deacon Jack just tried to concentrate on his driving and keep an eye out for deer, gators and wild hogs on the road.

As he guided the great, black Cadillac over a sandy stretch of Brunswick Road, the dust bellowing behind like churning smoke, Deacon Jack recited the Twenty-Third Psalm inside his head. Eli took his jackknife from his pocket and slowly and deliberately turned the sharp blade round the tip of his long, fat cigar. The end fell to the floor and rolled next to Deacon Jack's foot. Eli put the knife into the pocket of his vest and with his thumbnail struck a match and puffed. As usual, he had been drinking. The others in the car were quiet because they were embarrassed by what Eli had done at the ceremony, but they were more embarrassed for him than for themselves – embarrassed because he did and said things and didn't care what the Devil or anybody thought. And what outrageous thing had he done or said this time? When it had been his turn to say a few patriotic words, Eli had told the whole U.S. Navy and half of Georgia that as happy as he was to have the contracts, the Navy's job was to sail battleships and not to fly balloons, and then he went on to say that President Wilson's "high-flying ideas" came from paying too much attention to people like the Women's Christian Temperance Union.

"Doris, I order you to quit spoiling Richard! That's why he's so goddamned prissy. He ain't no girl; time you quit treating him like one. Come on Jack! Step on it."

Eli was in a hurry because he and his young friend, Max Maxwell, had planned to go hunting, and long-winded politicians had made the ceremony at the naval base last forever. His complaint that Doris spoiled Richard was constant. And yes, she did protect the crippled boy, for she had reason to. But Eli was ashamed of his effeminate son and would have done anything "to make him into a man." Eli had just announced that Richard was to accompany him, Max and Eli's two prize bird dogs on their quail hunt, and, as usual, his wife had meekly protested while the boy said nothing.

"That young Max, now he's a good example for young Richard here to follow," Eli said to his wife while really stating the opinion for his son to hear.

When they pulled into town, both Doris and Richard thought Eli had forgotten his plan to take Richard along, for Eli had been dozing; but as they crossed the Altamaha River Bridge and drove down Malachi Street, Eli awoke, sat up and said to Deacon Jack: "Take the rest of them to the house and then we'll go on to Mister Max's place. You can hitch up the ole mule and get them dogs. And boy, I want you to hurry 'cause we ain't got all day."

Jack did as he was told. He went to the barn, parked the car, hitched the mule to the wagon and put the orange-spotted bitch and the black-spotted dog in their pen on the back. As Richard watched his father get the shotguns and other gear from the trunk of the big black sedan, he looked around Max Maxwell's fish camp. How Richard hated it all: he hated the old shacks with their rusty, tin roofs; he hated tobacco-chewing Max Maxwell who always called him "young laddie"; he hated the smell of stinking fish; but most of all, Richard hated his father. Soon they were in a field near Max's camp and the dogs had picked up a scent.

"Come on boy!" Eli barked at his son. "Come on, you gonna make us miss a shot!"

The black-spotted dog ran toward the edge of the field, nose to the ground, sniffing so loud he could be heard fifty yards away. The dog darted into the swamp and was lost in a thicket of palmetto.

"Come on, goddamn it! Ole Bumble, he's on a scent!" Eli shouted back to his son, and he and Max followed the dog into the swamp.

The swamp was formed by a creek that flowed into the Oconee River just upstream from where Bumble entered. There was never much rain in early August and the stream could easily be waded. The dog surfaced from the palmettos and, still sniffing the ground, splashed across the creek.

"Hell! Bumble's lost the scent," Max said, adding, "Where's that bitch?"

Eli replied, "Don't know. Let's cross. Goddamn it! Where's that boy?" Then he shouted, "Richard! In here, boy! Come on! Get your sissy ass 'cross the creek!"

The dog picked up another scent and was so excited that he ran through saw briars and cut his tongue and mouth. They followed at fifty paces as the dog ran crazily, his bleeding snout to the ground. When they reached the edge of a cornfield on the other side of the swamp, they saw the orange-spotted bitch. She was frozen into a point. Eli motioned for Max to move to the left. Then Bumble appeared and he too froze, pointing toward a clump of mulberry bushes. Max crept to the left. Eli readied his shotgun and with his thumb pushed off the safety. It was then that Richard hobbled to the edge of the field, gun across his chest, and charged through the saw briars, which tore open his knuckles and covered his hands in blood. When he saw his father, Richard quickly wiped his eyes with the back of a bloody hand and his jerky motions spooked the dog. The dog broke his point and pounced into the mulberry bushes, causing a great flutter and Max unloaded both barrels at the scattering birds, but missed.

"The sorry, goddamn son of a bitch!" Eli shouted.

Just as the dog came from the bushes Eli lowered his gun, fired and the shot burst into the dog's rear. The beast jumped into the air and ran first this way and then that. It turned round and round, yelping, trying to get to his bloody behind.

"That'll teach 'em to break his point," Eli said, fury lacing his voice.

"Yeah, if'n he don't die first," Max Maxwell said disapprovingly under his breath.

At sun-up, when Eli made his rounds, he always took Bumble. Yes, the dog had lived, but now he would cower and hide at the sound of any loud noise and if he were to hear the blast of a shotgun he would pee all over himself. Bumble's hunting days were over and, as shameful as it is to say, he became a mere pet. But wouldn't you know it, Eli himself had nursed the dog back to health and the dog had become his constant companion. Deacon Jack had told Cora that it was the only Christian thing that Eli had ever done.

One morning, as Eli and Bumble were driving to the turpentine still, Eli told Bumble that it was going to be a hot day and then Eli talked about the new vat that the workmen had been installing at the still. Yes, Eli talked to the dog and he did it even when he was sober.

The Negroes liked to talk about that and some said the dog talked to Eli.

Each day began in an ordinary, almost predictable way. Eli and Bumble would go to the mill and to the still and, usually, to the brick factory and the bank. In the early afternoon, when it was too hot to do anything else, they would go home and Eli would sit in the kitchen and talk to Cora while he ate dinner. Then Eli and Bumble would have a nap. Eli would sleep in the hammock on the back porch and he wouldn't even pull off his boots. Bumble would take his nap under the fig tree that sat beside the porch, behind the summer kitchen, and he would usually sleep until he heard Jack ride by on his bicycle around four. In the late afternoon Jack liked to go to the cafés in Africaville and do a little preaching, and Bumble liked to go along. If Jack didn't go, Bumble would go out anyway and roam all around Altamaha until midnight. When he would get back to the Benjamin place, Eli would already be drunk and passed out and his wife would sob, his sons would hide and Cora would cry: "Lordy, Lord! Whatever is gonna become of Mista Eli."

When Eli and Bumble arrived at the still that morning, the crew was just leaving for the woods where they would gather the tin cups from under the gashes cut into the sides of the pines. From the cups they would pour the resin into barrels that sat on the back of mule-drawn wagons. If the crew wasn't gathering they would be slashing, which means that they would be taking their bushwhacks with their ugly hooked blades and slicing open the trees. Then they would place tin cups under the gashes to catch the oozing liquid. The Negroes waved and Eli raised his index finger in recognition. He stepped down from the truck and held open the door, waiting for the dog to jump out. Then he called Deacon Jack.

Eli and Jack walked into the still. Bumble followed behind. They stood in the shadows before the great iron vat that reached nearly to the top of the tin roof. They could smell the resin bubbling inside and its vapors condensing in the coils of copper pipe that twisted and turned overhead. Eli told Jack that he needed some stump. Stump was moonshine whisky, at least that's what the Negroes called it and Eli liked to call it by its Negro name. It sounded better that way. Jack didn't want to have anything to do with stump – didn't because he was a deacon – but he was not opposed to getting it for Eli under the circumstances. Jack always bought the whisky because it was a Coots who sold it. And Jack was right: Eli shouldn't be seen buying anything from a Coots.

The man who sold whisky was Shorty's brother and although his real name was Springs, everybody called him Jaybird, or Jaybird Springs. They called him that because the hump on his back made him spring along like a bird and he even encouraged them to call him that by the way he combed his hair – swooping it up into a point like the feathers on a jaybird's head. Jaybird sold liquor from the back of his blue Packard. He sold it from the curb near the railroad tracks in broad daylight, right there in the middle of Altamaha. In 1926, Altamaha County was dry; the churches and the bootleggers liked it that way and Jaybird Springs Coots was becoming a rich man because of it.

Next, Eli and Bumble drove to the mill. There Eli always left Bumble in the truck. He didn't like to see the dog run around and piss on all the stacks of new lumber. He went inside the mill, joked and talked with the bookkeeper and foreman about the new-fangled motor trucks he planned to buy for pulp wooding. The trucks were to have donkey engines mounted on a cable spool on the back for winching the heaviest logs – logs as fat as the girth of a horse and too big for two strong men to lift. The fancy trucks were called skidders because they could just skid along over felled trees or thick clumps of palmetto palm and go through mud like tanks in the Great War.

Then Eli and the foreman walked into the shed where the great saw sliced the logs into boards. High above the tin-topped shed, above the smoldering sawdust pile, higher than anything else in Altamaha, the great stacks bellowed smoke and sometimes spewed fire. The smoke smelled like the tar in the burning sawdust and the fire looked like it was being spit up from hell. The whistle let out one long and two short blasts. This told the town that it was almost eight and that work would begin in ten minutes.

There came a day in that late summer of 1926 when Eli and Bumble neither made it to the brick factory nor to the bank. And Richard, who managed the bank, was happy when his father did not show up. He never knew what his father might say to embarrass him. That day, instead of completing his usual rounds, Eli revved up the engine of this truck and roared away from Benjamin House. He turned onto Main Street and crossed the Seaboard Railroad tracks so fast that the truck went airborne and almost got away from him as he turned right on North Seaboard and then again as he took a sharp left on the road that ran parallel to the river and the Macon and Savannah tracks. Shortly after passing Max Maxwell's fish camp, he aimed the truck at Shorty's house as if it were a rocket shot out of hell. Eli blew the horn until someone came to the door. It was Vera Ola.

Vera Ola was sobbing through the screen. Eli jumped out, leapt to the porch and snatched open the door. There she stood, with a bruise on her cheek and blood crusted on her swollen lips, with Collie, her little son, hanging onto her leg.

"Where's that sorry son of a bitch?"

"The Thigpin girl – he's with that Thigpin girl again. And now he's gone and made her pregnant. They're likely at the general store," she sobbed.

The so-called general store was a store that was really a tavern owned by the Cootses. It was called the White Spot. That's where Eli went as fast as his truck could go. Shooting down the dusty road, Eli reached under the seat, pulled out a pint jar and took a great swallow of the clear liquid. He wiped his mouth with the back of his hand and told Bumble, "I'll kill that white-trash bastard!"

The still, Max's place and the mill were but a blur as the truck sped by, leaving behind a cloud of dust. They crossed the tracks to a dirt road that ran along the city docks. Eli cut through the Piggly Wiggly loading lot and turned onto Malachi Street, crossing the Altamaha River Bridge. By the time the truck was on Brunswick Road and had passed Pine Bluff Cemetery, Eli was driving so fast that when he reached the White Spot, the truck skidded into the porch and jarred the whole building.

Old-man Luther Coots stuck his head out of the door and said, trying to be friendl, "Son-of-a-gun, if it ain't Mister Benjamin." Then he turned and shouted to his son, "Colman, you better get your natural ass outta here. Run, Colman. Run!"

Eli heaved himself from the truck, sprang to the porch and nearly flung the screen door off its hinges. As he stood in the center of the room he saw Shorty's dusty, black shoes sticking out from under a curtain that was used to hide a row of slot machines whenever a Christian, or even a preacher, showed up.

At first Eli said nothing, but made a weak smile, as if he were about to say something friendly. Just as old Luther Coots was about to tell Eli that his son had left town, Eli bolted to the curtain and snatched it aside. And there was Shorty, his open hands begging, his eyes pleading. Like a panther from the Altamaha swamp, Eli tore into him. Shorty covered his face, but Eli hit him beside his ears. Then, grabbing him by his shirt, Eli dragged him out and pushed him over a stack of cans. Shorty was in the center of the store on his knees about to beg Eli to stop when he received the toe of Eli's boot in his mouth. When Eli pushed him over and he fell to his back, there was a great burst of air and several teeth blew out of him.

"Get up you trashy pile of Coots shit!" Eli hissed at him and glared at the others who were there looking on. "If you ever come close to my sister again I'll shoot your chicken-shit ass off. And if the rest of ya'll don't like it, I'll just kick your asses right now!" Then Eli spit on Shorty, unbuttoned his pants and pissed on him.

Time passed. Vera Ola and her little son, Collie, came to live at the Benjamin place and Eli retained the services of Durden Fowler Sr., the best lawyer in the county, to begin divorce proceedings. Life had returned to normal. As usual, Eli was sitting at the table in the summer kitchen drinking coffee, talking to Cora and waiting for the sun to rise. It was then that they heard a whimper through the screen door.

"Lord help us, Mista Eli. It's po' ole Bumble," cried Cora.

And it was Bumble lying there on his side the way dogs do – there on the bloody porch – trying to lick his behind and looking like he looked when Eli had shot him. Eli squeezed through the screen door, for the dog had lost so much blood that he was unable to get up and move out of the way. In the half-light Eli could see that someone had cleanly severed Bumble's tail – had cut it completely and cleanly about an inch from where it had joined his body.

When Eli went to the truck to get his pistol, he found the tail on the seat. He just looked at it, left it where it was and reached under the seat for his .38. Then Eli walked back to the porch, placed the pistol behind the dog's left ear and fired. Quickly, he went to the truck and stood in the shadows so that Cora would not see his tears. Once he had composed himself, he went back into the kitchen and told Cora to have Jack bury Bumble under the fig tree. Then he got into the truck, closed the door and roared off.

Eli saw Shorty's blue Ford parked in front of his house. Walking past the car, Eli saw on the back seat an open toolbox and there, sitting on top of the clutter of other tools, a pair of bloody tin snips. The window was down so he just reached in, picked up the snips and when he got to the door of Shorty's house, started banging the snips on the wall. Finally, the Thigpin girl came to the door. Yes, she was pregnant, for you could see it under her bathrobe. She swore on everything she could think of that Shorty was not there. But then a door slammed. He was there, alright. Eli handed the Thigpin girl the snips and the bloody tail and shot off after Shorty.

Shorty went under a barbed-wire fence and ran down the railroad tracks. Although Shorty was younger, Eli gained on him, and when Shorty got to the still, he staggered up the steps, ran across the loading dock and into the dark building. He fell over a barrel and lay there panting. He could hear nothing but the bubbling vat and the liquid running through the pipes; just as he was catching his breath a light flashed in his face.

"What you doin' in here, Mista Shorty? You know you ain't got no biddness in this here still." It was Deacon Jack. "You get yoself outta here right now or I'ze gonna call the law."

"Nigger, you just shut yo ugly black mouth. Ya hear?" he hissed, scrambling to his feet. Then Shorty snatched the flashlight from Deacon Jack and flung it against the wall. He pushed Jack into a stack of cans and disappeared into the darkness. Deacon Jack got up, asking the Lord to guide him, and fumbled his way to the office and switched on the lights. Then he saw Eli stepping inside from the loading dock.

"Where's that son of a bitch?" he hissed, and Deacon Jack pointed in the direction of the vat and its great swirl of coils and pipes.

When they got to the vat, they heard Shorty high up on the catwalk that ran around the top. Eli didn't even try to get him to come down; he just slowly started up the ladder. When he was near the top, Shorty ran to the ladder and tried to kick Eli off, but when his blows did not stop Eli and Eli kept coming, Shorty panicked and ran around the catwalk to the other side of the vat. When Eli reached the catwalk, he unhooked the ladder and pushed it off; it clanged to the floor there beside Deacon Jack. Shorty went round and round the catwalk. Eli slowly followed. The fumes burned Eli's eyes and when he stopped for a second to wipe them with his sleeve, he saw Shorty pick up a hammer. He felt the wind as the spinning steel and wood flew past his ear. He heard the hammer bounce off the tin wall and splash into the vat, and he imagined it disappearing into the thick, bubbling resin. As Eli moved closer he could see Shorty's green eyes widen and catch the light. The fumes made tears stream down Eli's face, but he did not feel them, and when he was just a few feet from Shorty, he looked at him and smiled. It was then that Shorty lunged at him with a screwdriver and sunk the steel shaft into Eli's shoulder. But at the same time, Eli came down with the sharp blade of his jackknife and its point caught Shorty just under his left ear, slicing across his Adam's apple. Blood burst from Shorty's windpipe. He tried to say something, but only gurgled. In a spew of dark red, Shorty tumbled into the amber resin.

Eli nodded to Deacon Jack politely, and Deacon Jack brought the ladder. Eli climbed down from the vat, left the still, got into his truck and drove to town to knock on the sheriff's door. Soon the sheriff was at the still, standing on the catwalk and he, Eli and Deacon Jack watched Shorty, spread eagle, turning in the steaming currents, frying like a fritter. The next day, when they fished Shorty out, he quickly hardened and so was preserved like a pair of bronzed baby shoes. Because his swimming-like posture was unalterable, the Cootses had to get a carpenter to build a special coffin for him.

Eli went to jail for manslaughter, but after six months they transferred him to the county chain gang where he was given the job of sitting astride a mule, guarding the Negro prisoners who were slinging weeds on the opposite side of the road from the whites. It was not long before Eli was allowed to go home on Saturday nights, yet he was required to return to jail after church on Sunday, which, of course, he was required to attend.

To protect the Benjamin fortune, Eli had handed everything over to Richard before going to jail. When his father was finally released two years later, Richard claimed that his father was an incompetent drunk and refused to sign the papers that would have restored Eli's fortune to him.

The people in Altamaha still talk about it. Nobody knows for sure how Eli found out about Shorty beating up Vera Ola. Some say that Cora told him; after all, she was told everything. But the Negroes say that Bumble told him. Everybody knows that the dog rambled all over town and must have seen and heard many things. Anyway, Eli didn't make his rounds anymore. He just sat on the back porch behind the summer kitchen and drank liquor until he fell asleep. One afternoon, he just drifted off and tumbled from his hammock into the fig tree, breaking his neck.

Because Malachi and Jessie had been lost in the Altamaha River and because Brother Rayburn's remains had been sent to Milledgeville, the Benjamins had no cemetery plot. Yes, they simply could have bought one had it not been for one fact: the Cootses owned every acre of Pine Bluff Cemetery and the Benjamins were not about to buy anything from any Coots. And anyway, the Cootses would not have sold any Benjamin an acre of land for all the money in the Benjamin bank. They would not have sold it to them even if it had been in the middle of Big Alligator Swamp. So Eli was kept in the Altamaha icehouse for almost a month until the Benjamins found a solution to their problem. Finally, the Benjamins – at a high price – bought the land next to the cemetery, and to this day all of the Benjamins are buried outside the cemetery walls.

Hamilton placed a floppy into the slot of Mo's laptop and saved the chapter. Then he took his pen and wrote on the label "Ch. I Altamaha."

# WORLD DEVELOPERS

When Hamilton, Mo, Andy, Starman and the Dikshits arrived in New Delhi they found the place dry, dusty and hot, a notable contrast to what they had been experiencing in sticky, sweltering Singapore. The timing of Mo's previous commitment to participate in the tennis tournament in New Delhi happily coincided with what Dicky had called his "pre-conference business" at the Institute for Human Development. He invited them all to New Delhi for a three-day stay before the start of both the tournament and the conference. They all agreed that it was a grand opportunity for them to see the sights, and since they had been offered free lodging and free evening meals at the Institute, no one could complain about the price.

It was not just the weather that was different. In Singapore, a draconian program promoting efficiency and order was winning the war over what previously had been the random and benign chaos of rural life in an urban setting. In contrast, New Delhi, not to mention Old Delhi, was a kind of urban-barnyard hybrid. Yes, I do refer to the many sacred cows on most every street, roaming casually and chewing their cuds wherever they liked: whether they are in the middle of a clogged intersection, in the midst of the traffic flow at a roundabout or among the many pedestrians on the sidewalks. The rest of their group had been to India before, but what struck the new visitors – Hamilton, Starman and Andy – about New Delhi, in addition to the ubiquitous, ruminating bovines, were the hoards of moving humanity.

Upon his noting the contrast of the two cities, Hamilton concluded that nothing appeared to have been happening in Singapore, whereas in New Delhi, everything seemed to be in flux.

"The crowd! Just look at it!" Hamilton shouted out over the clap, buzz and hum. "It looks like something I used to see under the microscope in biology lab. But then I couldn't hear them – too far away for that."

"You're right," Starman replied. "What you see is a single organism with distinguishable but coordinated parts. They look like bacteria!"

"Dicky told me about this place in Old Delhi, a shrine to Gandhi. He's among the greatest of my heroes. And this was true for ole M.L.K. as well. If you get right down to it, Gandhi was a greater influence on him than Jesus, if you ask me. And I'll tell you what: I'd take Gandhi over Jesus any day. That's a place I want to go. What's it called?" Andy asked.

"It was, and still is, called Raj Ghat. I can take us there," Mo replied.

"Great," Andy said, "Dicky said that Gandhi was cremated there after he was shot in '48."

"Yes, and when we go there we can see the actual pistol that was used to shoot him. They have it on display," Mo replied.

For two days they played the tourist game. They walked along the broad Rajpath, or King's Way, with its ornamental ponds. They visited the garish Birla Mandir, a temple dedicated to Lakshmi, the goddess of prosperity. And they wandered amongst the throng in Old Delhi looking at old, dark, skinny men repairing shoes, selling herbal medicinal cures or reading horoscopes from an enclosure no larger than a cardboard shipping box containing a typical North American refrigerator.

On their last day in New Delhi, Mo, Starman and Andy went to a place called the Red Fort. Dicky was attending to business, Jeri was visiting a friend and Hamilton had decided to spend the day in his and Mo's room working on *Jud's Story*. Mo had been a bit annoyed by Hamilton's refusal to accompany them to the fort and was also somewhat irritated because Hamilton would not allow her, or anyone else, to read *Jud's Story*.

Mo remembered visiting the Red Fort years before and she insisted that Starman and Andy see it. They all enjoyed the strangeness of the old Mogul edifice, but the heat drove them away. Besides, they were supposed to meet Dicky at a travel agency at a place called Jan Path Lane, a place where Dicky said cheap tickets could be bought. The next day, Hamilton, Andy, Starman and the Dikshits were to travel to Jaipur by train. In a few days, when her tennis tournament in New Delhi ended, Mo, who already had her plane ticket, would join them.

The three of them found walking difficult in the chaos of people, bicycles, rickshaws, cars, buses and cows, but Dicky's directions were clear and easy to follow. They located the place and found Dicky, who bought the train tickets. When they finished, Dicky insisted that his driver drop them off at a museum of medical and dental instruments from early Mogul times.

At dinner, Hamilton, Starman and Andy were on the terrace adjacent the dining room having drinks and waiting for the others to arrive. The Institute was in a part of the city known as Golf Links. It was a beautiful location, seemingly a world away from the shabby mayhem that was most of New Delhi. Apparently, Andy had thought about the contrast and found it disturbing.

"No fair, Hambone! Not fair to have all of this finery in the midst of this misery," Andy groaned.

"Fair? What do you mean by 'fair,' Unc?"

"Now, just what'n hell do you think I mean?"

"Well, the problem is that 'fairness' is about getting what you expect. We expect to get what we deserve and think we deserve what we desire."

"You know what your problem is, Hamilton. You need a cause. You need to believe in something big."

"Big, eh? Give me an example."

"You know goddamned well what I'm talking about, something like ... like freedom. Yes, freedom. Something big that causes you to ... to be free."

"You mean something that forces you to do things, something that, in this instance, forces you to be free? Right, Unc?"

"Enough of your professor shit, Hambone. What kind of fascist idea is that? And by the way, I'm not your fuckin' uncle."

At that moment Dicky entered, greeted them, went over to a cart of bottles and glasses and poured himself a Scotch. Then he walked back over to where they sat. Looking distraught, he pulled three newspapers from his case: *The Hindustani Times*, *The London Times* and *The International Herald Tribune*.

"Bad news, I'm afraid. Khomeini has put out a fatwa on that Rushdie fellow, and Rushdie is in hiding. Some are suggesting that he is here in India."

"A fat what on who?" Andy asked, both not hearing correctly and confused.

"Rushdie is one of our novelists. He made quite a name for himself back in England, you see. He wrote a book about the founding of India in 1949, but he has now written something that has landed him in big trouble with that Ayatollah fellow."

"So, the Mad Mullah's put out a contract on him?" Hamilton replied.

"Yes, a virtual death sentence, I am afraid," Dicky answered, wrinkling his brown brow and sipping his drink.

The administrator of the Institute by the name of Malik – a short, bearded, middle-aged man in a light blue, vested Nehru jacket, tan collarless shirt and long, skirt-like trousers – had come to announce that dinner was ready. He had been standing by, listening.

"Pardon me, gentlemen, but what can one expect? This man Rushdie has not only insulted the Prophet – peace be upon him – but he has blasphemed against the Holy Koran. And it is the duty of every Muslim to defend the Holy Koran," Malik said politely and firmly to all of them, but then when finished, looked pointedly at Dicky.

For a moment everyone was silent. Then Dicky spoke: "But I find this rather extreme. Rather over the top. Do you not think that ..."

"Doctor, I have come to announce dinner," Malik interrupted, muttering under his breath as he walked away, "Allah Akbar!"

They went into the dining room, found Starman already seated. As Starman rose to greet them, Jeri and Mo walked into the room.

"I found Mo lost in the halls," Jeri said, laughing. "I was just telling her that when her tournament is over and she gets to Jaipur, Dicky will give us a guided tour of the city. And that meanwhile, we will take good care of Hamilton."

Jeri's hair hung past her shoulders, the way western women wore their hair decades earlier. In fact, if one were to consider it, Jeri's appearance – her hair, her beads, her white Indian-cotton smock, her dangling silver and jade earrings and her Buffalo sandals – evoked the romantic styles of an ethos that, like a ghost, refused to go away. But then Jeri could be marked as an American who merely had spent much time abroad and had retained the styles of the era in which she had departed.

"It really is too bad you will miss the conference. There will be many progressive people there," Jeri said, looking at Mo. "But as I said, we will keep an eye on Hamilton."

The meal was a Taiwanese-inspired fish curry done in coconut milk and lemon grass, served with a good Sauvignon Blanc from Australia and an even better chardonnay from Chile. The Institute's cellar of fine wines was something rare for India in 1989, so Dicky told them. Malik, who did not approve of such and who had been standing by at previous meals, was nowhere to be seen.

While the Institute was an opulent building, the bedrooms were surprisingly small with poor air circulation. There was no fan in Mo and Hamilton's room and it was too hot either to lie under the sheet or for them to touch, so they lay on their backs, naked, trying to stay as cool as possible.

"Hammy," Mo said, using the name by which she had come to call him, "you heard what she said about keeping an eye on you."

"Who?"

"You know who. She did say it, and I don't like it. I'd rather die than lose you. And about the book, if you won't let me read the story than at least tell me what it's about."

She turned to him, smiled and reached over and stroked the newly returning hair on his head.

"It's about Jud, but it's also about what makes his story possible, the part that is always there but rarely written about. I guess, since I'm really the one pretending to be ole Jud, I'm what makes the story possible. So, I guess I'd better begin with me. Let's see, the story starts in a town in Georgia, the place where my father met my mother in 1943. My father was an aviator in the Royal Canadian Navy and had been sent to Glencoe Naval Air Station in Brunswick, Georgia. He was sent there to train with his American counterparts in anti-submarine warfare. My mother worked in the library on the base."

"So, they fell in love and ..."

"Yes, and all that. But it really was not all that simple. My father had both the wrong nationality and the wrong religion. He was neither American nor Baptist, and my grandmother Fowler did not like any of it. She refused to cooperate in any way. Also, my mother was only eighteen. Well, when he finished his training and it was time for him to leave, mother left with him. They traveled by train, as most did then. They first went to Atlanta, then to Chicago, from there to Winnipeg and then on to a little place called La Pas."

"The Paw?"

"Yes, the Paw, but spelled P-A-S. It was the closest place that had a train near Cumberland House, the village where my father was from. My parents were met by Uncle Fred, whose full name was Fred Ouest, actually de l'Ouest. My uncle was a traditionalist and so insisted on using the original family name that came from our Norman, voyageur ancestor. Hey, that's where I got my red hair."

"Voyageur?"

"Yes, the ones who opened up western Canada by canoe. They were mostly French Canadian. Fur traders. Hudson's Bay Company and all that."

"Interesting, and so romantic."

"Yes. My uncle was a Roman Catholic priest, so Uncle Fred was Father Fred as well. Uncle Fred taught at the reserve school in Cumberland House and was among the few whites who lived there. The day my parents arrived, my father's brother married them. A week later, my father stepped back on the train and began his long journey to Halifax to do his duty in the North Atlantic. Uncle Fred took care of mamma – got her a job working in the Hudson's Bay store. She waited and waited. Finally, when the war was over and my father had returned, I was born – but not until 1948. I went to school in Cumberland House and was taught by my uncle. Later, I went to high school in a place called Carrot River."

"Carrot River? Strange name."

"Yeah, but it's stranger that I eventually ended up in Toronto, then in England, then back in Toronto, and now I'm lying naked beside the most beautiful Mohawk in all of India."

Mo reached over and grabbed him.

"Oh no, not the Red Rider!" He squealed.

"Shh, they'll hear us," she whispered, laughing. "Promise me that you'll never call me Mohawk again!"

"This is the beautiful Palace of the Winds," Dicky said to them as he pointed up and behind him with the open palm of his hand. He was proud of the building and sounded as if he had built it himself. He closed his eyes as he talked, smiling.

"The Raj had it constructed in 1701 so that his many wives could sit in those bay windows and observe all that went on in the city below. This is indeed a fine structure, as I am sure you will agree. Did you know that 'fine' and 'fair' in English come from the Greek kalos and is traceable further back to the original Sanskrit? It pertains to the appearance of a thing, but to the appearance only. When we say that a thing is 'fine,' we mean that it appears as we expect it to appear, or ought to appear, and that it is noble or beautiful, which the Greeks called kallos. To say that a thing is fine is also to say that it is fair. Thus a thing can appear to us as fine or fair without necessarily being true or good. Today, that which we consider fair has more to do with the adherence to abstract rules or slogans and less to do with aesthetic judgment or fineness. It has nothing to do with justice, which instead has to do with drawing the boundaries that make both fairness and fineness possible. Come with me and I will illustrate for you what I mean."

The ethereal structure was pink as was the rest of the old city of Jaipur, and this is why it is called the "Pink City." But the Palace of the Winds is not really a building. If you were to step to the side of its honeycombed front, as Dicky was doing and urging those crowded around him to do, you could see that it was a mere facade. In other words, there are neither sides nor a back to the tall edifice and its roof is the clear sky above.

"It's like a Hollywood set," Jeri said.

"Actually, as you can see, the Raj had scaffolding and stairs erected behind. There the ladies and their eunuchs and courtiers would enter and sit under parasols. From those heights, untouched by the world, they could marvel, ridicule and criticize all that went on below them."

Among this crowd around Dicky were Hamilton, Starman and Andy. They had arrived the night before, tired and sweaty, and had joined the Dikshits at the former residence of another Raj, whose regal place had been converted into a hotel called the Rhumba Palace. Unlike the Palace of the Winds, this palace has four walls, a top and a bottom required of actual buildings. They had slept well in beds with mattresses of down and the cool night air of the Rajasthan desert. It had been a relief from the discomfort of New Delhi and the long, dusty train ride to Jaipur.

After Dicky's tour, Hamilton, Starman and Andy climbed into an old gray Mercedes along with the Dikshits. The car was provided to them by the university. The other guests waited nearby for an orange Volkswagen van. When the five of them were in the car, Jeri insisted that Andy swap seats with her, saying that Andy would be better able to see in the middle seat beside Dicky. Andy, quickly detecting her motive, was annoyed, yet accommodated her. Jeri took what had been Andy's seat in the back between Starman and Hamilton. Hamilton felt Jeri snuggle her body into his. He yawned and looked out the car window.

There were craftsman and merchants along the street: tinkers, cloth sellers, silversmiths, potters, a dentist and an old hag reading horoscopes. A beggar woman with a deformed child came to Andy's window. Pitifully, she winced at Andy, but before she could hold out her hand Dicky said something to her in Hindi and she scampered away like a skinny bitch carrying a pup.

"They maim the children at birth," Dicky said, "a disgusting, but common practice. The child is not likely hers. She has probably bought it."

"And this is the twentieth century?" Andy gasped.

The others were loaded into the orange van and then the two vehicles maneuvered through the traffic and out of the city. Soon they rolled into the desert and up into the dusty mountains. It was close to noon and the sun was hot. Dicky talked on about this and that and they all asked questions, but said little else. Dicky sounded like a book. Hamilton was sleepy and dozed for moments here and there. Jeri kept glancing at him, but he did not notice. The road was curvy and bumpy, and they continued to climb higher. At one point, the grade was so steep that passengers in the van had to get out and walk up the mountain road. While the passengers trudged up and reloaded into the van, the car waited at the top. The Mercedes' diesel engine knocked, knocked again, and they were on their way.

They stopped at a restaurant, a former shrine beside a blue lake at the foot of the dry mountains. In the lake were small cupolas that looked as if they were floating on the surface of the water like the lily pads that surrounded them. To the side of one cupola were two water buffalo, both in the water up to their necks, lazily grazing on the lotus flowers, pads and their long, ropey roots. Their keeper was asleep on a rock.

They dined on samosas, curry, cucumbers and yogurt. When they finished, they sat on the rocks, drank sweet, milky, masala tea and looked at the lake and mountains beyond. Dicky pointed to a reddish building surrounded by a wall running along a ridge halfway up a mountain and then to a structure above and to the side that dazzled in the rays of the sun.

"That's it," he nodded, "the fort and the Amber Palace. It is only a short drive from here," he added for the sake of the passengers of the Volkswagen. Meanwhile, Andy had ordered a drink and became agitated upon learning that the restaurant did not serve alcohol.

When they arrived at the parking lot below the ridge where the Amber Palace sat, they experienced a great contrast between that location and the serenity they had left at the restaurant down the road. The place was humming with business. They were surrounded by buses, cars and pack animals – mostly camels, buffalo and donkeys. They could hear the buzz of commerce coming from the bazaar that sat in a grove. Men shouted the merits of their commodities, many of them articles that could be taken up to the temple for sacrifice: milk, butter and varied grains of many colors. There were stalls of flower bouquets, fruit and garland after garland of marigolds. Souvenirs were for sale at stalls surrounded by tourists, many of them Japanese: dolls dressed liked fierce Rajasthan warriors, plaster statues of Shiva and ashtrays with pictures of the Amber Palace.

"We have something very special planned," Dicky said to all of them as they stood together in front of the van. "We have arranged for our visitors to have an elephant ride up the mountain to the palace."

"Elephants?" a plump Englishman from the group in the van asked with unease in his voice.

"Yes, my friend, elephants. I will assure you that there is nothing to fear. They are as tame as kittens. They are deeply in love with their masters and will die to satisfy their every wish. You have nothing to worry about. Believe me," Dicky further assured him. He then instructed all of them to meet back at the van in ten minutes and said that he would take them to the elephants. "Go to the bazaar," he said, "and buy something to sacrifice."

This was the first time since they were all in Singapore that they had seen Dicky without a tie. Still, he was elegantly attired in a tan bush jacket and trousers, like a Brahman in imperial gear.

They walked into the grove toward the bazaar. Andy and Starman, who were fascinated by the colored grains, wandered off together into the section that sold items for sacrifice. Although they were of opposite temperament, a common world somehow connected their very different tastes, manners and cares. They had become friends. As Hamilton heard their conversation about Walt Whitman become involved, he decided to buy garlands of marigolds for Mo and ambled off alone.

The stalls of flowers stretched through the grove that followed along a dry riverbed and ran at the base of the mountain, ending at a trail that twisted up to a ridge. All along the side of the mountain the world was orange, yellow and green – the colors of the marigolds. Hamilton found what he wanted, purchased about a half a dozen garlands, which he would present to Mo when she arrived. After Hamilton paid for the flowers and draped the strings around his neck, he realized how foolish he had been. By the time Mo arrived, the flowers would be dead. Then he looked up and there across the stall, smiling at him, was Jeri.

"You know Hamilton, with that mustache and red hair, you really do look like that bird back in Singapore – the big one we saw on the tower that escaped from Birdland."

He laughed and replied, "Come over here; I have something for you."

Jeri walked around the stall, all the while her eyes glued to his, and stopped in front of him. Hamilton could feel the heat from her body. When he looked down, her face was so close to him that he could tell she had had some problems with her skin at an earlier age. But it wasn't that bad. In fact, she wasn't bad, Hamilton thought as he draped three garlands around her neck and freckled shoulders.

"There," he said awkwardly.

She told him that the others had grown tired of waiting and had gone on without them. She suggested they could go up to the palace along the trail and ride an elephant back down.

"I guess I let the time get away. Oh, what the hell."

He smoothed his mustache and laughed. Then he took her by the shoulder, turned her in the direction of the path and said, "Let's go, California girl. You lead."

When they reached the trail, she took his hand and pulled.

"Come on, I'll race you!" she cried, looking down and laughing.

She ran on before him and he followed. After a short while they stopped, both panting. Playfully, as if she were about to fall down in exhaustion, Jeri leaned into him. They stood on a flat area of path next to a small pool filled with yellow lilies.

"How long will you stay in India – you and her?" she asked, as she pulled back and propped herself upon a rock.

He told her that they could only stay for a month, for that was how long Mo had arranged to be away from her work. Then Jeri asked if he would then return to Singapore and he replied that he didn't know, it had not even been discussed.

"And you and Dicky? You'll go back to England, after the season in Singapore, I mean?"

"Oh, I don't know. I'm so tired of England. Maybe I'll go back to the West Coast."

"What about Dicky?"

"Dicky? Well, we can't seem to get it together. He wants this. I want that. My life seems to be floating away, and I seem to be just standing there watching it drift by. Oh, don't you miss America?"

"No, not really. I'm Canadian, remember?"

They started up the trail. Often, at steep places, there were stone steps and a rope banister. Jeri continued to walk in front and when they were on the steps Hamilton could see up her dress. Her legs were lean and tan and she wore thin, silky, white underpants. He glimpsed honey-colored hairs around the edges as she mounted each step.

When Jeri reached a platform, Hamilton ordered her to stop. When he got to where she stood, he put his hands on her shoulders and moved her aside, stepping up and around her. As he looked down at her, his eyes fell upon her garlanded breasts. Her tight-budded, aroused nipples were showing through the thin Indian cotton of her dress.

They both laughed, breathing hard, and he turned her around saying, "Look at the view."

They faced the grove and the buses and cars far below. Hamilton took the three remaining garlands from around his neck and dropped them around Jeri's shoulders.

"I garland you in the name of Krishna," he proclaimed, laughing.

She turned back toward him, looked up at him and smiled.

"I am forever grateful, Lord Krishna."

Hamilton, being Hamilton, did not see her close her eyes and pucker her lips to be kissed. He had already darted up the trail, energized, bouncing along like some young satyr.

After about two hundred steps, on the next flat spot of earth, Hamilton stopped and gazed across the top of a small, dry hill to the lake below where they had eaten lunch. He saw Jeri come around a rock and follow the twisting path slowly up toward him. He knew that she knew that he was watching her. Then she stood before him, panting. She smiled and sighed. Beads of sweat covered her forehead and ran down her neck. She stepped closer, rested her arms on Hamilton's shoulders, closed her eyes and said:

"Kiss me."

I'll regret this, Hamilton told himself, pulling her toward him. Her tongue was like a separate being – alive and autonomous – darting, searching inside his mouth. She moaned from deep inside, pushing against and wrapping a leg around him. In a flash Hamilton saw Mo as she said she'd rather die than lose him. Jeri was tugging at his belt buckle and groping between his legs. As he scooped his hand under her dress and felt the hot damp of her crotch, he suddenly didn't care about the repercussions. Yes, the Red Rider was raring to get loose. Her tongue was in his ear and she opened her legs wider. Then their hands were like their tongues – wild beings with their own lives. Jeri was a cosmion. He melted into her. She had become the smell of marigolds.

But then it happened. It came from above them. Hamilton saw it lunge from the corner of his eye. Then he heard it shriek. He turned and saw its wide eyes and grinning face next to his. It had landed on Jeri's bare back and it grabbed her hair and tugged at the garlands around her neck. She screamed. Hamilton bolted from her, and as he did, he felt shame for pushing her away – shame washed over by shock.

"It's a monkey! A goddamn monkey!" he heard himself say.

There was more than one. They darted, jumped and snarled as they fought each other for the garlands. When they were gone, Jeri lay bleeding. Blood was all the way down the front of her white dress. Hamilton pulled off his sweaty shirt and placed it on the side of her head. A monkey had bitten off a piece of Jeri's ear. She sobbed.

"It's alright," he said. "It's alright. It's just the lobe."

All of that for nothing, he thought. Then he thought of Mo. She would have called it justice.

"Did you hear what the nurse said about those monkeys?" Andy asked, motioning with his skinny arm so as to include all of them. "She said that they were just mischievous. She thought it was funny."

"Oh no, she did not think the attack was funny. She felt awkward because it was her duty to defend the monkeys. Hanuman, the great monkey god of strength and a reincarnation of Shiva himself, is a most popular Hindu deity. Many Hindus worship the monkeys and protect them from harm. That is why the vendors were so politely shooing the monkeys away when they were relentlessly stealing their trinkets," Dicky chuckled.

"Ya'll won't believe what I've read. There's this temple where they worship rats! Says so right here in my guidebook. If you don't believe me, I'll show you," Andy earnestly responds.

"Well, not exactly, Andy," Dicky replied, "but indeed rats are considered sacred there. I gather you are referring to the temple Karni Mata, the temple at Deshnok?"

Andy did not remember the name. Dicky placed a chapatti on his plate, took a swallow of mango juice and continued:

"Perhaps we can go there. It's worth the trip. It is only a few hours from here by bus or car. Perhaps after the meetings?"

"Yes, when Jeri returns," Starman said, "and by then Mo will be here. We could all go. Would you take us, Dicky? That would be great."

"Yes, dear Starman, I would be delighted to take you, but I must tell you that Jeri will not be returning to Jaipur. I tried to tell her that there was no reason for her to fly back to Delhi. The medical facilities here are altogether adequate. But she does not listen to me. We will see her back in Delhi. Well, I suspect we will."

For a moment they were all silent, but finally Starman spoke up:

"So sorry about that, Dicky."

"Oh, no matter," Dicky replied. "Deshnok is on the Jodhpur road. It is on our way back if we go by bus. Here, Starman, try the chutney."

They sat at long tables on the patio beside the university guesthouse. In addition to their party there were perhaps twenty others eating. These were their hosts and the other foreign visitors who were to participate in the conference. The table was covered with a variety of exotic dishes and most of the guests ate with a mixture of curiosity and caution.

At first, the conversation had been subdued, but after awhile it was established that most of the guests spoke the same language. Soon their speech and manners became animated. Indeed, the language was English, yet spoken with an esoteric vocabulary. There was much talk of "movements, pressures and forces" as if they belonged to an occult system of hydraulics and described how parts of the world were to be swept up and transformed by the progressive wave of the future, while the rest just flushed away. This, as it turned out, was the language of "development."

To Hamilton's left sat the pink Englishman who had been worried about the elephants, and whose name, they learned, was Lloyd Lastmann. He was to deliver the first of the three opening talks. The woman sitting to Andy's right was to speak after Lastmann, and at the last minute, Dicky had dropped in Hamilton to deliver the third speech. His lecture was to be on the Russian polymath, Bogdanov – the inventor of cybernetics, the science of control.

Lastmann and the lady on the other side of Andy leaned over Dicky, Hamilton, Starman and Andy, and talked to each other in this progressive tongue. Others who knew the language listened, mostly differing to them, but occasionally joining in. Hamilton, Starman and Andy, even Dicky, were regarded as mere obstacles around which to talk. Dicky had found this amusing, but the other three were annoyed. The talk was about the "force" here and that "pressure" there and how what they call "the Movement" must continue to "struggle."

"The internal contradictions will eventually pressure the reactionary forces and bring about their own inevitable elimination," one of them said.

Andy was craning his long, scrawny neck and cupping his ear. Hamilton could tell that he was listening hard. Hamilton blamed what he heard on Andy, and Andy, somehow on Hamilton. But as one might guess, neither said this to the other.

After lunch, they were in an airy auditorium – airy because there was little difference between the inside of the room and the outside. There was no glass in the windows. It was nothing but open space. Even the doors, when there were doors, were left wide open. Birds flew in and out of the room with no boundaries to inhibit them, and although there were many whirring ceiling fans, for some reason the birds did not fly into them.

Dicky, or Doctor Dikshit, Conference Coordinator, officially welcomed everyone, especially those who had come from so far away. He then introduced the first speaker, Lloyd Lastmann.

Lastmann's main theme was communication. For him, communication was everything:

"People are not really different from one another, they just communicate differently. There are no conflicts, just miscommunications. All messages communicated are equally valid; that is, one message is neither more valid nor better than another, or less valid or worse. Moreover, there is no such thing as better or worse in itself; there are just different messages. That which is better or worse can only be measured by the effect of the message. Different messages, while of equal value in terms of their content, lead to conflict because they are different."

Thus, he concludes that the problem of conflict arises in the way people communicate:

"World conflict leads to world conflict," he said, pleased with his phrase and smiling big at his audience. "The problem lies not only in the different meanings we derive from messages, but in messages themselves being different. Thus difference itself is the basic distortion that leads to conflict! So what we need to do is get rid of difference. The eradication of difference is what we call 'understanding' and better understanding can be acquired through better communication."

When he finished there was a moment of silence and most everyone waited piously. He continued by elaborating on the relationship between miscommunication and an inequitable distribution of the world's resources. Finally, he concluded:

"We have the power to bring this understanding to the world and rid it of inequalities or, said another way, to wipe out differences. All we have to do is develop the consciousness of the world's people – to empower them. This we can do through various techniques of communication that we already have. We must rid ourselves of the differences that separate us from one another. This perfectly developed equality will be found in a world where there is neither rich nor poor, male nor female, child nor adult, human nor animal; where there is no north or south, east or west; where down is up and up is down; and where there is no receiver or giver of truth, but instead where everyone gives and receives the truth. A fully developed world is one in which everyone will be the truth and the way. The way to this new world is through perfect communication, which, of course, means to understand one another perfectly. And the truth is that we really are the world."

The speaker stood smiling, wallowing in the applause.

"What the hell was this guy talking about?" Andy asked Starman.

"Communication, or so it sounded," Starman replied. "What do you think Hamilton?"

"Yeah, sounded like communication to me. Chatter, talk, whatever you want to call it."

They were shushed by someone directly behind them. Mummers of approval were buzzing about the room. And then the next speaker was introduced.

"On behalf of the Institute for Human Development, I would like to present to you Doctor Mary Aleo, political and environmental activist and chairperson of The International Council of World Development in Indianapolis, Indiana. But of course, most of you know of her work ..."

Doctor Dikshit continued to dollop praises upon this speaker. Finally, with a generous sweep of his hand, and stumbling to get the words right, he finished: "The title of her talk is 'Hegemonic Heterosexual Masculinity and Human Development.'"

"Hedge what?" Andy asked, leaning over toward Hamilton and Starman.

The speaker had already begun and again somebody behind was shushing them, so Hamilton just shook his head.

The tall woman was made even taller by her red, high-heeled shoes. Her long, dark-brown hair was streaked with gray and she wore a red silk dress and long, dangling silver earrings with some kind of red stones. She had deep-red painted lips, a hard face with a long nose and, due to what was likely time spent in a gym, a hard body to match. Hamilton guessed her age to be forty-something, but then because she appeared to be in such good shape, her face looked much older than her body. Hamilton was sitting close enough to see a small tattoo just above her ankle – a picture of a green and blue Earth with "ONE WORLD" written just under it.

"...they are not neutral. Masculine and heterosexual behavior have no biological base; rather, they are social, economic and political. Who says you have to be this way or that? Those in power are the people who say this. Who is in power? Heterosexual men with macho behavior are in power. The hegemonic gender obedience to masculine behavior insures competition with other men and the subordination of women and other less masculine males. It brings forth violence toward these subordinated groups and their exploitation. In other words, hegemonic heterosexual masculinity promotes imperialism and is an obstacle to real development."

At this point the speaker had to stop for applause, but it was peculiar that the gesture of endorsement and appreciation was exhibited only by a portion of those present – by that part of the audience of western origin. This argument must be so advanced, Hamilton joked to himself, that it can only be understood by people from the developed world. She went on, elaborating first this point and then that.

"The gender regime is tied to the present system of production and power. It seriously affects the type of development we bring to the underdeveloped world. But a qualitatively better society can be visualized without this gender oppression and terrorism. Who says that men have to be men and women have to be women in the traditional sense? Hegemonic masculinity does. But we have it within our power to wipe out these oppressive dissentions, these differences that underpin the imperialism of the West. We don't have to be mere men and women – male masters and female slaves. We can be anything we want. There are no limits ..."

Finally, her speech was over. Most of the westerners clapped enthusiastically; the non-westerners applauded politely.

When Dicky introduced the visitor from Canada, Hamilton rose from his seat and walked to the lectern. He stood for a moment and looked at his audience, waiting for them to settle down. He did not appear as he often did: casual, joking, perhaps even frivolous. Hamilton began:

"My intention was to speak to you about Alexander Bogdanov, one of the original Bolsheviks, a writer of science fiction, a man associated with the embalming of Lenin and the inventor of cybernetics, the science of control. I was going to talk about the science of control as it relates to what some people today refer to as 'development.' Instead, I have decided to talk about why and how we can talk about development and control in the first place.

"First, I would like to consider the development of our control and then reflect on the control of our development. The latter, of course, is the topic that the other speakers have considered.

"The English word 'development' first came into our vocabulary during the latter part of the sixteenth century, that period in our history which marks the beginning of the scientific, or modern, era. To develop is to uncover various means that have lead to particular ends. It is, therefore, to expose what were once mere possibilities that lead to various actualities. In other words, development is revealing the possible in relation to the actual in this means-ends relation. What is this means-ends relation? I call this the historical process, and these moments, or parts, of the past that have lead to our present, I call history itself.

"So when we speak of development in terms of our species, in terms of planetary development, or 'world development,' then we see that the word 'development' has everything to do with understanding human history.

"In order for us to see the meaning of this 'understanding of human history' it is necessary, first, to uncover how it is possible to think of history as development. When we can see how it is possible for us to do this, then we will also see how we can control history and thereby eradicate it.

"Let us begin by breaking down how it is possible to uncover the means-end relation that is the historical process and to recognize these possibilities that have become actualized as history? To do this, we must ask the question: What are the possibilities that must pertain in order for things to be as they are and not otherwise? In order to provide an answer to this question one must be excluded from those possibilities that comprise the historical process. So obviously, the answer to our question is that we recognize a possibility only after it is over. The possible, therefore, is always seen as moments of the past. Hence, we find the possible by identifying the conditions that necessarily led to the actual present. This identification of the conditions that reveal the present is called memory, and memory is history. But history, or memory, is realized only when it has ended and the possible is fully developed. This is the meaning of history as development, and, in its more vulgar but less self-conscious form, history as progress.

"When we consider 'history as development' in light of this, we see several things. First, as I have already said, we see that history as development is the relationship of possibility to actuality. Next, we see that because we cannot recognize possibility until it has seeped into the past and been resurrected into the real or actual, then to speak of history as development is to speak of it as if it were, at least in principle, over. I repeat: To talk about history as development is to speak as if history has, at least in principle, ended. I say 'in principle' because principles are but possibilities too. Simply put, while parts of the world still exist that have yet to be what we used to call westernized, then modernized and now developed, in principle, the transformation is there, but not yet actualized. We shall return to this point later on."

"What in hell is Hamilton talking about?" Andy asked Starman.

"I haven't a clue," Starman whispered.

And Hamilton went on:

"The end of history would, in effect, be the identity of possibility and actuality – of the ideal and the real. It would amount to the co-penetration of thought and action, or said in a more esoteric way, the coming together of wisdom and power.

"Classical philosophy recognized that thought and action made no sense without the other. Were it not for Achilles' heroic actions, Homer would have had nothing to sing about, and had it not been for the poetry of Homer, we would not know of the great deeds of Achilles. But both pagan and Christian classical philosophy warned that thought and action were never to be equated. In other words, while they are related, their relation must remain ambiguous. But the modern project itself is to co-penetrate thought and action. I use the sexual metaphor here, for the result is just as unpredictable as sex. The result of co-penetration is modern science, or to use its more accurate name, technology.

"So what is technology? One can begin with this thoroughly modern word and try to discover its meaning synthetically. Technology is a compound of two Greek words: techne and logos. Techne pertains to making and logos to knowing; thus, we have to practice – to act – on the one hand, and to perceive – to know – on the other. But technology is not a compound in word only, for it is a compound from this co-penetration of making and knowing. Technology is the progressively rational – efficient – development of means to ends for humans and cause and effect for nature. The former has to do with practices – action – and the latter with perceptions –thought.

"Technology has as its project the transformation of nature both human and nonhuman. Efficiency, the goal of technology's projected development, is, and can be measured as, the progressively diminishing difference between those means and ends or causes and effects. Thus, technology is (1) self-referential, (2) relatively autonomous, (3) progressively sovereign and (4) tends toward the systemization of nature both human and nonhuman.

"If the relative difference of means to ends were ever reduced to zero, or to complete efficiency, then technology would be a totality – a complete system – like a kind of cybernetic world state. This, of course, would be the highest stage of world development.

"Now let me be a bit more concrete and talk about what kind of ideas might be related to the kinds of action that results in the development of our technology. Let's start by asking where ideas are located. The answer would be – even for someone who had misinterpreted Plato – that ideas are to be found in the brains of humans.

"So, where then do our actions occur? They occur in the historical and empirical world rather than in the world inside our heads. So, then, how does one get the world of ideas located inside our heads to square with the real world of everyday life? The answer is that we inseminate our ideas into our will and give birth to "ideals" – ideas that can act – and with this action we transform reality so as to make it identical with the idea of the reality we desire. This is history as development.

"Now what are these ideals to which I refer? Perhaps the best examples of these ideals are 'liberty, equality and fraternity,' that battle cry of modernity – the shibboleth used to justify the actualization of the possibilities of history as development. Those French revolutionaries sought to end history and have it start over again by creating a new world, the endeavor of all revolutionaries."

"What bullshit," Andy snorted.

"Andy, please!" Starman whispered in his ear.

"But the peculiar thing about these ideals is that we seem to be unable to hold the three of them together at the same time. And because we find it difficult, if not impossible, to justify at the same time the actualization of a possibility in terms of the three ideals of the equation, we tend to focus on one ideal to the exclusion of the others.

"The desire to focus on one ideal for justification of history and, at the same time, to exclude the others, leads to conflict. I refer to the kind of conflict known only to our century: ideological warfare. Ideological warfare is a kind of conflict resulting from the portion of the equation that we choose for justifying the actualization of the possibilities of history. If we choose liberty, we get liberalism. If we pick equality, the result is socialism. And if our choice is fraternity, or we might even say 'culture,' then we have embraced fascism. But the three ideals taken both together and separately are the elements of the same equation of development. And since the actualization of the possibilities of history is what we mean by 'development,' then we can say that the crypto-religious wars of the twentieth century have been, and yet are still conducted in the name of 'development.' The Soviets claim to have the best plan for developing the globe and so does the West. So, let me be clear, this is what the so-called Cold War is really about.

"Since history must be over in order for us to recognize the principles that have lead to the actualization of it, then, in principle, everyone is free, equal and from the same family. This only means that we are capable of not only visualizing a world where this would be actual, but of making the world this way. In other words, now that history is, in principle, over - or to be more accurate, dead - with our technology we are capable of controlling development. And now, with our technological prowess, we can enlighten the few remaining areas of the world that are still dark with backwardness. Backwardness is about boundaries. Our technology neither recognizes nor respects boundaries, whether they are human or nonhuman, historical or geographical, human or animal, animate or inanimate. The one and only thing recognized and respected by technology is efficiency. Efficiency is both the measure and the measurer of technology – its purpose and its judge.

"This 'enlightenment' is merely the elaboration of efficiency in the name of liberty, equality and fraternity. So, as we shall see, we can control history. This is to say that the limits, or differences, that heretofore have stood in the way can be removed. The limits pertain to ways of seeing things and doing things; in other words, they are the perceptions and practices that stand in the way of development. Indeed, in our time there are, in principle, no limits. Granted, we may for awhile replay the combinations and permutations of the contents of the garbage can containing the detritus of history. But in the end, we will tire of replaying moments of history and will do whatever is efficient. Eventually we may even come clean and confess that our actions are committed in the name of this newly revealed god, Efficiency. Alas, the age of ideology is passing with the twentieth century and the age of efficiency is upon us."

Hamilton stopped and looked out at his audience. They had been very still, but with Hamilton's moment of silence, they suddenly became restless and began to mummer and whisper. Hamilton caught a glimpse of the other two speakers. Although people were talking around them, they were silent.

Lastmann, who was naturally pink, had turned red. The woman introduced as Doctor Mary Aleo glared at Hamilton, but the Englishman just looked and blinked.

Hamilton continued:

"I know that I have been speaking in rather abstract terms, and I thank you for your indulgence. Now I will try to be concrete, appeal to common sense and perhaps, if you will permit, even be a bit crude. I will tell you what I think the world will look like when we have removed all these limits and the globe has become fully developed.

"But before I do this, I should like to thank the two speakers who spoke before me for their illuminating lectures. In fact, were it not for progressive people such as these, people such as myself would have no clue as to what development is all about. So, I could not have agreed with them more, and because of what they said, and the visions of the world they described, there is little left to do except to proceed with the kinds of projects that reflect the values expressed in their speeches.

"Considering that which remains on the program for world development, I will describe what the fully developed world will look like. In other words, I would like to tell you what to expect when the principles of liberty, equality and fraternity are fully universalized. What remains of applying these principles, I leave to others more worthy of the task.

"The first manifestation of universalizing these principles is 'niceness.' Niceness has to do with pleasantness, tameness and domestication. At the end of history everyone will be nice, and we will all know what to expect from one another: niceness. All our days will be alike. They will all be nice days when what we expect to happen does, indeed, happen.

"The next thing that characterizes the universalizing of these principles is 'whiteness.' It is as if our differences will die along with our history and we all will be resurrected as white people, at least symbolically we will. We will have turned all the black, brown, yellow and red people into white people. We will dress like white people, eat like white people, play music and make love like white people. This is not to say that the various ways of seeing the world and acting in it will simply vanish. Only that which cannot be transformed and appropriated will vanish. This is but another way of saying that at the end of history, those things that previously made us different from one another – race, culture, class – will no longer matter. What remains will be there for all to choose. Life will become mere style. Only style will matter.

"White people are western people, and, for ill or good, the most developed people in the West are the Americans. Perhaps we should stretch this a bit and be more inclusive by using the term "Euro-Americans," for all nice, white people will become Americans. Thus, the third characteristic of the fully developed world is 'Americanization.' In this I include the Russians, who sit at the eastern boundary of the Western Empire – the less developed side – and who have had the misfortune of stressing a less productive moment in the equation, the element of equality. This has made them nothing more than poor Americans. But there is no real difference between them and their rich cohorts; or, as we once could say, they are metaphysically the same.

"The fully developed world at the end of history will be safe. That is, it will not be a dangerous place. Our experience tells us that if we are to rid ourselves of danger, then we have to abolish the unpredictable, for the unpredictable, because we cannot plan for it, is dangerous. Thus, to make the world safe, thereby ridding it of the accidental or unpredictable, we must eradicate spontaneity, spiritedness and sportiveness. These are the basis of 'maleness,' and it is maleness that has always been the harbinger of danger. So the new realm of public safety must be bereft of maleness; and therefore, the last characteristic of a world at the end of history is 'femaleness.'

"So this world at the end of history will be nice – that is, domesticated or tame. It will be white – non-mysterious, non-secretive, open, sincere, shallow, transparent and inclusive. And since it will all be western, than there will be no eastern, no southern and no northern. We all will be the same. We will be homogeneous like the members of one big happy family. In this world, this family will all be equal in that all will be fully developed and never again will anyone have to envy or resent the West. And since the danger of maleness will be eradicated, the new world will be so safe and secure that no one will remember ever dreading, longing for or fearing the future. With the eradication of fear, there will be no need for seriousness or for politics, and seriousness and politics will be replaced by entertainment. In this world of entertainment, the future will become like the past – a story already told. And then the story will become a progressively forgotten bad dream. Thus the future will have come, and then be gone forever, and the universal and homogeneous world at the end of history will be one eternal world of nice, white, American women."

"The squaring of our ideas with our actions is the key to entry into, as Hegel called it, the "New World." I speak of the development of our planet by the progressive power of our technology. Technology is the risen Christ, and development is His Prophet and the harbinger of the Advent of His Holy Spirit.

As Hamilton paused, he noticed the restlessness in the audience and heard the Englishman groan. He held up his hand asking for silence and proceeded.

"Yet, as inefficient as it may be, there will be resistance, probably desperate and violent resistance. The past cannot be eradicated without a last fight. Yes, some folks will be much annoyed by this. These unhappy people are those who do not want to be like everybody else and who do not find the new world of entertainment amusing. These people find a world devoid of seriousness abhorrent and will refuse to give up politics. They will kick and they will scream and, indeed, they will blow things up. But in the end, efficiency will prevail and those who refuse to be transformed will perish. So do not despair, for now that history has died the globe can be transformed into a fully developed planet."

"Good God," Andy muttered.

Again there was a great restiveness in the room. Hamilton had stirred everyone up, and by the time he sat down, people were whispering, talking and leaving.

Dicky arose and walked over to the lectern.

"Thank you professor ... thank you Doctor West for a most illuminating talk," he said, his voice rising as the exit from the room became a flood.

"Do we have any discussion? Do we have any discussion on any or all the papers? No? No. Well, in that case, we will dismiss. Please do not forget that our round table will begin tomorrow at ten. I guess we will save our discussion for then. And, oh yes, for those of you who wish to go to the Eco Village for the evening, the bus leaves from the guesthouse at five. It will return in time for our luncheon tomorrow. Thank you."

The bus was far from full. In fact, there were fewer than twenty people on the bus – all of them from the West. The Indians had left. It had turned out that the rush from the lecture hall had not been caused by anything that Hamilton had said in his speech. No, the inattention, the whispering and the hasty departures had been brought about because of a rumor circulating in the audience. It had been reported that Rushdie was hiding in the area and some were saying that he was hiding in a Hindu temple and that Hindu temples were to be blown up by enraged Muslims. So, the temper of that particular conference on world development held at the university in Jaipur in 1989 was being determined less by acrimony and more by fear.

Most of those who had attended the conference had left. As a result, fewer had decided to go to the model village than had been expected. Since Andy and Starman were among those to stay behind, only Hamilton and Dicky were there with the small group. Hamilton noted that Lloyd Lastmann was on the bus and was sitting several seats behind him and Dicky.

When they arrived at the village, children ran to the bus and followed the little group. A village elder showed them a biogas plant, a solar-powered thrasher and streetlights operated by solar cells attached to the tops of their poles. The children got closer and closer to Hamilton, but he did not notice until one reached up and asked to stroke his short, red hair and large, crescent-shaped mustache.

"Moini, Moini," the child said.

Hamilton was startled, but did not stop the boy.

"What's going on?" he asked Dicky.

"The youth is saying to his friends that you are wise. They have never seen red hair before and although you do not have much of it, what you do have they associate with divinity – and then there are those red whiskers."

That evening they were taken into the largest building in the village and the elder, who spoke some English, told them that it was time to eat and that something special had been planned for them.

"It is not something special to eat. That is not what he means. It is something else that is special," Dicky interpreted.

They were placed in the front of the room, all sitting on the floor facing a box covered with a pearl-studded shawl embroidered with a picture of blue-faced Krishna and his entourage of cow-eyed girl admirers. The elder, as if performing a feat of magic, looked at his audience, smiled and snatched off the shawl. There stood an old Zenith television encased in a blond oak box. The elder walked around the set, opened the doors and turned the switch. To Hamilton's surprise, the images were in color.

"Solar power," the elder announced proudly, adding that they were happily participating in India's official program of zero energy dependency and radical self-sufficiency.

At that moment, the food was brought. Each received a banana leaf upon which giggling girls scooped rice. There was also yogurt, chapattis and a hot vegetable curry. They all sat silently, eating while being observed and watching a video rerun of the Bill Cosby Show.

After the meal, when they were standing outside drinking sweet, milky, masala tea, Lloyd Lastmann came over to Hamilton and interrupted the conversation he and Dicky were having with the elder.

"What you said today was offensive. You should know that when I return to Essex, I will write to both your institution and to your professional association and ask that you be censured for your outrageous behavior. Professor Mary Aleo is doing the same, and so are at least a dozen other people. You'll never receive a travel grant again. We'll see to that."

Hamilton replied, "So where is the Virgin ... sorry, Mary whatever her name is?"

"I can't believe you said that. I ..."

"She is probably at the hospital with her sick child and partner. They had a child with them," Dicky interjected. "She said that her partner and the child drank the water. I called the doctor for her and sent her over to fetch them by taxi. Yesterday – before they got sick, of course – I heard her say that the business about the unhealthy water in India was some kind of conspiracy."

"Oh, how awful!" Lastmann said as he blinked and wobbled off.

That night, about two hours before dawn, the village was awakened by screams and cries.

"Oh, God! A monster!"

They all rushed from their beds toward the communal outhouses – the direction from which the screams were coming. It was the Lastmann.

"Oh, how awful! How terrible," he sobbed as he pointed toward the cracked door of an outhouse.

The beam of Hamilton's flashlight caught the line of open ditching behind the outhouses that ended in a tunnel, which led to the biogas tanks. He sliced the beam along the edge of the trees and behind the buildings, but nothing was there. Then Hamilton and Dicky went inside the outhouse and Hamilton shined the light into the hole in the wooden seat. Then he bent over and peered inside. There, in the beam, was a pink pig with a dollop of shit on its head. The pig looked up at him with happy, beady eyes and blinked. Hamilton later told Dicky that he could swear the pig was smiling.

Hamilton had been surprised when they returned to Jaipur, for he had expected to find Mo at the luncheon. He had left a message at the desk for her to meet him there. Hamilton hurried across the lawn and then across the campus and hailed a taxi. The taxi stopped at the hotel and Hamilton paid the driver. He ran to his room and slowly opened the door, but the room was empty. He went back downstairs to the front desk.

"Miss Pangolin? Have you seen a dark-haired American lady?"

The clerk looked up, "Yes, sahib, the lady, she left. It was some time ago. She was transported by taxi. I remember well, for when she told me that she was with you, I gave her a letter posted to you from New Delhi, I believe. And then several hours later she came here and presented me with the same letter I had given to her."

The clerk handed an envelope to Hamilton. Hamilton's name and the address of the hotel were written across the front and the envelope had been torn open. Hamilton held the note in the light so he could read the childish handwriting.

Hamilton dear,

We must not deny our feelings. Could we have a life together? We must at least finish what we started. I am staying at the Institute. Call me immediately. Can't wait. A fire burns between my thighs.

Have a nice day,
Jeri

"The letter, it arrived for you by special courier. The lady, she said I was to give it to you. Something is wrong, sahib? I hope not bad news?" the clerk asked.

Hamilton looked at him and, with a break in his voice, asked where Mo had gone. The clerk said he did not know, but that perhaps the taxi driver could be found. They did find the taxi driver, asleep in his cab under a Mimosa tree beside the hotel. Shaking his head from side to side, the driver told him that he remembered the dark-haired American lady. Hamilton handed the man five hundred rupees and the man lowered his head gravely.

"She act crazy, sahib. I am sorry. She says to take her to men, and she has very bad language and she very drunk. I am sorry, sahib."

The driver looked down again, embarrassed, and said that he would drive Hamilton to a place called the Hotel Ashok.

Hamilton found Mo in a hotel room. She was on the floor next to the toilet, face down in a pool of her vomit.

"Mo, please!" he begged, shaking her. "Mo! Please! Please, wake up! Speak to me! Mo, please!"

She opened her mouth, licked her lips and sighed, "Hamilton, you bastard."

Hamilton told her everything, trying to persuade her that there was nothing to his brief tryst with Jeri – telling her that Jeri was crazy and that, even if the monkeys had not attacked, nothing would have happened. Mo knew that the first part was true and that the last part was a lie, but had let it pass. Then she told Hamilton that she was pregnant, that she had learned this from the doctor at the tennis club in New Delhi.

"We'll take care of it when we return to Singapore. I'm too old to have another child," she sobbed. "I didn't even think it was possible. Besides, who in their right mind would want to give birth to a child at ... what do you call it? At the death of history?"

They held each other, laughing and crying, quaking in love and forgiveness.

# RAT CITY

"Hamilton, you're not only reactionary, you're fucking racist. I don't think even Jud would get up and say the kinds of things you said to all those people," Andy said, exasperated. "You know what I think, Ham? I think that end of history crap has messed up your mind. And I thought you'd changed for the better. Hamilton, you just didn't have the right to do that."

"Right? Right means power, nothing more and nothing less. If you say you have the right to do something, all you mean is that you have the power to do it. Ticks you off, eh Unc?" Hamilton replied, smiling.

"Screw you, Hambone. You and your globalization shit."

"Globalization, now that's a neat word. Where did you get that, Unc?"

"Just a word that popped into my head. Like everything else it's just a goddamn word. Just something I made up. And by the way, I'm not your fucking uncle."

"Guess you're right. 'Unc' is just a word, but like you say, it can mean whatever I want."

This is what they said to each other at breakfast before Andy and Starman left for an ashram at a place called Mount Abu. They sat in the sun on the terrace of the Rambagh Palace, sipping coffee from Royal Doulton demitasse cups. Under the surface of all the finery was the smoldering presence of former masters. Hamilton changed the subject. He worried that what he just said to Andy might have been a bit too heavy handed, and secretly he was still having uneasy feelings about the kinds of things he had said the day before. He also did not want to do anything that might upset Mo. She still was recuperating and Hamilton had left her asleep in the room, but she could appear anytime.

Hamilton and Mo spent the next two days at the hotel. Mo tried to help Hamilton with his tennis game, but he was a hopeless pupil.

"It's not a hockey puck!" Mo shouted at him from across the net.

The hotel did not have a tennis pro and there was nobody on the nearly deserted courts who could have been a fair match for Mo. But she located an ancient serving machine and Hamilton tinkered with it until he got it to fire the ball across the net, at least some of the time.

In the mornings and late afternoons, Hamilton would take a chair and table to their little balcony and, with a borrowed extension cord for Mo's computer, wrote more of *Jud's Story* on her laptop. From where he sat, he could hear the machine serving the balls and, looking down on the courts, could watch Mo gracefully swatting them. If he gazed out he could see both the Pink City and the dry hills and mountains beyond. The sky was the color of a wood duck's egg.

Starman and Andy had made some day trips, thus Mo and Hamilton had not been seeing them until dinnertime. Hamilton invited Dickey to have dinner with them at the Rambagh Palace. Over dinner, Dicky reminded them that they were to return to Delhi via Deshnok and see the Karni Mata Temple. Andy was happy Dicky had neither forgotten nor had changed his mind, but while the smiling old Brahman had often done the former, he had not done the latter for many years.

Hamilton still felt awkward about the conference. By most accounts it had been a failure, and he knew that in part he was to blame. But then the Rushdie factor had been the main reason for its going sour. Hamilton did not know what to expect when they returned to the university. He thought that he might face fireworks, but when they returned, he found that most of the conference attendees had left, and those who remained snubbed him.

"Yes, they have all gone because you set off that bomb, and when you did, nothing else could be said." Dickey sighed, saying, "I've never had the courage to say what I saw; but in my old age, at least I am associated with it. So now, my name is mud. And guess what? I like it."

"Are you sure about that?" Hamilton asked, smiling.

"Sure. I am retired. You know, Hamilton, the trouble with those people is that they have too many ideas and not enough concepts," he answered, grinning at Hamilton.

"Sorry, Dicky, but what is the difference between an idea and a concept?" Mo asked.

"Ideas just float about. They are not anchored to anything. They are like ghosts, my dear – abstract, elusive and as private as our desires. Concepts are rooted in reality, in experience. They are concrete, alive, and people can talk about them because they mean something. After Hamilton's speech it became apparent that many had come to the conference merely to have it recognized that they were loyal to certain ideas. They wanted to find others who embraced the same ideas as they did and join with them in plans for spreading those ideas and denouncing those who disagreed with them. These people are like their ideas: one-sided, inflexible ghosts. When they heard what Hamilton had to say, they felt betrayed by their expectations. They didn't come to hear that! They came to display their virtues, and your Hamilton ruined it for them because they would be required to think in order to meet his criticism. Thinking is something most of them neither have the capacity for nor the courage to engage in. Thinking requires risk, but with no risk, there is no life."

The next morning, Hamilton sat on the balcony writing. At noon he took an autorickshaw to the university and lunched with Dicky. That afternoon, when he was taking his jog in the desert, he thought about what Dicky had said the evening before about risk and life. He thought about risk, and he thought about Mo and her being pregnant with his child. He thought about how much he loved Mo. He loved her so much that it hurt him to think about it.

That evening before dinner and after showering, Hamilton and Mo lay together in bed. Hamilton was just about to doze off, for his run has made him pleasantly tired, but then Mo brought up the subject of risk and Dicky's talk the night before. They decided that risk revealed what is hidden and, in the end, forces the admission that one does not know the future. It is because of risk, they concluded, that the future – no matter what it brings – is both dangerous and wonderful.

"Mo, what if we take a chance and keep this child?"

The words just shot out of Hamilton, and he was astounded at what he had said. For a moment Mo didn't answer, but reached over and stroked his bare chest.

"Hamilton, what are you saying? You could allow a child to come into the world at the end of history?" she laughed, shaken.

Before Hamilton could reply, there was a knock on the door. It was Starman and Andy. They had returned from Mount Abu and came to take Hamilton and Mo to dinner.

"Come on you two. We'll be waiting in the bar. Andy has had ten too many already. Let's eat," Starman said, laughing.

"Yeah, now that we're back, ya'll can start having fun again. You two act as if you are married or something. It's disgusting," Andy joked.

After dinner, in anticipation of the journey the next day, Mo went to bed. She was tired. After all, she was pregnant.

Hamilton, Starman and Andy went to the bar for coffee and brandy. Starman and Andy told Hamilton about what they had seen at Mount Abu – about a yogi who was buried in the ground for half a day and a blue-eyed American with long, graying blond whiskers and locks. He had been in India since 1968.

"He sat on a rock for hours, and was so still he could have been dead. While he talked to us, only his lips moved. He didn't even blink," Andy said.

"Well, maybe a few times," Starman interjected, first rolling his eyes and then looking affectionately at Andy.

"Yeah, he referred to America as the Old World and said he would never go back. He was naked and he could erect and relax his dick at will," Andy added, laughing.

"Big day tomorrow. Rat City," Hamilton announced.

Hamilton was tired, but before he went to sleep he wanted to read over the last chapter he finished writing, the second chapter of *Jud's Story*.

"Good night, guys," he said and left.

## CHAPTER II
### DEACON JACK, THE POPSICLE MAN

What I want to tell you about took place well over a decade after Eli had died and perhaps fifteen years after Collie's mamma had brought him to the Benjamin House to live. What I want to tell you about took place well over a decade after Eli had died and perhaps fifteen years after Collie's mamma had brought him to the Benjamin House to live. Yes, that much time had passed since Shorty had fallen into the vat of resin and Eli had tumbled off the porch and broken his neck. I can tell this story because when I was growing up in Altamaha I heard bits and pieces of it, and when I was older and had moved away, Uncle Andy talked about it from time to time – floating in, as his stories usually do, on a tide of Scotch.

Over these years, Altamaha, like everywhere else, was suffering through the depression, but both the churches and the bootleggers were still in business. Springs "Jaybird" Coots was still selling liquor from his Packard car parked near the tracks, and righteousness was still sold from every pulpit in town.

Doris had grown old and she was placed in an institution called the "Bethel Home for Ladies." She was soon forgotten about and, eventually, she died. Vera Ola, too, had aged. Her nerves had become so shot that she could no longer raise Collie, and, for a time, Cora looked after him. But then Cora was getting up in years herself and had become so skinny that her face was pointed and she could wear Collie's clothes. Her hair became so gray, long and tangled that it looked like an angry thunderhead was hovering over her. One day, after all those years, Cora simply announced she was quitting working for the Benjamins and she began root doctoring full time.

Richard, who remained a bachelor and had become even more crippled, was spending more late hours at the bank, though during those years he was making little money. He was busy just trying to hold on to what he had. To Richard's credit, and to the benefit of the town, he had become scoutmaster. Ewell, my father, had recently finished college at the Citadel in Charleston. He had been commissioned an ensign in the U.S. Navy and was in flight training down at Glencoe Naval Air Station. Uncle Andy Ray, who just turned sixteen, had finished his last year of high school and couldn't wait, as he put it, "to leave the idiocy of rural life."

At that time, Collie would have been about fourteen. For quite some years, due to Vera Ola's nerves and Cora's absence, Collie just did what he pleased. Just like his daddy, Collie was a crazy son of a bitch. And I can see him just the way Uncle Andy said he was. I can imagine him standing on the Altamaha River Bridge, leaning over the rail – him and two other boys – and spitting into the water. They were pretending that their spit was German bombs, the kind that the Nazis had been using in Spain, and they would make that whistling noise that falling bombs make as the gobs of spittle sailed downward toward the reddish-brown water. And then, as their spit hit the water, they would say "KAPOW." The boys would watch the water swirling and rippling around the iron legs that supported the bridge, following the shore to the rotting boards and pilings of the abandoned Benjamin docks.

Earlier that day, the three boys had stood at the "V" – upstream where the Ocmulgee and Oconee rivers joined to form the Altamaha. On this peach-colored, clay bluff they had stood pissing, letting their own waters mix with the eternal ones of the river. They stood at the very spot where it was said that the Spanish had buried their gold, but because greed is a more powerful emotion than piety, it long had been forgotten that this spot was also the place where the Indians had buried their dead. The boys had dug and found nothing – not even a bone, much less a doubloon – and pissing in the river was an act of defiance and revenge against the unyielding past, as was their standing, right there, in the middle of town, leaning over the bridge and spitting into the river.

"In Baxton, they say that somebody got the gold, got it a long time ago and took it far away. They say that the Indians put a hex on it," said the tallest of the three boys, who was from the town of Baxton, upriver. He was visiting his grandmother in Altamaha. His name was Wayne "Chick" – for "chicken" – Fowler; and because he was the tallest, he didn't even have to stand on his tiptoes to lean over the side and spit. He was tall, but he was also skinny. The boy next to him wore new high-topped basketball shoes. They were black with white laces and shiny moons on each ankle. His name was Grady.

"Yeah, that's right. You could just feel it. You could just tell that there was ghosts or somethin' there. That's what the colored people say. You could just tell," the tall, skinny boy named Wayne said.

"So you think it was the Indians what put a hex on the gold?" Collie Coots asked. And Wayne answered:

"Well, I don't know, but that's what they say up in Baxton."

"People up in Baxton, they don't know shit," Collie replied, wrinkling his face as if smelling something bad.

"Well, maybe ... maybe it ain't true. Maybe the Indians didn't do the hex," Wayne laughed, "seeing as how they's always drunk and everything. But we know there was gold there." Wayne didn't like either himself or his town insulted, but he was afraid of Collie Coots.

"Sure, there was gold there," Collie said looking dreamily downriver. "There was gold there and I know what happened to it." He stood on his toes, pulled himself up on the rail and spit.

"You wanna know what happened to it?" Collie asked, knowing that Grady and Wayne would say "yes" and beg him to tell them.

"Well, okay," he said, not waiting for an answer, "I'll tell you, but it's gotta be top secret. The secret is that a nigger got it."

"A nigger got the gold?" Grady gasped.

"A nigger?" Wayne echoed.

"Yeah, a nigger. And you wanna know what nigger?"

"Yeah. What nigger?" Grady whispered.

"Well, I'm not sure that I oughta tell you that," Collie said, glaring at Grady as he cleared his throat and spit again into the water.

From the apex of its tall, arched span, the bridge provided a panoramic view of the town and all the surrounded it. Collie looked down the bridge in the direction of Confederate Veterans' Memorial Park in Pine Bluff Cemetery, which sat on the little knoll where the bridge began. The heat rose in crooked waves from the tar and gravel street. He let his eyes follow a tobacco truck as it passed them and went on across the bridge and into town. Collie's gaze followed the truck to where the street stopped at the tobacco warehouse. Then, for a moment, his eyes went back to the street and he watched as people poured out of the picture show, indicating that the Saturday-afternoon serial was over. Some of the people squinted in the glare of the sun and others shielded their eyes with their hands, for sunglasses were not yet in common use. Some crossed the street and the oozing tar stuck to the soles of their shoes. Others stood and talked. Collie sighed. The clock on the Coca-Cola sign on the top of the Piggly Wiggly food store said it was four, but the clock on the Altamaha County Courthouse said it was not.

Then Collie's eyes fell upon a man crossing the Seaboard Railroad tracks near the road that passes the Benjamin mill. He pedaled slowly as Collie watched lazily and the other boys looked upriver and were quiet. The man was on a bicycle of sorts – the kind that is attached to a cart and driven from behind. He passed a block of clapboard houses that long ago Eli had built for mill hands, but that eventually had become occupied by Negroes. By this time, the mill hands had moved into what was called the "Benjamin Estates," a housing project constructed with Benjamin lumber and Benjamin brick bought with New Deal money.

The man went south on Main Street instead of passing East Park, the new name given to what used to be Africaville. East Park sounded better and it had looked better on the forms that the city of Altamaha had filled out when it applied for government funding to extend its sewage system into the area of town where the Negroes lived. In East Park, there were no new houses and all the paint were peeling and their tin roofs were becoming red with rust. But like nowhere else in Altamaha, there were flowers in East Park. There were flowers in pots, tubs and buckets and in containers made from rubber tires. There were even flowers planted in beds outlined with upturned Coco-Cola bottles or brightly painted rocks. There were daisies and marigolds and there was the excessive hydrangea, but mostly there were petunias.

Collie watched as the man pedaled. The clock on the tower at the courthouse struck four. The man pumped the pedals slowly and steadily, and as he did he kept his eyes pinned directly in front on the hot, tar road and paid no attention to anything except that which he saw inside his head. He appeared to be floating, silently, almost motionless. Then, without looking, he crossed Malachi Street and headed in the direction of the bridge. He drifted across, looking neither this way nor that. He neither rung his bell nor blew his whistle, and no white children ran behind the cart with the picture of the bright, green, dripping popsicle painted on the side. There were no shouts. There was no "Gimme a red one" or "I'll have me a purple one and an orange one" and there was no "Does your wife really doctor with roots and talk to the dead?" No, there was nobody but Deacon Jack and his cart and the heat rising off the road.

The cart was an inch thick – a wooden box insulated on its inside and out with tightly packed chicken feathers covered with tar paper and then clad with white-painted tin. It was cooled inside by a contraption that Deacon Jack had devised and is known technically as an absorption refrigerator. Coal inside a small chamber boils water concentrated with ammonia and the gas given off is collected in copper coils that Jack had salvaged from the abandoned turpentine still. In these coils the pressure causes the ammonia to condense and freeze and the freezing pipes absorb the heat from the dark interior of the cart. Inside, dry ice – frozen carbon dioxide, or "hell's ice," as they called it – formed. Deacon Jack always had little pieces of it for the children who were nice and did not tease. He would put the ice in a Dixie Cup with water, and the water would bubble as if boiling. Black coal smoke would escape from the smoke stack at the front of the cart and the whistle that was located on the top of the stack was blown by steam. The water that remained behind in the boiler passed into a container where it became reabsorbed with pure ammonia vapor and pumped back through the heat exchanger that Deacon Jack operated with a lever located on the crossbar of the bicycle. And then the cycle started all over again.

Usually when you saw Deacon Jack, he and his wonderful cart were surrounded by children. The top would be open and billows of steam would be escaping from the cool inside and crashing into the hot air outside. This collision was so great that one wondered if someday he would open the door and the abrupt clash of cold and hot air might produce a violent storm – a small, localized thunderhead

Disorderly Notions

that might even generate tornados and grow into a small hurricane right there over the cart.

"There he is!" Collie hissed.

"Who?" Grady asked.

"Who does it look like? Missus Roosevelt?" Collie sneered, but Grady did not understand and did not answer, so Collie said, "Let's go!"

The two shot off, shouting for Wayne to get the shovel they had used at the "V" to look for gold. They ran off the bridge and down the road and into the town toward Deacon Jack and his popsicle cart.

"Gimme an orange one," Grady shouted after Deacon Jack.

"You got a banana one?" said Collie.

"I want a banana one too," Wayne called after them, copying Collie.

But Deacon Jack did not stop. In fact, Deacon Jack didn't even look at them. He just kept on pedaling with his eyes pinned to the road, a trail of black smoke coming from the stack and following lazily behind. Deacon Jack kept on pedaling and the boys kept on shouting and running behind the cart. They became more and more tired and fell farther and farther behind, shouting "Wait! Wait!" Jack doubled back and went across the bridge and turned at the cemetery. He went up River Road toward Great Alligator Swamp.

"You nigger bastard!" Collie yelled, and then he blew through his teeth, saying, just as he had heard adults say: "Who in the hell does that nigger think he is?"

Finally, looking for excuses, but not finding one for being ignored by a Negro, the boys gave up. With heavy legs, they headed back toward town.

When they got halfway down Malachi Street, Collie, making his voice strange and low, whispered, "He's the nigger what got the gold."

After a second of silence, Grady asked if this were really true – if this was the secret Collie had kept from them. Collie said that yes, it was the secret. Deacon Jack was really the nigger who had stolen the gold.

The boys passed the courthouse and the Farmer's Mutual Exchange and then they went into the parking lot in front of the great, tin tobacco warehouse. First they were lost in the jumble of vehicles: huge trucks piled high with bales of tobacco tied up with sheets made from sewn-together gunny sacks; wagons hitched to skinny, irritable mules; and trucks and cars stuffed and covered with bales. Then they emerged at the back of a crowd that had gathered to watch a ventriloquist and his one-man, one-dummy minstrel show. The black-faced dummy was named Jimmy Zulu. Jimmy – who sometimes wore a top hat, sometimes a baseball cap, frequently an aviator's cap and occasionally a gray fedora or a Panama – had a joke for each change of headgear. But the boys had heard them all and were no longer interested in listening to the cigarette-smoking dummy or in taunting his master as he held up a bottle of brown elixir and had the dummy say that it was good for everything from syphilis to senility.

Collie took the shovel from Wayne, hid it under a pile of tobacco bales and motioned for the two boys to follow him through one of the loading doors into the warehouse. Inside, they could see the long rows of baled tobacco spanning the length of the building. Tobacco buyers from the big companies up in Carolina walking along, following an auctioneer who was singing and shouting, "I have twenty, give me twenty-one, two. Do I have three? Four? Six? Do I hear seven? Seven! Sold to Ligget and Myers!" – or Philip Morris, or American, or to Export or some other tobacco company with a far away, exotic sounding name.

Clouds of dust churned up as the buyers inspected the golden leaves. It went up the boys' noses and burned their eyes. But the dust and smell did not bother the buyers, and although they were completely drenched with sweat, they wore stylish, expensive clothes and two-toned shoes, gold watches and rings with diamonds. Outside, along the street, their big cars were parked and a few were driven by Negro chauffeurs with gray uniforms and high, black boots. Their fancy clothes, flashy jewelry, money and cars helped many of the buyers to win more than a date with many an Altamaha girl and bring shame to more than one of Altamaha's wives.

Tobacco season lasted for only two months, and then the buyers would take their fancy clothes, their expense accounts and their endless supply of bourbon, get into their big cars and disappear up into Carolina until the next season. Then the great, tin box would stand empty except when it was used for basketball. There were lines marking off two courts, one at either end of the building; one for the white team and the other for the Negro team. But basketball was played outside when weather permitted. This was preferred because the splinters in the warehouse floor impaled many feet and the floor was especially rough on the boys who had no basketball shoes and played barefoot. So usually – except for those two months of tobacco season – the building was like a great, silent, empty grave.

In the center of the building was an office – a little wooden house built around a scale that appropriately was called the "scale house." When the bales of tobacco arrived from the farms they were weighed. When they were sold, the weights were checked again before they were carted to the doors that led to the train tracks and loaded into boxcars to be shipped out.

That afternoon, beside the scale house was a tall, muscular Negro standing with his hands on his hips as he talked to the crew who were pushing hand trucks. Then he picked up a clipboard and walked to one of the doors that lead to a boxcar out on the railroad tracks. He began talking with a white man.

"It's tha nigger. The one what thinks he's white," Grady said.

"Who?" Wayne Fowler asked.

"Chick, you people from Baxton are all ignorant. The niggers call him Black Strap Jack and he's got that name 'cause his mamma is a nigger woman what used to work for us and his daddy is that Popsicle Man. He's trying to tell that white man what to do. We ought to fix 'em. Thinks he's shit on a stick."

The boys jumped through one of the loading doors and when they were on the tracks, Collie ordered that Grady and Wayne follow him up a ladder on the side of a boxcar. They climbed on top of the car, scooted along behind Collie down the catwalk and, from there, they jumped on the tar roof of the warehouse. Then they ran over the roof to the other side of the building.

"He ain't over here," Grady said.

"I know where he went. This way. We'll sneak up on him," Collie ordered, jumping off the roof and landing on a pile of soft tobacco bales.

The others followed. They crept around and then they saw him. He was walking toward the restrooms, clipboard in hand. Although he was much larger than the boys, he was not too much older than them. "Who does he think he is?" Grady sneered, copying Collie.

Black Strap Jack went into one of the three tin outhouses – the one marked "COLORED" – and locked the door from the inside. The boys hid behind some bails. Collie, who had quickly formulated a strategy, gave orders. He took a piece of hemp twine, the kind used to tie tobacco bales, and wound it tightly over and under a big nail on the wooden door and another across from it on the door frame. After silently binding the door shut, Collie smiled in self-satisfaction. Then he shouted to Grady and Wayne, who he had stationed under a chinaberry tree behind the tin building, "Fire one!"

Grady unleashed a handful of hard, green chinaberries toward the ventilation hole at the top of the tin wall. The berries slammed against the tin like bullets from a machine gun. They could hear the angry screams inside the tin shack.

"Fire two!"

Wayne let loose his berries, but he did so in haste and all his berries missed the hole. The effect of his poorly aimed projectiles was a battering like a rain of ball bearings driven by a storm against the tin wall. The shouts became louder. Collie, who had retrieved the shovel from where he had hid it, swung it as hard as he could against the side of the tin building.

"Fire three!"

BLAM! He hit it once. BLAM! Twice. But before Collie could get off the third swing, Black Strap Jack kicked open the door.

As the three boys ran behind the outhouse, over the tracks and then off in different directions, Black Strap Jack stood outside the door, fastening his pants. When he finished, he looked up at the crowd of laughing white people and walked away, saying nothing, trying to hold back his tears of shame and anger.

"Until you can quit fighting in Sunday school, you'll have to work at the mill. I'll be getting you up at seven and we'll see how you like shoveling sawdust all day. That'll help you to remember that Benjamins have good manners," Richard said to Collie. Yes, something had to be done about Collie, and Collie's Uncle Richard would do it.

"Well, he started it. Besides, I ain't no Benjamin!" Collie whined.

"Yes, you are, Honey," his mother said. "Course you're a Benjamin. Just because your name is Coots, that doesn't mean you're not a Benjamin. Your mamma's a Benjamin! Don't be common, Colman. Don't you ever let your mamma hear you talk like that again!" Vera Ola cried, as she usually did when she tried to protect Collie.

She had good reasons for trying to protect him. Just as I said, ever since Cora had left, Collie had gone wild. Richard, who had no children of his own, found that he delighted in his efforts to tame Collie. It was his duty to the good Benjamin name.

How Collie hated the Benjamins. He hated Andy because he never said anything and was always reading books without pictures. He hated Ewell because he had that dumb name and thought he was shit on a stick when he wore that white, Navy uniform. He hated his mother because she was always crying and talking about being a Benjamin. He hated Cora because she was a nigger, and niggers are stupid and dirty. But most of all he hated Richard. He hated him and he would get him.

For over a week, Collie shoveled sawdust into the boiler that heated the water to make the steam that turned the great blade that sliced the logs into boards. He did it along with a Negro named Lolly. When Collie got bored, which was just about all the time, he tried to get Lolly to talk. But Lolly didn't like Collie and Richard had told him to keep the boy working. Every time Collie would ask a question, Lolly would tell him, "Boy, I don't play." When Collie would slow down and complain or curse, Lolly would say, "Boy, Mista Richard ain't gonna like you loafin' and cussin'."

Collie was afraid not to cooperate at least some. He was afraid that if he didn't his uncle wouldn't let him go on the upcoming scout trip to Savannah where they would march in the Labor Day Parade. So he did some of what Richard said and the next week, with the help of his mother, he was allowed to stop shoveling sawdust. But Collie couldn't help it and the very next Sunday he gave the same boy a bloody lip. The boy's mother told Richard and Richard said that Collie could not go to Savannah, and Collie shouted, "He started it!"

It was that Sunday afternoon that Grady and Wayne came by to get Collie to go to the afternoon picture show. Collie had no money, but thought that since "The Ten Commandments" was playing that Richard would give him some. But Richard laughed and said he didn't care what was on; said he didn't care if Moses himself was at the theater, Collie wasn't going to get a penny. So Collie went out back and told Grady and Wayne to follow him, he knew where some money was. They took off down the path through the kudzu behind the Benjamin House. The path twisted around through the broad-leafed vines. More often than not, the path was a tunnel burrowing under the vine-covered trees. Eventually, the path opened into a clearing along the river in which sat the African Baptist Church.

The boys looked down at the river and saw a crowd of Negroes — some on the bank and others wading in the water. They all wore white and the boys could see the blackness of their skin showing through their clothes. They stood for a moment and watched a man out in the water up to his waist. The man was holding a girl who was holding her nose. The man was looking up to the sky and talking. Then he shouted something and dunked the girl backwards into the water.

They followed the path on along the bank. At the next clearing, they stopped at a one-story wooden building, painted brown and trimmed in white, standing under two great, live oaks. Over the padlocked door was a sign — an eagle painted gold with "B.S.A." across its crest and the words "BOY SCOUTS OF AMERICA, TROOP 33" written just over the motto: "BE PREPARED." Like the door, the windows were sealed for the summer — their shutters closed and nailed tightly to the sills. Collie walked around the building and the others followed.

Under the building, Collie spotted a four-foot long, rusty, iron pipe.

"See that pipe? That pipe there in the sand?" Collie pointed and looked at Wayne, who looked away. "Chick, you go under there and get it. No, Chick, there ain't no snakes under there." And so Wayne went and got it.

Collie placed the pipe between the shutter and sill of one of the windows at the backside of the building and, with all his weight he pulled down. The shutter would not budge, but then he told Grady to help pull and the bottom hinge started to move. The nails gave way and the shutter hung loose and dangled like a hanging man. Collie placed the pipe under the top hinge, closed his eyes, grunted and snatched. They jumped back and the shutter fell to the ground.

"How we gonna get in?" Grady asked, tapping on the glass, hoping that somehow the glass would be perceived as an impenetrable obstacle that would avert what they were about to do.

"Easy. Chick, come here," Collie ordered. Wayne went. "Bend down. I'm gonna get on your shoulders."

From Wayne's shoulders Collie could see the latch. The window was locked. Collie made Wayne put him down. He took the pipe and smashed all of the glass, even knocking wooden frame out of the window.

"There," he said matter-of-factly. "Lift me up. I'll pull ya'll through."

Soon they all stood in the shaft of light pouring in from the broken window, bisecting the dark interior of the house. They stood beside the wood stove, half in the light and half in the dark, saying nothing. They were afraid to talk lest they be heard by whatever might be in the blackness on either side of them.

"The lantern," Grady whispered.

"What lantern?" Collie asked.

"There's always one on the scoutmaster's desk. He always keeps it there. Right there," he said, pointing in the direction of a desk, the outline of which could be made out by their adjusting eyes.

"Yeah, I see it," Collie said, speaking more loudly now. Stepping over to the desk, he felt for the lantern. Then he ran his hand beside the lantern and felt the matches. His face glowed as he grinned in the flame of the wooden match – the long and thick kind the scoutmaster said scouts were supposed to use. He raised the glass on the lantern, placed the match inside and the room was bathed in yellow light. But when Collie adjusted the wick, the yellow changed to white and the bright colors in each corner appeared to them magically as if they were seeing them for the first time.

Each corner had been designated for a patrol. There was the "Tiger Patrol" in green with its yellow tiger head, the "Panther Patrol" in red and black and the "Bear Patrol" in brown and orange. Then there was the "Rattlesnake Patrol" in white, black and purple. Although Collie had never made it past tenderfoot, for some reason, it made him proud to look at the coiled, enraged viper. Yes, both he and Grady were Rattlesnakes.

"I'll get the Tigers; Grady, you take the Bears. Get the Panthers, Chick." Then Collie went over to the green and yellow corner and started kicking over the chairs. The others did the same. But they left the Rattlesnake Patrol untouched. Wayne threw a chair into a shuttered window and as the last shards of glass tinkled to the floor, he looked back to see if Collie had seen him. But Collie paid Wayne no attention. Collie stood beside the wood stove and was placing the lantern on its top. Then he began to unbutton his fly.

"Looks like a good place to piss," Collie laughed, holding his still prepubescent penis between his thumb and index finger. "Scoutmaster Richard's gonna like it when he lights the fire."

He squeezed, increasing the pressure behind his stream, and reared back, straining and aiming at the freshly lain fire that awaited the first chill of fall.

"Yee yow!" he said as he urinated over the coal and wood.

Then, pissing as he went, he strutted over to the desk and brought back to the stove a box of rubber bands and a bottle of rubber glue. He told Grady to piss in the half empty glue bottle and when Grady had finished, told him to toss the bottle of glue and urine into the stove. Then he threw in the rubber bands.

"Ever smell piss on a fire, Chick?"

"Yeah," Wayne lied. "Really stinks."

"There it is! Over there behind his desk!" Collie said as he nodded to the wooden trunk.

"Told ya'll," he laughed.

The trunk had been some boy's father's sea chest; it was sturdy and had a strong padlock. Collie stood there studying it and then told Grady to give him the pipe. Collie swung hard and banged the lock until the wood screws gave way. The lock and hasp hung down like the head of a dead chicken. He grabbed the hinge and lifted the top of the chest.

The light spilled in. At the center of the chest they could see two kerosene lanterns identical to the one they were using. There was a length of rope tied in a series of two half hitches and to the right of the lanterns and under the rope, were three books. Collie reached into the box and took the book that had the picture of the scout in his campaign hat, shorts and high socks looking up and waving at the airplane flying over his camp site. The name of the book was Scouting Today. Collie threw it into the direction of the ruined home of the Bear Patrol and then he lifted the next book, A Manual for the Modern Scoutmaster, tossed it aside and looked to the other side of the box at the gray and maroon ledger embossed in gold. It read: LEDGER, 1931–1938. He picked it up and flung it behind him. It hit Wayne on the shoulder, but Wayne said nothing. There, under where the ledger had been, reverently folded in the shape of a tri-corner hat, was the flag, and under the flag, a blued metal box.

"There it is," Collie said. "Just like I told ya'll. Yep, that's it alright." He reached under the flag, took the box and placed it on the desk. The light from the lantern reflected on the satin metal surface. The brass key was tied to the box by a string. Collie took the key and as he inserted it into the lock, he told them that it would contain all the dues the scouts had paid for the previous year.

"Yeah, and it ain't even stealing cause they're yours anyway," Wayne said.

Collie told him to shut up and Grady was trying to figure how much dues he had paid in the previous year, thinking he would just take that. Then the top sprung open and there was nothing but a fat envelope inside.

"Don't look like money to me," Grady said.

They all had expected silver coins. Embarrassed and angered, Collie remembered that Richard was always telling them about the interest their money was earning, yes, earning at the Benjamin Bank of which he was President and Chairman of the Board. Collie knew at that moment that the envelope could not contain money. He held it in the light and tore it open. There, in the light of the flickering lantern, were several dozen photographs of young boys. All of their little penises were erect and while most were hairless, a few sported early pubescent fuzz. Most of them were naked, but a few wore strange items of clothing. One wore a matador's hat, white stockings and those little bull fighter's shoes with satin bows, his face covered by a mask. A mask just like the Lone Ranger wore, Grady said, and Collie told him to shut up. Another was in a pair of rubber Wellington boots – rubber boots and nothing else. Then there was one wearing the war bonnet of a Sioux chief.

Grady and Wayne were afraid, but Collie was not. "I know what to do," he said. "We'll write him a letter and get money for the pictures. He's got plenty. He owns a bank. I oughta know, I'm a Benjamin too." Then he thought about the pictures and what he had just said. "We'll take them to the "V" and bury 'em. Then we'll send the letter. We'll get 'em," he said, and for emphasis he took the pipe and flung it at the wall where it crashed into the Scout's Oath, just under the lines, "I will keep myself mentally awake and morally straight."

Grady and Wayne headed for the window, but Collie told them to wait and started undoing his pants. He squatted over the wooden chest. Collie grunted. "There," he said, but the other boys were already outside. Collie stood, wiped himself with a page torn from the ledger and glanced down at what he had done inside the chest. What he saw was a well-formed turd lying across a stripe and touching two stars of Ole Glory. He shut the chest, blew out the light and left with the blued metal box and its contents tucked under his arm.

With bribes of extorted treasure and threats of extreme violence, Collie persuaded the two boys to go with him and bury the box at the spot where the two rivers meet. While they covered the box with the dark swampy earth, Black Strap Jack and a girl watched from behind a clump of palmettos. They had left the church and paddled Jack's boat upriver to the "V", behind which was the top of an Indian burial mound that served as a hideaway for their frequent lovemaking.

From that height, in the clump of palm, Jack watched the boys' boat cross from Max Maxwell's fish camp.

When the boys had gone, Black Strap Jack uncovered the metal box. In its place he buried a Mason jar. Inside the jar he put a spooky note that said whoever found the jar would have a hex cast on them for disturbing sacred ground. He signed the note as if it had come from the Indians.

In their haste, the boys had not thought to keep a picture to include with the extortion note, and in two days returned for the photograph of the boy in the war bonnet. But when they returned to the "V", they uncovered not a metal box, but the jar containing the note.

Black Strap Jack and the girl would have liked to have been there to see the boys read the note about the hex. Black Strap Jack burned the photographs in his mamma's wood stove and gave the metal box to his daddy, Deacon Jack.

It was the last week of summer and had it not been for the frequent thunderstorms, it would have been the hottest time of the year – late August. Not a pine needle was moving; every thing was limp and slow. But the rains had begun; thus, it was the end of the dog days, or so they called them.

Ewell, my father, was home on leave. Soon he would be catching a train and going all the way out to California where he was to learn how to fly airplanes off the decks of ships, but that was something new and it was secret. Vera Ola, as usual, was suffering from bad nerves, but she was particularly distressed because she had learned that Cora had died of a stroke. Andy was happy and was packed and ready to go up to Macon and begin his freshman year at Mercer University. Richard was suffering frequent attacks of anxiety, for a fisherman had discovered the vandalism and robbery at the scout hut and the sheriff was blaming Gypsies. And Collie, since the note in the Mason jar had been found, had dreamed every night of ghosts in war bonnets.

Yes, the Gypsies were in town. But since it was late August, this was not unusual. They came as they always did, in their big, pastel-painted cars and house trailers, with their Ferris wheel and merry-go-round. They came with their silver bullet that always got stuck upside down and with their swing-a-ling that – just the year before – had flung a young girl from Baxton clear over the top of the silo at the Farmer's Mutual Exchange. The Gypsies brought along their throwing games, shooting games and their slimy people with tattoos who talked through their noses like Yankees. And just like the year before and the year before that, there was Madam Utte, the teller of fortunes, Mister Ram the Wise, who knew everybody's weight and

Wildman Willy, who never cut his hair, was chained to a stake and who bit the heads off chickens and cats. On the last day, he always chomped off the head of a big, brown-and-yellow rat-snake. There were the freaks and there were the relics: the calf with two heads and Napoleon's penis in a pickle jar.

The fair always came at the same time and was located in the same place, at the field behind the tobacco warehouse and the Farmer's Mutual Exchange at the end of Malachi Street; and it stayed there for one week. As usual, the last Saturday night was set aside exclusively for the Negroes and, for this reason, it was known as "Colored Night," but some of the white people referred to it as "Nigger Night." This was a night for marking time in Altamaha: "You know, I can't remember; did that happen before or after Colored Night?" they would ask. It was also on that night that the white people always blocked off Malachi Street and had a dance on the Altamaha River Bridge. Over the twang-twang of the street dance, the white people could hear the pink-pink of the fair and they always speculated as to what went on up the street and behind the tobacco warehouse. Some said that there was boxing and wrestling, and even rooster and dog fights. Some said that there was a beauty contest and that the Negroes crowned a king and a queen and that people paid money to watch them do things together. In my opinion, hardly any of those things happened and the truth is that these stories were invented both to humiliate the Negroes and to make the whites ooze with envy.

That particular year something different happened. It happened the day after the fair left town. School would start the next day and Wayne Fowler's parents were supposed to come over that night. After supper, they were to take him back to Baxton. The boys were under the bridge, where their club of three had started meeting. Wayne had just taken his "final test," as Collie and Grady called it, and Wayne was anxious to become a full member and to be told what Collie referred to as the "top secret." The final test had been for Wayne only. After all, he was from Baxton and not from Altamaha.

Collie didn't like to admit it, but it was Grady who had thought of the final test. This was because Grady's mamma kept chickens and the Benjamins did not. Grady and Collie had stood in the henhouse and covered their mouths to push back the giggles while Wayne pulled down his pants and entered the squawking chicken. But they had not been quiet enough and Grady's daddy, who was upset when people made noise on Sunday, ran toward the henhouse yelling. They had bolted out the back and had gone into the kudzu. From there they went to the bridge. Collie lingered on the bridge and collected the three longest and driest cigar butts that had been left behind after the street dance the night before. They sat there under the bridge puffing, and Wayne couldn't wait to learn the top

Disorderly Notions

secret. He was just sure that it had to do with the thing about the Indians and the note about the hex they had found. It had started raining.

"The top secret is ..." and then Collie paused and took a puff.

Wayne opened his eyes wide, Grady shifted closer.

"The secret is that the Indians ain't dead."

"What d'ya mean ain't dead?" Grady asked.

"You heard me. You ever noticed how you can't tell the difference between an Indian and a Gipsy?"

"Well, my Grandma says ..."

"Fuck yo Grandma, Chick. She don't know nothing," Collie laughed.

"Well..."

"Well, you ever noticed?"

"Yeah," Grady said, making it sound real secret and mysterious.

"No!" Collie howled, "You couldn't 'a noticed, 'cause there ain't nothing ta notice. People don't know it, but there ain't really no difference. Gypsies is just Indians that gyp you. That's all. Most people don't know that, but you can tell. You wanna know how you can tell?"

"Yeah," said Wayne.

"Yeah," said Grady.

"You hear 'bout that nigger woman, the one what was the root doctor, the one that was the Popsicle Man's wife? Well, you know she died? And she died cause of the hex."

"The hex?" Wayne asked.

"Chick, you don't remember nothing. The hex because old Jack got the gold. That's what made her die. The Gypsies, who are really the Indians, were just here ... here with the fair. They were just making sure their hex had worked. You saw 'em didn't you?" he asked, looking squarely at Wayne Fowler, who was nodding.

Then they heard it. There was a ring and then a toot. The boys came out from under the bridge, scampered up the slick bank and stood in the drizzle watching. He was coming along the road beside the tracks, he was pedaling slowly and keeping his eyes pinned to the front and his mind only on what was inside his head. A trail of black smoke followed him.

"Let's go!" Collie ordered, and Grady and Wayne shot off after him. He turned down Malachi Street and went in the opposite direction toward the tobacco warehouse. He blew his horn and tooted his whistle. "Wait! Give us a popsicle. Wait!" But he did not wait.

When the boys finally reached the deserted parking lot, he was nowhere to be seen. Then, just as Collie said, "That lowdown black ..." Grady pointed down toward the mud.

"Tracks!" he yelled.

They followed the tracks. Behind the warehouse, under a chinaberry tree, was the cart.

"Where'd he go?" Grady whispered.

"How the hell should I know? But there's the cart. If he's not going to sell 'em anymore, guess we're just gonna have to take us one. Think I want a grape. We'll pay him later."

They walked over to the cart, looking for him as they did.

"Chick, Grady will give you a boost and you reach in and get us one. Be sure you get me a grape." Collie ordered Wayne.

Grady boosted him up and Wayne opened the top. A great cloud bellowed from the dark inside. For a moment, Collie and Grady stood back and watched him, and then Grady stepped back over to the cart and held Wayne's legs so he could reach way down into the bottom of the cart. It was when Grady was helping Wayne reach deeply into the cart that Collie noticed the box. It was on a shelf near the handlebars, and one might have thought that it was just an ordinary metal box for keeping money, except that it was blued. Collie flipped open the lid and there he saw an old photograph of a young Negro woman dressed in white. At that moment, they heard the slap of tin. It was Deacon Jack. He had just come out of the door with the sign that said, "COLORED."

"Hurry! Let's go!" Collie shouted.

Wayne, who had not seen Deacon Jack, thought Collie meant to hurry up with the popsicles and Wayne could not see because half his body was upside down as he groped inside the dark, white box. But then Deacon Jack saw them, and Collie and Grady started to run. Suddenly, desperately, Wayne bolted from the dark, cold box. He staggered and fell, and then sat on the ground. Deacon Jack stood over him, looking down at him expressionless. Wayne's face was white – white like ice. He dropped his head and peered at his hand. And in between his gripped fingers were tufts of wiry, gray hair.

Hamilton took a floppy, inserted it into the slot and saved. Then he wrote on a label "Ch. II, Deacon Jack, the Popsicle Man" and stuck the label to the floppy.

"Can't you just imagine?" Mo said. "It's just like what the maharajah would have served the king's viceroy when he came to Jaipur on royal business."

Mo was referring to the breakfast. It was as English as any breakfast one might be served at a manor house in Kent. The rattan table was covered with a white linen cloth and the table was lain with yellow and green Spode china. Mo looked at the pattern on the eggcup. It was strewn with the kind of flowers one might see in a Home County garden. In fact, the restaurant in the

Rambagh Palace where they were having breakfast was called "The Vicar's Garden."

Hamilton carefully spread marmalade over his toast. Then he took a sip of his Earl Grey tea and looked across the table at the others.

"Mo and I have something to tell you. Actually, we have several things to tell you."

"Yes, to be exact, there are three things," Mo added happily.

Starman and Andy stopped eating and looked at her.

"Well, for goodness sake, go on. Tell us," Starman said.

"The first thing is that Mo and I are getting married," Hamilton announced.

"I knew it!" Starman laughed. "I just knew it would happen. I can always tell about these kinds of things."

"But wait. There's more," Mo laughed.

She looked at Hamilton and then at Starman and Andy.

"We're going to have a baby," she told them.

"Oh, my God! That's great," Starman said, clapping his huge, black hands together. "Before you get married?"

"No," Mo said to him. "We'll be married right away, but it takes a while for a baby. Starman, I am pregnant."

"So are you going to do this back in the States? In Singapore? Canada? Where?" Starman asked.

"Oh no, not back in the States. My parents are dead. I haven't been there in over a decade."

"So, Canada?"

"No. As a matter of fact, we are going to be married in China."

"China?" Starman replied.

"Yes. We thought that might surprise you. Hong Kong, actually. You see, I'm still married, technically anyway. We never divorced for tax reasons. Well, my ex-husband – or is it husband? Whatever he is, he lives in Hong Kong. He and I will have to be legally divorced. Hamilton and I are going there to have it done. It's quicker and easier that way. Then we'll be married in Hong Kong."

"Will he cooperate?" Starman asked.

"Sure. He'll probably even be the witness," Mo laughed.

Hamilton reached across the table and took her hand. From the looks of it, no one would ever guess the power with which her hand could grip a tennis racket. He held the delicate tips of her fingers and noticed the points on her ring catch the early sun.

"I'm declaring that this is now an engagement ring," Hamilton laughed.

"Yes, the durian ring. It's altogether appropriate. The durian, the lover's fruit!" Mo said, smiling at Hamilton.

Then she leaned over the table and kissed him on the cheek.

Throughout all of these revelations, Andy had said nothing. When Hamilton had left to meet Dicky to buy the train tickets and Mo had gone to the room to pack, Starman asked Andy why he looked so glum. Andy pushed up his glasses and lit a cigarette. He told Starman he had warned Hamilton that he and Mo were moving too fast. Something was just not right.

"And I oughta know," he said. "Tried it four times myself and each time I stepped in shit."

"Leave it to you to be vulgar, Andy," Starman scolded. "You should be ashamed. Come on, be happy for them."

The five of them waited silently while the bus was being loaded. Although it was still quite early in the morning, the sun was blazing. Everything was a washed-out yellow. They had arrived in Bikaner the night before, too late for them to see the colors of the Thar Desert. They had all been exhausted from the long train ride from Jaipur, and the few hours they had to sleep at a hotel next to the bus station had been a welcomed relief.

The driver opened the door and said something to the knot of passengers as they filed into the brown bus. Dicky had already become sentimental about everyone's imminent departure, the dissolution of their group and his own departure from India back to England. He stood at the door beside the driver as if he were a guide welcoming everyone aboard. Well, he was their guide, and they were his guests. That's the way he wanted it and he would not have had it any other way. Wise old Brahman, Hamilton thought and smiled.

Hamilton stepped up after Mo. Her white dress was bathed in the morning glow. As Hamilton sat, he lightly brushed her cheek with his lips. He was pained by his immense love for Mo.

"Look. There, on that roof," Mo said, pointing toward the bus station, "Look at that peacock."

The bird then spread its tail, showing the pattern that resembles the innumerable eyes, which, in Hindu mythology, are taken to represent the starry firmament.

"Yes, I know, they are everywhere in Rajasthan," Hamilton replied.

He placed his big hand over her hand that wore the ring. He could feel the spikes of her ring in the center of his palm. They all sat in silence as they rode along a road potted with holes. They passed battlements and walls of pink stone. At the top of a hill, they could look back and see the town of Bikaner. In front of them was a dry valley surrounded by low mountains. Mo snuggled into Hamilton's shoulder. They both dozed and from time to time heard the drone of Dicky's voice:

"The temple we are going to see is dedicated to a fifteenth-century mystic. It is said that she was the incarnation of the goddess of power."

"What bull," Andy grumbled, taking a puff on his cigarette.

"What about the rats?" Starman asked.

"I know that Andy doesn't believe such stories, but since it is you who has asked, Starman, I will tell you that the rats are reincarnated family members of the mystic. The mystic's relatives inhabit the bodies of the rats, and when the rats die, they again become human. You see, it is like a cycle, and the whole thing starts over again.

"Yet, there is a better story. Yama, the god of death, was beseeched by Karni Mata to raise from the dead the son of a teller of tales. When Yama refused to meet this plea, Karni Mata reincarnated all dead storytellers as rats, and because all humans are storytellers, this deprived Yama of human souls."

"Who says?" Andy taunted.

"Oh, I do not know who said it. I doubt if anybody knows. You see, it really does not matter who said it, or if indeed it was ever said at all; the important thing is what it means." Dicky said, smiling at Andy.

The bus stopped and they all walked toward the silver gates of Karni Mata. They stood and looked at the carvings cut deep into the marble. Above them, an umbrella of gold crowned the top of the temple. As they approached the silver doors of the sanctuary, they could see an image of the goddess of power standing on a crescent moon, the rays of the sun bursting over her head. The goddess was flanked by a pair of sniffing rats.

"So this is Rat City," Andy scoffed.

They passed through an arch and, following Dicky, removed their shoes. The great room was silent. The floor was black-and-white marble squares worn by centuries of shuffling feet. The stones were cool. They could hear the scurrying rats, and then they saw them gathered around the sanctuary, concentrated in an area where pastel-colored rice and other grains had been put before an altar. In a golden bowl was ghee – clarified butter – an offering favored by the gods. Rats clustered around the bowl and another silver one next to it. Their hundreds of overlapping tails were like gray-brown lace cast across the floor. Dicky told them that the silver bowl contained sweetened milk and that it symbolized sperm, while the ghee represented the fire in the female womb. Mo held Hamilton's thick arm tightly.

Suddenly, and for no apparent reason, a large, brown rat bolted away from the bowl containing the white liquid and charged straight for Mo. First she jumped up on one foot, then on the other and, with the third step, came down with her whole weight upon the back of the squeaking animal. Reddish-black blood oozed from the rat's mouth and made a stream toward the bowl containing the ghee. Soon, it surrounded both bowls. The blood darkened the white marble squares and its thick warmth seeped between Mo's and Hamilton's toes.

"Oh God! How awful," Mo said, holding her stomach as she stepped from the dark river of blood.

At that moment, a man with a mustache and wearing an orange turban appeared before her. He looked at her fiercely, but then, as he spoke, a faint smile came to his lips. His voice was strange and guttural. Dicky told Mo that she must put some money in the man's open palm and that the amount of money does not matter. Mo reached inside her purse, took out a 5,000 rupee note and placed it in the man's hand. The man bent down, took the dead rat by the tail and unceremoniously left, leaving a trail of blood behind.

"Don't feel bad my dear, it is a rare but blessed event. The man is grateful. You have freed a human soul from the body of a rat and that soul will be with you until it is reincarnated. The money is like giving alms, and the goddess will repay you," Dicky consoled her, smiling.

The turbaned man soon reappeared. He held out his hand, but this time there was something in his open palm.

"Take it my dear, it is yours. A payment from the goddess," Dicky whispered.

It was a two-inch gold figure of a rat with its tail making an 'S' behind it and its sniffing nose held into the air.

The trip back to Bikaner was sweltering. They could see the heat rising off the desert in crooked vertical waves and the sky was a dull white. Dust was everywhere. They could feel it inside their noses and eyes, and they could taste it on their tongues.

When they arrived back in Bikaner, they almost immediately boarded a train for Jodhpur. Late that night, when they arrived in New Delhi, they were all pleased to have the journey behind them.

At the High Palace Hotel in central New Delhi, Dicky dropped by to say farewell. He told them that Jeri had already left for London the night before and that he would be taking the night flight to Berlin in order to visit his son, a major stationed there with the occupying British Army. Dicky spoke with a mixture of sentiment and melancholy about the wedding plans for Hong Kong, saying that were it not for his having to go to Germany, he might have even considered going along with them. Hamilton noted that Jeri had been left out. There was regret in Dicky's statement, and it was obvious that Dicky was avoiding returning home.

Dicky and Hamilton were alone for a moment on the balcony. They stood at the railing, looking down at the traffic and, across the brown grass, at the cud-chewing cows.

"While you are correct about much, often what you say is not true," Dicky said. "Sometimes your heart is not attached to your head. I think grace will come to you, but it will come through suffering. I want you to know that I know that you slept with my wife."

"No, I ..."

"She confessed. But you are not the first one, and I forgive you."

The old man smiled sadly, extending his hand to Hamilton. Too stunned to reply, Hamilton took it.

Starman and Andy were supposed to meet Mo and Hamilton at Nirula's restaurant, one not far from the High Palace Hotel. Hamilton looked at his watch. Starman and Andy had gone to the travel agency on Janpath Lane to purchase tickets home. Hamilton had reminded Andy and Starman not to even consider Aeroflot, assuring them that they would find many other reasonable ways of getting back to England and to America.

Mo and Hamilton sat and talked about the previous night. Mo had had a bad dream. In fact, she had had what they used to call "night terrors." Hamilton had awakened to muttering, and when he realized that Mo was not in the bed, he sat up and could see Mo in the dim light from the street. She was in the corner facing the wall, naked, and he heard her talking in a low voice that did not sound like her own. It had taken Hamilton some time to wake her. She had called Hamilton "Judah," a clear reference to a conversation they had the day before about Judah P. Benjamin. Mo had urinated on herself and on the floor.

While waiting for Starman and Andy, Mo told him about her dream. She had been flying and talking with God. Mo said she thought her medication needed adjusting and that her being pregnant had something to do with it. She planned to go back to the clinic before they left New Delhi.

When Starman and Andy arrived at Nirula's, they both smiled the kind of smile that reveals they had a secret.

"Well, what is it? It's written all over your faces," Mo said, smiling at them.

Andy lit a cigarette. He took his time. Then he looked across at them.

"We've decided to go to China with you."

Hamilton and Mo both looked at Starman.

"Yes," Starman said, "it is true. We don't want to miss the wedding. We already have our tickets."

# ROACH RANCH

"Daniella, Daniella Tucker's her name. She was a student in the school of architecture and I met her when she began auditing my lectures on Bogdanov. She was fascinated with Alfred Jarry and André Breton, and with Bogdanov, of course."

"Breton, the artist?"

"Yes, and Jarry, a nutty playwright. They were part of a crowd of people in Paris during the years between the two world wars. They knew of Bogdanov and he knew of them. During the early thirties at the Sorbonne, in a famous seminar on Hegel, both the anti-art movement and Bogdanov were discussed extensively. Some of the anti-art people, including Breton, attended the seminar. Well, so much for the lecture."

"Oh, no. That's very interesting. But what about the girl?"

"Oh yes, the girl. Well, that's exactly what she was – a girl. She was almost half my age. She was half Irish, half French Canadian, and as frail as a bird, but pretty. She wore those wire-rimmed glasses and her hair was auburn. Although she was from Montreal, she spoke French only when she was excited. And she had one of those diamond studs ..."

"Where?"

"In her nose."

"I'll bet."

"Anyway, she attended my lectures and then it seemed that everywhere I went she was somehow around. She was interested in me, and I knew it, but I wasn't so sure that I was interested in her. With all the fanaticism about sexual harassment, being cautious seemed like a good idea. And then, on a spring day, she invited me to her place for lunch. I just said to hell with it and agreed to go. After all, it was she who had taken the initiative."

"Yeah, sure," Mo laughed, playfully slapping Hamilton on his bare chest.

"She lived alone downtown, but not exactly in a student district. It was a nice, large apartment. Her family had money. She had her paintings hanging all over the place. She was more interested in painting than in architecture. There were a few good ones too – erotic and dreamy."

"Did you love her?" Mo asked, moving a finger among the sparse clump of hairs surrounding a nipple.

"No."

"So what happened?"

"Well, what happened, happened fast. Before summer came, she was living in my house and her pictures were all over my walls. I got reckless, I guess you might say."

"But you enjoyed it?" Mo asked, smiling, but serious.

"Yes, oh yes, I'll admit it. I had just never even imagined doing anything quite like that. I had always been so careful. So, I just fell into it and let things happen as they might.

"One night, when a girlfriend of hers was visiting, I overheard their conversation. I suddenly realized how young she was and what an old fool I was being. Immediately, I panicked. I tried to break it off. I tried to get her to move out. She screamed and cried; she begged and bargained with me. Finally, in June, when she left for Montreal to visit her family, I packed up all of her stuff and shipped it UPS to her parent's home in Westmount."

"That was good of you."

"But at least I paid for it. Cost a fortune."

"How magnanimous!"

"Yes, that's me, always the gentleman. Then I put my house up for sale. Pretty drastic measures, eh?"

"You took the chicken's way out, I'd say."

"Yes, I know. The guilt really got to me. For a while I just didn't care anymore. I wallowed in self-loathing for quite a while. When I sold my house, I moved into my office. And suddenly, to my surprise, I realized that I was really having fun. Then Daniella charged me with sexual harassment and the dean got on my back. He would have fired me if he could have. My chairman came up with this early sabbatical idea – getting me out of harm's way by packing me off to Russia and then, when that failed, to England. I do appreciate it. Guess he thought I'd gone nuts or something."

"Wonder why? You bad boy!" she said, nudging up against him. Then she looked up at Hamilton. "Really, Hammy, you were a scoundrel. You won't ever do that to me, will you? You won't ever leave me, will you?"

"No. Never," Hamilton told her, and he meant it.

They listened to the rain. Hamilton asked Mo if the baby was kicking and she told him no, it was far too early for that.

When morning came, Mo tried to wake Hamilton, but he was dreaming that his face was between Daniella Tucker's thighs and she was saying, "Mon Dieu! Mon Dieu!"

The window of their room opened into an airshaft and the rain has been pouring down its four walls and into a drain outside. The sound was like a mountain stream in spring. It had been this sound, together with people shouting in Spanish, that had awakened them. The shouting was coming from down the hall – from a room full of Filipino girls who had stayed up all night. But the shouting was merely punctuation for the music that the girls played over and over: Stevie Wonder's "I just called to say I love you" was becoming all too familiar to Hamilton and Mo.

Hamilton's confession, and their restless sleep from the shouting and the music, occurred in a place called <u>Kowloon,</u> an area located just across the bay from Hong Kong. Their hotel was called the Chungking Mansions, an establishment suggested by the travel agent in New Delhi as a good place for people who want little money to go far. Andy and Starman claimed to be short of funds and had liked the idea. They had never planned to stay long in the roach-infested hotel, only until Monday when the Gibraltar Export Company would be open. Gibraltar was the business owned by Mo's husband – and Mo planned to just show up unannounced.

"And boy! Will he be surprised to see me!" Mo had told everyone with a laugh.

Andy dubbed the hotel "The Roach Ranch," but the fact that the hotel had thin walls, dirty communal toilets and was generally a thirteen-story fire trap did not matter to Andy. Many different types of people from all over the globe were staying there, and Andy was able to easily acquire much useful information, such as where to find the best bargain on Johnnie Walker. The young people with whom Andy talked had returned from the People's Republic and told him about its wonders. Andy got it into his head that he was going there, and he tried to persuade the others to go there with him. If they would not go, he told them, then he would go alone. After all, China was a real communist country, not one like the U.S.S.R., which Andy always said had betrayed its glorious past since the days of Stalin.

On Sunday, the day before the night of rain and shouting girls, Mo, Hamilton and Starman had taken the ferry across to Hong Kong. Much to everyone's surprise, Andy said that he would rather stay behind. When pressed, he said he had fallen victim to diarrhea and needed to stay at the Chungking Mansions. This, of course, is always an excuse with which no one ever takes issue. After the three of them wandered around Hong Kong looking for a cheap and large enough jacket for Starman, they rode a tram up <u>Victoria Mountain</u> to an overlook high above the city. From there one can <u>gaze over</u> Hong Kong, Kowloon, and, in the distance, see Macau and the Chinese mainland.

Mo stood at a wall with the mist and clouds to her back and Hamilton's eyes turned from the view to her. He stepped back and for a moment watched her as she listened to Starman tell a story about the Japanese invasion of Hong Kong during the war – a story mostly about the fierceness of the Japanese. Hamilton took Mo's camera and looked through the lens at the two of them with the view of the city in the background. Hamilton focused the lens on a smiling Mo. God, Hamilton thought, she looks like an angel. Then he smiled, amused at himself

Disorderly Notions

for thinking that. He had had many unusual thoughts lately, and he blessed the coincidence that had brought Mo to him.

Meanwhile, a Hong Kong businessman and his guest from Taiwan had stopped Starman, asking him if he played basketball for the NBA. During their conversation the man had suggested a restaurant near the Hong Kong-Kowloon ferry dock. Thanking the businessman as he departed, Starman asked him what he thought it would be like in a few years when the People's Republic took control of the island.

"This will never be," the man had replied, "Hong Kong will always be British."

When they came down from the mountain, they decided to go to the restaurant suggested by the businessman. The restaurant was in a part of Hong Kong called Aberdeen – a community of floating houses. The restaurant was really a great barge decked out to resemble a Mississippi riverboat. It contained a grand salon with exquisitely painted screens depicting graceful white cranes, Chinese lanterns and elaborately carved fire-breathing dragons. The meal was excellent. Starman said it was like San Francisco, Hamilton said Vancouver.

When the three of them returned to Kowloon, they could not find Andy at the hotel, but they were not alarmed, thinking he had probably found some cozy bar. Starman went out for a walk, Mo read the *Sports Illustrated* she had bought in Hong Kong and Hamilton worked on the next chapter of *Jud's Story*. Eventually, Mo fell asleep. Hamilton turned off the laptop and the light and crawled into bed beside her.

That morning, once Mo finally brought Hamilton from his shamelessly carnal dream about himself and the student, Daniella Tucker, Mo and Hamilton hurriedly dressed and made their way down Nathan Road. They went in the direction of the waterfront, wanting to catch the ferry to Hong Kong. It was Monday and the Gibraltar Export Company would be open. On their way to the dock, they stopped in for breakfast at a place called the New World Center, and when they passed McDonald's they saw Starman sitting alone at a booth in the back. Starman did not notice them until they were standing over his table. When he finally looked up, they saw that his face was expressionless and his eyes were red.

"Starman! What on earth are you doing here? What's the matter?" Mo asked.

"I didn't sleep a wink last night."

"Why?" Hamilton asked, "What's wrong?"

"Andy. That's what's wrong. He came in drunk last night. He had been out with those Filipino girls and brought three of them into the room. I was in bed, but he didn't care. They were jabbering in Spanish and putting their hands all over one another and pulling at me lying there in the bed. Then Andy bought out one of those disposable cameras and started taking pictures of them and me. I kept telling them to go away, that I was trying to sleep and the pictures wouldn't take anyway because he had no flash. But do you think he'd listen? They finally left, but only to go to their room across the hall. Then the music started. It must have been about four. You should have heard it."

"Yeah. We did hear it," Hamilton said, suppressing a smile.

"I'd almost fallen asleep when one of the girls started screaming. Turned out she was screaming at Andy. Andy came back into our room and locked the door, and the girl banged on it and shouted at him. I asked Andy what she was saying, and he told me he had made her mad because he took a picture of her wearing nothing but her underpants. 'Would be just like a bathing suit, but without the top,' he said he told her. Imagine that! And at his age!"

"So then he left?" Hamilton asked.

"No, then he went into this tirade against me. He said that he had suspected that I did not like girls. He called me a pussy, and then he went to sleep."

"I'm so sorry Starman," Mo said.

"Oh, don't be. I don't like girls. Not like that ... not like he meant it. But then that's my business. He really didn't have to call me that. Andy's so vulgar."

"Yes, he is. And you're right, that's your business," Hamilton said. "Just forget it. He won't remember anything about it. Besides, that sort of thing makes no difference to Andy. Not really."

"I don't care."

"Oh, I know you don't. When he's sober he doesn't think like that. So it wasn't diarrhea after all," Hamilton said, and he and Mo both smiled.

Mo teased Starman, telling him that he was speaking in a different accent. Starman, weakly smiling, admitted that he always reverted to his Alabama speech when was tired or when he was angry. After calming Starman down, they told him that they would meet him and Andy around six and bring with them news about their upcoming wedding. They wanted everybody to go to the houseboat in Aberdeen.

"We'll celebrate. Maybe Gowey will come along and foot the bill," Mo said, adding that he could certainly afford it.

Mo was referring to her husband, Gower Roburg. Starman tried to appear enthusiastic, but he was still hurt. Yet they all knew that he would soon forgive Andy.

The offices of the Gibraltar Export Company were on a street not far from the docks. Mo and Hamilton entered, and they were met by an officious English-colonial type, Gower Roburg's secretary, a Mister Teawaddle. At first he took issue with who Mo said she was, but then reluctantly told her that Mister Roburg was not there and would not be back for a month. It turned out that Mo's estranged husband was on a business trip to London and New York. Mo was terribly distraught.

"We should have called ahead," she kept saying as they rode on the ferry back to Kowloon.

They considered their options and concluded that because of the great expense of air tickets from Singapore to Hong Kong, the only rational choice was for Mo and Hamilton to remain there in Hong Kong until Gower Roburg returned. And this is what they said they would do.

When they reached the Chungking Mansions they found Starman acting as if nothing had happened the night before. He had had a nap, and Andy had apologized. Andy did not know that Mo and Hamilton had heard the story about him and the Filipinos. He cheerfully suggested they all go around the corner to an Australian bar, get some real western food and drown their disappointment about Mo's husband being out of town.

Hamilton thought he'd explode from all the Foster's Lager and bangers and mash. He and Mo left before ten, and Andy and Starman returned to their conversation about that peculiar institution: slavery in America.

The next morning, Hamilton and Mo joined Starman and Andy at McDonald's for breakfast. Mo and Hamilton expected to hear about whatever plans they had made for their departures back to England and America, but they heard otherwise.

"We're going to China," Starman said with a smile. "Andy and I decided last night. In fact, we're all going. You too. Why not? We're so close and you can't do anything until what's his name returns. It's so much cheaper than Hong Kong."

Starman was excited. Mo and Hamilton looked at each other. Mo gave a little shrug.

"Sure. Why not?" Hamilton said.

It took two days to get their visas from the Chinese. Mo, Starman and Andy did some sightseeing, and Mo spent an afternoon on the indoor tennis courts at the Kowloon Athletic Club. Andy spent most of his time in the bar drinking and reading a fat book on China that he had borrowed from the library at the American Embassy. Hamilton spent his days at McDonald's in the New World Center finishing the third chapter of *Jud's Story*. As it turned out, McDonald's was a good place to write. They even let him use an electrical plug under a booth at the back so Hamilton did not have to use the battery. There was no way he could have worked at the Chungking Mansions. The Filipino girls down the hall had changed to a night shift, and so they played the Stevie Wonder telephone song, giggled and jabbered in Spanish all day long.

# CHAPTER III
## DOG DAYS

It was always said in Altamaha that most of the Indians along the river died in a massacre, but nobody knew the details. I guess if anybody really had wanted to know, they could have asked the few Indians that were left. But nobody did. The Indians lived down on the edge of Great Alligator Swamp on the Oconee River. They neither thought of themselves, nor did anyone ever think of them, as a part of the town. They dwelled in obscurity in their tar-paper shacks on land nobody cared about, and they were only ever seen quietly watching the world of whites and blacks from the riverbank, roadside or jail cell. While this remnant of the once-great Creek tribe was ignored, their ancestors were far from being forgotten. They were celebrated, even championed, for the citizens of Altamaha had chosen to name their baseball team the "Savages."

The Altamaha Savages wore the war bonnet of the Sioux tribe on their uniforms and they frequently ran out on the field announcing themselves with blood-curdling Apache battle cries. For four of the nine years since World War II had ended, the Savages held the regional title. But, of course, there was not a real Indian on the team. The closest thing they had to an Indian was the dim-witted manager's helper and mascot: Jake Bailey. He was a local Negro, and it was said that he had Creek blood in his veins.

The Savage's ball club had come from all over. Most of the players were free agents from other small towns in Georgia, Alabama, Florida and South Carolina. The first baseman had been sent down – or "farmed out" – by the Atlanta Crackers, the right fielder by the Macon Peaches and the shortstop, who people said was being watched by the Chicago White Socks, was from Havana, Cuba, and he had been farmed out by the Jacksonville Jaxs.

Although it had rained every day for the previous week, the corn on the sides of the road was parched a light brown by the dry, scorching days before the beginning of the rains. Whenever it was dry enough to put a tractor or mule into a field, the corn would be harvested. The night air felt sticky and thick like the greasy vapors rising from a hot griddle. Five of us drove along the highway that night: Uncle Richard at the wheel; Uncle Andy – our family war hero who lived in New York – riding shotgun; and sitting in the back seat, my younger cousin Hamilton, our common Uncle Durden Fowler and, of course, I was there as well.

Yes, finally, I, Judah Anubis Benjamin III, formally enter my own story. I say "finally" for where one begins is, in a way, just as absolute as where one ends and, if you think about it, the conditions for entry are the most baffling of all. This is why it has taken two chapters for us to get here. Before I could enter my story, the conditions that made my entry possible had to be accounted for – well, at least the conditions that matter. So now we ask ourselves why it happened as it did. The dog's truth, as my Uncle Andy always said, is that it could have happened in an infinite number of ways and might have ended up in infinitely different conclusions. But this is the wondrous and mysterious part of any story; how, with all those possibilities, things happen as they do and not otherwise.

It was 1954. Nobody played baseball during the days in August – not even on Sunday afternoons. Although the rains had already come, the days were still far too hot. So, muddy field and all, that night baseball was played. The Savages lost a doubleheader to the Baxton Bombers. It was on that dark, sticky night that we hit the cow.

Uncle Richard and Uncle Andy were having an old argument about the New Deal. Uncle Richard argued that it had been a communist plot. Uncle Andy laughed like a madman at his older brother and then, being serious, said that it wasn't at all communistic, but that it should have been. And then Uncle Richard told him that he should be arrested by the F.B.I. because he was un-American, swearing that he was going to turn his brother in himself.

My cousin and I were sitting in the back seat, one of us on either side of Uncle Durden. The big, green 1952 Chrysler swashed through the damp night while Uncle Durden dozed. That was when Andy yelled:

"Watch out! Shiiiiit!"

It was the lead cow. The one that carries the bell and that has the yoke around her neck to keep her from jumping fences. She lay across the hood, her head against the windshield on Uncle Richard's side, her hind feet hanging off the side where Andy was sitting with his elbow stuck out the window, which, upon collision, had become covered with soupy dung.

"You boys okay?" Durden Fowler asked.

We, wide awake and astonished, meekly nodded our heads over the bellowing and groaning of the cow. The engine was dead. We all got out and tried to push the car off the highway, but it wouldn't budge. The grill was crushed back into the steam-spewing radiator and the right fender had crumpled into the tire. A farmer came in his pickup and took us to a store where Uncle Durden called the state patrol. Uncle Richard called the night watchman at the mill and told him to send a pulpwood skidder out to get us and tow the car back to Altamaha.

When the farmer took us back to the car, the state patrol had already arrived and the officer had shot the cow behind the left ear with his .38. Then the men took the dead cow by the legs and dragged her off the hood. Uncle Andy directed the farmer's bumper to the back bumper of the Chrysler, and the farmer pushed the car off the road. It was funny to see that state patrolman with his shiny black boots and his spiffy campaign hat bending double and slapping his knees as Uncle Durden told him about the cow shit getting all over Andy's elbow.

"Welcome back to Ja Ja!" the patrolman laughed. "Ja Ja" meant Georgia. "Now, Andy, that's what ya get for staying up there so long with them damn Yankees!"

As it had happened, the state patrolman had gone to high school with my uncle.

When the skidder arrived, we all got into the cab next to Lolly Bailey, the one-eyed driver that the night watchman had sent from the mill. I sat in Uncle Richard's lap and my cousin Hamilton sat in Durden's. Andy helped Lolly and the farmer hook a cable to the frame of the Chrysler and hoist its front end high into the air. We took off into the night with Uncle Andy hanging on to the skidder's door while standing on the running board outside. But this didn't keep him from talking. Andy just stuck his head into the window as we swept along the highway in the skidder. I tried to listen to my cousin answer all of Andy's questions about life up in Canada, but I couldn't help it and dozed.

When we crossed the Altamaha River Bridge, Uncle Richard said, "Wake up, boys. We're home," and Lolly drove us down deserted Malachi Street. We took a quick detour by the Fowler house and let Uncle Durden off. He had to argue a case in court early the next morning. But Hamilton and I did not get out, for we were going to spend the night in the big backyard at the Benjamin place. We had made a tepee so we could sleep outside like Indians. We went back onto Malachi Street and soon we were pulling into the parking lot at the tobacco warehouse.

The big trucks were still. Some stood empty, waiting for bales of tomorrow's tobacco. Others were loaded and at daylight would pull out of the lot and head north for Carolina. I had never seen the tobacco warehouse at that hour. It was as sad and as silent as the grave.

"Take the car inside and we'll see about it in the morning. I'll call Moxley's Filling Station and tell 'em to pick it up."

"Yessa, Mista Richard," Lolly said.

"Where 'bout's Black Strap?"

"The Black Strap, he inside."

Lolly pulled up to the warehouse and stopped, the wrecked, green Chrysler swinging behind. He took the skidder out of gear, yanked up the brake, hopped out and slid open the great warehouse door. Then he returned to the skidder and drove inside.

Tobacco bales lined the long, tin building from end to end; there was a vehicle here and there and hand trucks were scattered about, but no one seemed to be around.

"He asleep in da scale house," Lolly said, referring to the little office in the center of the building.

Black Strap Jack was the night watchman and weigh master during tobacco season. He had a cot inside the scale house. The skidder rolled along between rows of tobacco, its engine roaring under the roof and between its tin walls, making the warehouse vibrate like a great, metal box.

"Get this muffler fixed!" Uncle Richard shouted as the walls and roof rattled and shook.

"That noise is for those poor bastards with overdue loan payments to let 'em know Richard's coming to collect!" Uncle Andy yelled, laughing.

When we reached the scale house, Lolly stopped and switched off the ignition. Silence. Then Lolly jumped out and walked quickly to the scale house. We could hear him say,

"Hey, Strap, we gots us a big, hurt, green bird," referring to the wrecked car hanging behind.

Lolly disappeared inside, but few seconds passed before we heard him groan. We watched as he stumbled backwards from the house as if being pushed by an invisible force. Lolly turned, stood up straight and looked at us. His eyes were bulging and he was gasping for breath, trying to speak. Then he fell to his knees and vomited.

Uncle Andy told me and Hamilton to stay in the skidder. He and Uncle Richard got out, walked past Lolly as if he were not there and entered the scale house. I looked at my younger cousin.

"Come on," I said.

I don't remember where my uncles were or what they were doing. I don't remember anything except what I saw. And what I saw, I shall never forget. There was blood – blood splattered and smeared on the pine lattice and black, thick, pooled blood on the floor. There was a bloody pillow on the white sheet covering the cot and prints of a bloody hand, shiny and slick, streaking down the glass covering the great, round face of the scale. Just behind the scale, wedged deeply into the wooden desk, was the ugly, curved blade of a bushwhack, its handle pointing toward me.

Then I saw him. He was in different places. Under the cot, I could see the top of his head, but the other part of him was in the center of the room. He was on his back with an ice pick driven into his crotch up to its handle. Yellow receipts were scattered everywhere. They had spilled from a blued metal box that lay open on the floor beside the tip of a severed hand.

When the Japs had attacked in 1941, Black Strap Jack had been almost thirty. When he heard the news, he left the skidder sitting beside the mill and took his entire crew to the recruiting office next door to Bud's Amusement Company, the movie theater, on Malachi Street.

The petty officer behind the desk asked them to step outside. He picked up the telephone and called his superior at Glencoe Naval Air Station:

"Sir, I got me six niggers here. Say they wanna join up. What am I 'posed to do?"

Black Strap Jack and the rest of his crew went to Negro boot camp at Fort Benning, Georgia. When training was over, everyone except Black Strap Jack was assigned to Fort Dix, New Jersey for orderly and valet school. It was because of his leadership qualities recognized during training that Black Strap Jack was sent to North Carolina. Fort Bragg, North Carolina was the home of the 82nd Airborne, and Black Strap Jack was "volunteered" for duty with the newly formed Black Hawks, the all-Negro paratrooper regiment. Six months later, with buck sergeant stripes on his sleeves, he shipped out for England.

He and his outfit fought in Africa and then in Italy. He was captured near Naples and the same day he escaped. He was fortunate; the Germans did not take Negro prisoners. Two years later, in the invasion of Northern Europe, the Black Hawk regiment swooped from the sky with General Gavin's 82nd Airborne and landed on the Germans at Arnhem, a strategic town where the Rhine separated Holland from the Reich. There, beside the river at a pumping station, with his platoon shot to bits, Black Strap Jack knocked out a German machine gun nest and was wounded in the arm.

One hot, October afternoon in 1945, Black Strap Jack got off the bus in Altamaha. He stood in the dust and shielded his eyes from the sun. Across his left shoulder was a braided, powder-blue cord and around his neck was a scarlet silk ascot, symbols of the 82nd Airborne Division. On his sleeves were the stripes of a staff sergeant and when he looked down, the Bronze Star, the Purple Heart and a nest of campaign ribbons shone in his dazzling jump boots. Black Strap Jack was the most decorated soldier to return to Altamaha.

Nobody met him. Cora had been dead for years and Deacon Jack, who had never recovered from her death, spent his last days in the insane asylum up at Milledgeville. It was not until the bus was well out of Jacksonville and already across into Georgia – somewhere near Waycross in the Okefenokee Swamp – that Black Strap Jack realized he had no place to stay in Altamaha. When the authorities had come to take Deacon Jack away, he burned down the cabin beside the river, so Black Strap Jack had no home, and Negroes did not stay in the New Altamaha Hotel. I'll go see Mister Richard, he thought, and bunk in the night watchman's hut at the mill.

Black Strap Jack stood proud and erect, his service cap cocked smartly over his left eyebrow, just as it was supposed to be. He hitched his duffel bag over his shoulder, walked down the dusty street, crossed the railroad tracks and went off toward East Park. He walked past Boss Dog's Tavern, and the boys with an old putter, trying to sink a dirty golf ball into a hole dug into the sandy ground, almost snapped to attention as he raised his hand, touching his cap. He walked on. Everything looked as it had four years before.

He stopped in front of a screened door with a tin sign bisecting it and smiled at picture of a white girl eating a slice of buttered "Sunbeam" bread. Yes, he had seen it before too. And yes, over the door was another sign indicating that this place was still called the Silver Moon Café. He went inside.

"Ya'll looky here! As sho as I is livin' and breathin', if it ain't the Black Strap Jack hisself!"

The woman was as round as a wash tub and her skin was a satiny, almost purple-black. She ran over and engulfed Black Strap Jack before he could get his bag through the door. Then everyone came and the girls hugged him and the boys and men patted him on his back. The fat woman made him sit and brought him a big glass of iced tea and a plate of pork chops, corn bread and collard greens.

"Anybody's been killing all them Germanies for four years gotta be hungry!" she exclaimed, as if for all those years he had been too busy to eat.

"But you do have some place to stay. You coming to my house. My niece from Alabama, she's there. Oh my! Strap, you'll sho like her."

Then everyone made Black Strap Jack tell just how it was to jump out of an airplane and land in a nest of Nazis.

Four weeks after he arrived, Altamaha had a ceremony to honor her war heroes. The event was held in the center of town, just in front of the railroad tracks and between one short and one tall palm tree. It was held on a flatbed railroad car, used as a stage. The governor of the state, who was running for re-election, was most happy to be the guest speaker. After the minister of the First Baptist Church prayed for the souls of Altamaha's fallen sons, the governor pulled off his blue seersucker coat, loosened his tie and rolled up his sleeves. He flipped his cigar into the air and it landed among the fronds of the shorter palm tree. Then he stuck his thumbs under his red suspenders, reared back and bellowed:

"Sho I stole, but I stole for you. And now that America has whipped the Nazis and them sneaky little Japs, we gotta think about the great state O' Ja Ja!"

The mayor stood and clapped, the crowd cheered and the other people on the flatbed stood and cheered too. There were perhaps twenty whites on the flatbed. Behind and to the left of them were six blacks. They were soldiers, sailors and marines – all of them proud and happy to be home.

First, the mayor introduced all the white boys. Then he brought five recipients of the Purple Heart up for special recognition. The mayor asked the superintendent of the Negro school, known to all as Professor Jackson, to come up and introduce the six Negro soldiers and to pay special tribute to Staff Sergeant Black Strap Jack, recipient of the Bronze Star, the country's second highest award for valor, just under the Congressional Medal of Honor.

Last, the mayor brought Uncle Andy to the podium and announced that he had won the Flying Cross for heroism under fire as a pilot of his B-17 during twenty-three sorties over Germany. The mayor asked Andy to tell everybody how it had been to live for a year in a Nazi prison camp, but Andy just said that it had been boring and reminded everyone that their loss in the war had been nothing compared to that of the Soviets. The mayor politely thanked him and was glad to see Andy sit down.

For a week longer Black Strap Jack wore his uniform around town, and when he finally bought himself civilian clothes, he did not feel right in them and made up his mind to re-enlist. But then there was Maudy Mae. Yes, the fat woman had been right when she said that Jack would like her niece. The girl from Alabama was small as a sparrow and had a voice that tinkled when she laughed. She made people cry when she sang in church. She was pretty too, and had it not been for the shriveled arm and hand – a defect since birth – she would have had many boyfriends. But one deformed arm and hand did not matter to Black Strap Jack and he proudly took the shy girl to all the cafés. The two jived and drank iced tea at the Silver Moon and he taught her how to play pinball at Boss Dog's. When it was late, they would go hear a new band called the Cool Breeze that played at an all-night place called the King Koon Klub – the KKK – the name being a cunning device for infuriating the white-trash element.

One night, after Jack had taken Maudy Mae home, he met Lolly Bailey at Boss Dog's. Lolly liked to go out with Jack, for in those days as long as Jack was along, all the tea and even beer they could drink was free. It was that night that Jack told Lolly he was in love with Maudy Mae. Lolly replied that this was no secret to anybody and that Jack had been acting as if he had died and gone to heaven.

Black Strap Jack took Maudy Mae to Bud's theater to see a movie called "The Texas Masquerade," starring Hopalong Cassidy. When it was over, they came down from the balcony – the area some of the whites called "Nigger Heaven" – and there in that dark corridor, they heard a sneer.

"Well, if it ain't the war hero hisself."

It was the voice of a white man. Black Strap Jack turned and recognized him.

"Hey, Collie. It's ..."

"It's Mister Coots to you, Boy. War's over. They ain't no heroes no more," he sneered.

Jack looked down at Collie, who was almost a head shorter. He said nothing. Collie laughed at his own joke, as did someone with him whose identity was obscured in the darkness.

Collie Coots, too, had just returned from service. He had been a seaman in the U.S. Navy and had spent most of the previous three years chipping paint, washing dishes and cutting lawns on the base at Hampton Roads, Virginia. The Navy knew better than to let Collie within a mile of a ship. He had not attended the ceremony that had taken place a month before, for he had been in the brig serving the last days of a sentence he had been given for public drunkenness and insubordination. The Navy had happily discharged him.

Richard had congratulated Black Strap Jack, saying how proud he was of "both boys in the family," referring to him and Andy. For good reason, he had left Collie Coots out. Richard always talked like that, leaving Collie out. Black Strap Jack told Richard how he had cried when he received Andy's letter telling how my father Ewell had, in the very last month of the war, been shot down over the Pacific and never found. Richard said that whenever Jack was ready he could start work; his old job was still waiting for him.

So in a few days, Jack got his old crew together and they started to work. They enjoyed the work like never before, for the crew had been transformed into an exclusive club of the only Negroes of Altamaha who had traveled to exotic places and who were associated with great and exciting events. But most of all, these five men were led by a true war hero.

The fat woman from the Silver Moon Café threw a big party for all of them. They drank until all the beer was gone and sang late into the night – white people's songs that they had learned in the war and made their own.

Early the next morning, as Jack sat in his new Ford skidder, he looked at the flowing river and thought about that world he had left behind – a far away world with destiny he had helped shape. He told himself how glad he was to be home, that Altamaha, while not perfect, at least seemed to be more or less set straight and turning right. It might wobble, but it was his. He revved up the engine and he felt the power of the machine merge with the power of his own body. No, for that instant, it was the vitality of life itself that animated him, the world and all that was in it. Jack was strong and proud and his world was overflowing with possibility.

His thoughts turned to Maudy Mae. He admitted to himself that his mother, had she been alive, would never have approved of the girl. Cora would have said that deformed people cause hexes. His mother, though now long dead, always badgered him. Sometimes he thought of her as he worked in the woods, or she appeared in his dreams, ready with advice. Early one foggy morning as he walked along the banks of the Altamaha, he even thought he saw her waving at him from the opposite shore. He had honored his mother, but now she had passed away and even though she might yet let her objections be known from the other side, Black Strap Jack vowed that he would marry the girl with the tinkling laugh and the songbird voice. He loved that shy girl from Alabama and she was going to have his baby.

He was home, alive and happier than he had ever been. The red water glistened in the rising sun, and Black Strap Jack closed his eyes and smiled. He had been to hell, but now he was home. Yes, Jack was back – back like a ...

BLACK PHOENIX

On the liver peach banks of the Altamaha
grew Black Strap Jack from his bone-faced Ma

Like the pushing pulse of the flow in his arm
with its puff-up breath banging
back and again with air-scrape noise,
Wet Red will be there when he wakes in the morn
to slap in his eye today and yesterday
and the day be after
when needled light speckles his face
and the heat of the day seeps through the pine
the black of hand flips the key
and the motor of his skidder is set free

Black Strap Jack was a pulpwood nigger
and there weren't no nigger in the swamp no bigger

From oozing morns til scalding noons
from half daybreaks til night runs in
Jack pops the bulge in his upper arms
to load logs on the skidder truck
then night has come and day is gone
clean shirt, point-toe shoes
and head hatted with stingy brim
Jack be cool, Jack be cocked
Jack be ready to come and jive
and to Boss Dog's black man drive

Nothing is faster than a skidder
piloted by the hands of a pulpwood nigger

The only hook with the sweaty day
the resin holding fast to his neck
but this no matter none to Jack
whose day is gone

whose night has come
who'll bust the town
who's ready to lay
who'll screw the squeals from Maudy Mae

When screw is done and jive is had
turns the mind a fickle sad

Roll by yourself, bunged-up skidder
take home to Ma your drunk-tired nigger

The morning tongue is tipped with brown
and knees they flex on oily hinge
the gut is filled with flutter air
all recall the bumbling binge

Get up get up
you cloud of scrounge
and to your daybreak hear
the gobbling snout rasping
the raw-bellied place you sit

Fine fine for a young buck
to get hisself a nightly fuck
but you yourself you rightly know
the younguns you'll have, the way they'll grow

Maudy Mae's got that twisted arm
flecked with knots and gnarly boned;
shriveled fingers loosely hang
like lizard's paw of five-clawed fang

Leave her alone you stupid boy
leave alone your tainted toy
forget forget the crabby claw
forget the bite of your point-cheeked ma,
you, Jack, have work to do
tonight, again, you can screw
flex your arms
strain your back
you nigger are Black Strap Jack

Black Strap Jack was a pulpwood nigger
and there weren't no nigger in the swamp no bigger

Black Strap Jack and Maudy Mae were married in the African Baptist Church. Maudy Mae had been so happy that she had broken out in song. Black Strap Jack had grinned, closed his eyes and his chest swelled under the hero's medals pinned to his uniform. When he looked up at her, he thought that he would melt.

Everybody said that it was the most beautiful wedding ceremony ever held in Altamaha, and they all were so glad that Maudy Mae had decided to be married there and not over in Alabama where nobody knows how to do anything right. Other than for Black Strap Jack and the black-robed minister, everyone at the wedding wore white – the men in white shirts set off by black ties and the women in white dresses and brightly colored hats.

After the ceremony Maudy Mae's aunt led them all in a song called "Shall We Gather at the River?" They all filed out into the summer day and gathered at the river. There were many verses to the song and they sang them while they seated themselves at long cedar tables under the mossy oaks. Some of the verses were made up at the moment, and the river in the song simultaneously was the River Jordan and the eternal flow of God's love. They ate sandwiches made with pineapple or with tomatoes or with cheese and pimento. There was cool, crisp chicken and iced tea. Yes, the Altamaha had become their River Jordan and beside it they ate, drank and, for a time, washed their sins away.

Then Jack and Maudy Mae spent their first night in the white-frame house that Richard had built for them on the original site of Cora and Jack's cabin beside the river. They sat on the porch until the crickets began and then they went into the house and Black Strap Jack lay beside his wife – she full inside with their baby. They overflowed with love for each other.

Jack got up before the sun rose over the pines and, as usual, was the first to arrive at the mill. This he had learned from the army: If one is to be a leader, he must set a good example. He woke the night watchman, opened up the sheds, shoveled some sawdust into the fiery furnace under the boiler and went to check out the skidder.

The crew always got into the woods before the sun became hot and they often were finished cutting by noon. On the crew were two bushwhackers, men who were responsible for slashing away the vines and palmettos so that the sawmen could get to the trees. The bushwhack itself is a kind of axe, but its blade is curved and its end flows backwards forming a hook, like the feathers on the head of a jaybird. The hook is for slashing, the blade for cutting. When the pines were felled, the bushwhackers would slice the limbs off the trunks so that the sawmen could cut the trees into eight-foot sections. Then the larger logs would be hoisted to the bed of the skidder by the wench and, in pairs, the men would take turns throwing the smaller logs to another pair of men, who would stack them on the bed of the skidder.

The work was hot, sticky and dangerous. Trees sometimes fell on careless men. Once a sawman got his foot sliced off by a bushwhack, and on several occasions men had been bitten by rattlesnakes. But none of these things ever happened on Black Strap Jack's crew. His crew had a perfect safety record. He always said that men made mistakes when they were tired, and this is why he always rotated with his men to allow them time to rest. When Lolly took a crew out, he would just sit in the cab of his skidder, work the winch and watch a bit, but mostly read comic books. But not Black Strap Jack, and his men loved him for it.

They would pulp wood all fall and winter. In the spring they would plant saplings so that Richard could take advantage of the government's reforestation program. In the summer – during tobacco season – the crew would push the hand trucks stacked high with bales of tobacco. They would take the bales to be weighed, line them up in long rows on the floor to be sold, weigh them again and load them into boxcars and trucks to be taken to Carolina. No matter what the crew did, or where they did it, Black Strap Jack was their chief and they were his loyal tribe. They would have killed and gone to hell for him, as some men had already done.

The next year, at the end of tree-planting season, Black Strap Jack and Maudy Mae's baby was born. If one were to have gazed upon it, one would have seen no hint as to the species of its parents. Like the outcast beasts of the book of Leviticus, it was beyond category. But the tiny, miss-shaped thing was his, and for the month that it held on to life, Black Strap Jack fed it, changed it and rocked it to sleep. Its mother became hysterical whenever she was forced to look at it.

Seeking solace after the baby's death, Maudy Mae's aunt asked the preacher if the baby would be made perfect in heaven. Grimly, the preacher had told her that that kind of baby would not go to heaven because it had no soul. Because the preacher would not allow the baby to be placed in consecrated ground, the burial had to be done in the cover of darkness. Lolly went to the cemetery with Black Strap Jack. In early-morning light, at the edge of the graveyard and almost under the church, Black Strap Jack dug the hole, took the little box from Lolly and, placing it inside, covered it with the sandy earth. Despite what the preacher had said, Lolly prayed for the baby's soul, and then marked the grave with a concrete block. As they walked back along the river, Black Strap Jack told Lolly that he had secretly named the baby C.J. Lolly asked if Jack had named the baby for his mother and Jack just nodded, letting Lolly think that. Jack had defiantly named the baby Christ Jesus. The name was at the same time recognition that his mother would have been right about the hex, but with that name, Black Strap Jack had cast a curse over the name of his mother, over the world itself and over the world to come.

For almost eight years after they buried the baby, Black Strap Jack lived in quiet sadness. When Cora appeared to him from the other side, he ignored her. He did not care even if the preacher had been right when he said that the twisted child was a punishment of God. He could live without the memory of his mother and even without God. All he needed to live was his wife, for life itself did not exist without Maudy Mae.

Despite Black Strap Jack and his wife's terror of repeating the reproduction of his God-forsaken son, their desire for each other was so strong that, from time to time, it assuaged grief and cancelled all caution. With their intensity and frequency of love making, one would have expected the emergence of a tribe. Yet nothing happened and they eventually decided that their sadness had rendered them barren. With this conclusion, their terror subsided, and because they thought their love would never be concretely manifested and carried into the future, great weariness set in.

The weariness stayed for those eight years. Everyone noticed it. After awhile, some even forgot how different Black Strap Jack had been when his world had been right and he had been happy. But the weary sadness left one evening when Black Strap Jack and Maudy Mae were sitting on the porch. It had grown dark enough to see the fireflies, hear the bullfrogs croaking and the first cricket chirp. They sat barefoot. Black Strap Jack was tired; but on this night, Maudy Mae told him she was going to have a child. His weary sadness left and he became strong and proud again. A new light brightened his long, gloomy world. He knew that the child would be right, that the child would be a boy – a special, shining boy.

The very essence of Collie Coots was resentment. It was the purest part of his protoplasm, the marrow in his every bone, the fiber of every ounce of his flesh, and the deepest hole in the darkest nook of his soul. This essence, though hidden in the interiors of his being, was revealed by his words and shown by his deeds. From this resentment, revenge and hatred were born.

Collie did not like the way the world was. Because he was unable to change the world, he wanted revenge against the conditions that had allowed it to be the way it was. He hated the Cootses because they were like him. He hated the Benjamins because they were not. He hated them both because they were from whom he had been issued. He hated Altamaha because it was the place where he had appeared and the place where who he was had been revealed to others. But also, Collie hated Altamaha because he had come back there and had not remained elsewhere, where people did not know him. He hated himself for coming back, hated himself for being like he was and hated all of them for making him like that. He resented everyone in Altamaha – every white, black, man, woman and child – for not forgetting things he had said and done, and for not recognizing the worth of wise words he had never spoken and great deeds he had not performed. Collie hated it all.

After he served his sentence in the brig, Collie was discharged and given his separation pay and a train ticket to Altamaha. He moved into his old room at the Benjamin place and for a month, until his money ran out, hung around town. He spent most of time at Moxley's Filling Station and at the juke joint out at Max Maxwell's fish camp. He seldom took meals even with his mother, but then, Vera Ola was often sick and did not go to the table. He never saw Richard, who always worked late and who never used the door on the side of the house where Collie and Vera Ola's rooms were.

So Collie came and went as he pleased. When his money ran out he tried to find a job, but the people of Altamaha knew Collie and were neither interested in him nor his stories about his exploits in Hampton Roads, Virginia. No one wanted to hire Collie Coots. Most didn't even want to talk to him and those who did talk to him did so only because he was part Benjamin. Finally, because of Vera Ola's persistent nagging, Richard employed him.

Collie was given a car – a dark-blue, 1941 Chevrolet with "First Benjamin Seaboard Bank" painted on the side. His job was to drive to Savannah twice weekly with two armed guards and bags containing deposits. On other days, he delivered and picked up messages, legal documents and anything else the bank wanted picked up or delivered. Collie tried to make what he was doing seem respectable. He would always wear a tie and his new two-toned, brown-and-white shoes. He started carrying a big ring of keys on his belt and, at times, smoked a wooden-tipped Tampa Jewel cigar. Often he would comment on whatever it was he was supposed to pick up or deliver, speaking as if he knew all about it. But, of course, this did not work. Everyone in Altamaha knew exactly who Collie Coots was.

One day, when he and the two guards were coming back from Savannah, Collie stopped in at the beer joint next to a place called Kent's Pool. He and one of the guards got drunk and went into the swimming pool in their clothes. The other guard, tired of being ridiculed for not doing likewise, got a ride home. Mister Kent tried to keep Collie and the other drunken man from driving off in the Chevrolet, but they did it anyway. They left Kent's Pool and were on their way to the White Spot when Collie failed to take the sharp fork at Brunswick Road before the Altamaha River Bridge. Losing control, Collie drove the Chevrolet over a whole row of headstones in Confederate Veterans' Memorial Park. The drunken guard broke his arm, the United Daughters of the Confederacy threatened to sue and the bank replaced the headstones, junked the car and fired Collie.

Collie went to Florida, but before everybody was used to his being gone, he was back. With him was a fellow who claimed to be from Miami, but who, it later was learned, was really from Jacksonville. The two of them showed up at the New Altamaha Golf and Country Club. It was the club's first annual awards day. Collie and the man who claimed to be from Miami were both as high as Georgia pines. When they began heckling an undertaker named Strickland, who was acting as the master of ceremonies, they were asked to leave. They did leave, but only after being shoved around by several of the men and the master of ceremonies said that he was going to call the county sheriff, who Collie knew would delight in seeing him behind bars.

After the white convertible with its Florida tag screeched down the road and the ceremony resumed, someone noticed both Collie and the man from Florida down on the green at the first hole. To get their attention, Collie took the flag out of the hole and waved it into the air. A woman shouted, "Oh, look they are back!" and the ceremony stopped once again. Everyone looked down the fairway at them. This was when Collie bared his bottom and the man from Florida pissed into the first hole.

They were just passing through, I guess you could say. They certainly knew better than to stay around Altamaha after what they had done at the Country Club. It was said that they made their way down to Savannah and that Collie got a job measuring farm land for the government. After all, Collie was a veteran. Years later I heard that because he did not like the sun, and because it was quicker than using a tape measure, Collie climbed trees and estimated the land he was supposed to be measuring. The government must not have liked this method of measuring land because Collie was fired. It was about this time that the man with the white convertible was caught passing bad checks and the police discovered that he was wanted for several things by numerous police departments across the South. Durden Fowler said that he read it in the Savannah Morning News.

For a few years, no one heard from Collie, not even his mother. It was later learned that he had landed a job with a crew that was building a bridge down near Brunswick, but he stabbed his foreman with an ice pick and he was sentenced to eighteen months in the Glen County chain gang. His mother was upset, but not nearly as upset as she was when Collie was released and showed up in Altamaha.

It must have been around '52 or '53. He was first seen down at Moxley's Filling Station, and then people saw him around Grady Platt's used-car lot. As it turned out, Grady Platt had let him stay there in exchange for cleaning up the cars. In the evenings he often hung out at Max's and, eventually, Max Maxwell hired Collie to run the bar out of his juke joint at the fish camp. This was a steady job until Collie started bragging and threatening the customers who didn't believe his stories. Max soon lost all of his customers and had to shut the juke joint down.

Collie went back to work for Grady Platt and, for practically nothing, continued to rent one of the cabins out at Max's fishing camp. Both Uncle Durden and Uncle Andy were old friends of Max's, and Max figured he was doing the Benjamin family a favor by letting Collie stay on. Indeed he was. Richard was secretly paying Max a handsome sum, and, if the truth be known, Max was a little afraid of Collie.

So things weren't too bad for Collie. Grady even sold him a car cheap. Collie started seeing his mother, but only occasionally, usually when he needed money and always when his Uncle Richard was not around.

The first time I ever saw Collie Coots up close was at the baseball game – the doubleheader between the Altamaha Savages and the Baxton Bombers. Sure I'd heard of him – heard about him all of my life – and from time to time I had seen him drive by in his old, black Plymouth. He didn't look at all like I had imagined. He was medium height and had olive skin and dark hair. He looked kind of like an Indian, I remember thinking. He wore two-toned, brown-and-white wing tips, a Hawaiian shirt and a Panama hat. He was smoking one of those little cigars with the wooden tip. He wasn't bad looking at all, not like I thought people who had been to prison were supposed to look.

Two other people were with him, a short man with a blond crew cut and a pretty, redheaded girl. Sometime later, I learned that the blond man was Grady Platt and that the girl hanging all over Collie, who couldn't have been more than sixteen, was Rose.

They came in and sat several rows below us. It was the top of the sixth in the second game, an unusual time for anyone to arrive. Then I heard Uncle Richard tell Uncle Andy that they were drunk. But Andy got up to speak to Collie anyway.

"After all," he said to Uncle Richard, "he is our cousin and he did live in our house for most of his life."

Uncle Richard just shook his head and mumbled, "Well, you go then. I'm staying right here."

Andy paid no attention. I watched him as he went down and shook Collie's hand and talked with him. I could hear little that was said, but I could tell that it was friendly.

At the bottom of the seventh, just before everybody gets up to stretch, the Cuban on the Savages hit a homer and tied the game. Everybody jumped up and screamed. Then, somebody passed a baseball cap around to collect money for the Cuban who had hit the homer. When the cap finally got around to Collie and Grady, they kept it. The person who had passed his cap around came to them and asked them to give it back. The owner of the cap was Jake Bailey, Lolly Bailey's brother and the team manager's helper.

"Why should I give it back? What you gonna do with all this here money, boy?" Grady asked loudly, throwing back his head and laughing.

"We gonna give it to Roberto, give it to 'em fo knocking that homer."

Then Collie spoke: "Hell, he ain't got no use for it. This here's American money. Spick Cubans got no use for American money. They can't even speak American."

"Come on," the girl named Rose said, "you boys give 'em back the money."

Collie ignored her and turned, looking at people around him, inviting them to join in.

"You know what I think? I think we ought to give this here money to the niggers, least they speak American. What you think, boy? Oh, but I forget, everybody says you is an Injun. That right, boy? A nigger Injun?"

"Hey, Collie," Grady laughed, "I think we oughta give this here money to this boy's church!" he said, snorting, slapping his leg.

I could feel the discomfort of the people watching this spectacle. The ball game itself seemed to vanish.

"That Collie is bad," Durden Fowler said. "Worse than all us put together."

"No, he's more than bad. I don't know what you'd call it, but it's more than bad," Andy said, and then he got up and went down the bleachers to where Collie was sitting.

"Collie," he said firmly, "why don't you give Jake back his money. Look around. The joke's not funny. Nobody's laughing."

"What this? You telling me what to do? You Benjamins think you're better than anybody else. You think you're shit on a stick and can tell everybody ..."

Grady cut him off in the middle of his sneer. "Come on," he said, "give it to 'em."

Collie glared at Grady, "Whose side you on anyway, you nigger lovin' son of a bitch?" He shoved the cap toward Jake, and Jake took it and walked away.

Disorderly Notions

No arrests were made until three weeks after the murder. When enough evidence had been gathered, the sheriff's car pulled up beside an unpainted house near the mill. The house was in the white section, but not far from East Park. The house belonged to Rose Thigpin's mother. After the deputy knocked many times and the sheriff had called out identifying himself, Rose's mother came to the door. She said that Rose was sick in bed, but the sheriff said that he had heard that one before. They made Rose come out, get into the sheriff's car and go downtown to the courthouse. They told her to sit in a chair beside the deputy's desk. The sheriff and his other deputy went to Grady Platt's trailer next to his car lot.

On the way back to the jail, Grady kept saying, "I didn't do it. I swear to God, I didn't do nothing."

Then they went out to Max Maxwell's fish camp, stopped at Max's house and the sheriff went to the door. Max told him that Collie must be there because his car was. When Max asked if Collie was in trouble, the sheriff said, "Yeah, that boy's in a heap of trouble." Then Max Maxwell told them that Collie was in the cabin down beside the river.

The sheriff and his deputy didn't take any chances, they knew Collie. They left the car running just in case. They knocked and the sheriff called out. Collie told them to come on in and they opened the door. Collie was just standing there in his under shorts.

"Bubba, you comin' with us," the sheriff said.

But Collie just ran straight into the sheriff and knocked him into the deputy. He darted out the door, jumped into the sheriff's waiting car and drove off laughing.

As one might imagine, there were alerts in six States announcing that a dangerous, armed suspect had escaped in the Altamaha County sheriff's car. The alerts described him as a dark-haired, white male in his thirties who was last seen wearing blue-and-red striped boxer shorts. Two days later, a fisherman noticed a long antenna sticking out of the Altamaha River down near Glencoe Naval Air Station. It was the sheriff's car, alright. When they towed the car to the garage, they found that it was out of gas. The next day, someone said they saw a man hiding down at the airbase garbage dump and the shore patrol went there to check it out.

Yes, it was Collie. They chased him out of the dump and into the area where the long runways are. Collie ran into a little red tin house in the middle of a field with "DANGER EXPLOSIVES" painted on its side.

"You Bastards come any closer and I'll make this place look like ground zero!" he shouted.

Two days later, when Collie finally gave himself up, it was discovered that Collie never even had any matches.

"Well, you can't eat dynamite and there wasn't nothing to drink in there but cans of paint!" he laughed as the sheriff cuffed him.

When the trial began, Andy came all the way from New York to be with his brother Richard, who had been smothered with shame and terrorized by the fact that they had to be witnesses. Among the other witnesses were Lolly, the state patrolman (the same one that shot the cow), the sheriff, his deputy and various people who had been with, or who had seen, the accused on the night of the murder. And, of course, the three accused were: Colman Benjamin Coots, Grady Tyler Platt and Rose Darleen Thigpen.

Much to their relief, Richard and Andy were excused as witnesses because they were closely related to one of the accused. Despite the fact that Hamilton and I had been witnesses, we were not called because of my close relation and our age – and Hamilton was already back in Canada by then. Anyway, as I said, not only was I related to the accused, I was too young. But I just could not leave this alone. And I must confess that as awful as my memory of it still is, it still attracts as much as it repels me. I wanted to know then, and I still want to know now, what happened and how and why it happened as it did.

I cannot give a personal account of the whole trial because I saw only the last day. But even if I had been there all the time, I could not have told you Rose Thigpin's or Grady Platt's side of the story. The reason is as plain as the nose on your face: they never came to trial.

Three days before she was to be called to testify before the court, Rose Thigpen learned she was pregnant. Right there in front of the doctor, she went crazy. She fell to the floor and started flopping around like a chicken with its head cut off. They had to tie her up with adhesive tape, give her a sedative and take her to the insane asylum up in Milledgeville. Sometime later, Uncle Richard said he thought she had died there, but Durden Fowler later told me this was wrong, that the Thigpin family was just saying this to stop all of the gossip about her.

But Grady did die. With his teeth, he ripped open his wrist, and, pretending to be asleep, he dangled his hand over one of those buckets full of sand they use in jails for cigarette butts. His life filled up the can and then overflowed, oozing over and making a black puddle on the concrete floor.

Although they never testified in court, there is a version of Rose's and Grady's story. There is nothing secret about it, for all of it is on public record in the Altamaha County Courthouse. Here are their stories, provided to me by my uncle, Durden Fowler, in the form of briefs of evidence.

Disorderly Notions

---

**ALTAMAHA COUNTY SUPERIOR COURT**
September term 1954
The State vs Colman Benjamin Coots, Grady Tyler Platt and Rose Darleen Thigpin
Being on trial for murder of Black Strap Jack
Filed in this office, August, 1954
P. Pierce Woods, Official Court Reporter

**EXHIBIT A**
Statement of the Defendant Rose Darleen Thigpin
Statement Sworn September 1, 1954


I, Rose Thigpen, residing at 102 Eli Avenue, Altamaha, Georgia, this 2nd day of September, 1954, in Altamaha County, Georgia, do make the following statement of my free will and in accord without any threats or promises toward me, and knowing that this statement can be used against me in case of trial.

That Saturday afternoon on August 16, Collie Coots and Grady Platt come to my house and picked me up in that black car Grady drives. They had already started drinking. My mamma, she tried to make me not go, but I tell her that not to worry that it'll be alright. Then I get in the car and go up town with them. We ride all around looking for Ella Kirkland, 'cause Grady, he wants to go on a date with her, but we can't find her nowhere and there ain't nobody at home at her house either.

Then we go over to Grady's trailer. That's when Collie tries to get me to let Grady see me naked, but I won't do it. Collie says that Grady has a camera, and Grady showed it to me. Grady said he just wanted to see the picture – that he'd show Collie how to work it. He said he knew how to make it into a picture hisself and that nobody would see it but us. I said no, that I wasn't about to let anybody take my picture naked. Collie got mad and said he was just going to take me home 'cause if Grady didn't have no date then he didn't want one neither.

But when we left, we saw Ella Kirkland sitting in Herschel Blackwell's car there at Moxley's Filling Station. We followed them out the Savannah Road and to Kent's Pool. We sat in the car and watched them go in. They saw us, but didn't say nothing, and we just sat there. Collie told me to go in and get us a Coca-Cola. He gave me some money and

I went in and brought the Coca-Colas back. Collie, he and Grady, they drank some whisky and chased it down with the soda. I didn't. Like I told you, I don't drink - drink liquor, I mean. The stuff makes me sick. It always makes people mean, and I'm sure, like the Bible says, it's a sin.

Then we went in and Herschel and Ella, they was in their bathing suits. We sat on them bleachers and watched them, and that's when Collie and Grady started making fun and laughing at Herschel, on account that Herschel, he can't swim but was making like he could. When they laughed, Herschel, he don't do nothing. Then he come over and tried to be friendly, but Grady told him that he wasn't supposed to be out with Ella and that he'd better watch it. Then Ella, she come over, and Grady said he wanted to talk to her and she said alright and they went over to the other bleachers and talked. Herschel, he acted like nothing was happening and just went back on in the shallow part of the bathing pool.

I don't know what Grady said to Ella, but she went in and got dressed and then she come out and we all got in Collie's car and drove off. Then we went to that place they call the White Spot. We went in and Collie and Grady played pool. Ella and me, we played the jukebox and danced with one another. Collie and Grady bought us both a hot dog and Coca-Cola, and Grady he kept putting whisky in Ella's. She kept drinking it, and he bought her another Coca-Cola and pretty soon she couldn't dance no more, got sick on the floor and we had to take her home. Then I told Collie that I wanted to go home too. Collie laughed and told me that I wasn't going nowhere but to the baseball game. He acted like he thought I was kidding or something. He just paid no attention, and we went on to Baxton.

I didn't like the old baseball game one bit. I had to sit there with all those people looking, and Collie and Grady was always making jokes. They kept leaving me there right by myself saying they was going to see a man about a dog, which everybody knows means you got to go to the bathroom, but I know they were going there to drink some more whisky.

Then the car wouldn't start and we had to get somebody to push us to get it going. We started on back to Altamaha. On the way, Collie and Grady was talking about where they could get some more whisky. Collie told Grady that they could get it from that Mister Coots, the one what they call Jaybird, who lives out past Max's fish camp. But Collie said that it didn't matter if he was kin to him, that ole Jaybird wasn't about to let them have it without any money.

Disorderly Notions

I told them that I didn't even have no money even at home. I told them I wanted to go home, but Collie told me to shut up.

Then Collie said he knew where they could get some money, that it didn't matter how late it was cause the colored man at the tobacco warehouse stayed there all night and he always had money. They'd get him to loan them some. No, I don't know what time it was. I don't have no watch, and I don't ever think about the time anyway.

We went to the warehouse. Collie he told me to sit in the car and to put my foot on that thing on the floor and to keep it there cause if I didn't, the car would stop running and they might have trouble starting it back.

They stayed a long time. Then I heard some yelling, and the car just stopped. I went in and they was fighting with that colored man. (Yes sir, the dead colored man in that picture.) I saw Collie take that bushwhack off the side of that skidder parked next to the little house and hit the colored man across the shoulder with it. (Yes sir, that there bushwhack.) I tried to make him stop, but he wouldn't.

I went on back to the car. I don't know where Grady Platt went. I never seen him again. I was so scared I was shaking. Then Collie come on out to the car. He was mad at me for letting it stop running. He made me push it down the hill so it would start. Collie said he would kill me if I ever told anybody what I saw, and I said I wouldn't ever tell nobody nothing. Then he let me off at my house. He'll probably tell you he didn't cause Collie, he likes to brag. I was so scared I was sick.

---

**EXHIBIT B**
Statement of the Defendant Grady Tyler Platt
Statement Sworn September 1, 1954


I, Grady Platt, live in my trailer on my car lot on Joiner Street in Altamaha, Georgia, this 2nd day of September, 1954, and do make the following statement of my free will and accord without threats or promises toward me, and knowing that this statement can be used against me in case of trial.

Well, gentleman of the jury, I know you'll be reading this 'cause I just know that we'll all be going to trial. They are gonna charge us with murder and I am not guilty.

On the afternoon of August 16, 1954, Collie Coots come by my trailer and we took us a drink and decided that we wanted to go to the ball game over in Baxton that night. We got in the car and went over to the Thigpin's place to get Rose. Then we looked for Ella Kirkland, who I wanted to go to the ball game with me. At first we couldn't find her nowhere, and so we went back to my trailer to get us another drink. We stayed there for maybe an hour. I showed that Thigpin girl my camera and told her how I develop pictures.

When we left we saw Ella with Herschel Blackwell. 'Cause I wanted to talk to her, we followed them out to Kent's Pool. I talked to her and she decided to come with me. We said bye to Herschel and left for the ball game. On the way, Collie said that he was hungry. We went in that beer joint they call the White Spot, the one out on Brunswick Road. He said "You wanna shoot a game?" meaning shoot some pool, and I told him I did. I kept beating him and he kept getting madder and madder and wouldn't quit. Finally, I let him beat me.

The girls were getting tired of waiting, and we was gonna be late for the game. We all had a hot dog and this is when Ella Kirkland gets sick all over the floor. And the man – I can't remember his name, but he's Collie's cousin – come over and he's mad and acts like it's our fault or something. He says we have to clean it up. Collie tells him we ain't going to and we leave. We have to take Ella home 'cause she is real sick, and then we leave again for the ball game in Baxton.

We get to the game late. One is already over and we watch almost all of the next one. Rose is complaining 'cause she don't like baseball, but it is not a good game anyhow. Before the game is over, we decide to go. Collie's car won't start, but a man pushes us with his truck and we get it started and go on back to Altamaha.

Collie and me want a drink before we go home, but don't have no more money. Collie says that colored man – the one that does the weighing at the tobacco warehouse – always had some in his metal box. He said that if we go over there and wake him, he would be glad to lend us some. So we go over to the warehouse. Collie tells Rose to say in the car and to keep her foot on the gas so it won't stop. We go in and knock on the door of that little house where they weigh the tobacco bales. The colored man (yes sir, he is the one in the picture), comes to the door. (Yes sir, he is the one they call Black Strap Jack.) And that colored man, he is mad.

## Disorderly Notions

"No, you cannot borrow no money," he says and he is not polite, not one bit.

He tells us that if we don't leave he's gonna call the sheriff. Then Rose, who has come in to tell us that the car cranked down, laughs and says that colored people don't know how to use telephones anyhow. This makes the colored man real mad. But he don't say nothing, he just looks at her and then at Collie and me. Then he turns to go get the telephone that's sitting on the desk next to the cash box by the big old scale.

"You pick up that telephone and something's gonna happen to you that is worser than what happened to your daddy," Collie tells him.

His daddy's the one that put his mamma in that ice box when she was dead. Anyhow, he did pick up the phone and Collie took his ice pick from his sock. (Yes sir, that's the ice pick.) Anyway, then he stuck that colored man in the arm. The colored man was real mad. He turned over the chair and charged out toward us. But then the colored man, he stops and looks down at his arm. There's lots of blood, and he was trying to stop it.

Rose and Collie, they had run behind the skidder what was parked next to the little house, and I seen Rose give Collie a bushwhack that she must have got out from the skidder or something. (Yes sir, that's the bushwhack.) The colored man, he didn't see them 'cause he was trying to stop the blood. Then, she says, "Here, use this," and then Collie, he taken it from her, he hits that colored boy 'cross his shoulder. Right here.

I get scared and I say that he ought to stop, but Collie, he don't listen. The colored man, he gets up and goes into the little house, but before he can get the door shut good, Collie sticks that there hook that is on the end of the bushwhack into the crack so the colored man can't close the door. Then Collie goes in there. I can hear the colored man yelling and can hear the bushwhack hitting him, but I can't see it. Then Collie comes out of the little house and puts that metal cash box on the floor. He hits it with the bushwhack and it comes open, but there ain't no money, just yellow pieces of paper. So Collie throws the box back inside the little house and we go out the door. (Yes sir, that's the metal box.)

Well, I guess that's when I get so scared I run off. I must have gone out of one of them loading doors beside the boxcars. The next thing I remember, I was out on the railroad tracks near where that there turpentine still used to be.

I tried to get him not to do it. I really did, and I didn't do nothing myself. When I finally went home it was turning light. I was so scared I couldn't sleep. I have told you the truth, I swear to God I have, and if I didn't, I would not say that 'cause I have found Jesus and have declared him to be my savior.

---

Collie Coots was represented in court by the court-appointed counsel, Mister Wayne Borden of Baxton. Even if Mister Bordon had not been so young, Mister Borden could never have done much with Collie's case. Even Cicero couldn't have done anything with it. That's what I heard Uncle Durden say. He said that all Wayne Borden could have done to help Collie was to tell him not to say "nigger" in court, since there were all those Yankee reporters and, besides, a lot of the white folks in Altamaha didn't like to hear that word either. Collie pleaded innocent, but, of course, everyone knew how things were likely to turn out.

It so happened that, on the night that we discovered Black Strap Jack's body in the scale house, Uncle Richard had not known what to do, and, in a panic, we had fled the scene and went straight to Uncle Durden's place. Uncle Durden had called the sheriff and met him at the warehouse. Although he was the county prosecutor, because Durden Fowler had been a witness to the crime scene, he had taken himself off what otherwise would have been his case. The bench appointed Mister William Darby instead, Durden Fowler's law partner.

The summer had ended. The tobacco men were gone. The pink-pink sound of the fair no longer plucked the air, and with its passing went the rumors of sly Gypsies, pervert Yankees and communists with names that end in "ski." School had started. Ah, but it was Columbus Day, and the whole class had gone on a field trip that morning. We had gone to Bud's theater to see a picture about Christopher Columbus. I was amazed to learn that he was really an Italian. Then we had the rest of the day off.

Every night at supper, I had listened to what Uncle Durden said about the trial, and I knew that the trial was likely to end that afternoon. So I found myself a place in the big chinaberry tree beside the courthouse. My place was in the forks where I could see into the second story of the courthouse where the courtroom was. I lay there among the cool leaves and berries; I had the best seat in the house. I could see them, but they could not see me. The balcony was filled with the colored people and the rest of the courtroom was filled mostly with Yankee reporters and country people who had come to town to hear the trial.

By the time Collie took the stand, I had become quite comfortable in my perch high in the chinaberry tree. It seemed the birds had even come to accept me. I could see the bailiff present the Bible to Collie. I heard Collie make a fuss because, for whatever reason, he did not want to place his hand on it and say "So help me God."

To this day, I do not know why he did this. But I am sure that most everyone there thought that he did it because he did not believe in God and that he may even have been employed by the Devil. But I think that there are two other likely possibilities. He may have thought that if there really was a God, then Collie Coots had the right to be pissed off with him. Or, Collie may have put up a fuss because he knew it would deeply insult and thereby anger everyone who witnessed it. But alas, whatever his motives, Collie had taken his stand.

"Well, Colman Coots, now that we have finally got that matter settled perhaps we could settle a few others," William Darby said, standing there in his elegant, blue seersucker suit, black-and-white wing tips and red silk tie. He smiled. "So, Colman Coots, pleading innocent, as you have done, let us establish a series of actions that culminated in this ... ah, event that you declare was authored by your very own hand."

"Okay, Bill what'd you wanna know?"

"It would please the court to know your relationship with the now deceased Grady Platt and then to tell us what took place on the night that the, ah, event took place?"

"Grady Platt I have known since we were little. That night, he said he wanted to go to the ball game with me. It was a doubleheader over in Baxton. I went by his trailer and he said that we ought to go get the Thigpin and Kirkland girls and carry them over there with us. I said that was a good idea. We went over to the Thigpin's house and picked up Rose – that's the Thigpin girl's name. Then we tried to find Ella Kirkland, but there was nobody at home, and so we decided to go on back to Grady's trailer and have us a drink. Grady showed us his camera and we just sat around there and talked for a while."

"You just talked?"

"Well, yeah kinda."

"What did you talk about?"

"Grady tried to get Rose to have a drink, but she said she didn't like to drink. Grady said that she didn't know how to have fun, and she said that she did and that you didn't have to drink to have a good time. Then she asked Grady if he wanted to take her picture with that camera, and she meant without any clothes on. He, at first, thought she was kidding, but I knew she was not. I didn't like it one bit, but did not stop her. She goes in the bathroom and comes out all naked. She lies on the sofa in all kinds of different ways, and Grady, he keeps snapping the camera. I just watch and don't say nothing, but when Grady suggests that they go do something in the bedroom, I tell him no, that Rose is dating me. Rose says that is right, that all Grady can do is take her picture. She didn't know, but Grady had already told me that the camera didn't have film in it."

"And then, Colman Coots, what did you do?"

"Well, then we went on out to the car and saw Ella Kirkland in Herschel Blackwell's car down at Moxley's Filling Station. Grady was mad, and we followed them, but they didn't see us. We went out to Kent's Pool. Grady talked Ella Kirkland into leaving that Blackwell boy and going with us."

"And then?"

"Then we headed out for the ball game, but Grady, he gets hungry. We stop at the White Spot for something to eat. We go in and Grady talks me into playing pool with him. I don't really want to 'cause he is too easy to beat and I always feel sorry for him. But we play anyway and I let him win a few times. Then I go on and beat him so we can go to the ball game. That is when Ella Kirkland gets sick, and we have to take her home. Grady should not have given her that whiskey. She ain't used to it. Grady had no reason to be mad at her."

"And what happened after you dropped off Ella Kirkland?"

"Then we go on to the ball game in Baxton. We get there late and nothing was really happening. We joked around for a while with that colored fellow that works for the Savages baseball team, the colored fellow they call Jake Bailey. They call to him to stop talking to us and get back to work – you know how he is – and then we left and drove back to Altamaha. We left before the game was over, but it didn't matter. Wasn't any good anyhow."

"What did you do after the game?"

"Well if you wait a minute, I'll get around to that, Bill."

"Okay then, go on."

"We got on back to Altamaha and Grady says he wants a drink before we go home, and I say that since we ain't got no money that we had better forget it. But then he suggests that we go out to Jaybird Springs Coots's house, and that, because he is related to me, he'll let us have a pint of whiskey. I say that it don't matter that he is kin to me, that he ain't letting nobody have liquor without no money. Then Grady asks me if I know that ... ah ... that colored man what stays at the tobacco warehouse during the tobacco season. I say sure, I know him, and that I'm sure he'll let us have five bucks till tomorrow. We figured he'd have money in that cash box."

"So, then what? What happened at the tobacco warehouse?"

"Give me time, Bill. So, when we got to the warehouse, I told Rose to stay in the car and keep the motor running. It was always choking down. Besides, the thing wouldn't start when we tried to leave the ball game over in Baxton. So Grady and me, we go in. I knock on the door and this colored fellow, he comes out, and he is rude to us. He tells us that he's going to call the law and we'd better get out of there."

William Darby walked over to the prosecution table and retrieved a photo of Black Strap Jack in uniform. He held it up for both Collie Colman and the jury to see.

"Yeah, he's the one in the picture," Collie said. "Anyhow, I ask him if he knows who I am. He says that sure, he knows me. But, you know, I bet he never really knew who I was. I should've told 'em, but I never really had time to think about it. He started pushing and calling us sorry white boys. He kept saying it, and I ain't about to let anybody call me that, especially somebody like that."

"And?"

"And then he pushes me again. I took that ice pick that was on the edge of the desk in the scale house, and I held it up."

William Darby was displaying for the jury an ice pick wrapped in a clear, plastic evidence bag.

"This object that I have just displayed to the jury is called an ice pick. What the court wants to know, Colman Coots, is whether you have ever seen this object."

"I don't know about that one, but I do know what an ice pick looks like," Collie said.

"Does it look like the ice pick that you might have used to stick the victim in his upper left arm?"

"Okay, I took that ice pick and I told him if he didn't leave me alone that he was going to get it."

"Thank you, Colman Coots. And then what did you do?"

"What did I do? Well, he wouldn't stop coming so I stuck 'em."

"In the arm?"

"Yeah, first I stuck 'em in the arm."

"What else happened?"

"Well, we all ran 'cause ... 'cause ..."

"Because of what?"

"'Cause he was really mad. Not that I was scared of him, but you know how big he is. So Rose, when me and her ran over around the back of the skidder what was parked beside the scale house, she gives me this bushwhack that was attached to the truck just above the running board."

William Darby returned the ice pick to the prosecution table and appeared before the jury with a large, transparent evidence bag. He turned and walked a few paces, stepping toward Collie.

"Is this the bushwhack?" he asked, holding it high before thrusting is at Collie.

"Looks like it."

"And then what did you do?"

"What did I do then? What do you think I did? I told him to stop. He didn't, so I hit 'em just hard enough to stop 'em, but it wasn't enough. He started back into the scale house and I was sure that he was going to get a gun or something. He locked the door."

"And?"

"Well, I had to stop 'em so I stuck the blade in the crack between the door and the ..."

"The jam?"

"Yeah. And I got it open."

"So then?"

"I ... I ..."

"You what? What did you do?"

"Goddamn it, Bill! Just give me a goddamned minute. Okay, I hit 'em."

"And you hit him again?"

"Yeah."

"And again?"

"Yeah."

"Exactly how many times did you hit him?"

"Hell, I don't know."

"You relieved him of his left hand, not to mention his head."

"If I did, I didn't mean to cut it off."

"And then you pinned his crotch to the floor with the ice pick. Right?"

"What would you do if a nigger was trying to kill you?"

At that moment there were gasps in the court room especially from the balcony where the Negros were seated. Then the room was abuzz with murmurs. William Darby held up his hand asking for silence and when the commotion abated but did not completely stop,

The judge slammed down his gavel and shouted: "Order!"

"Let me remind you, Collie Coots, that it is you who is being prosecuted in this court of law. It is I, the consular, who will do the questioning. Now, it would please the court to know what Grady Platt was doing all of this time."

"I don't know 'cause I don't know where Grady Platt went."

Reporters had begun to leave the room, presumably scrambling to find available telephones.

"Order!" the judge shouted. "I'll have order in my court!" He slammed the gavel down twice.

"Okay," William Darby asked, "Where do you think Grady Platt went?"

"Well, I've been knowing him since we was little. I can tell you right now that Grady is scared to stand up for hisself. He just ran away. There wasn't no money anywhere, but then, even if there had been, it was too late to borrow it."

"That is it, Collie Coots. I think we have heard quite enough."

"Fine with me, Bill."

"Your Honor and gentleman of the jury, if it would please the court, I have no further questions and will forgo my closing comments."

"Mister Borden, as public defender it is your privilege to speak?" the judge said.

"I have no further questions, Your Honor, and I too wish to forgo this privilege, Your Honor."

The judge had the bailiff bring the jury into the room, and then he told the defendant to rise. But Collie just sat there until the bailiff took Collie's shirt at the shoulder and pulled him from his seat. Collie faced the jury, glaring.

"Gentleman, have you reached a verdict?" the judge asked.

"Yes, Your Honor," the foreman, who had risen, answered in a shaky voice. "We, the jury, find the defendant guilty as charged. We recommend no mercy." He sat down.

"Gentleman," the judge said, "there is no reason to retire. I am ready with the sentence."

The courtroom was quiet. Collie cleared his throat, looked around and smiled. I thought I even heard him laugh.

The judge looked at Collie. "I hereby instruct the sheriff of this county to transport Mister Coots to Atlanta immediately after this trial. Tomorrow at sun-up, as is the custom in this state of Georgia, you, Colman Coots, shall die in the electric chair. You may speak, if you so choose."

Collie rose and looked at the judge, then glanced around the courtroom. Finally, looking directly at the jury, cleared his throat and smiled. His eyes were cold and sharp, and as he spoke, his voice did not waver or crack.

"Well, you've done it, all you God-fearing people of Altamaha. You've judged me now, just as you've judged me all my life, and you will continue to judge me as long as somebody remembers Collie Coots. You people are so good ... You ..."

"That is quite enough Colman Coots!"

"You really think you're something, don't you, Herman?" Collie sneered, addressing the judge. "In fact, all you people think you're shit on a stick! Your God, he ain't paying no attention to you. In fact, he really don't give a ..."

"Bailiff, get him outta here!" the judge shouted.

The deputy blackjacked Collie Coots and they threw him into the car and drove him to Atlanta.

# UPRIVER

The train followed the tracks into the yard and came to a stop with a bang and a hiss. They had arrived in Guangzhou, a place once called Canton. They gathered their bags and filed out of the car with the other passengers, making their way down the platform, through the terminal and into the square. People were everywhere – everywhere to be seen, touched and smelled. The sun was setting, and the air was chillier and damper than Hong Kong.

Hamilton hailed a taxi. Andy, who had acquired information from the bartender at the Kowloon Athletic Club, told the driver: "White Swan Hotel." The driver held up his hands indicating that he did not understand, but then Mo drew a picture of a swan on the back of Andy's matchbook, and the picture worked.

The White Swan was a thick building and perhaps ten stories tall. The fat, bright thing was a trove of excess in the midst of a squat, crumbling city. In the granite and lava-rock foyer were great tropical trees: mimosas with orchids breathing from their branches, banyans with viny roots and several varieties of palm. Amongst the trees was a waterfall.

"It's like Birdland," Starman said.

"Yes," Mo replied, "except this time we are the exotic birds."

Andy snorted and laughed, but his attention suddenly turned elsewhere.

"Look, I'm buying Starman a drink; you and Mo book us in. Okay?" Andy said to Hamilton.

Hamilton shook his head letting Andy know that he thought him incorrigible. Andy and Starman left and Hamilton and Mo went to the desk. They inquired about a room and were shocked to learn the cheapest one was over two hundred dollars, or the equivalent in "tourist money" they had acquired when crossing the border. The clerk informed them that there was only one room left.

"School outing," the clerk had said, amused. "No school in Hong Kong. Nice holiday for kids, yes?" he said.

"What are we going to do?" Mo asked, turning to Hamilton and ignoring the clerk.

"Don't know," Hamilton answered, "but we're not going to stay here."

They went to find the bar to discuss the matter with Starman and Andy. The bar was accented by a whirring strobe light. A Chinese band played a tune by Guns and Roses, and leagues of young Chinese danced or stood around talking and posturing. The place throbbed. Most of the young people from Hong Kong were just a shave from being "clean cut." They looked healthy, used impeccably polite English and were conscious of the styles of that time, as was evident by the clothes they wore. This was quite unlike the Asian gangs of Toronto, with their hoodies and absurdly baggy pants, Hamilton had concluded.

They found Andy and Starman standing at the bar talking to a sandy-haired man with a red baseball cap pushed back on his head.

"Hot damn!" Hamilton hears the man say as they approach. "Bushwhack Jinkens! I saw you take out that Georgia quarterback in the Sugar Bowl in 1974."

"1975," Starman corrected him.

"What did they say? That you were the meanest linebacker that ever wore a jock?"

"Well, that's what the man wrote. I thought it rather silly," Starman replied.

"Hot damn! Can't believe it. Bushwhack Jinkens, right here in China! Man!"

As he said this he took the bill of his cap and pulled it down almost to his eyebrows, as if needing to shade his eyes from Starman's brilliance. "Chiefs" was written across the front of the cap.

"Meet Rusty," Starman said to Hamilton and Mo. "He's from Kansas City. He's working over here with an oil company."

"Yes siree. Imperial Oil. Our rigs are up near Fuzhou. My buddy and me, we been seeing the sights. He's visiting me. He's from K.C. too, but we didn't know each other 'til we was in Nam. Now if that ain't some shit! Been all the way out to Tibet. Now that Tibet, I mean, that's really something. And we got two more weeks! Don't know yet what were gonna do. Esso gives everybody who works here this little ticket ..."

"So where is this friend?" Hamilton stopped him.

"Oh, he's out shooting. That's what he calls it, but it really means that he's just out taking pictures. He's always doing that."

"In the dark?" Andy grumbled.

"Oh, he's got one of them fancy video cameras. Don't matter, day or night, he can take pictures at any ole time. He takes 'em of just about anything you can think of. So what's ya'll's names?"

They told him their names, but as little as possible about who they were or what they were doing. It did not take much to satisfy him, for Rusty asked few questions.

"So you've been to Tibet?" Andy asked as he lit a cigarette and pushed his glasses up on his nose.

"Yes sir, we been to Tibet. Man, now that is really some place! And you don't have any trouble getting in there. Not now, anyhow. Not like they say it used to be. Little paper work, that's all. Yes siree, they just love the good ole American dollar. And these Chinese, they call themselves communist! Man, you just wouldn't believe it. It's just like being on the moon – Tibet, I mean. And the sky burials ..."

"The what?" Mo asked.

"Sky burials. Well, that's what they call 'em, but there ain't really any burial. When you die there, they can't bury you 'cause the dirt's all frozen and stuff. And there ain't no wood, so they can't burn you up or anything like that. So they do it with buzzards."

"Buzzards?" Starman asked.

"Yeah, that's right. They use buzzards. What I mean is that they come by each morning and they put all the dead folks in a cart. Then they take 'em up to this place on the side of this mountain and put 'em on a flat rock. And the dead people, they'll be naked. Then they take these long ole knives – machetes or something – and they split open their heads. Somebody told me that this is to let out the soul. Well, that's what they think, anyhow. And next, they turn them over and hack open their chests. Me and Rodney, we seen 'em. They give the heart and liver to the biggest birds. But you know, they're real good – the birds, I mean. Good, kinda like well-trained dogs. They just sit there 'til they're told to move. It is really something!"

"Oh God!" Mo said covering her mouth, almost gagging.

"Then they strip off the skin, cut the meat off the bones in hunks and put the hunks in baskets that they dump on a platform. They know just what they're doing," he said earnestly. "And I kid you not, the birds don't do nothing 'til they're told to. They just sit and wait. Then they eat every lasting bit, except some of the bone. After, men come along and crush the bone up and burn it on a little fire.

"We saw it – Rodney and me did – and he got some real good pictures of them doing it too. Boy did that make 'em mad – him taking pictures and all. That Rodney, he takes pictures of just about everything. One day he's gonna make a movie, just you watch. You know, they didn't pay us any attention 'til he took out that camera. Then they started yelling and waving their arms, and when Rodney didn't quit they come running and throwing bloody hunks of meat at us."

"Did you get hit?" Hamilton asked.

"I didn't, but Rodney, he got it right behind the left ear."

Starman said that this was the most disgusting story he had ever heard.

"Well, see you around, Rusty. Have a good time. We gotta go see a man about a dog," Andy said

The clerk agreed that they could leave their bags next to the desk while they decide what to do. The four of them sat down in chairs near the man-made jungle in the hotel lobby. Mo said that if they could not find a place to stay then she would be perfectly happy snoozing in the lobby of the White Swan Hotel, adding that this would allow them to get an early start in the morning.

"Start to where?" Andy asked.

"Upriver to Guilin – the place where they have those strange mountains. You were the one who told us about them. You read about them in that book," Hamilton told him, annoyed with the old man's forgetfulness. It made him wonder what he would do if Andy were to have a stroke, or something worse.

The clerk came over and informed them that if they did not mind staying in a new part of the hotel that was not yet fully furnished then he could let them have two rooms for the price of one. They would have to wait until later that night in order for him to have the rooms ready. After they agreed to take the rooms, the clerk told them that he could even sell them tickets for the boat to Guilin and he suggested a restaurant owned by a friend where they could go for a good, reasonably priced meal. He drew them a map that would take them to the restaurant and stacked their bags behind the counter. They thanked him, letting him know that they meant it. Andy tried to tip him, but he refused.

"Do you suppose that awful story about Tibet is true?" Mo asked as they walked along the river, following the directions on the map the clerk had made for them.

"Well, the book that I read about China – the one I got in Kowloon – didn't say anything about it. Sounds like a crock, if you ask me. And Tibet is not really a part of China, not culturally anyway," Andy said, backing up his statement with statistics.

Hamilton thought Andy sounded as if he were reading directly from his book. So much for his worry that Andy might be losing his marbles, Hamilton thought, now his memory is like a Xerox machine.

"Bet it's quite a place. Wouldn't mind going there," Andy concluded.

The city was lit dimly and all was a dirty glow through the moist air. They strolled beside a low, crumbling wall that ridged the bank and were met by many people who appeared not to notice them. They entered the restaurant at the conjunction of the Pearl and Xi rivers on the water's edge, near the gentle arch of an ancient span.

After they had been seated, Hamilton noticed a monkey sitting on a platform in a back corner of the restaurant. The animal picked at its fur and paid them no attention. The waiter at their table noticed that Hamilton was looking at the animal. He went over to the platform and took the long chain that was attached to the monkey's collar and gave it a sharp jerk. The monkey stood and looked at them, its eyes bulging and mouth gaping. Then it turned around, sat back down and resumed its business of picking nits.

"Oh, look. The poor thing," Mo said, sadly.

One of the waiters was bent over and slapping his thighs while laughing at the spectacle. Mo stood up and glared directly at him. When he sheepishly disappeared into the kitchen, Mo sat back down. Another waiter appeared at their table with a pad of paper and a pencil ready to write. His look was both quizzical and ironic, as he knew what he was supposed to do despite the fact that he did not know what to say. The waiter smiled – at first, nervously – but everyone in their party looked at him and then looked at each other and laughed, the waiter laughed too. It was a polite, measured laugh. Without a common language to communicate, the waiter simply ordered for them. The food did not look like any Chinese food that they had ever seen before, but it tasted good. There was rice and greens, which were served with some kind of curry sauce.

Everyone was relaxed. Starman joked about what the man named Rusty said about him in the bar. Andy, since being reminded of their trip up the Li River, talked about it with excitement and authority. Hamilton and Mo overflowed with love for each other. Although Mo was not due until September, they really did feel the baby move the night before. Mo told Andy and Starman about this, and Starman asked them about a name.

"Who knows," Mo laughed, "we might even name him after you. Right Hammy, darling?"

"Well, for all the black people named after white people, I think it only fair," Starman said, smiling.

"Yeah, call him Bushwhacker," Andy added.

"Don't you dare!" Starman implored them with mock solemnity. "I bet it will be a girl."

"Not a chance. I wouldn't mind, but not a chance," Hamilton replied.

"He's right," Mo agreed, but she did not explain.

Mo looked across at Hamilton, reached under the table and took his hand. She smiled and sipped her green tea.

"Where in hell is Kansas City, anyway? Look, I'm serious. I don't know. I'm Canadian."

"Well," answered Andy as he exhaled a puff of blue smoke, "Kansas is in the middle of nowhere, and Kansas City is in the middle of the middle of nowhere. It's not even in Kansas. Not most of it anyway. It's in Missouri. It's neither east nor west, neither north nor south, or maybe you'd say it's all of them blended together. So Kansas City is nowhere, but it's nowhere because it's everywhere. Just like in the movie, you go to Kansas to get to Oz."

"Yes, the yellow brick road," Mo said.

"Yes, my dear," Andy replied, adding, "So, now you know Ham."

The old bastard was calling me "Ham" on a regular basis, Hamilton thought. Nobody but his father had ever done that. It bothered him, yet he liked it. And it bothered him because he liked it. Well, he had known Andy just about as long as he could remember. And yes, Hamilton had now known Andy longer than he had known his own father. In fact, he knew Andy better too. Fair enough. Fine, he thought, the ole commie redneck can call me whatever he liked.

"See. There he is! Ain't he as big as I said!"

It was Rusty. With him was another man. They walked over to the table.

"This here's my buddy Rodney. He's the one I was telling you about – the one that's gonna make a motion picture someday."

Rodney was neither tall nor short, in his early forties and in shape. His black, down jacket was unzipped and T-shirt said "K.C.K.C." on one line and "Kansas City Karate Club" under that. His baseball cap was black, and on its bill were the gold leaves seen on military caps. The front of the hat said: "Vietnam and Damn Proud of It." His face came to a point, and his eyes were small and sharply focused. He made Hamilton think of a rodent.

"Hey. How ya'll doing? Didn't think I'd be seeing other Americans here."

He glanced at Hamilton.

"He's not an American," Starman laughed. "He's from Canada. He did not even know where Kansas was. And she's from Singapore," he said, motioning to Mo.

"Canada. Ha! Same thing. Who they think they're kidding. Still America. And I know you ain't from Singapore, I know Americans when I see 'em."

"Well, I guess in China all of us look alike," Starman laughed, trying to dissipate the tension he felt invading the room.

Rodney smirked at Starman, but did not reply.

"China's really outta sight!" Rusty said. "Ain't nothing like this back in ole K.C.! No siree. Just like the fucking movies! Oh sorry, ma'am."

"Yes, it is unusual," Starman replied dryly, in his best Tidewater accent.

"Well what the hell you expect it to look like? Fucking Africa?" Rodney said through his teeth, glaring at Starman.

Rodney followed Rusty across the room and they sat down at a table in the far corner.

"Six pee-joes," Rusty shouted to the waiter while holding up six fingers.

The waiter looked puzzled and motioned to the other waiter, who had just emerged from the kitchen.

"Hey, you heard the man. Bring us six pee-joes!" Rodney ordered, almost shouting.

"Ah, pijiu! Pijiu!" The one waiter said to the other, and they both laughed.

Their waiter brought them six-quart bottles of beer, and for awhile the men sat and quietly drank.

Starman and Andy tried to discuss the next day's departure; Hamilton and Mo said little and from time to time glanced at each other and smiled. The company that they were keeping made them all uncomfortable. Hamilton looked at his watch; it was getting late and the boat for Guilin was to leave at six in the morning. They all were ready to leave the restaurant, but when Hamilton looked around for the waiter, he was not in the room.

A loud shriek came from the back of the room. The monkey jumped from his perch and crouched on the top of a table. It showed its teeth and shrieked again.

"Did you get 'em?"

"Fuckin' eh I got 'em! Oh sorry, ma'am. Go over there and stir 'em up again."

The one called Rodney lowered the video camera and walked across the room. The monkey ran across the table and jumped back to his perch, dragging its chain behind. Then Rodney squatted beside the edge of the table and rested his forearms on its edge, steadied the camera and aimed it at the monkey.

"I figure his chain goes about to the middle of the table. This oughta be good!"

Hamilton could hear people behind him laughing nervously and speaking in hushed tones. He did not turn around to look, but since there were no other customers in the restaurant, he assumed it to be the waiter and maybe the cook.

The camera flashed. The monkey sprang. When it reached the extent of its chain, the animal was snatched backward and flung to the floor. Then it was up again, jumping to the table and retreating to its perch.

"Look at that little bastard! Man, did we get 'em going or what?" Rusty shouted.

Rusty placed his thumb over the top of his beer bottle, shook it, walked over to the monkey and sprayed beer on the cowering beast. The camera flashed. The monkey's limbs spread and it was in the air, flying toward the camera, but then, in midair, it was jerked backwards and hurled into the wall.

"Ain't this some shit?" Rusty laughed, turning his head around and looking at the four of them. "We ain't got nothing like this back in ole K.C.!" he said, as if to complement China and the monkey at the same time.

Hamilton tried to restrain himself by holding his body to the bottom of his chair with both hands. When he could no longer bring himself to listen to the taunting of the beast, he loosened his fingers and started to rise. Starman was already up. The waiter, jabbering denunciations at Rodney and Rusty, ran across the room, unhooked the chain and disappeared through the kitchen door with the monkey clinging to him like a terror-stricken child.

"Got it all!" Rodney announced to everyone, "got every goddamn bit of it."

Andy left more than enough money on the table to cover the bill and motioned for the rest of them to follow him to the door. Hamilton and Starman left reluctantly, as they were uncertain that the poor animal was safe from the game that Rusty and Rodney had imported from Kansas City.

"Not even gonna tell us 'bye'? Look at 'em. The candy asses," the one named Rodney said.

"Hey Rod, think we ought to tell 'em?"

"Tell 'em what?"

"Tell 'em that over here it grows sideways."

They both laughed as if Rusty had invented the dumb old joke.

Somebody guessed that there must have been at least five hundred people aboard the boat, but that was a claim that could not be substantiated, for the four of them were the only non-Chinese aboard and that meant they could speak only among themselves. Not being able to talk with the other passengers wasn't really a problem; they just did what they saw others doing. When they stepped aboard, they gave the woman their tickets and followed the crowd below where there was a large room with two-tiered, shelf-like beds lining the walls. Like everybody else, they walked over and picked out a bed. They choose two sets of bunk beds to share. Hamilton noticed that the bunks on either side of them had not been claimed and thought that perhaps the Chinese were being polite, allowing them excess space because they were guests, or that maybe the Chinese were shy around foreigners. It also occurred to him that they had simply been shunned.

They lay in their bunks looking out. The dawn made the buildings along the shore change from drab gray to yellow. The boat shoved off, and as the city slid past, they could see the bridge near the restaurant where they had been the night before, but no one mentioned this, for the experience at the restaurant was best forgotten. They soon left Pearl River behind and entered the Xi, traveling upstream toward the city of Wuzhou. Fisherman moved about on shore, and several long, low fishing boats came near. Their own boat's whistle blasted, and a fisherman waved to someone on the boat's bridge above them.

They went up to the deck, but soon Mo got chilly and everyone returned below to their beds – everyone except Andy, who soon appeared below, very excited.

"Ham, you won't believe this! I just saw the Virgin Mary!"

"Getting started early today, Unc?" Hamilton asked, smelling Scotch.

"Don't fool around with me, Hambone! It's Mary, that woman from the conference in Jaipur. You know the one. She's on the riverbank watching our boat. Come on. I'll prove it to you."

Finally, Andy persuaded Hamilton and Starman to go up on deck with him.

"I swear by the dog! Goddamn it! She was right there. She was there beside that big tree next to the building back there," Andy said, pointing. "And I know you won't believe this either, but that woman we saw at Birdland with the baby in that thing on her back, the one that was with that guy letting out the birds, she was with her too. She had the baby with her and all that."

Hamilton and Starman humored Andy, acting as if they believed him, but Andy knew what they were doing and told them to go to hell.

They spent the first day dozing, reading and walking on deck to breathe the clean, chilly air. Mo said that it was wonderful not knowing what was coming next. They all agreed. They had become fast friends.

The next day, Hamilton went to the upper deck. On the stern, in a secluded, sunny spot in a crevice between tarp-covered bags of rice, he plugged the battery into Mo's computer and began the forth chapter of *Jud's Story*. Starman and Mo talked quietly, played Gin Rummy and drank many cups of green tea from a great tank resting on a cart in the center of the room below. Andy spent much time on the bow of the lower deck. They all knew what Andy was up to.

Starman went for a stroll in the late afternoon and found Hamilton writing. He told Hamilton that he had seen Andy standing on the bow, shouting lines from Whitman to the crew up on the boat's bridge. When they reached the lower deck, they saw him punctuating the poet's words with the pointing finger of his raised arm.

"From pent-up aching rivers / From that of myself without which I were nothing ... And ole Walt he's the best goddamned poet since ole Billy himself. My nephew Jud, he said ole Walt was just some kinda fairy. Ah yes, he was a fairy, but the ... Ah hell, who cares?" he shouted, arms outstretched as if the bow of the boat were a stage and he were an actor delivering a Shakespearean soliloquy.

Suddenly he stopped, pulled a plastic shampoo bottle from the pocket of his tan trench coat and took a big swig. He pushed his glasses up on his nose, looked up at the amused Chinese and grinned. When he saw Hamilton and Starman, he quickly shoved the plastic bottle into his coat. They walked over to him and Hamilton argued with him. Finally, Andy allowed them to lead him below. Mo was able to talk him into eating some rice and drinking a little soup. Then Starman and Hamilton lifted Andy into his bunk, and Mo covered him with his trench coat.

"Bushwhack Jinkens, you're a good man. Ham, you are a naked chicken fucker," Andy muttered, laughing himself to sleep. He snored mightily.

They were all awakened by the bumping of the engines reversing. It bumped again, and then there was silence. They had stopped and the boat had docked. It was almost dawn. They gathered their things, but by the time they got Andy moving, the boat was almost empty. They crossed the gangplank alone, and in the near darkness they saw the crowd stealing into the dark town. Hamilton felt disoriented, for none of them had expected to get to Guilin so soon, and certainly not in the dark. Hamilton observed that somehow like ghosts, all the passengers had disappeared.

"The man at the Kowloon Athletic Club told me wrong. I'm sure he said it was a two-day trip," Andy grumbled.

They all agreed with Andy, humoring him. They walked up a street, and finally, not knowing where they were and having nowhere else to go, they sat on a low wall under the yellow glow of a street lamp. There they remained until the sun rose.

In the tan light, a solitary figure walked toward them carrying a great pack on his back. The person was a young Australian who was going in the direction from which they had come. He told them that they were not in Guilin, but in a town called Wuzhou, and that the large boats could not go further upriver on the Gui that time of year because of silting. Those passengers who wanted to go on to Guilin were supposed to continue by bus. He told them that he had arrived by barge, a slower but more pleasant way to travel. He suggested that they do the same.

By mid-morning they were on a barge. The engine of the tug knocked, turned over several times and finally caught. It maneuvered into place behind the long, rusty barge, and they were on their way up river.

The barge was loaded mostly with food – greens, cabbages, oranges – and caged animals – raccoons, cats, dogs and snakes. It was all for the best restaurants in Guilin. In the center of the barge was a bamboo hut. It had a woodstove made from an oil drum inside, and there was a long table and scattered chairs. They sat at the table and watched through the open windows as the banks passed.

The land had become steep, and the vegetation lush. It drizzled and as the day waned, the hills on either side grew into mountains, and the lushness became jungle. The air had turned sweet and warm. They were surrounded by water, mountain and misty sky. They could hear the regular knock of the tug's engine, and sometimes, when the barge made a sharp turn, they could smell the sugary diesel from the smoke that had just been behind them. The water churned up by the tug's powerful screws was red like the earth and so thick with silt that no white showed in the tug's wake. They pushed further and further upstream, slicing deeper through the mountain gorges and green jungle.

The sun finally came out. Starman took his chair out to the deck and snoozed. Mo and Hamilton sat at the table and continued their game of Gin Rummy. Andy had also moved to the deck and was sleeping on a bale of hemp.

In late afternoon, they were all served soup and rice. Hamilton bought Guilin beer for all of them except Mo, and again Andy described for them a picture he had seen in the fat book he read in Kowloon. The picture was of the landscape of the area where they were going. He told them that the mountains will look like spear points rising from the earth. He sounded excited, and Hamilton and Starman listed and asked him questions. Mo seemed distracted, even melancholy.

That night, the barefoot man who had prepared their food brought mats and quilts and spread them along the floor. He hung a great mosquito net over them. The four of them slept side by side and the next morning awakened to the sound of birds. The engine was quiet and the barge was still. It was dawn.

They were tied up to a dock. Men brought on boxes of vegetables, rolled on oil drums and took off some automobile tires. Hamilton went to the rail and looked out over the wide river at the mountains surrounding the boat. Yes, their pointed shapes appeared to have forced themselves from the earth. The river had changed to the color of mother-of-pearl. The vegetation, while still lush, was no longer jungle-like; rather, it had become a blend of cultivated green fields, woods and mossy foliage on the sides of the tooth-like mountains. The green blended into cloud where the earth reached up and touched the sky.

"My God! I've never seen anything like it. It's beautiful," Mo said, adding, "but I expected a bigger town."

"Mo, dear, this is not Guilin," Starman said. "This is a place called Hungshui, but we're close to Guilin. I reckon by my map that Guilin is maybe twenty miles away."

Hamilton thought Starman sounded a bit like Dicky, who was always addressing Mo as "dear." Andy had been doing this as well. Oh well, Hamilton said to himself, "dear" had a pleasant quaintness about it. Of course, he did not say this to anyone.

"Why don't we just stay here? No place could be more beautiful," Mo suggested, only half serious.

"You know," Starman replied, "I was just thinking the same thing. What do you think, Hamilton?"

"Okay, by me. I'll go wake Andy."

"Will he agree?" Mo asked with a little laugh, her silver earrings flashing in the rising sun.

"Has to," Hamilton smiled. "He's out numbered."

They stayed in a hotel that had once housed a regiment of Red Guards. It was now an "enterprise" that assembled bicycles, which, in consideration of the expected new tourist trade being promoted for places such as the Guilin area, they planned to rent to the tourists and sell them in the newly opened free market. The workers were all of two families, which were related to one another by many marriages. They were friendly people, yet clearly ill at ease, for few westerners had yet to visit Hungshui. The man who operated the front desk was eager to practice his English, and the rooms were clean, simple and had hot water for showers.

Their first five days in Hungshui were like spring. Unfortunately, those were the days Hamilton spent mostly indoors writing chapter four of *Jud's Story*. He apologized to Mo and the others, saying that he was "on a roll and must go with the momentum," but Hamilton realized that it was more than that, for he had been swept into the vortex of Jud's possible world – a world of memory and wonder. However, some afternoons he did go out into town or the tooth-shaped hills with the others. Every evening they ate at what had become their favorite restaurant – a little houseboat floating on the Li and tied to the town dock. They call it "Bob Something's" after the restaurant in Singapore. At night, Mo and Hamilton made love and talked of what their life together would be like. But they made no decisions; they were too happy.

# CHAPTER IV
## NIGGER LOVER

"What the hell's going on?" Uncle Andy asked, referring to the traffic on the Chattahoochee River Bridge. It was backed up for at least a mile.

"Hey, what's happening?" I asked a man who was walking back to his pickup parked behind us.

"Some crazy woman done jumped off the bridge. State troopers say when they stopped the truck she was in, she got out holding a baby. And a man and little girl, they got out too. They say she just climbed up on a sofa that is in the back of the pickup and jumped right out into the air and over that bridge – jumped over that rail while holding that little baby. The Alabama State Police done taken the man and the other little girl off in the police car. State troopers and the county sheriff, they looking for that woman and that little baby that she jumped with. They some crazy people in this here state. And they was white folks too. You boys ain't from round here. I can tell that," he said, pushing his new white Stetson back on his head.

"You're right," I answered, trying not to make him suspicious. "We're from Altamaha."

"Altamaha. Oh yeah. Over there in South Georgia. You know, they was saying something about Altamaha up there on that bridge. But I can't remember. You had any niggers come through there yet – on the bus I mean? You know them niggers that wants to ride up front where the white folks ride?"

As usual, I did the talking: "Nope, none have come through there yet. They're probably too scared."

"Yeah, maybe so, but you boys wanna know somethin'? Us folks in Alabama don't know about ya'll over in Georgia. Know what people 'round here call Atlanta?"

"Call Atlanta? What do they call Atlanta?"

"Yeah, we calls it 'Niggerlanta.' That's what we calls it. Cause all the trouble comes from over there and ..."

"Well," I stopped him, "Atlanta is a long way from Altamaha."

"You right! Ya'll just like us down there. We ain't gonna have no trouble cause we got a strong Klan, and our niggers, they know their place. Well, see you boys. Ya'll come back to Alabama now."

"Okay. Bye." I said.

As the man walked away, Uncle Andy, who had not uttered a sound, said through his teeth, "Redneck bastard. Just as soon kill you as look at you."

My uncle could not have been more right, for if that man had known where we had been and what we had been doing, we may never have crossed that bridge. Yes, Uncle Andy and I had to be careful. That was why I always did the talking. I could easily speak in such a way as to raise no suspicions, but my uncle had lived up north and in British Honduras, and for the past year he had been living in Atlanta. He was teaching there at Atlanta University, an almost exclusively Negro institution. He even had a Negro wife. Well, she was from British Honduras, but still, she was a Negro.

But mostly, Uncle Andy had a hot temper and couldn't help saying what he thought once he began talking. Nobody in Altamaha except for me and my other uncle, Durden Fowler, knew much of anything Andy had been doing. But people knew enough. Some people had a name for people like Uncle Andy. The name was "nigger lover," and the nigger lover was the most despised of all men, despised because he had turned on his own kind. To some, a nigger lover was lower than a snake.

Finally, the traffic moved and we crossed on over into Georgia and through the border city of Columbus. When we were on the open highway, I put the pedal to the floor and my red Volkswagen Beetle took us to a farm just outside the town of Americas. We had been to Opelika, Alabama, near the Georgia-Alabama state line, and we had attended a rally of the Klu Klux Klan. We had information to give to a civil rights sympathizer who owned the farm. His name was Jordan.

I don't know exactly how this man Jordan felt about all that was going on, or why he was doing what he was doing. I met him only briefly, so I will not try to guess. But I know how Uncle Andy felt. He said you had to get at the root of the problem: private ownership, or what he called "the modes of production." As he put it, "the way you make a living determines with whom you associate, and this, in turn, shapes the way you see the world." Andy said this to me many times, for he really believed you had to change the whole society, and, as he saw it, you had to get rid of private property to do it. I had never heard such ideas before and must say that I was impressed with his insight.

When things started to change down South, my uncle had moved from New York to Atlanta. I thought at the time he was just teaching there, but I later learned differently – learned that he was working with what he called the "Movement." As Uncle Andy saw it, it was through the Movement that racial segregation would be ended and society changed – changed swiftly and thoroughly.

My Uncle Durden had a different opinion. He said that what was going on in the South was the South's problem, so he thought the problem could only be solved by Southerners – Southerners both Negro and white – and that it had to be done over a generation. He felt that some of the people from the North who were going to the South with Andy's Movement, while well meaning, were, like Andy, misguided. He often said that Uncle Andy "didn't know his ass from a green blackberry." Although they once had been fast friends, as you might have guessed, my two uncles no longer got along very well.

The KKK rally had been held on the field at the Opelika baseball stadium. There were hundreds of people there, most of whom did not wear the robes and pointed hats of the Klan, but who were definitely in league with them. Before dark, there was a sort of picnic. By this I mean that the ladies of the Klan auxiliary had set up booths to raise money by selling baked goods, fried chicken and sandwiches. A concession stand was opened to sell hot dogs and Cokes, and a band played gospel and country music. The food was good, especially the chicken.

Once, a nice little lady with white, wavy hair said to us, "Land sakes, I don't believe you boys are from around here."

I told her that, indeed, we weren't and that we had come all the way from Georgia to attend the rally. Then I complimented her on her chicken and told her that her permanent looked good. When she asked Andy something, I said:

"Ma'am, he can't hear; German bomb, you know. Shell shock. He's my daddy, and I take him everywhere with me. He don't think too straight either."

She said that she was so sorry and told me that he was fortunate to have such a loyal son. She was a kind lady.

When darkness came, a great cross was lit just behind second base and the Klan marched in from behind the fence. At the front were three flags: the American one, the Confederate one and a white flag with a cross – the flag of the Klu Klux Klan. They all had torches. Uncle Andy said he hoped they would catch their robes on fire.

The procession went to the infield and their khaplin – their way of spelling "chaplin" – asked God to help them carry out their holy mission – the mission of keeping the white race pure. There was shouting and clapping and the Grand Dragon of Alabama gave a talk about how they were going to block all the bridges on the Chattahoochee River.

"This is how we gonna keep those kinda niggers from coming here to Alabama. By keeping those kind out, we not only will be doing ourselves a favor, but we'll be helping the good Darkies who live in the great state of Alabama," the man had said.

Yes, we had gone to that meeting to learn just what those people were up to. And we had found out, and this was the message we took to the Jordan farm near Americas, Georgia.

We left the Jordan farm late and didn't get to Altamaha until after midnight. I dropped Andy off at the Benjamin House. I went on home and, because I had lost my key, Uncle Durden had to get up and let me in.

The next morning, I got up early to go down to the Southern Pine Café. I knew I'd find Uncle Durden there, for he had been there almost every weekday morning since the end of World War II. Indeed, he was there talking with the usual crowd: Bud McGiverly, the dentist; Jack Vann, a farmer; and Hubert Beasley, a house painter.

We talked about the high school football team, speculated as to who would play in the World Series and commented on what the tobacco harvest had amounted to that year. They wanted to know what I had been doing with myself now that tobacco season was over, and they asked me when I was planning to go back to the University of Georgia where I was soon to become a senior. My reply to the first question was a lie, and my answer to the second was the truth. I had a great urge to tell the whole truth, to tell them just what I'd been doing, and then when they showed horror, to explain to them that they were wrong and I was doing what was right – right and just.

Then they started talking about an incident that had taken place the day before. As usual, my Uncle Durden did most of the talking. People in Altamaha liked to hear him tell things, and most people would take seriously what he said, even if they disagreed. After all, he was still senior county prosecutor and he knew more about almost anything than anybody in town. I can't sound exactly like him, but this is something like what he said:

"Three days ago – let's see, that would have been Monday – Dotty Thigpin calls my office. She said that daughter of hers, Rose, the one who was involved in the murder years ago, had just appeared out of nowhere. Now when she said 'nowhere' she meant just that. She said she hadn't seen Rose since they released her from the asylum up in Milledgeville. And she reminded me that wasn't more than six months after Collie Coots went to the electric chair. It's true; Dotty's daughter just appeared on the proverbial doorstep, holding the hand of this little girl and carrying another, who was barely old enough to walk. There was a red Ford pickup parked under the pecan tree in the front yard, and there was a man asleep at the wheel. The truck, she said, had an Alabama tag."

Now, this is the way Uncle Durden told it. He told the story as if Dotty, that girl's mother, was talking, and like Dotty had told it on the phone. He said the woman told him that her daughter just said:

"Hey, mamma. Me and Lester, we got us a problem."

And then Dotty said she told her:

"Rose, you are a walking, talking problem."

Then she asked her who Lester was. It turned out that Lester – Lester something – was none other than the man sleeping in the truck.

"We waited there under the tree 'til you woke up. Didn't want to bother you. Then we saw you come in the kitchen and make coffee," Rose said to her mother.

"What kinda trouble you in, Rose?" her mother asked her.

"Well, we had our baby die on us, and I didn't know what else to do. And we got the baby in the cooler and ..."

"You got what?" Dotty said.

Disorderly Notions

As it turned out, there in the back of the truck, along with a liver-spotted bird dog, was the dead baby that they had brought all the way from Alabama. They had put the baby in a plastic garbage bag and had iced it down in a rusty, old Igloo cooler that Lester used for fishing. Rose explained to her mother that the baby had died and that they didn't have money for a proper burial. If they had gone to the welfare people, she said, they would have taken her children away again.

"Rose, you want some coffee?" Dotty said.

"Yes, mamma, I do want some coffee," Rose said.

Then Dotty grabbed the little girl's hand and said to Rose:

"Rose, go wake that son of a bitch in the truck."

Dotty didn't know the little girl from Adam's house cat. In fact, she had never laid eyes on either of her grandchildren. The truth was, she had never even heard of them.

Dotty called Billy Strickland to arrange for a proper funeral, but Strick – as everybody called him – told her that no undertaker would even consider performing a burial without a death certificate and that either they go and get one or they could just drive on down to Great Alligator Swamp and bury the baby themselves in the Altamaha River.

"You know how ole Billy Strickland gets sometimes," my uncle said.

I guess he was referring to ole Strick's temper.

That's when Dotty called Uncle Durden and he made the arrangements to have the baby taken around to the hospital. Sure enough, when they got back to my uncle's office, he looked at the death certificate and the coroner's report showed that Rose wasn't lying. It said: "Cause of death: rat poison." So he called up the funeral home. Strick said to tell them to go ahead and bring the body over there. Uncle Durden told him that he'll send him a notarized copy of the death certificate.

My Uncle Durden went on:

"Well, Dotty musta got to feeling real bad for her daughter. Somebody said they saw Rose with her mother down at Coots Department Store and that poor Rose was as ugly as homemade sin. She looked like she had not eaten for about a year, and those two raggedy younguns looked even worse. The smallest one was said to be two, but wasn't even housebroken yet. Sad bunch, they were."

Well, that's how my uncle put it. Granted, it's not exactly right, but it's close enough. When he went on to tell the rest of the story, he said something like this:

"Yesterday I get this call from Billy Strickland, who was mad as hell. He asked me if I know where my client is and I tell him that I have lots of clients and would thank him if he would quit shouting and tell me what client he's talking about. He said he's talking about the client who stole his furniture. Finally, Strick said that he's talking about Rose Thigpin. I tell him that Rose is not my client, that I merely did her mother a favor, and did it for free – or as we lawyers say: pro bono. Thank you very much," he added.

There is no use in going into more detail about how mad ole Strick was – my uncle says everybody knows how Billy Strickland can get mad.

Here's what happened after: The baby had been laid to rest in the funeral parlor – one of the small parlors for little funerals. It used to have a statue of an angel on either side of the place where they put the coffin and, hanging on the wall behind it, a picture of Jesus raising Lazarus from the dead.

During the night, Rose and that Lester fellow went in there and took everything in the room except for the casket with their dead baby in it. I guess they figured it was a pretty even swap. Among what they took was a green velvet sofa, two chairs, a coffee table, a big, fat Bible and two lamps. But the thing that made Strick the maddest was their taking the two Plaster of Paris statues of the angels and that picture of Jesus. Dotty told my uncle that when they left her house, they also took a rifle and a bust of Elvis, and that the rifle was the one that her great-great-grandma had shot a Yankee with.

My uncle called the state patrol for Strick, and they caught them just as they were going across into Alabama. They stopped them right in the middle of the Chattahoochee River Bridge. The Georgia state patrol came up from behind and they met the Alabama county sheriff in front. It had rained that day and everything got soaking wet, including that big picture of Jesus raising Lazarus from the dead. Strick told my uncle that all of it was ruined. They couldn't find the rifle anywhere. The Georgia state patrol later said Lester finally confessed that he had swapped it for a tank of gas.

When the police met them on the Chattahoochee River Bridge, they made them get out of the pickup. Without any warning, Rose put her baby on the sofa that was sticking out over the tailgate and then she got up there herself. She picked up one of those angels and the baby, and she jumped. My uncle told us that as she sailed over the side, they heard her say that she was flying to heaven.

My uncle went on to say that the Alabama State Police took that Lester fellow to Opelika for questioning. Uncle Durden said that when he talked to the officer over there, the officer told him that Lester was about as smart as a run-over armadillo. He would do just about anything any white man told him to do. They gave the little girl to the welfare office, gassed the bird dog and impounded the truck with all of the furniture. My uncle told us that Strick said he didn't

Disorderly Notions

care about the furniture, he had plenty of theft insurance, and, besides, they could probably use the furniture over there in Alabama anyway. He did say that he was going to get that angel back if it was the last thing he ever did. They were still dragging the river for the bodies, but even if they found them, they would not find the angel, my uncle told us, because Plaster of Paris dissolves in water.

Everybody at the Southern Pine Café agreed that everybody in Altamaha had always known that the Thigpin girl was touched in the head. Nobody should have been surprised at what she did. But somebody pointed out that nobody over at the state line knows anything about her, and they are bound to make a big thing of it in Alabama.

The whole time Uncle Durden was telling this story, I wanted to tell them about how Uncle Andy and I were there on that bridge and almost saw all of it ourselves.

Later that day, I was sitting in the lobby of Uncle Durden's law office reading a *National Geographic* when Uncle Durden shot through the room.

"It's the Freedom Riders. They're at the bus station. Let's go!" Uncle Durden shouted at me.

I followed him outside, and we got in my Beetle and headed to the bus station. They were there alright, sitting at the front of the bus and looking down at the crowd of people surrounding them. The windows were closed and so was the door. The sheriff stood in front of the closed door.

"Don't know how much longer I can hold 'em back, Mister Fowler. They wanna get to them Negroes in the worst way. And there's that pickup what is blocking the bus."

There were shouts and curses. The windows of the bus were spattered with egg and spit. One man had an axe handle, another had a baseball bat. I saw another man hold an opened pocket knife up so that the Negro looking down from his window could see it.

"Edgar, don't you tell me that. 'Course you know who's truck that is. If you don't order him to move it, there's gonna be hell to pay," Uncle Durden calmly said to the sheriff.

The sheriff looked relieved. Now Uncle Durden would be blamed. The sheriff ordered the truck moved, and the bus began to slowly pull out of the station.

"You boys go home," Uncle Durden said to the crowd.

"Nigger lover," somebody grumbled as the crowd was leaving.

It was at that moment that I noticed a man taking pictures. The pictures that would appear in all of the papers the next day. One headline would read: "Altamaha County Prosecutor and Nephew Rescue Freedom Riders." I was so proud.

The next day I left for the University of Georgia up at Athens, but because Andy had lost his license for drunk driving, I had to detour through Atlanta. But I didn't care if I had to go out of my way, I'd drive Uncle Andy anywhere. On the way, he told me that my appearance in the newspaper was going to have an effect that I had not expected.

As he lit his cigarette and pushed his glasses up on his nose, he said:

"You know that your Uncle Durden will never be re-elected as county prosecutor. In fact, he's gonna have a hard time there in Altamaha from now on. Probably would have a hard time in Savannah – even in Atlanta."

"He'll never leave Altamaha," I said.

Andy laughed, saying that yes, Durden would not leave, but that he would be doing lots of deeds, wills and collections for the *Atlanta Journal* and the *Atlanta Constitution*. Except, of course, his Negro business would improve.

I dropped Uncle Andy off at his and his wife's apartment in a faculty-housing building on the Atlanta University campus, and then I drove on over to Athens. As I was driving, I worried about the uncle who had always been like a father to me. After my mother died of a stroke a few years ago, any strength and purpose I've been able to muster would not have been possible without my Uncle Durden standing behind and guiding me.

Classes were to start in a week and it was the beginning of fraternity rush. I belonged to the AKs, the Alpha Kappas, but known to all as the "Ak Aks," just like the World War II anti-aircraft gun. Despite this frivolous nickname, the AKs took themselves quite seriously. They said that their organization was not really a fraternity, but referred to it as an "order," indicating that, at least in their opinion, it was not a mere social club. Of this they never tired of reminding anyone, informing students that their order had been founded by a band of Confederate veterans who had served under Jeb Stewart in the Army of Northern Virginia. They venerated this founding as if it were some holy event, and they considered themselves to be the progeny of their founders and to have some kind of mystical covenant with them. They espoused the virtues of the Old South as they perceived them: chivalry, honor, patriotism and all that.

The Alpha Kappa house was the stateliest mansion on Fraternity Row. It was a replica of "Tara" from the movie, and it had been bought and was maintained by their always-loyal alumni. The glorious past, as they thought it to have been, mattered. Every effort was made to protect and preserve this past and its virtues and to have them recognized and venerated. A great many of the boys came from small towns, and just about all came from old southern families.

I'll admit that it was because of my family that I had been asked to join when I first arrived at the university. There had been an article in the *Atlanta Journal* and *Constitution Sunday Magazine* about the end of the War Between the States, and it was mentioned that some relatives of Judah P. Benjamin lived down in Altamaha. Somebody in AK checked with the United Daughters of the Confederacy and was told that, indeed, this was true. I guess they never found out that ole Uncle Judah was a Jew.

When I had first arrived there, it never had entered my mind that I would join a fraternity. I had planned to do only two things: to run the half-mile and to study American literature. But the AKs instructed a high jumper to recruit me, and I quickly found myself enamored with the idea of becoming a bona fide southern gentleman just like him.

Their parties were fun. Some claimed they were the best on campus. There were the proper parties and then there were the others. At the others, you never knew what you would see. Sometimes my brothers would have what they called "pig parties," to which they would invite girls that were thought to be socially unacceptable and physically less than attractive. At one party, I remember seeing a brother stir his martini with his dick. And when everyone was drunk enough, they would always start chanting, "Pig party! Pig party! Oink, oink, oink!" and the girls – usually unsuspecting freshman – would always cry, and, if possible, leave. I am sure some left with wounds that probably are not yet healed.

Then there were the proper parties, the most grand of which took place in the spring. It was called the Plantation Ball, and to this expensive affair were brought only the best girls – or as they were fancied, ladies. Those AKs who could would grow beards, and we would all dress like characters on the set of that movie. We would dance around, the girls in hoop skirts and the boys in Confederate officer's or planter's dress, and when the party was over everyone would form a great circle and sing "Dixie" in a slow and reverent way until tears streamed down our drunken faces. There was one ball where the Negro band refused to play the tune, and, finally, walked off leaving the ball without a band.

As I arrived, I pulled my little red Beetle around to the back of the fraternity house. Music was blaring from a record player. I remember it well. It was a tune by a Negro group called the Hot Nuts, and they were known by the song that was playing: "Nuts, nuts, red hot nuts. Get 'em from your peanut man..." I unloaded my stuff on the porch and went into the back door of the fraternity house. Then I stepped into the kitchen to speak to the cook, a

Negro woman who had been working there for at least twenty years.

"Juddy boy," she said, "I was hoping that somehow you wasn't coming back. Boy, you's in a heap of trouble around here."

I was absolutely flabbergasted. Nothing like this had ever occurred to me. I stood there looking at the terror wiped across her black face. It was fear and also shame – shame for her because she worked there and fear for me because she hated me for suddenly making her life confused and fearful, too. She was warning me and, at the same time, she did not know what she must do. Both she and I knew at that moment that things would never be the same again.

They grabbed me from behind. There, on the kitchen floor, before the cook's eyes, my brothers pulled off my pants and smeared a mixture of analgesic balm and indelible, purple dog medicine all over my penis and nuts. The high jumper, whom I had called my "big brother," took a spoon and smeared the burning goo on my anus. They sang with the music: "Nuts, nuts, red hot nuts..."

Finally, I think it was when the music stopped, they quit and let me go. I stood up. I burned with embarrassment, rage and analgesic balm. I looked down at my socks and new Bass Weejun loafers. They were covered with the purple stain, as were my legs, shriveled penis and the tail of my expensive Gant shirt. The cook had fled the room, but you could hear her sobs.

"Saw you nigger lovers in the paper and on TV," the high jumper said.

They all laughed.

I ripped the fraternity pin from my shirt, placed it on the kitchen counter, picked up an iron frying pan and screamed "Chivalry, Honor and Country." I smashed the pin with the pan and dared them to come closer. Then someone must have hit me.

When I awoke, I was still naked from the waist down. My clothes, books and my old radio – all that I owned – had been thrown into my car with me. The whole left side of my face and the back of my head throbbed. I found the key in my pants on the seat beside me, started the car and, with my bottom half still naked, drove away. I was crying. I was confused.

For the longest time I did not stop. Just after I crossed over into South Carolina, I went down a country road, pulled over and put on my pants. I will never forget how I felt as I stood on that dirt road in the rain. It was a feeling I had never felt before. I felt hopelessness. And on that road I realized that I had died, or at least part of me had. I do not know why I did it, but I continued to drive north, stopping only to relieve myself and to gas the car. I drove all the way to Canada.

I had never been to Canada before. When I crossed the border at Niagara Falls, I stopped and called my cousin Hamilton West. He told me how to get to Toronto and to his apartment near the university.

When I got to Toronto, I got lost and Hamilton had to come on the subway to find me. I had never been in a city that large. I had never ridden a subway. But I was lost in more ways than this.

I told Hamilton what had happened and showed him the purple stains. I guess my confusion bordered on hysteria, but I was tired and I was desperate. I think Hamilton could understand some of what I was feeling. He had spent much time in Altamaha and knew something of the mysteries of that world. I talked with my younger cousin for hours and learned that the three years between us now seemed to make less difference. We talked until it had grown dark, and Hamilton, who played on the freshman hockey team, had to leave for practice.

After about a week in Toronto, Hamilton persuaded me to call Uncle Durden and Uncle Andy and tell them what had happened and where I was. I am sure Hamilton had been urged to do this, for I know he had called Cumberland House. I know Aunt Becky had told him to try to get me to call Georgia. I think Hamilton had probably felt disloyal to me for his interfering.

When I called Durden, he didn't act surprised, but then, nothing ever surprises Uncle Durden. He told me to stay as long as I wanted and that he would send me a hundred dollars. If Durden had known what I had done with Uncle Andy over in Alabama, he would have been mad with me, so I said nothing about it. Until this day he has no idea that I almost saw that woman jump off the Chattahoochee River Bridge with her baby and that angel.

When I called Andy in Atlanta, he was delighted with my story about what had happened at the fraternity house. He had told me many times how disappointed he was with me for associating with people who he said were just upper-class Klansman. He said he couldn't help me if I needed money because he didn't have any, but he gave me a list of names of people in Toronto and told me to call them.

I made one call to a woman named Miriam Underfelt, who told me, much to my surprise, that she had been Andy's second wife for a brief time. She also informed me that she, along with the other people whose names were on the list, belonged to a group called "The League of International Socialists (Marxist-Leninist)." I never called her again and conveniently lost the list. Even considering the things Andy had told me during our trip to Alabama, I still found it hard to believe that Uncle Andy was really one of those people.

Before Andy hung up, he told me that the Jordan farm had had its barn and silo shot up with .50 caliber machine guns. The papers said that the local unit of the National Guard was suspected. Andy said big things were planned for Alabama – big events, like marches. When I later learned about my uncle's friends, I was glad to be in Canada and not in Georgia near my uncle who had always had a special hold on me.

Money was a problem. While I could stay on the sofa in Hamilton's apartment for a while, a mere hundred dollars would not last me long. I could only work illegally, which was a big surprise to me. Americans are often astounded when they find that national borders actually pertain to them. I also learned that my Beetle could not be sold in Canada, and if I wanted to sell it, I would have to take it back to the States. So I did. Hambone – Hamilton's nickname since we were kids – and I drove down to Buffalo and I sold it to a sleazy used-car dealer for half its worth. We took the bus back to Toronto. That night we had a big party to celebrate my new fortune.

There was another problem: It would be just a matter of weeks before the university notified my local draft board that I was no longer a student. Only days later, they would draft me, if they could find me. If they couldn't find me, they would issue a warrant for my arrest. After all, just a few years before, all of the highways in Georgia had been full with a convoys going to Florida for what looked like the invasion of Cuba. And now, things were hot in Southeast Asia. Let me tell you, where I come from people are very serious about defending their country, and my being a Benjamin would make no difference. In fact, because of the incident at the bus station, there would be people on the draft board who would just love to see me arrested for draft evasion.

For my first month in Toronto, I tried to have a good time and put my problems out of my mind, but it wasn't long before the little money I had began to disappear. For a couple of weeks, I sold my blood at a quasi-legal clinic down in Chinatown on Dundas Street for fifteen dollars a pint. One day, when they were extracting my life fluid, I noticed a dirty, red-nosed man on the cot beside me. The man must have felt my eyes on him, for he turned toward me and, in a voice harsh from cheap wine, told me not to go to sleep. I was puzzled and asked him why.

He laughed and said to me, as if I were crazy:

"'Cause if you go to sleep they'll keep on draining it. I know this guy they did it to. Found him in the alley the next morning. Took every last drop. Blue, he was."

I didn't believe the story, but hearing it was enough to make me end that form of enterprise. And too, because of the great drain on my last resource, I was feeling a bit peaked. Hamilton talked to one of his coaches, who knew the owner of a tavern called Brunswick House where hockey teams had been patrons forever. I got a job washing beer glasses. Because no tax was taken from my illegal wages, the money was enough to live on, and all of my food was free. It was a grand but shabby old thing. It was customary there to buy two glasses of beer at a time, and locals often got up on stage and sang, cracked old jokes or played the piano and accordion. I found the place a wonder of urban, democratic foolishness, something I had never experienced before. It still stands there on Bloor Street, and whenever it is necessary that I go to Toronto, I always return to that tattered old dive.

I liked being in Toronto with my cousin. It was different. Perhaps Canada was like the North in my country, or England, I conjectured, but since I had just passed through the former and never had been to the latter, I really had nothing to which I could compare it. But this did not matter; what did matter was that I was in a different place, with my cousin Hamilton, and being there gave me a chance to step back and catch my breath. Yet, while the world I had left behind seemed to be spinning so fast that it was going out of orbit, it never even occurred to me to stay in Canada. It was not my world.

So, after almost two months, I said farewell to my cousin and rode the train to Windsor, Ontario. It was fall and the trees were vibrant golds and reds. I had never seen the changing of autumn leaves before and, to me, they did not look real. I especially dreaded crossing the border into Detroit, because I feared that there was a warrant out for my arrest, but then nothing happened. I boarded an express bus for Atlanta, and soon we pulled into the fast lane of the I-75 and headed due south. When I awoke, Appalachian pines surrounded me.

Late that day, I, along with the bus full of Detroit Negroes, arrived at the downtown Trailways station in Atlanta. I walked up to Peachtree Street, found a phone booth and called Uncle Andy. His wife answered. When she realized that it was me who was calling, she started to cry. Andy was in the veteran's hospital; police dogs had nearly ripped off his left arm in Alabama.

I was allowed to visit Andy at the hospital the next day. He was in better shape than I had expected and felt good enough to tell me how angry he was at me for leaving Canada and coming back to face the draft.

"But you went," I protested.

"Yes," he snarled, "but I went to fight the fucking fascists. I'm still fighting them, goddamn it! So, now what are you gonna do?" he asked.

"I'm going to join up," I said. Then I added, "At least if I join up I'll have some control as to what might happen."

"I figured you would do that. No, you won't have any more control. They'll do with you whatever they want. In a few months, when you're fed up with killing for Coca-Cola, you'll realize what you've done. But then, you've always been a little slow. For you, it might take a little longer. Juddy boy, listen to me. Leave. Call Hamilton right now and tell 'em you're coming back. I'll buy you a plane ticket."

I went into a recruiting station in the post office in my uncle's neighborhood on the south side of the city.

"Bet you people have been wondering where I've been," I told the sergeant, who I think was a Puerto Rican.

He found my name on a computer print out, took my draft card that said I still was a student and drove me in his army car across town to the United States Army Induction Center. It was located in what had formally been the huge, brick Sears and Roebuck central warehouse on Ponce de Leon Avenue in downtown Atlanta.

The sergeant was very friendly, but acted as if he didn't trust me. He walked to the door with me and placed me in the hands of another sergeant. This other sergeant politely escorted me to a great room with hundreds of people sitting at tables and filling out forms. Soon I, too, was in there filling out forms and then taking tests.

After a long and boring day, I found myself on an army bus being driven to the old Briarcliff Hotel, which the U.S. government had leased as a holding station for inductees like me. They fed us mess hall food and assigned us a room shared by four people. I had three black roommates from South Carolina. No, there was no formal racial segregation in the U.S. Army. In fact, that night we all went to a bar on Auburn Avenue, in the heart of the Negro section of Atlanta, and got drunk.

"White Boy," one of them said to me as we staggered toward a bus stop, "you sho better be glad you with us."

We were up before dawn, showered, fed and ordered on a bus to the induction center by seven. There we were measured, poked, probed and stuck. That afternoon, they began some arcane procedure of segregating us into groups. I found myself to be among a small minority of white boys within a large group of Negroes. Everyone struck me as exceptionally physically fit.

Finally, they had us get dressed. While we stood in clusters of about fifty, they then made us take an oath to protect the Constitution against all enemies, foreign and domestic. After this, they herded us into a warehouse that opened into loading docks. We were told to form a line. Nobody knew what was happening. And no one dared ask.

At the top of our line were two sergeants. The one holding a bull horn wore the beret and jump boots of the Airborne. The other was from the Marine Corps – I could tell by his brownish uniform. The paratrooper was black and the marine was white. The marine walked down the line and tapped every other man on the shoulder. The fellow in front of me was tapped, as was the one behind. Then the marine walked back to the front of the line and took the bull horn from the paratrooper.

"Alright," he growled in a cracker accent, "all you men I tapped on the shoulder form another line right here and follow me to the buses. We're going to Parris Island. Stand proud, and congratulations! You have just volunteered for the United States Marine Corps."

That's strange, I thought. Aren't the Marines part of the Navy? The Navy is not drafting anyone. There were terrible groans from the instant marines and great sighs from those of us who had not been chosen to "volunteer." When the new marines had left, and after we heard their buses pull away, the black paratrooper shouted right into the face of an enormous white boy:

"What you smiling 'bout, you ugly motherfucker? We gonna bust yo white ass. You and all the rest of you honky and nigger mamma's boys gonna wish yo daddy had'a stayed outta yo mamma's drawers! Straighten up that line and get yo candy asses on them buses! I can't believe that you is the sissies they send to us to make into troopers! I'm gonna make sure that you wish you was never born!" Again, he screamed into the face of the same white boy, "I'm gonna personally throw yo prissy ass outta a chopper and you gonna be cut up by the trees, and yo guts is gonna be scattered across the swamps and the gators and the cottonmouths gonna fight the buzzards for yo white hide. Now move it out!"

And indeed, we did move it out. The buses left Atlanta and, because of what I guessed was due to road work, we took a detour west and then south, following the Chattahoochee River. At LaGrange, we crossed over into Alabama, and at Opelika, we turned southeast and crossed back over the river, back into Georgia at Columbus. As we got to the top of the bridge, I wondered if they ever found the Thigpin woman who had jumped into the Chattahoochee clutching that plaster angel and her baby. I wondered if they ever made it to heaven. But then I was embarrassed at having such thoughts – those thoughts about heaven and all.

As the sun set, our buses pulled into Sand Hill, that portion of Fort Benning where they were sending inductees who, after a special boot camp and A.I.T. (Advanced Infantry Training), would be "volunteered" into the Airborne or the Air Cavalry.

In less than two months, I had learned how to kill with my bare hands.

After having labeled the floppy and placing it into its case, Hamilton thought about something Mo had said when they had been making love the night before. In the middle of it all, she had abruptly frozen.

"Mo. What's wrong?" Hamilton had asked.

"Nothing," she sobbed.

"Nothing? Then why ..."

"I'm so happy," she said. "Hamilton you won't ever leave me, will you?"

"No. We'll always be together."

She lay perfectly still, but tense.

"Hamilton, there are things about me you don't know. And I must tell you these things."

"Look, love," Hamilton said, an edge to his voice, "it's not as if we are kids. It's not healthy to dredge up all this stuff. Nobody can or should know everything about anyone else. It is just not healthy. Nietzsche says that the healthy organism is one that can forget. That's why history ended. It ended because we remembered too much."

"I don't understand," Mo said, sobbing hard. "Do you still love me?"

"Still love you? That's absurd. Of course I still love you," he said, rolling off her and lying on his back. Then he pulled her to him, and she lay there crying on his chest.

As the next morning waned, Hamilton worried that he had been selfish by staying in the room and writing when he should have been with Mo. Yes, he should be with her that very minute. Selfish bastard, he thought. He got up from the computer. He undressed except for his briefs and shoes, wrapped a towel around his neck and walked along the balcony to the shower. He caught a look at himself in the mirror. His hair was growing out. It was a rusty red, but it had more gray in it than before.

When Hamilton had showered he spotted Mo from the balcony. She also saw him and shouted:

"I think I've had it with the exercise. I've had a fine walk, but I had to let the great Star go on by himself. I'm pooped. Andy's gone to Guilin. Bet he's out of Johnnie Walker. He said he'd meet us at Bob Something's tonight."

Andy had news that Guilin was just a large, dirty city with nothing much going for it.

"We've seen all there is worth seeing right here in Hungshui," he said.

He told them about his conversation with a very helpful fellow from the China Tourist Agency and suggested they go to Tibet.

"It will take only one day to make the arrangements. It's cheap and not too cold because it's so dry."

Andy turned and looked directly at Hamilton.

"And it's really different. Just like the man in that red cap said – it's like being on the moon."

He tried to bribe an answer out of Hamilton and Starman with the Scotch he had bought at the Friendship Store in Guilin. Hamilton and Starman gladly took the Scotch, but changed the subject.

The next day, Mo and Hamilton ambled through town. Although it was cool, damp and cloudy, many of the front doors were wide open to the street, as if to show off the order and cleanliness of their interiors. Hamilton and Mo looked on as a baby cried and a grandmother quieted it. They walked along the river and through a round hole in a masonry wall. Mo said that Andy told her the round holes in the walls are called "moon gates" and have special religious meaning and are associated with high culture and wealth. During the Cultural Revolution, the Red Guards made a great number of the round gates square.

"Tried to square the circle," Hamilton replied.

Mo thought it was a joke and laughed. Hamilton chose not to explain further.

The gate led them into a courtyard where young men played video games with names such as *Final Fantasy* and *The Legend of Zelda*. They must have come from Hong Kong or maybe they are copies, Hamilton and Mo speculated.

Mo was taking Hamilton to a place she had previously visited during Hamilton's writing binge. They walked through a bamboo thicket and up a winding trail on the mountain. They frequently had to stop to rest; Hamilton insisted, for he did not want Mo to take any chances. When they reached the top, they stood under a green and red pagoda-like roof and gazed below at the cloud-shrouded mountains rising from the earth. There were cultivated patches of new, green growth, and the gray river twisted through the hills and fields.

"What did I tell you, Hammy darling? Isn't it as beautiful as I said?" Mo asked, smiling. "Doesn't it just make you want to fly?"

When they returned to town they met Starman on the Main Street. "I have been looking for you two," he said. "Let's go to Bob's and get something to eat. Ole Andy's still in the sack."

They made their way down to the river and into the houseboat, which they found to be empty. Mo pulled out her Cantonese phrase book so that they could order; they decided on bok choy and noodle soup.

Starman and Hamilton left to go to the restroom. The public toilets were a few blocks uphill from the river, just far enough to give them time to get there and back before the soup arrived, they said. On their way back down the hill, about four town blocks above the river and restaurant, they had a clear view and could not believe what they saw.

"It's them," Starman said matter-of-factly. "It's those barbarians in the baseball caps."

"Those bastards," Hamilton said through his teeth.

The sound of explosions filled the air – rapid, chaotic reports rather like the sound of an automatic rifle firing. The men in baseball caps were setting off fire crackers on the dock in front of the restaurant. Hamilton and Starman watched them prance around, laughing. The one named Rusty slapped the other on the back, and then they went inside the restaurant. They acted as if they owned the place, Hamilton thought.

As Starman and Hamilton entered the restaurant, they saw the rodent-faced one, Rodney, sitting at their table and facing Mo. Something was going on; Hamilton could tell by the expression on Mo's face. Suddenly, Mo got up, took her bowl of hot soup and dumped it over Rodney's head. He jumped to his feet, knocking over his chair, and screamed while smacking his hands on top of his head.

"You fucking bitch! And I was going to ask you to leave them and go with us!"

Rusty came to Rodney's side, but Mo looked at him and he immediately shrunk under her glare. Then Rodney spotted Starman and Hamilton.

"Well, if it ain't the mounty and the sambo. Look what your squaw's up and done."

"You have worms on your hat," Starman said calmly, referring to the noodles absurdly adhering to Rodney's baseball cap.

"Where'd you learn to talk like that, boy? They not gonna believe me when I tell 'em I seen a coon in China? I'm just gonna have to show 'em."

Rodney moved toward the video camera that was sitting on the corner of the next table. As if he were swatting a fly, Starman swiped up Rodney's hand. Rodney screamed as he rose off his seat to the tips of his toes. For what seemed like a very long moment, Rodney appeared to be in suspended animation – almost in immaculate ascension. When Starman finally let go, he fell to his knees, holding his hand as if it were a dead bird. His face was a grimace of agony and wet tears. After a long silence, Rodney hissed:

"I'll get you, you motherfuckers. You just wait."

No one said a word until they were almost into the courtyard of their hotel. Then Hamilton spoke:

"So why did you dump your soup on the creep? What did he do?"

"He put his hand under the table and into my crotch, that's what he did!"

"We have to leave. We have to leave now," Starman said.

"Yes, the bastard's crazy. I'd like to ..." Hamilton started.

"Yes. He is crazy, and when he said that he would get us, he meant it," Mo interrupted.

"Well, I'm not worried about him," Starman replied. "It's me I'm worried about. Next time I won't just crush his hand. I won't be able to stop."

"Stop what?" Mo asked.

"Stop myself from killing the son of a bitch. Bushwhack Jinkens, remember?"

They got Andy, hired a car and left for Guilin.

# SKY LAND

They tried to explain to Andy why they had to leave so quickly, but because he had not seen what had happened in the restaurant, he did not understand. Besides, Andy and stubbornness were born twins. As far as Andy was concerned, they had made plans without consulting him and then dragged him from his nap and forced him into the car. He pouted all the way to Guilin. The rest of them did not talk much, and from time to time, Hamilton could feel Mo shudder and he would pull her tightly to him.

As they approach Guilin, Hamilton commented on how dirty and drab the city was. Mo said that even the drizzle looked filthy. Andy turned around and reminded them that he had told them so. Then he said to the driver:

"Turn there! There at the bridge, Goddamn it!"

The driver did not understand a word he said, but because he was the same man who had driven Andy to Guilin before, he understood what Andy wanted.

The driver eased the car through swarms of cyclists and eventually stopped at the curb in front of a wet, gray-tiled building. There was a lone sign written in English out front: "HAPPY CHINA TRAVEL AGENCY."

"Okay, Starman, since this trip was your idea, you pay the man and tip him good for putting up with my bad manners," Andy said.

"Whose idea?" Mo asked, anger lacing her laugh. "It is pretty obvious what you are doing. Seems it's you who has had the big idea of our going to Tibet. Is that what this is about?"

"Well, I'd have thought we might have discussed it first, but then you just snatched me out of bed before I had the chance to tell you what I had found out about going there. So yeah, this is what it's about."

Although it had been unspoken, what had happened at the Hungshui restaurant led to much interest in a drastic change of location. After doing the required paperwork and paying for their tickets, they were driven to a hotel built thirty years before by the Russians. The hotel was damp, cold and expensive. The front desk insisted that they pay in American dollars.

At nine o'clock the next morning, they were awakened and taken to the airport. They departed for Chengdu on a converted transport plane.

They were met by a car and driver at the Chengdu airport. Unable to interpret the agenda that determined what was happening to them, they rode in uncomfortable silence. The car stopped at a hospital. There they were informed by a small female interpreter wearing a surgical mask that they must undergo a physical examination.

"Yes, we must check heart pressure, lung strength and blood weight. Tibet very up. Very, very up. Bad up," she said urgently.

"She must be crazy!" Andy muttered to Hamilton, knowing that at his age and with his alcohol- and tobacco-racked body he would never pass the test.

But their going to Tibet suddenly became a quest for Andy, and just when he was beginning a tirade, Mo spoke up:

"There is no way that I'm going to be examined by a bunch of strange doctors that I can't even understand!"

Then they all began to protest.

Although the Chinese had legitimate fears that an abrupt ascent to 12,000 feet could be harmful, in the end they showed that they cared more for the four-hundred American dollars that the trip cost each of their visitors than they cared for safety. So everyone received an abbreviated exam – a blood pressure check – except Andy, who the Chinese found convenient to overlook altogether.

Later, at the airport, they almost missed their connecting flight to Lhasa. Andy had insisted on going to the Friendship Store for a large supply of Johnnie Walker, an irregularity which caused the airport police to examine everyone's bag. In the end, the authorities held the flight until the search was over.

"Guess you think we're gonna bootleg the hooch," Andy snarled at the scowling official as he stuffed several bottles of Scotch back into Andy's bag.

Remembering Andy's ill fated confrontation with the official in India, Hamilton told Andy to shut up. Andy did shut up, but told Hamilton to kiss his ass.

But it was not long before Andy's mood changed altogether. Although it was one o'clock, Andy had become naughty like an exuberant child. The plane was empty except for a knot of passengers who looked like they might be government functionaries. Andy spoke loudly, ignoring the Chinese altogether. He shouted across the aisle to Hamilton and Mo:

"Don't you just love to go to exotic places? Isn't this something? Hambone, just think what Jud would think! We are going to the top of the world! Here Ham, ole nephew, have yourself a drink."

On his way to the restroom, Hamilton met a man in the aisle and stepped aside to let him pass.

"Excuse me please," the man said in perfect, unaccented English.

The man, who was Oriental, asked Hamilton where he came from. From that – as what seemed to be man's intention – they began a conversation. Hamilton learned that the man was from Vancouver and he had been contracted by an American publishing house, in a joint venture with the Chinese, to undertake the publishing of a coffee table book on Tibet. He described himself as a photo-journalist and said that his name was "Wing."

At dawn they began to circle. The sun turned the snow on the mountains pink. When the sun rose higher, they could see that the sky was clear and blue.

As they left the airplane, Hamilton took a breath of the fresh, thin air. The silence was as pure and as profound as the air itself. On all sides, they were surrounded by mountains. There was nothing but empty space aside from the rectangular hanger at one end of the runway. The hanger looked like a lonely coffin, Hamilton thought. His eyes followed its roof line to the brown-and-white mountains and into the clear sky. There seemed to no life except for the circling birds.

Soon they were on the tarmac, standing beside the plane and waiting for their baggage. The Chinese, except for Mister Wing, huddled together ignoring the four of them. Mister Wing stood beside Hamilton, and Hamilton introduced him to the others. Because it was so dry, no one had felt the cold yet, and Mister Wing left his red parka open. Hamilton noticed the way he was dressed: jeans, heavy hiking boots, plaid-green flannel shirt and a blue, wool V-neck sweater. The clothes were North American and from the West Coast. Mister Wing told them that he had been educated at Reed College in Oregon and at the Emily Carr College of Art and Design in Vancouver. This fact was corroborated by his casual manner, which was characteristic of that part of the world.

A truck roared up to the tarmac from what appeared to be nowhere and stopped directly under the airplane. Then a door opened and men began to load the truck with boxes. They placed the baggage beside the truck, and a man motioned for the passengers to claim it. Then a dusty, green military bus rambled up. They began to follow the Chinese, who were beginning to board the bus, but a soldier ordered them to stop. Just as Starman was joking that this was all they were going to see of Tibet and that it was time for them to re-board the airplane and leave, an equally dusty, black Red Flag sedan drove up. A man in a blue Mao suit, with the buttoned military collar, hopped out. He gave a little bow, took his cigarette from his mouth and smiled.

"Allow me to introduce myself with you. I am Mister Xu. I am from the Tibetan Friendship Committee. I pleasure to be guide for you."

The five of them got into the sedan, assuming this was part their unknown itinerary. As the sedan drove off, Mister Wing asked the man who called himself Mister Xu how far it was to Lhasa.

"Lhasa two hundred kilometer," the man replied, smiling.

"That can't be right," Mister Wing muttered to Hamilton. "It's not nearly that far."

They followed the twisting gravel road. Soon they caught up with the bus, and then the truck caught up with them. They drove along together at even intervals like a troop of well-drilled soldier ants. The dust was a fine, tan powder that bellowed both in front and behind. Hamilton wondered how the drivers could see to operate the vehicles, and at such great speed.

In less than an hour, they saw Lhasa in a valley below. As they descended into the city, they could look up at the acropolis-like Potala Palace on a crest of red stone. Mister Wing told them that it was first built in the seventh century and was over one-hundred meters above Lhasa. He said that a thousand years after it was constructed, the fifth Dalai Lama, newly enthroned as the leader of Tibet, began to renovate it, along with Tibetan Buddhism. The renovation took many decades to complete.

During the night, at the guest house where they had been taken, Mo awoke from a dream. She did not know where she was. She had dreamed the dream familiar to all of us – the dream of falling. But unlike the way this happens in the dreams of most of us, Mo had dreamed she was falling up and not down. When she told Hamilton, he at first joked saying that nobody falls up, as that is both oxymoronic and physically impossible. After thinking about it he said, he considered that perhaps, in her dream, Mo had experienced the absence of an up or a down. It took Hamilton over an hour to calm her.

Andy also had a bad night. He awoke with chest pains. Starman and Mister Wing, who were sharing the large room with Andy, assured him that he was suffering the effects of the altitude and his body would gradually adjust. But the next morning, when Andy decided to stay in bed, no one argued. His color did not look good.

After their breakfast of eggs, rice and tofu with chili sauce, Mister Xu walked briskly into the dining room and found its center as if the room were a stage.

"Good Morning from the Tibetan Friendship Committee!" he proclaimed. "Today, for education, we go to a fan factory and a hydroelectric factory. For the fun, we go to Tibetan village where you will ride a pony. Tibetan cowboy!" He laughed.

On the way to the hydroelectric facility, Xu gave a long and heroic account of how, in 1951, the Chinese had liberated the Tibetans from backwardness and superstition. Then he presented them with buckets of statistics to prove that Tibet was being developed into a progressive part of China. When Hamilton asked Xu what their altitude was, Xu replied that it was 16,000 meters.

"That's impossible," Mister Wing laughed. "16,000 meters is nearly 50,000 feet! It seems like ten, perhaps twelve, thousand feet is more like it. Yes, I'm sure. I remember reading it."

Xu did not reply, but instead glared first at Mister Wing for laughing at him and then at the others for witnessing it.

The sedan turned off the main gravel road and made a steep descent into a valley. When a river came into view, Mister Wing pointed and said:

"This must be a tributary that flows into the Lhasa River. The Chinese have dammed up several of the small rivers and made a series of hydroelectric power stations. They've made an ecological mess, too."

He ignored Xu, as did they all.

There was nothing extraordinary, or even interesting, about the facility. The equipment looked new, but its design seemed old. There were about a dozen people inside the facility, and none of them looked busy. The water was backed up by a dam, and there was a perpetually frozen lake about a mile long that snaked between two brown-gray mountains near the city. Its slick surface was caused by mist that rose off the surface when it came into contact with the intense sun. The lake experienced a continual freezing, melting and re-freezing.

"That's what we call 'black ice' back in Canada," Hamilton said. "It must be the slickest surface known to man."

Xu interrupted and again began to lecture them on the proud accomplishments of the Chinese and the progress they have brought to reactionary Tibet. He began to speak louder, but the idle workers could not understand a single word Xu said, and the rest of them had stopped listening altogether. When Xu finished, Hamilton began to talk again about the frozen lake of black ice.

"Black ice can stop you dead in your tracks and make the whole world spin out of control," he said.

On their way to the fan factory, Mo asked if the others found it strange that fans were manufactured in a cold place like Tibet, where there was absolutely no use for them.

Angrily, Xu interrupted:

"This is the second largest fan factory in all of China! There we make 500 fans a day. 500,000 each year."

"Yes, Xu, that is exactly what she means. Isn't it strange to make fans here and to make so many of them?" Starman added, trying to reduce the acrimony that had developed between themselves and their host; but Xu did not understand, and his resentful gaze cut into Mo.

"Xu's arithmetic is wrong again," Mister Wing said about some other "fact" Xu stated as they left the factory and got into the sedan.

Xu barked an order at the driver and they left. For the next half hour they talked about Mister Wing's days in Oregon and how Vancouver was becoming an Oriental city. Mister Wing had many questions for Mo about Singapore, Starman about America and Hamilton about life in Canada's heartland. Silently, Xu smoldered.

By the time they reached the village, they were tired. Hamilton's watch flashed eight o'clock, but it was really just after midday. In Tibet, as well as in all of China, time is the same as that of Beijing. They left the sedan and followed Mister Xu down a trail beside a dry creek bed. The brown landscape was treeless, the sky bright blue and the air thin. Mo felt faint, forcing them to stop twice. Her morning sickness did not always come in the morning. Hamilton worried about her overtaxing her strength in the rarefied air.

The village consisted of a dozen square tents of felt and leather. Hamilton speculated whether the scene had been staged just for their visit. A row of chairs on a bed of rugs formed a line in front of the tents. The chairs faced a flat, grayish steppe surrounded by the snow-topped mountains. They were seated by a woman in a red dress and a beaded necklace; silver and turquoise dangled from her ears. Capes of rich fur draped the shoulders of the men, and they wore red boots with turned-up toes. The woman brought a bowl of scalding liquid and ladled it into cups.

"This is beer, believe it or not," Mister Wing told them. "It's made from yak butter. I've read that it's not bad."

He looked at Mo, who was wincing, and laughed.

"Try it," he said. "It'll warm you up."

Yaks appeared from behind the tents, and on their furry backs were brightly colored blankets and black saddles from which tinkled hanging bells. The riders, who also wore those embroidered felt boots with turned-up toes, descended from their yaks and for a few moments vanished into a tent while their yaks stood by passively. The animals were black and white. They reminded Hamilton of the hybrid Holstein cows that his father had crossed with wood bison. Yes, these yaks were about the size of the North American buffalo. Then, bowls of food appeared on the table, accompanied by the sounds of gongs and cymbals. The riders galloped off as fast as their lumbering yaks could go, which was fast if one takes the size and the anatomy of the animals into account.

There were pickled eggs, yogurt and mutton boiled with hunks of fat on the table. There was also tsampa, the staple food of the Tibetans, which consisted of grains, mostly barley, mixed with butter and tea. Both Mo and Starman gagged. Mister Wing ignored the food altogether. While trying to get Mister Wing to tell him more about the mysteries of Tibet, Hamilton ate with abandon.

According to a letter that Mister Wing had received back in Vancouver from the China Tibet Tourism Bureau, the next day was supposed to consist of a visit to the Potala Palace. He guessed, and the others agreed, that all of them probably would be doing the same thing. Mister Wing, who had only two weeks to make his photographs, told them that he would refuse to complete his project if they did not get another guide. He said that if Xu appeared the next day, he would speak to the proper authorities at the Tibetan Friendship Committee. He told them that it would be impossible to complete his assignment if things did not change, and change quickly. Hamilton noted that he had not yet seen Mister Wing take his camera out of its case.

By the evening they were all exhausted. When they got back to the guest house, they found Andy alternately drinking Scotch and taking oxygen that had been made available in three large canvas bags in each bedroom.

"At this altitude it doesn't take much Scotch. Look at the money saved," Andy laughed, adding, "and beside that, by itself oxygen is so bland you don't notice it, but mixed with Scotch, man, it's supercharged."

No one thought he was funny.

After Andy passed out and Mo and Mister Wing had gone to bed, Hamilton and Starman went out for a walk. As they walked along, looking at the palace perched on its hill and frozen in the moonlight, Starman asked Hamilton if they should be concerned about Andy. Hamilton replied that worrying about Andy was a waste of time, for Andy had always done what he wanted to do and he would not listen to anyone. Starman then asked Hamilton when he was going to let him read the book he was writing. Hamilton told him that no one could read it until his cousin Jud had read it. He was not nearly finished it, anyway.

"I'm sorry. It was presumptuous of me. My curiosity got the better of me, and I have absolutely nothing to read. Mo and I were talking about it today – about not having anything to read," Starman said.

"Starman tells lies," Mo said the next morning. "He lies about himself all the time. He denies who he is. He tries to hide it even from himself. Don't tell him I said so."

"No, I would not even think of doing that. But really, what a surprise, I never thought I'd hear you say anything against Starman," Hamilton said with a mix of teasing and earnestness. "I thought you were great friends."

"Oh, we are. Hammy, this is nothing against him. It's just an observation. He almost never talks about himself and when he does, I just sense that he might be lying. He denies who he is and where he came from. He always looks at the world through a squint. Come on darling, we all know that."

"Well, if you ask me, I'd say that Starman is a gentleman – a self-made gentleman, but a gentleman nonetheless. To me, that's the truth about Starman."

"Well, with that I can't argue. He is a gentleman."

"Yes, but there are gentleman made and gentleman who make themselves. I get your point, Mo."

"Morning, Miss Pangolin, did you sleep well?" Andy asked.

"Yes," she laughed, "as a matter of fact, I did. I dreamed a great weight had been taken off my shoulders and I was soaring above the mountains and into the clear air. Of course, you did that last night. We all saw you."

Everyone laughed.

"You must be one of those ancient Tibetan witches," Mister Wing said to Mo, smiling. "It is said that witches and shamans can fly. Their souls become released from their bodies and soar from place to place, and even from time to time. Flying is how they get around, or so it is said."

"Andy is one of those shamans," Mo said, laughing and looking at Andy, "He flies most every day. He's usually aloft by mid-afternoon."

"You better believe it," Andy laughed, "but my problem always comes the next morning, like right now, when I realize I've crashed and now I'll have the Devil of a time taking off again."

Then Xu appeared.

"Did I hear someone speak of the devil?" Mister Wing asked, looking up at the guide. "Where to today, oh wise one?"

"We go to the Potala Palace for you to see for yourselves decadence of the Dalai Lamas and monks during reign of superstition and exploitation," Xu answered with deep conviction as he stood over the table, meeting their eyes earnestly.

"Perhaps he'll tell us what they did with all those superstitious monks," Mister Wing said.

Xu did not appear to understand.

Hamilton, Mo and Starman squeezed into the back of the Red Flag sedan. Andy sat up front with the driver and Xu. When they were out of the jumble of streets and on a straight road, they could see the palace looming ahead. It dominated Lhasa like a great, white tyrant sprawled upon the red hill. They turned back again into twisting streets, and the eyes of every Tibetan they passed fell upon them. Finally, they could see the palace again, and the driver stopped the car at the base of the hill. They got out of the car and followed Xu to a winding path. They began their ascent.

After about ten minutes of slow but steady walking and two stops to accommodate Andy, they came upon stone steps. When they climbed no more than fifty of these steps, they had reached a great, flat rock that served as a resting place and overlook. From there the steps forked off into two paths.

"Perhaps the Chinese were right. Maybe we should have let them examine Andy. Look at him," Mo said, nodding downward.

Andy had stopped about a third of the way up and was panting and holding his chest. He was bleeding from his nose.

"I'm going back with him. He can't do this. He'll have a heart attack," Mo said.

"Yes, it's the altitude. The nose bleed is common. Why don't you get Xu to go with you? He can talk to the driver and tell him to take you back to the guesthouse," Mister Wing suggested.

"No. That's not necessary. I'll just say 'fandan' to him and he'll understand. Besides, you guys can't get off that easy. You don't want to disappoint Xu," Mo said, trying to make light of what she thought could develop into a grave situation.

Now she had to steel herself for arguing with Andy; she needed to argue just enough for him to save face.

"We now go!" Xu said without discussion, and he started up the path leading to the right.

Xu looked back at Starman, Hamilton and Mister Wing, who were watching Mo and Andy descend the steps and ignoring Xu.

"We now go," Xu repeated, but louder this time.

Mister Wing barked something at Xu in Chinese, and Xu reacted as if he had just had cold water thrown in his face. He turned and hurried away, vanishing as the path turned.

"What did you say to him?" Starman asked.

"Oh, nothing much. I just let him know that I knew who he was – an ignorant peasant – and that we had no interest in following him anywhere. Now he knows who's really the boss."

"So what will happen if we take the other path?" Starman asked.

"I don't know. Probably nothing," Mister Wing said, smiling.

"And where will we end up?" Starman asked.

"Who knows, but who cares? Let's do it," Hamilton answered.

Both paths clung to the side of the hill and were bordered by low stone walls. After they had walked along for several minutes, they could see that the farther they went, the more crumbly the wall became. Finally, at an outcropping of rock that jutted into the sky, the path widened. Where it continued around the side of the hill, there was no wall at all.

"God! What's that smell?" Starman winced, covering his mouth and nose with his hands.

At the back of an open area and into the side of the mountain, was a cave. Like all caves, it was dark, but the sun was bright enough that they could see some distance into its mouth.

"Shit," Hamilton gagged.

"Yes, I see what you're saying. Ah, what you're smelling, I mean," Mister Wing replied, his mouth and nose muffled into the sleeve of his parka. "Oh yes, human excrement. It's a shit cave. Must be the place where the waste from the palace ends up. Let's get out of here!"

Once they took the path around the hill, they were no longer affected by the smell. They stopped and gasped the thin, clean air.

"Look!" Starman said, pointing down into the city. "Look, the black sedan. There they go – Mo and Andy. It was so good of her to do that."

"That's Mo. That's just the way she is," Hamilton said.

For a time, they stood there and watched the car. After it had vanished from their sight, they proceeded along the path, which had become steeper and narrower. All three of them had unzipped their jackets, for the bright sun had heated the stone face of the hill.

At a ragged set of steps, they stopped and looked out through the clear sky at the snow-capped mountains.

"Good God! Look at that!" Starman said.

"Beautiful, eh?" Hamilton replied, thinking how he wished Mo could see what he was seeing.

At the top of the steps they found themselves behind the palace, and while looking for a way inside, they came upon a man with a shaved head. He was leading a yak pulling a cart laden with a great, clay pot. Thinking they might follow him, they stopped to wait for him to finish what he was doing. He lead the yak over to what looked like a well or cistern, and after backing the cart over its edge, he pulled a handle and the contents of the pot surged and sloshed into the well.

"That clay pot is full of excrement!" Mister Wing told them. "That hole must lead to the cave."

They backed farther away. From a good distance, they followed the man and his cart along a path and under an arch. The man stopped the yak at some steps, glanced back at them and vanished into a darkened doorway. Hamilton lead the way up the steps and then through a narrow alley that made him think of a medieval bazaar without people. High up they could see bright sunlight. Soon the passage became wider, and above them loomed the walls of the white palace. Finally, they saw its flat, sprawling top. When the twisting alley completely straightened and became a wide street, they saw Chinese-styled roofs of other buildings. The roof tiles were covered with gold. Suddenly, they were in the midst of crowds of people gathered in a wide courtyard.

The space was surrounded by red buildings with windows and balconies encrusted in gold. Many of the people wore wide-brimmed hats – Mister Wing said were pilgrims – and there was the odd monk in a saffron robe and with shaved head. They all ambled about, lazily talking.

"Must be the courtyard where the Dalai Lama made his pronouncements," Mister Wing told them. "I've seen pictures of all of this."

For the first time, Mister Wing took his camera from his bag and snapped pictures. It was soon apparent that the pilgrims did not like what he was doing. An old woman came over to him and shook her finger in his face, at which time he returned his camera to his bag.

"Well, I don't know how anybody would be able to shoot here," he said, shrugging his shoulders.

Mister Wing tried to orient them by what he could remember from his research, but in the end, they just wandered about. They entered a gate that passed into a dark hall, which opened into a room where people lay prostrate before altars and bumped their heads on the floor.

Soon, they found themselves in a better lit room that Mister Wing identified as the Great West Hall. It had become apparent that Mister Wing had finally figured out where they were. He seemed delighted with his new role as guide, and with humor and authority he answered every question Starman and Hamilton asked.

"Most of the Dalai Lamas are buried in those stupa-tombs," Mister Wing told them. "Well, they're not buried really; they're salted and dried in a lotus position and then encased in a special alloy – a kind of metal powder that is a mixture of gold and bronze."

They followed Mister Wing down a corridor. As they walked, he told them about everything along the way:

"Now we'll go to the Dalai Lama's bed chamber, provided we can find it."

Mister Wing learned from an official that the bed chamber was under renovation and not open for visitors, but he was told that they could go to the Dali Lama's summer palace and was given directions. But Mister Wing thought it was a good idea for them to return to their guesthouse, check on Andy. He proposed that they visit the summer palace in the afternoon. Hamilton liked this proposal, for he hoped that Mo would want to come along.

They followed the road that the official told Mister Wing would lead back to town. Along the way, they spotted a gray stone building.

"It's a monastery," Mister Wing said. "Look there, there on the side of that mountain."

Starman took off his glasses, cleaned them on his sleeve and replaced them on his nose. Shading his eyes and squinting, he looked in the distance.

"There, Starman. Where those birds are circling," Mister Wing said. "Do you see it, Hamilton?"

Hamilton answered that yes, he did see it.

"That frozen lake is the one we saw from the mountain where the fan factory is," Mister Wing said.

When the three of them arrived at their guesthouse, they found Andy sitting in the lounge looking at the pictures in a Chinese magazine. His color was better. They told him what they had seen at the Potala Palace and their plans were to go to the summer palace in the afternoon. They had been told it was an easy excursion. Andy assured them that he was feeling fine and said that he wanted to go along. Andy told them that Mo was in the bedroom. She had said that she was tired.

When Hamilton opened the door and crept in, he could see in the bars of light from the shutters that Mo was curled up in the bed. He noticed that there was a floppy lying beside the laptop. She had been reading "Nigger Lover," chapter four of *Jud's Story*. Hamilton was angry; she had no right to read the story. He started to wake her, but then changed his mind and left the room. You did leave it lying out on top of the metal box, he told himself, and she had had nothing else to read. Don't be such a bastard, he scolded himself, ashamed.

"She's asleep. She didn't sleep well last night. We'll go without her," Hamilton said to the group when he returned to the lounge.

Mister Wing had been right when he said that the Chinese had falsified the map, but eventually they got there. The Dalai Lama's summer palace was on the edge of town, but it was only about a mile from their guesthouse. The area around the summer palace was a mess, for the Chinese had littered the place with oil drums, construction materials and piles of rubble.

"Guess this tells us how much respect they have for the place," Mister Wing said.

They went through a white gate with a tiled roof. On either side were porcelain lions, which were white like the gate, but adorned with bright colors –

red, gold and green – wonderfully ordered. Coming from the disordered outside was like crossing over from one world into another.

The summer palace did not look a like palace or temple, for it was built to human scale and stood only two stories high. The doorways were carved and painted. No one was around. They walked across the courtyard and entered the house. Mister Wing led them down a hall, and then they stood at the entrance to the Dalai Lama's bedroom. A red velvet cord stretched across the entrance, but they could see inside. Upon Mister Wing's suggestion, they stepped over the cord and entered the room.

There was a late-1940s or early-1950s Philips radio and record player in a huge wooden console. Hamilton looked down at the record on the turntable: "Buddhist prayers, manufactured in India. 1953." On the console, beside the turntable, was another record: "The Ink Spots." It was from the same year and made in the United States. There was an electric fan and an iron bed. Yes, the Dalai Lama, an exceptional human being, alas, was but a man. This, it seemed clear, was the very point the Chinese were trying to make in their displaying the most intimate part of his private environment. Like all men, he was incomplete, and this was illustrated by the commonness of his private quarters. But what is the private, if not the mundane, Hamilton thought. And though the Dalai Lama is a man, he pretended to be no more. The Chinese missed the point.

"The simple dignity of this place brings shame to those who would have revenge on the Dalai Lama," Mister Wing said quietly.

"Yeah, but whatever shame is left in the Orient we'll help them get rid of. Our guilt is the cure for their shame," Hamilton said, looking at Mister Wing.

"Yes," Mister Wing laughed, "the West has a surplus of that."

"You sure shamed Xu," Andy said to Mister Wing. "Starman told me what you said."

"Why were you so reluctant to speak to him in Chinese; except, of course, when you wished to insult him?" Starman asked.

"Xu is a barbarian – a mere peasant. It's he who doesn't speak Chinese."

"You mean he doesn't speak Mandarin?" Andy asked.

"True; but moreover, Xu is a Puritan from a vanishing ersatz China, which is bound to be lost in, and shamed by, what is to come."

"Ersatz China?" Starman asked.

"By that I mean the communist one. And don't expect the real China, the one before communism, to return. I suspect the new one will look a lot like us," Mister Wing replied.

It was dark when they returned to the guesthouse. Hamilton was surprised not to see Mo sitting in the lounge. When he went to look for her, he found their bedroom door ajar. As he pushed it open, even before he switched on the light, he sensed that something was wrong.

"Mo," he whispered, his voice cracking.

One of the beds was partially stripped of its covers, and the floppy for "Nigger Lover" was on the dresser beside the laptop. The contents of Hamilton's shaving kit and Mo's cosmetic bag were both scattered on the dresser. On the mirror above the dresser was a childish scrawl in red lipstick. The smeared words read: "RAT MAN." As Hamilton walked over to the wall, his foot bumped a glass on the floor. He picked it up and smelled it: Scotch.

Panicked, Hamilton hurried into the dining room and told the others what he had seen. Andy told him that he had just discovered that a bottle of his Johnnie Walker was missing.

Mister Wing went into the kitchen to see if the housekeeper knew anything about where Mo had gone or what had happened. He soon returned to the dining room and told them what the housekeeper had said:

"She told me that Mo had been acting strangely. She was wrapped in bed covers and holding a large bottle. She said that Mo had talked to Xu, and she thinks that Mo might have gone to find some ... 'rat man.'"

"Rat man! Who the hell is that?" Andy asked, looking at Hamilton.

Hamilton replied that he had no idea, but that she had scrawled the word on their mirror.

"There is more," Mister Wing said. "If I understood her correctly, the housekeeper told me that Xu told Mo that maybe this rat man, or whoever, was at the Potala Palace. She thinks that Mo has gone there to look for him. She was still wrapped in a blanket and carrying a bottle."

"My Scotch!" Andy said, blaming himself.

"Yes, one would assume. And guess what? The housekeeper is Xu's wife," Mister Wing replied.

Mister Wing returned to the kitchen to find out from the housekeeper where Xu went. Reluctantly, the housekeeper went to get him. When Xu appeared in the kitchen, he looked at Mister Wing. Through the open door, Hamilton could see that Xu was smiling.

"You want to know? I tell you. The lady, she drunk. I try stop her, but she want to find him. Him, he is the one," Xu pointed toward Hamilton, who was in the dining room. "She must tell him something about ... about 'rat man.' I do not know this rat person. She keep saying the flies, they come. The 'well flies.' A fly in well? And she talk about 'rat person' and 'rat man.' I do not know these people. She have so much drink. I afraid she go lost, so I get driver to take her."

"You mean you told the driver to take her to the Potala Palace?" Mister Wing shouted at him.

"Yes. I think she become lost. I ..." and then Mister Wing shouted at him in Chinese.

They got into the car. Mister Wing must have told the driver where to go and to go there quickly, for he drove fast.

"What did you tell Xu? What did you say to him in Chinese?" Andy asked.

"I told him that I was going to the Tibetan Friendship Committee, and I was going to get him fired."

"And what did he say?"

"He said that he was the Tibetan Friendship Committee."

"What do you suppose Mo means by the 'rat person'?" Starman asked Hamilton.

"I have no idea, unless she was referring to that creep back in Hungshui with the black baseball cap. He looks like a rat. Remember, we all talked about that? I've seen her like this once before. She did something like this when we were in India. She becomes somebody else. She can't drink. I don't understand the whole story, but Mo seems to have extreme moods. She takes medication for it. The medicine works just fine, but not with alcohol. God, I hope that creep from Kansas is not around here."

"No. No, that's not possible. He ain't around here. Starman fixed his ass. So, why do you reckon she took my Scotch?"

"I have no idea, Unc."

When they reached the Potala Palace, Mister Wing told the driver to wait. Andy was staying in the car and told them not to worry; he would make sure that the driver did not leave.

Everything glowed with a blue edge. The moon was almost full. Mister Wing had borrowed a flashlight from the driver, but it was not needed. He switched it off and stuffed it into his pocket. Hamilton, Starman and Mister Wing hurried along the winding path. The white palace loomed over them and soon they reached the stone steps and began to climb. When they came to the fork at the overlook, Mister Wing asked which way they should go. For whatever reason, Hamilton's instinct was to go right. Mister Wing, who was more composed than Hamilton, suggested they take the left path, for it would at least be familiar. Hamilton reluctantly agreed and started up the left path. Remembering the condition of the path, Mister Wing took the flashlight from his pocket and gave it to Hamilton. As Hamilton and Starman walked in the moonlight, they could hear no sounds except the earth crunching under their feet and their own voices calling her name.

Hamilton looked down and saw the car and the city. Above him, the snow-capped mountains were lit up by the light of the moon. Directly under him, he saw where the steps lead to the overlook and the path divided. Then they reached the cave. In the same motion, Hamilton buried his mouth and nose into his sleeve and switched on the flashlight. Mo screamed.

"Well flies! No, please! Please! Well flies!"

Hamilton flashed the beam inside the cave. The voice was not Mo's, and yet it was Mo. Just inside the mouth of the cave, she sat bundled in a sheet and blanket. She clutched an almost-empty bottle of Scotch to her breast.

"Here," Hamilton said, and gave the flashlight to Starman without taking the beam off Mo.

She wore no shoes. She was filthy. When Hamilton moved closer, she suddenly stood and the blanket and sheet fell to the ground. Mo was naked.

"No! No, please! Please, rat person! No, not the well flies. It was the rat man!"

Hamilton stepped closer.

"Mo, it's Hamilton."

She shrieked, "No! No! No! No! Please! No!"

Hamilton reached for her saying, "Mo, Mo, love."

She swung the bottle at him and it grazed his temple. He staggered and reached for her again.

"Noooo!"

Her scream sliced the air. She darted past Hamilton, ran into Starman, knocking him aside, and then quickly scrambled to the tip of the overhang. Before either of them could respond, she turned and faced them; yet, she looked right through them. She was clutching the bottle in one hand, and in the other they could see the gold rat – the rat that had been given to her in India. She brought the rat to her lips, kissed it and looked upward, smiling. Then she turned around and casually stepped off the overhang, falling into the sky.

They placed Mo's body in an empty bedroom at the guesthouse and waited for morning. Andy had tranquilizers and tried to get Hamilton to take a pill. Finally, after much argument, Hamilton took one and stopped shaking.

The next day, the officials came and Mister Wing translated. Time and time again, the officials reprimanded them for not complying with the wishes of Mister Xu. Although neither Xu nor his wife were anywhere to be seen, it was obvious that Xu had spoken with the officials.

The officials told them that arrangements were being made for them to fly with Mo's body to Beijing. From there, the people at the American Embassy could take responsibility. However, they were told that they must wait two days for a plane to arrive, and that, meanwhile, they could continue to keep Mo's body in an unheated bedroom at the guesthouse.

With tears running down his face, Hamilton bathed the filth from Mo's body and covered her with a fresh sheet. He tried to remove her ring, but her arm had been broken and twisted by the fall, making her fingers so swollen that the ring could not be removed. Hamilton sat in a chair next to her. He sat there for hours. When he finally fell asleep, Starman picked him up as if he were a child and took him down the hall to his bed.

In the early morning, Hamilton awoke to his own sobs. In his dream he had heard a voice saying:

"Who is worthy to open the book?"

He knew in his dream the rat man had spoken.

"Come and see," the voice roared, and then he heard her scream.

That day, Hamilton was in a daze from both the drugs and the shock. Although the others tried to prevent him from doing so, Hamilton spent most of the day sitting in the chair beside Mo's body.

Starman and Andy gathered up Mo's things and discovered that her purse was missing. Andy said that they must find the purse, reminding Starman that in it were most of their traveler's checks and money, for they had given them to Mo for safekeeping. They looked everywhere, but they could not find the purse.

Andy and Mister Wing looked for Xu and his wife, figuring that the housekeeper might know where it was. Mister Wing also wanted to have the pleasure of telling Xu that when he arrived in Beijing, he was going straight to the Canadian Embassy to file a complaint against the Chinese government. He wanted to see Xu squirm, but neither Xu nor his wife were ever seen again.

They had so drugged Hamilton with Andy's pills and with the last of the Scotch that night that he had to be taken to bed. At first he was unconscious, but for most of the night he dwelt in the twilight between wakefulness and sleep. In that shadowy void, the screams came again and again. Finally, he found himself sitting up in bed with Starman holding him.

"I'm alright," Hamilton told him. "I'm okay, you wondrous black star."

The screams Hamilton had heard had been his own.

Once Starman had returned to bed, Hamilton sat up, looked down and pressed the button on his watch. The illuminated pulse blipped; it would soon be dawn. Hamilton stepped out of bed, found his parka and groped down the hall through the dark. He hesitated before the door of the bedroom where Mo's body lay, but then he opened the door and felt for the light switch.

"She's gone! Mo's gone! Have I gone crazy? Oh, tell me I've gone crazy. Tell me she's not gone."

He fell to the floor and sobbed with his face in his hands. Then he crawled on hands and knees to Starman's door and soon Starman was holding him and telling him that it was okay; he had been dreaming.

Andy came, as did Mister Wing, and the three of them followed Hamilton to the unheated bedroom.

"You haven't gone crazy, Ham. God, she really is gone," Andy gasped as he stepped into the room and stood over the empty bed.

"Come on, Hamilton. Don't argue," Starman said firmly, taking him by the arm.

Andy and Starman guided him back to his bedroom and made him take another pill. Finally, he became quiet.

"It's the way the body reacts to shock. He'll sleep," Mister Wing said. Then, when he was sure Hamilton was asleep, Mister Wing looked at Starman and Andy and whispered, "Xu! He's responsible for this."

"What do you think Xu did with her?" Starman whispered.

"Sky burial," Mister Wing answered.

"God! We have to ..." Andy gasped.

"Look," Mister Wing stopped him, "you stay here and watch Hamilton. We'll see what can be done, if it's not already too late."

Starman and Mister Wing went out into the night, ran across the city, past the rubble strewn area of the summer palace and up the hill toward the gray stone monastery. The sun came up as they reached the monastery. Yes, they were too late.

Vowing never to tell Hamilton what had really happened, they returned to the guesthouse. The three of them told Hamilton that the officials had had Mo's body cremated, and then they flew to Beijing.

Mo's purse was never found, so Hamilton and Andy had to go to their embassies and request emergency funds. The day after they arrived in Beijing, Mister Wing and Starman flew on to Hong Kong. The day after that, Starman took a flight on to London and Mister Wing returned to Vancouver. Before he left, Starman wrapped his heavy arm around Hamilton's neck and, with a crack in his voice, said:

"Call me at Oxford when you return to England. You have the number."

Then he stepped back and held out a big hand. There was something bright in his palm. It was Mo's ring. Starman looked at Hamilton, eyes welling with tears, and Hamilton took it.

# CENTER OF THE WORLD

To the medieval Chinese – medieval by western standards – China was both the physical and the metaphysical center of the world. Khanbaliq, its capital, was the center of that center; and the palace of the Great Khan was the navel of the navel of the navel of the body of the world. In 1275, Marco Polo visited this imploding Chinese kingdom and wrote in his diary that the Great Khan employed five thousand astrologers and prognosticators in the palace. From the palace, these men could stand and view the world as if from the hub of the universe; their gaze into the future could radiate out in all directions. Thus Khanbaliq was both a standpoint of all standpoints and a standpoint without standpoint.

In the last year of the second last decade of the second millennium, when Hamilton and Andy were there, not only had the name of the center of the center of the world changed from Khanbaliq to Beijing, but the center of this center had moved down the street from its previous location, which is now known as the Forbidden City. Centers shift, and the new site, in this "new" time, was known as the Beijing Hotel. While the hotel had some of the finery and even pomp we associate with palaces, all the astrologers and prognosticators were gone.

For the most part, Hamilton and Andy had come to the Beijing Hotel for practical reasons. In those days, despite the fact that it was a time of economic reform, American Express had yet to open an office in Beijing. Even if there had been an office for American Express, without the numbers of the lost traveler's checks, Hamilton and Andy could not have recovered their losses. They were just about broke, but much to their good fortune, the Beijing Hotel took VISA.

In spite of himself, given his communist leanings, Andy regarded this to be a real stroke of luck. Andy was pleased because as long as they could use Hamilton's credit card, Andy didn't have to rely on an emergency fund from the American Embassy.

"You never know about them," he had told Hamilton.

If Andy went to the American Embassy to see about an emergency fund, it might end up like that time in Mexico City when he had gone in the American

Embassy to see about a medical matter. They nailed him for the taxes he had refused to pay, which were financing the Korean War. And after all, the fund was really a loan, and Andy didn't believe in credit, much less credit from the U.S. government. Better to borrow from Hamilton and cable his bank back home for money. Anyway, Hamilton said that he didn't care and that Andy could do whatever he wanted.

Hamilton, who was paralyzed by grief, didn't consider money at all. Time would have to pass before he would be able to travel again, and the Beijing Hotel was just the place to bide time and let Hamilton heal. Also, Hamilton remembered that he and Mo had learned from the secretary at Gower Roburg's office in Hong Kong that the Gibraltar Export Company had an office in Beijing. Mister Roburg was to stop there on his way back to Hong Kong.

Yes, they would have to wait for Mo's estranged husband. Hamilton insisted on it. He felt that he must deliver the terrible news in person. Hamilton intended to confide in him and tell him everything. After all, he told himself, Gower Roburg had also loved Mo once. And yes, he would even tell him about Mo being pregnant with his child. Hamilton had decided that he would answer any question Gower Roburg might ask. No, he would spare him nothing. Hamilton had even imagined their finding comfort in each other's grief.

As it turned out, no matter what one might guess, it didn't happen that way. Like most things of importance in China in those days, the office of the Gibraltar Export Company was in the Beijing Hotel. When Hamilton had first gone to the office, he was told by the pretty Chinese secretary that Mister Roburg would not arrive in Beijing for four or five days. After five days passed, Hamilton was informed that Gower Roburg had telephoned and that he had already learned of the tragedy from his Hong Kong office. They had been informed by the Chinese government. Hamilton was disappointed, but Andy was much relieved.

For a while, Hamilton continued to take Andy's tranquilizers, and some nights he would drink on top of the pills in order to sleep. Andy, being knowledgeable about such things, was worried enough to tell Hamilton that he had no more pills and flushed those that remained down the toilet.

For Hamilton, these first days in Beijing were no different from the nights. Over and over, Hamilton dreamed of the Virgin standing on the moon. But the moon was not a crescent, rather it was full. Angels were chipping away at its bloody surface with hammers and chisels, cutting the heavenly body with machetes and chain saws and banging it with jack hammers. They were hollowing out its inside and making its round surface square. Then the angels wiped away the gore and reverently polished the six sides of the moon with feather brushes and cloths of silk. Once the moon was made a metal box, the angels fed the Virgin the blue viscera from the insides of the moon's body with silver spoons. Lifting her purple robes, the Virgin stepped upon the heavenly body, and, as she gazed at the firmament, she held to her breast a golden rat. When Hamilton beheld her, he looked upon the face of his aged mother. His mother lifted up the top of the box and placed the heavens and the earth inside. Then, followed by a host of angels, she disappeared into its interior. The box-moon shined in infinite space. From its internal glow, Hamilton heard the voice of his father – God the Father – announcing in a prairie accent that history was dead.

This dream came to Hamilton at all hours and it appeared always the same. He would wake each time to a great burning on the site of the tattoo on his back. Contrary to what one might have expected of Hamilton, he never attempted to interpret the dream. He didn't even reflect upon it. Rather, when it came, he just watched in wonder and horror and, with no dread and in absolute silence, embraced his destiny.

Then one night, after spending all day sitting at the desk in their hotel room and tapping on Mo's laptop, his dream appeared less vivid and intense. When he awoke, the site of his tattoo did not burn. After a few more days, he began to note that the more he wrote, the less frequently the dream occurred. Somehow the world of *Jud's Story* provided an alternative to that other world – the world glowing in the sorrow of empty, infinite space. Maybe, he told himself, through his sojourn in the world of *Jud's Story*, he would better understand how things had come to be the way they were. What this specifically had to do with Mo and his coming to terms with her death, he did not know. Probably nothing, he thought, but the writing was keeping him alive and sane.

One might not have expected Andy to be so understanding, but Andy's kindness and patience would have been apparent to almost anyone. Hamilton, however, was too smothered in grief and confusion and too absorbed in *Jud's Story* to notice much that was happening around him. Finally, after their second week in Beijing and the day before Andy's money was supposed to arrive from his bank in New York, Andy tried to bring up the subject of their departure from China. Hamilton refused even to talk about it.

"And what the hell are you going to do? Live forever as a recluse in the Beijing Hotel? Goddamn it, Hambone! You ain't Howard Hughes! One day that VISA card's gonna expire. I don't know nothing about those cards, but I do know that they don't have an infinite amount of money in them. Have you thought about that? I'll be dogged if I understand you sometimes! Come on Ham, let's go home."

Eventually, Hamilton agreed to leave, but to leave only after he had finished *Jud's Story*, and he would return only to England so that he could collect from Rodger and Jud the money he and Andy were owed for winning their bet. Also, he said he would return there only by train and by no other route other than the one through Siberia.

"We can't arrive there 'til spring," he said. "Otherwise, we lose the bet."

For a while longer, Andy gave up and continued to humor him. At first he had difficulty getting Hamilton to leave their room, but at the beginning of their third week Hamilton started wandering around in the hotel. "This little world has everything one could possibly need," he exclaimed dreamily to Andy, who was again scolding him for not at least getting out to see the sights.

That cosmion that is the Beijing Hotel consisted of three buildings. The first was built by the British, the next by the Americans and the last by the Russians. They were joined together in chronological order, so that when Hamilton went from shop to shop, bar to bar and restaurant to restaurant in each segment of the hotel, he had the sensation of venturing through time. Yes, it was a bit like evolution.

Hamilton whacked off his mustache – bits of it, that is – and without as much as a comment, wore it around in ascending degrees of eclipse. Funny enough, the Chinese took it as the latest western style, but the westerners in the hotel were either astonished or appalled and treated Hamilton like a pariah as he went about the hotel with a mustache on the left half of his face. At the end of the third week, much to Andy's relief, Hamilton finally cut the whole thing off. He explained to Andy that his great crescent mustache had merely been waning like the moon. If Andy had thought the statement crazy, he did not say it. Maybe he said nothing because of the way Hamilton looked. He looked like a denuded bull without his horns.

One night toward the end of the third week, while Hamilton waited for Andy to come to dinner, he ordered for them both. He chose "dog in casserole" for Andy, and for himself, "webs of camel's toes." When the food arrived, Hamilton acknowledged that he had planned the joke and announced that he was ready to see the Forbidden City. Yes, Hambone was beginning to act like his old self, and Andy was so pleased that he did something he thought he would never do: he ate dog. They sat there laughing, and Hamilton told Andy about the outrageous joke he and Jud had played on a dean at the university.

After they left the dining room, they went to a place in the oldest section of the hotel called the Red Bar. They sat for hours drinking Heineken beer, and Hamilton talked about how much he admired Starman and said that he really would get in touch with him when he returned to England. Hamilton was making sense, and Andy was relieved. He had shuddered at the thought of being stranded in China with a madman on his hands.

The next day, they went down the street to the Forbidden City. In those days, it was opened to anyone who wished to enter, provided they paid the fee. They crossed over a bridge and under a great portrait of Mao.

In 1403 the Emperor Yongle renamed the old capital of the Great Khan "Peking." It was said that in the same year, a mysterious Taoist priest descended from the sky and presented the Ming Emperor with a plan for the city. This plan was in accord with the celestial forces, and the heavenly order of the city was reflected therein.

There were moats surrounding walls, walls within walls and moats within moats. In the east there was the Temple of the Sun and in the west, the Temple of the Moon. To the north was the Temple of the Earth, and to the south was the Temple of Heaven. In the center, toward which everything implodes, is the Forbidden City – the "Great Within," as it was once called.

In that center of the world, Andy and Hamilton found an open-air bazaar. The most prominent items for sale were fans.

"Told you so," Hamilton laughed. "This is how it ends."

At the risk of triggering one of Hamilton's discourses about the end of history, Andy answered him:

"Nope. Hambone, you are wrong. There are just too many contradictions. Someday soon, the shit's gonna hit them fans. Maybe this thing you call history has immigrated, or maybe it's unemployed for now. Maybe it's just playing dead. But, no, it ain't over yet. You just wait."

Andy's money finally arrived. Anticipating an argument, Andy built up his courage and bluntly told Hamilton that it was time to leave. To his surprise, Hamilton just said, "Okay." But then, before Andy could say that he had found a reasonably priced flight to Vancouver, Hamilton informed him that it was time to see about the tickets for the train.

"I've changed my mind about not leaving until *Jud's Story* is finished," to which he added cheerfully, as if to please Andy, "I'll charge up the batteries and I can write on the train and in Moscow too. That way I can finish it off and keep my promise to Jud."

Andy thought Hamilton had forgotten all about the train. He was astonished.

"Now it's the train again, and it's also Moscow? Where in hell did you come up with those ideas? And come on, Hamilton, your promise to Jud? What in hell are you talking about?"

"Now you come on. Jud has never let me down, and I'm not about to do that to him," Hamilton said with conviction.

Then he laughed, saying that the train went to Moscow anyway. Besides, there was a man in Moscow he needed to meet – a man named Koldomasov.

"You know, I've told you about him. Bogdanov saved his life," he added matter-of-factly.

"Okay, Ham, I don't know 'bout this Koldomas or whatever his name is, but what the hell you going to use for money? They ain't gonna let you ride the train for free just because they love your royal Canadian ass. And there's this little matter about eating. And you can bet the Soviets don't take VISA."

"Well, as close as I can figure it, you owe me about seven or eight hundred dollars. And that, Unc, is my low figure."

Andy was so furious that he left the room and went to the bar. He sat there thinking about what could be done and concluded that he would have to abandon everything he had ever stood for and tell the people at the Canadian Embassy that they had a lunatic running loose in Beijing. The Canadians will just have to deal with him, and Hamilton will be out of his hands. But then Andy remembered Hamilton telling the story of how he recently had been denied permission to enter the Soviet Union. Andy smiled. The Soviets aren't about to change their minds now. He would just let things take their own course, he decided. He had another Scotch and returned to their room.

"Who in the hell is this Bogdanov, anyway?" Andy asked Hamilton.

Hamilton did not look up from the computer, but Andy could tell that he was smiling.

"Oh, you know. I've told you about this guy. He's the one who invented cybernetics – the science of control. I've written a book about him."

"And he embalmed Lenin?"

"Well, not exactly," he replied. "But he was in on it."

And, without missing a stroke, Hamilton returned to *Jud's Story*.

# CHAPTER V
## ROUND TRIP

The war in Vietnam had begun for the Americans in 1954 when the French lost the battle of Dien Bien Phu and evacuated that country. The U.S. involvement started with a few military advisors to South Vietnam – a state created by the United Nations - and was followed by irrational increments through the mid-sixties. By then it already had become a runaway train. Vietnam, for the Americans, truly was an incremental war, as if its policies were guided by some built-in self-referential, and thereby autonomous, mechanism. By the mid-sixties the United States had over a quarter of a million troops there. The new president, Lyndon Baines Johnson, was basing his decisions on advice from his Secretary of State, Robert McNamara, who was using the Pentagon's computers for modeling the war. They thought that they were in control of a war that was really controlling itself.

As one who had acted as squad leader on many patrols and sometimes as right-door gunner on a Huey chopper – the warhorse of the 1st Air Calvary – I had seen my share of action. My finale came when I was about as "short" as I could have been. During my last two weeks in Nam, I was taken off the gun and two choppers dropped my squad in a jungle clearing. We were to give ground and air support to infantry blocking exit trails from Cambodia used by the North Vietnamese and Viet Cong troops. This battle would become the heaviest action of the war so far and was coined Ho Krignou. My outfit was most heavily involved in the second of three operations supporting the 2nd Battalion, 18th infantry Division, which had moved into a place called An Loc and then to Quan Loi, a French rubber plantation. When this operation ended and my year "in country" was finally done, I considered myself to be one of the lucky ones – lucky unlike the left door gunner of my chopper who had taken a stray round in his left eye.

Because the war had heated up, the ports and airports were clogged with ships and planes carrying men and material to and from Vietnam. I was on one of those planes – a C-141 – with twelve other soldiers, a crew of six and a full load of occupied body bags in gray, steel coffins. We landed at Travis Air Force Base in California, and I was discharged at the Presideo of San Francisco. It had been exactly two years and one week since I had been inducted.

At the San Francisco airport, I sat in the bar waiting for my flight to Atlanta. From there I would fly to Jacksonville. I was not used to the air-conditioning and Jack Daniel's had failed to save me from a chill. I felt I needed to move about, so I gathered up my things and went to the restroom. Soon, I was standing before a row of washbasins, looking at myself in the mirror and thinking about how foolish I looked in my rumpled dress greens. In the reflection I saw a black man enter the room.

"Sittin' on the dock of the bay ..." he sang to himself as he bumped through the door, pushing a cardboard trash barrel on a dolly as he entered.

Impulsively, just as he passed behind me, I wheeled around and flung my hat into his barrel. He stopped, opened his eyes wide and looked at me. In went my tie, and I ripped off my shirt and heaved it into the can too. On the hook next to the mirror was my jacket with its shiny brass buttons, the Purple Heart, the campaign ribbons, the "hard five" Sergeant's stripes and the gold-and-black shoulder patch of the First Air Calvary. Slowly, and with deliberation, I took the green jacket from the hook where it hung. For a second, I held it over the trash barrel, and then I let it go. The man's mouth hung open and his eyes followed each move I made as if I were a stripper and he an aroused voyeur. Next went my pants. Last, I snatched my dog tags from around my neck and hurled them into the can.

"There, mother fucker!" I said, drunk and laughing in my jump boots, drawers and T-shirt.

"Now, ain't you somethin' boy! Ain't ever seen nothing like this!" he squealed, laughed and went on.

From my carry-on bag I took my jeans, put them on and left.

After a long wait and a change of planes in Atlanta, I arrived in Jacksonville. It was just past midnight. At the baggage return, I found my duffel bag with "U.S. ARMY J.A. BENJAMIN III, 254-60-7934" stenciled on both sides, and then I made my way outside. Just as I was getting on an airport bus, an M.P. came up to me and, suspecting that I was an AWOL soldier, demanded to see my identification.

I reached into my jeans and with both hands popped my discharge paper open before his face and said, "Look, you ugly prick!"

When I boarded the bus, a girl with long, greasy hair and granny glasses said, "Guess you told that pig!"

I did not know what she meant. Before I could respond, she must have realized who I was, or had been, by my short hair and shiny jump boots. She shrunk under my glare and fled from my silence.

Hot damn! I was out – out and back in the world!

At the bus station in Jacksonville, I fell asleep in a chair and dreamed of the rubber plantation where we killed them.

The chopper drops us in a clearing and we head into the trees, staying in the bush and walking parallel to the road of red mud. We see them cross. They wear black pajamas and straw hats – three of them. They are carrying bicycles chest-high as they scurry across the muddy, red gash, their elbows sticking out making them look like fleeing, frightened birds. They vanish into the grass.

We go down. Freeze. The radio man cups his hand around the phone, and in an Appalachian drawl whispers:

"Angel One, Big Green Angel, Angel One, this is Chicken Little. I read back: Coord 23-65-40-65-10-4. Roger and out."

Then we hear an engine. An APC – a ZIL-151 – comes from the grove of rubber trees and slides to a halt in the mud. They flutter from the grass, hook their bicycles to the side of the vehicle and get in. The engine whines. Just as it passes us, like a fire-spitting angel of death, the chopper swoops down on them.

Almost simultaneously, rockets hit the APC and the APC runs over the mine that we had planted on the road. The vehicle is blown into the air and lands on its side. I smell sulfur. My nose, my face, stings.

They scramble from the opening at the back. As we fire, the sulfur sharpness mixes with the sweet smell of burning human flesh. I gag. Something hits my helmet.

I awoke to a ringing inside my head. I rubbed my eyes and felt for my missing earlobe. Picking up my bag, I board the bus for Altamaha. Soon I was sleeping, but this time I did not dare to dream.

I yawned, sat up and looked out the window just as were crossing the Georgia-Florida state line. It was dawn. As we went through the Okefenokee Swamp and my eyes fell upon Spanish moss, cypress and palmetto palm, I had a funny feeling. Home.

We pulled into the bus station at Waycross. A fat woman sporting jeans and a tattoo got on, as did two black GIs. Their uniforms were that of the famed Eighty-Second Airborne. One wore a hairnet under his overseas cap; the other carried a radio, and until the driver made him turn it off, it played Motown – Gladys Knight & the Pips. The soldiers were followed by an elderly white man, obviously drunk, who the driver stopped because he did not have a ticket.

"And where are your shoes, Bubba?" the driver asked, and the man looked down at his dirty, yellow socks.

"I left 'em on the bus, boss. Ain't no crime, is it? And I had me a sleep."

"Where you going, Bubba?"

"Me, I'm a goin' ta Tampa. Goin' ta my ..."

"Well, this here bus is goin' to Altamaha and then on up to Macon. This couldn't be your bus. Let's see if we can find it." And the shoeless man followed behind the driver and they went into the station.

As the sun climbed into the sky, we rolled through pine woods and pecan orchards. I nodded and in my dream saw that all the flesh was blown off the Gook's face. And I saw myself wipe the blood from my own face and then vomit through my fingers.

As we passed Blackshear High School, I smiled. I remembered the afternoon the Altamaha High School debate team took on the team from Blackshear High, and I thought about our opponents – two girls who arrived at our school in a pickup with two sows in the back. The subject was something like: "Resolve that the federal government should subsidize the ailing railroads."

In the rebuttal, one of the girls had said: "South American countries have beautiful bird-like sounding names: Venezuela, Columbia, Paraguay, Uruguay, Brazil, Argentina, Bolivia, Ecuador, Chili and Peru."

What she had said had nothing to do with the topic and she had memorized it for another occasion. Thinking no one would notice, she used it. We won, which is not saying much, and because we knew no better, laughed and hooted and made fun of her.

We passed the Jesup High School and their football field and baseball diamond. When we reached the bus station, the driver went in and came back with a coffee.

On the other side of town there were fields, now fallow, mossy swamps and stands of scrub oak, pine and palmetto palm. I had been asleep when we crossed over the Altamaha River near the nuclear power plant, and I awoke as we were approaching town from the south. We passed the place where the road forked for Highway 280, which would take you to Savannah, and the charred remains of the White Spot. As we rounded a curve, Pine Bluff Cemetery came into view and then the Altamaha River Bridge. When the bus reached the apex of the span, I looked upstream. There was Great Alligator Swamp on my right and where Max Maxwell's used to be on my left. In between was the "V," the place where the then early-morning, misty river started. I was back. Home.

I hitched my duffel bag on my shoulder and walked onto Malachi Street. I passed the Piggly Wiggly and Bud's theater, and then turned at the courthouse. There on a bench, before a bed of dead calla lilies,

Disorderly Notions

killed months earlier by a rare frost, sat Jake Bailey. Jake was the former manager of the Altamaha Savages ball team – the one who had passed the hat for the Cuban ball player that night in 1954. He also was the brother of Lolly Bailey, who still worked for my family.

"Hey, Juddy Boy," he said.

"Hi ya Jake," I replied, and went on.

Long ago I had misplaced my key, so I stood at my own front door and knocked. Surely, Uncle Durden couldn't be asleep. I kept knocking. Although I had called him from San Francisco, knowing him he had forgotten, or he could be down at the Southern Pine Café arguing with somebody about something. No, he was there. I heard him.

"Goddamm it, Juddy Boy! Do ya have to knock so friggin' hard?" and he opened the door. "Boy, you almost as skinny as your po' ole uncle. You look like something the dog dug up! Come on in, boy! Let's shut this door."

His eyes filled. Briefly he turned and drew his sleeve across his face.

"Hi, Uncle Durden," I said.

I took his hand, and he put his other hand on my shoulder and looked at me.

"Hey! Glad you're back, son."

That day, mainly to show me off, Uncle Durden took me to dinner at the Southern Pine Café. He asked why I didn't wear my uniform, but I didn't have the heart to tell him what I had done with it.

I thought people might treat me, or maybe even treat both of us, coldly because of what happened a few years before when the Freedom Riders came to the bus station. But they didn't. Later, when I mentioned this to my uncle, he laughed and said that they soon forgot all about it. He guessed that I probably heard my Uncle Andy's version of the story. I realized that a Fowler or a Benjamin could do or say things that would have resulted in others being run out of town on a rail. Then I remembered how Uncle Andy hated Altamaha. Maybe this was one of the things he hated about it.

When I asked how Uncle Andy was doing, Uncle Durden told me that he had been arrested and had spent a few days in jail for dumping a whole plastic Clorox bottle of blood over some steps at the Pentagon. He said it had been on the TV National News. They said it was pig's blood. I could tell that Uncle Durden did not want to talk about Uncle Andy, and later I learned that they had a serious falling-out over the war.

That afternoon, after my uncle closed his law office, we walked over to Benjamin House to see my Aunt Vera Ola. The brown grass was too long and the azaleas were overgrown, and because no one had thought to pick its white flowers, the great camellia bush in the front yard was covered with wilted, brown, rose-like blossoms. The screens on the side porch were rotted. Some had even ripped open and hung down like pieces of dead skin. The house needed paint, and someone had left an ill-rolled garden hose on the porch beside the front door. I rang.

Finally, the door opened. It was Lolly.

"Well, sho nuff! If it ain't Juddy boy! Been over there soldiering in Vietnam. Boy, we sho been worret 'bout you! Come on in here, boy."

"Saw your brother," I told him.

"Jake? You know, Jake, he ain't no good. But Jake, he can't help it. He ain't quite right. He stay up in Milledgeville at the insane asylum as much as he stay here."

And then Lolly told us about how Aunt Vera Ola wasn't "quite right" either. But, of course, we knew that.

"I has to watch everything she do. She always wantin' to go over next door to Mista Strick's funeral home and see if he done a good job. Begs to go every time they's got a body. Well, the other day, I says alright, that I'd take her, but only if she promise not to say nothing to nobody. There wasn't nobody around 'cept Mista Strick, and he don't mind 'cause she's Miss Vera Ola. So, I takes her and they had po' ole Mista Moxley laying there dead and all, and she goes over and puts her finger on his nose and looks at me and says, 'BEEP.' But there weren't nobody in that room 'cept me and, well, Mista Moxley. But he dead, and it's a good thing too." Lolly threw back his head, rolled his good eye and laughed.

We walked down the dark hall as he talked on. The house smelled of dust, collard greens and age. I could hear a TV. Lolly opened the door and there she sat.

"Miss Vera, somebody here to see you."

"Well, don't just stand there, you silly old nigra. Move and let 'em in."

"Miss Vera Ola, looky who's here. Juddy done come home from the wa'. And he look so good!"

"I hope you killed a German for me and a Jap for your Uncle Richard. Don't just stand there, boy. Come give your mamma a kiss."

I walked toward her chair, but before I got there, her attention was diverted by the TV.

"And now, for this nice refrigerator ... or will you go for the box?" the TV host said. "Go for the box! The box! Go for the box!" The crowd cheered.

"Well, go for it," the man said to her.

Aunt Vera looked at me and said in her high voice, "He's right. The box. I'd take the box. You just don't ever know what's in a box. Now, a refrigerator is a kind of box, isn't it? You really don't know what's in there either. Usually it's food, but then it doesn't have to be.

No, I wouldn't take that refrigerator 'cause there might be a dead nigra woman in it."

"Vera Ola," Uncle Durden said, "you know who this boy is?"

"'Course I know who he is! And I'm surprised at you for being so impolite to your sister. Richard Benjamin you ought to be ashamed! My lands. You and that ... boy."

My Uncle Richard had died of a heart attack in the DeSoto Hotel in Savannah. That was in 1958. There had been some boy with him.

"Of course you do, honey. 'Course you know who he is," Uncle Durden said, smiling.

"Ha! You think I don't know my own boy. Collie, come give mamma a kiss."

"Miss Vera Ola that ain't Collie. This here's Juddy. Juddy Benjamin. He been off in the wa'. He been fightin' in them jungles ..."

"That's enough out of you, you uppity nigra. Everybody knows about your daddy putting your poor dead mamma in that ice box."

I spent the next year and a half up in Athens, at the University of Georgia, finishing my degree. I lived by myself in a trailer under a big oak tree on the outside of town. I had few student friends. In fact, I had no friends. As one might guess, the AKs were among the few groups on campus who made it known they supported the war, yet many of them had managed to avoid it by joining the National Guard. I was in no mood to hear some sentimental fool tell me how glorious it must have been to be a part of Pickett's Charge. Although most of those who had been there when I was among them were long gone, I'm sure the story of how I smashed my AK pin in the kitchen had become part of their local lore. Well, what the hell, they could just kiss my South Georgian ass.

As far as the majority of the other students were concerned, had they known I had been to Nam some would have verbally assaulted me and maybe even spit on me. Their numbers were growing. I hated their self-righteousness. There were times when I was nearly moved to violence. No, it wasn't a question of whether I was for or against the war, I was not going to listen to people screech and chant about us poor bastards who, for whatever reasons, had ended up in that corner of hell. But while I wanted nothing to do with those puritanical, spoiled children, neither did I seek the company of other veterans. What we had in common was something neither I nor they would want to talk about.

As I said, I had no friends. So for the first time in my life, I studied. And I really loved it. Sometimes I would get drunk and all night walk up and down the length of my trailer reciting Aiken, Yeats, Allen Tate or Ezra Pound. I grew especially fond of Aiken. Did you know he was born in Savannah and that he went back there to die?

When I finished my degree, I went north. While the direction was the same as my previous flight from the university, the circumstances were quite different. I contend that my last exit had been a direct result of a chain of calamities that had begun on the day the Freedom Riders came through Altamaha. And just when I thought that the chain might have run out of links, the Viet Cong invaded Saigon and Hue. These and other Viet Cong victories would be dubbed the "Tet Offensive." It was 1968 and the United States was losing the war.

Once, during this time, I saw cops gas-cheering demonstrators with North Vietnamese flags. There was a girl who dashed from behind a hedge and used what was to become a much favored tactic – flinging her still-warm shit at the lines of police. Not only was it effective against both cops and soldiers, but many thought it demonstrated revolutionary zeal.

Then, another Kennedy was shot and King was murdered in Memphis. That's when the fires started.

What people would come to call the "sixties" already seemed like a century to me – a century of bad, dishonorable and mostly dishonest history. I'd had enough. And this was what that second flight north had been about: I had to break that chain. Yes, God save us from the goddamned sixties.

Hamilton had both written and called me, suggesting I go to graduate school in Canada. I was interested, and applied. Hamilton took care of the details. On my way to Canada I decided to stop off and visit Uncle Andy. I had not seen him in almost four years, and, to tell the truth, I had avoided him because I knew how opposed he was to the war. With apprehension, I took the bus from Altamaha to Macon and from there a taxi out to the place known as Seven Bridges – a farm where Andy lived.

Seven Bridges was owned by Alcoholics Anonymous. Uncle Durden had told me as much as he knew about it, which wasn't that much. Andy had been there since Lotty, his wife, had fallen into the bathtub, hit her head on the faucet and died. They both had been drunk, and at the time, were fighting. The judge had given Andy a choice, and he seemed to have made the right one. Surly Seven Bridges was better than jail. But now he was in trouble again because of the blood incident at the Pentagon.

I walked from the road to the top of a hill. There, next to a weathered, white barn and a big, white farmhouse, I saw three men trying to coax a pig up a shoot that led into the back of a pickup. There was a fourth man sitting behind the wheel. It was Uncle Andy. I knew right away that if you stayed at Seven Bridges you had to work, because Uncle Andy was working. The truck began to move toward me. Beside the mailbox, where the lane turned into the road, I met Uncle Andy and the pig in the truck. He stopped.

"Jesus H. Christ! Am I having the DTs?" he laughed. "Juddy? That you, boy?"

"Well, last time I checked it was," I said.

I got into the truck, and we drove off.

That evening I had dinner with my uncle and the nine other men who lived on the farm. They were from all over. Some were my uncle's age, but most were younger. Three were black and there was one Mexican. The men affectionately referred to themselves as the "Once Drunk Farmers." The name, of course, had been my uncle's idea. He always tries to change the world by naming everything.

As we sat at the table, I remembered the last time I was on a farm with my uncle - the Jordan farm, near Americus, Georgia. When I mentioned the woman jumping off the bridge, Andy told the story to the others at the table. Someone asked if they ever had found the woman.

"Nope, it was as if she just vanished into the air, and the child with her," he answered.

As far as I could tell, my uncle was happy. I don't think I had ever seen him calm before, but that is the way he seemed to be at Seven Bridges. Calm. They all joked that there were no women around to cause trouble, but from time to time most of them went to town and some, undoubtedly, had liaisons with women. I would imagine that most of them did not always succeed in avoiding the bars.

The men had to agree to stay away from the farm no longer than one month in a year and to return sober. I don't know how strictly this was enforced, but I later found out that, in my uncle's case, he somehow got away with staying longer. When it came his time to vanish, Uncle Andy often went to Rye and visited Rodger at England's Benjamin House. In every pub for miles around Rye, Uncle Andy would throw a binge that people talked about until he returned the following year. In fact, and for good reason, to the locals in and around Rye he was known as "Bingy Benjamin."

The order at Seven Bridges seemed strangely monastic. It seemed a place out of time. Life was the slow, steady rhythm of the seasons. I helped the men do the many things that one does on a farm. It was haying time when I was there. We walked behind the tractor and loaded fresh bales into the back of a pickup. From there we took them to the barn and hoisted them into the loft. The men raised most of what they ate: pigs, cows and chickens, and for money, they raised exotic birds. These birds were sold to pet stores mostly in Atlanta and they fetched a fat sum from the frivolous rich.

The birds were kept in wire cages in a large, blue metal building behind the farmhouse. The cages were twelve or fifteen feet high and about as wide and long. There were four of them. These cages were on wheels. During cold weather they could be pushed inside the heated building. Andy showed me all of the birds in these cages. Some of the birds were fed seeds and others were fed meat. He knew all them by both their scientific and special names. It was the brood stock, the ones that they didn't sell, that had these special names. A wise-looking and stern, gray hoot owl was named Karl; a fierce bald eagle they called Vladimir; an exquisite, scarlet parrot with a great, hooked beak was dubbed Rosa; and a cunning, blinking and goateed vulture was Leon. Except for my uncle, none of the "Once Drunk Farmers" were politically sophisticated, and had they known that these first names also had last names, it probably wouldn't have mattered.

When my uncle had first come to Seven Bridges, he had instituted this calendar of saintly fowls. Andy quipped with self-mocking cynicism that no matter how covert and feeble giving names to the birds was; it was still an act of "revolutionary praxis."

Uncle Andy was pleased that I was going to Canada.

"Maybe the revolution will happen there. It's damned sure missed this place," he declared as I got out of the truck, adding that America was doomed to fascism.

I didn't agree, but then I did not argue either. We never mentioned the war, and never did we acknowledge that I had fought in it.

After a few days with my uncle, I checked in at the Atlanta Airport with a ticket for Toronto. In my bag I had a heavy, blued metal box that Andy had given me. It had belonged to my great-great-grandfather Malachi, and contained a few personal items of his. Andy said our ancestor had found it in the Indian burial grounds there at the "V" in Altamaha.

After I had been in Toronto for almost two years, and had completed a Masters degree in American Literature, I left for England. My studying at Oxford had been Hamilton's idea, for Hamilton had to be there himself. His university was insisting that he return to England in order to complete his doctoral dissertation. There was material at the Warburg Institute in London – material essential for his research. The university had granted him a two-year leave of absence because his finishing the dissertation was a condition of his continuing employment with them. Considering that my presence was not always conducive to maintaining the contemplative atmosphere that encourages scholarship, Hamilton took quite a chance in suggesting that I go along. He really was behind that proverbial Magic Eight Ball. But at that age, you take chances, even Hamilton took them then, and he especially did when I was around to encourage him.

As it had turned out, Hamilton spent more time at the Institute in London than he did at Oxford, yet we did get together on some weekends. Sometimes I would go down to London and we would take in a show or just hang around Bloomsbury near his flat. On other occasions he would come to Oxford, but since neither of the fellows with whom I shared rooms at Newfield College ever left, Hamilton always had to sleep on a short and badly sprung sofa. Finally, he just said:

"Sorry, Juddy Boy, I just can't sleep on the chesterfield any longer!"

After that only when there was a bed available did he ever come back. But the best times we had together, and I would even say some of the best times that either of us would ever have, were spent at Rye.

I could have gone to Rye earlier. Three years before, when I had visited Andy at Seven Bridges, he had given me Rodger Inksetter's address and telephone number. I guess I didn't call because I figured that, although Rodger Inksetter was a distant cousin, if he was a friend of my uncle, he probably was like those friends my uncle once had suggested I contact in Toronto. Yes, I figured that Rodger was probably a communist.

Hamilton kept telling me I should phone. When I finally got around to it, Rodger and I got along great. He told us to come any time and to stay as long as we liked. So, Hamilton and I made our plans for the week at the end of Trinity term. As it turned out, we did not go alone.

I had met her one afternoon in the public library of the nearby town of Abingdon. I had been walking along the river and when it started raining, found refuge in an overstuffed chair.

"Excuse me, sir, but you must wake up and quit snoring. You cannot do this in a library. You are disturbing the public!" she whispered.

"Well, I will stop snoring, but I will not wake up," I said. "You must be a dream and I don't want you to go away."

Her name was Gertrude – Getty, for short, and for mercy as well. Getty had a friend called Helen. After Hamilton and I had taken them out a couple of times, they agreed to accompany us to Rye.

Rodger was about as good a guy as you could find anywhere. I liked most everything about him. He had become the sole heir to the old Benjamin House and he erratically operated it as a bed and breakfast. He lived there with Marti his dark-haired, common-law wife, and Marti's eight-year-old daughter. Marti had both beauty and grace.

Rodger was a painter. At that time, he was full of hope and ambition, but also he had talent. His paintings are realistic, but, at the same time, the content of his work is both humorous and playful.

There is the picture of Marti over the fireplace, for example. Your eye naturally follows the curve of her reclining, nude figure into the background where, in a shadowy corner, Rodger is standing beside an easel and holding his palate and brushes. He's grinning at her. But this is the weird thing: Rodger is wearing the exact clothes worn by a Flemish painter of the seventeenth century who did a similar painting. As is often the case, the English do not always appreciate the genius of their native sons. So it was with Rodger. But the French loved him.

Rodger loaned us his old Morris. We put the top back and picnicked in the downs of East Sussex and Kent. In Rodger's dinghy, we sailed down the Tillingham to where it meets the Rother and took our chances in the Channel. We took long walks through the Romney Marsh and rode on the bike path over the hill and through the wood behind Benjamin House. When we got to Winchelsea, we swam in the sea.

Getty would let me do whatever I wanted with her. If I couldn't think of new things to do, she could. Hamilton's girl was less accommodating, but then my younger cousin was slow when it came to such things. We were young and it was wonderful. I remember thinking as I lay with Getty in a field of wheat that finally the chain had broken and those links of bad history were over.

Hamilton finished his dissertation early. He had worked like a dog. He wrote about a Russian physician, science-fiction writer and political theorist, Alexander Bogdanov. Later he would transform the research into a book that would be praised in the most exalted, if arcane, circles of academe. As a reward for himself, Hamilton took a cruise to the Azores. There he met a young lady from Toronto who he soon married, but to whom he stayed married for little over a year. I would never get to meet her and, from the very little Hamilton had to say about her, I never cared.

Hamilton followed the girl back to Canada and I, having already chosen a topic for my dissertation, began writing about the poetry of the American, Conrad Aiken. After Hamilton left, my only distraction was Rye. Rodger, Marti and I had become good friends. This is when I became fascinated with my ancestor, Judah P. Benjamin.

During the beginning of Michaelmas term, in what I had thought would be my last year at Oxford, I met Meg. Even today it is difficult for me to recall most of it. It happened fast, and it sunk deep, so deep that, at times, I can dredge but little of it up. When I can, what I find is elusive, abstract and attached by a fragile thread to the shadow of a memory – a ghost of my experience.

She was alone, gliding down the river in a punt. I was walking along the bank, hurrying, taking a short cut to see my tutor. I had noticed her, but had paid little attention. Then I heard her say, "Oh, shit!" and I knew she was American. She had dropped her pole into the water.

That's how it started – with me putting my notebooks there in the reeds, shedding my shoes, shirt and trousers and going after her. From that moment on, I've never really quit going after her, even after she fled, for my soul has never stilled. I know now that it was the intensity of my passion and my never-exhausting pursuit of her that in the end gave her flight. Meg feared that if I ever truly captured her, I would consume her.

We spent the morning drifting in the punt. In mid-afternoon, we pulled the boat to the bank and among lacy, soft ferns I lay between her open thighs and kissed the honey-colored down on her belly. We floated on the September air, hidden in a sea of green. All that day, we only drank of each other. Of another, I shall never drink more deeply. Then, as the evening stars began to shine, we returned to the punt and, with her entwined around my feet and our ill-distributed weight threatening to tip our bark, I poled back upstream.

Meg was on an exchange – "junior year abroad" was the name the Americans had for it – and at Oxford she was to study mostly art history and music. Although the term was just beginning, she had been in England since June and at Oxford since midsummer. As it turned out, being acquainted with all the places undergraduates congregated, she was more knowledgeable of the city than me. Although the people who went to these haunts were far too young for me, for awhile, I went along. I was so involved with Meg, and she with me, that we were seeing all things anew. It mattered less where we were than the fact that we were together. We gave so much of ourselves to each other that we were both complete. Ah, it was the meaning of "contentment."

We spent Christmas in Rye. Marti and Meg were soon acting as if they were sisters, and although Marti was dark and Meg honey haired, because they both were slim and sparkly eyed, they looked the part. I remember watching them in Benjamin House move around the room together, and then standing by the fireplace, discussing the painting hanging over the mantel, of which Marti herself was the subject. They moved around like two young cats.

Marti always made me think of a dark beauty I had once seen in Altamaha who had come there with the fair. For the first time in my brief life, just looking at her made mysterious juices flow within me. When looking at Marti, I often recalled this boyhood memory and its attendant manhood feelings. The association gave me the feeling that I had known Marti much longer than I had. But my desire for Meg was visceral, more primeval than those young stirrings I had for Rodger's wife. Somehow, I felt that I had always desired Meg, that my love for her was ancient, yes, eternal. I felt like that then and I still do now. And of this, I can say no more.

Only the four of us were at Benjamin House that Christmas. Marti's daughter had gone to London to visit her father for the holidays. Though there were a few paying guests at the time, the house was large enough that it never got crowded. We helped with breakfast, and Meg sometimes helped Marti make the beds. I usually accompanied Rodger to the market in Rye, to Hastings or to Winchelsea to get a part for his car, or to Brighton for art supplies. We never felt as if we were in Rodger and Marti's way. We helped them run the place. In fact, I had come to feel at home in England's Benjamin House, as much at home as if it were my own house. And why not? Had not it been owned by my great-great-uncle, and even named for our family?

Meg and I slept in one of the third-story bedrooms with a view of the sheep-dotted meadow. From the dormer, we could look into the garden and see the squat Martello Tower and the marsh beyond. Above the foggy green we could see the mist rising into the hill upon which Winchelsea sat. Below the hill was the path where, once, Hamilton and I had made love to our ladies from Abingdon.

On the plaster wall behind the bed, Rodger had painted a mural. I guess you could say that it was Rodger's "medieval world picture," at least that's what he called it. But really, it was a scene from the land of Cockaigne. At first, one saw thatched-roof houses, barnyards, a church and a tavern – a village scene of peasant life reminiscent of Peter Bruegel. But upon peering more closely, one saw a women heaving wash water from an opened window. Under the window two drunken louts were about to become drenched. There were ladies in veiled, peaked hats gesturing to bearded men wearing turbans. In a barnyard, a raffish goat was chatting up a young pig. There were knights astride Harley Davidson motorcycles. The sea was full of red-sailed boats flying banners inscribed in Latin gold leaf that proclaimed the end of the world. The sky was full of birds with feathers like the satiny details of Mogul ichnography, and there were multiracial cupids and an androgynous angel. The bearded and turbaned men wore goggles.

On our bed were down comforters. One afternoon, as Meg lay naked in the chill allowing me to make love to her body with my eyes, she said:

"Jud, I have a boy in my belly."

On the eve of the New Year, among the clutter of finished and unfinished canvases, we were married in the parlor of Benjamin House by Calvin, the communist mayor of Rye.

We found a little flat in a working-class district on the edge of Oxford. I continued to write on Conrad Aiken, and Meg went on with her seminars and spent long hours in the music studio and at the library and the museum. The baby was due in August.

Because both Meg's parents were dead, she received a monthly sum from a small trust. She would continue to draw monthly until she was twenty-one, at which time she could do with her inheritance as she wished. That time would not come for another year. Until then, her monthly sum would not be enough for three to live on, and my scholarship funds were running out at the end of term. As we were debating whether we should return to Canada or America, I was offered a one-year teaching appointment at the University of Sussex in Brighton. Since neither of us was ready to return, I immediately took it.

Soon after I learned of my job in Brighton, we spent a weekend there walking on the beach and browsing through the book and antique shops. Since Rye was so close, on the Sunday of that weekend we took the train down for a night. When Rodger and Marti heard of our plans, they immediately proposed we move to Rye. They insisted that there was plenty of room at Benjamin House and convinced me that a commute three days a week would be inexpensive and manageable. We agreed.

We moved to Rye in June and took the third-story bedroom with the view of the meadow and with the medieval world picture on the wall. That summer was our best time together. Other than my working occasionally on a dissertation and our helping out with the guests at Benjamin House, we had nothing to do but enjoy ourselves. We sailed in Rodger's boat, and the four of us explored the countryside in the Morris. The summer was enchanted and I was now certain that my chain of bad history had broken.

It delighted and fascinated me to think that we were actually living where my celebrated ancestor had lived almost a century before. I asked Rodger everything I could think of about Judah P. Benjamin. He told me all he knew and sent me to see several people in town, but about all anyone knew, including Rodger, was that he had lived there.

One day, after we had finished lunch at the Mermaid Inn, Rodger and I left the ladies talking at the table and walked to the top of the hill. There, in the graveyard next to Saint Mary's Church, he showed me where Judah P. Benjamin's family had been buried. Funny enough, in that Benjamin bone yard there was no Mr. Benjamin. When I asked why he was not there, Rodger told me that he had been buried in Paris in a famous cemetery. He said that someone had erected a huge monument at his grave. He did not know why the remains lay in Paris. I vowed then that I would find out.

Our son was born in August, the month most celebrated by the ancients. For me, because of my childhood, the month always harbored the future. It was the month of dog days and the beginning of the rains. I insisted we name our son Anubis Rayburn after my uncle. It also seemed an appropriate name in other ways. Anubis and Rayburn were names that had come down through my family, and, of course, Anubis was also my name. My great-great-grandfather, who had been the classiest of us all, had introduced the name into our family by donning his son Eli Anubis. Anubis was the messenger god of the Egyptians, the equivalent of the Greek Hermes. Some said that he could divine the future. Meg, while having no preferences of her own, thought the name odd, but when I suggested we could call him Burnie, she agreed. And Burnie did harbor the future. After August, our lives were changed forever.

As the autumn came, and then the winter, I was commuting to Brighton three days a week. Meg began to complain of boredom and often she was melancholy. I was sick with worry. Nothing I could do would make her talk with me. Despite the fact that there was almost a decade of age between us, I never anticipated our having troubles in our marriage. Looking back, I realize that it was my love for her that had blinded me. And then, when I was forced to come to terms with myself and to face the seriousness of these difficulties, I foolishly convinced myself that if only I could discover what it was that was making Meg so unhappy, I could change it. I was certain of this and desperately begged her to tell me the source of her melancholy. But Meg would say nothing except:

"It's not your fault."

During Christmas everything seemed to get better. It was Burnie's first, and Rodger and Marti did all they could to use this to help us reconcile our difficulties that had so quickly and unsuspectingly arisen between us. On Christmas day, Rodger donned a Santa suit and paraded around the studio handing out presents to us and to the guests he had invited for dinner. Although Burnie could not yet talk or walk, he giggled and cooed, fascinated by, but not knowing what to make of, the toys scattered about him. Meg was sitting in a green wing back. She smiled at him and then she looked up and smiled at me. Finally, I told myself – not thinking about the many times I had done so before – that everything was going to be alright.

There must have been twenty-five for dinner, far too many to sit at the table. The guests were varied. Some were local people such as the commie mayor and the cronies of Rodger's from the Pipe Maker's Arms and the Mermaid Inn. There were several people from London who had been in art school with Rodger.

Among this group were two youngish women from Brighton who were friends of Marti's from the University of London. I guess they somehow were attached. One of them got into an argument with a handsome young man who worked as a curator for the Ashmolean

Museum in Oxford. She was trying to badger him into agreeing that museums should acquire and display more works by women and other minorities. She declared loudly that the Ashmolean, like all other museums, was both sexist and elitist. His disagreement was made with such precision and grace as to make her look foolish. In her frustration and resentment, she became rude and abusive, but he was absolutely unflappable.

I had taken little Burnie upstairs. When he was finally asleep, I returned to the party and found Rodger carving the goose and telling a funny story about a party given some years before by one of the guests at Benjamin House that night. This guest was then a poor art student and all his friends were marveling at the lavish repast on the table in his dumpy flat. As struggling art students, none were accustomed to a meal fit for royalty. When they all had finished eating, the host informed them that they had not feasted on goose, as they had thought, but that the bird had been a swan. It turned out that their gracious host had liberated the fowl from Regent's Park, and since Regent's Park is part of the Crown Estates, they had literally eaten a royal bird.

When the story was over, and I finally managed to get through the dining room and into the studio, I saw Meg sitting on the floor beside the young curator of the Ashmolean museum. She was holding the glass bell that sealed the stuffed owl that my great-great-grandfather had sent my great-great-uncle. I could tell by their eyes that the conversation was intense. I saw more life in Meg than I had seen in months. I expected disaster, and disaster came.

During the days that followed I tried to talk with Meg. The days multiplied into weeks, and still she refused to talk. I begged and I bargained. Again and again, I told her how I loved her and how I would do anything to change things. When we made love, which was seldom, she was altogether undemonstrative. Even her responses were bereft of passion.

Meg never neglected little Burnie, but she did insist that I tend to him on Tuesdays and Thursdays – the days that I did not have to go to Brighton. I knew that I had no choice. She was going to Oxford whether I liked it or not, and, of course, I knew whom she was seeing there and what she was doing. Once I grew so angry that I thought of going to Oxford and attacking him. Another time I had a fantasy of finding them together and murdering them while they twitched in a lover's embrace. Not caring if Rodger and Marti heard my cries of desperation, I screamed at Meg and begged her to tell me what I had done wrong.

"Nothing," she replied calmly. "You've done nothing wrong. None of this has anything to do with you. It has to do with me. Why can't you see that? Now look, you've awakened Burnie."

At my lowest point, I had notions of doing myself in. Drowning appealed to me more than any of the other methods; after all, hadn't Lord Byron gone that way? I thought about lining the inside of my trench coat with lead sinkers and sailing out on a quick tide into the Channel and jumping into the sea.

Finally, one morning I awoke and knew that it was over and asked her to go. Two days later, on her twenty-first birthday, she took little Burnie and went to collect her inheritance and her future.

Marti told me that Meg had told the truth –I had had nothing to do with it. But, she said, the problem lay in the fact that Meg had been smothered by the weight of my love for her. She had feared that she was being consumed by my passion. She had no choice but to get out from under my weight. She needed to still my passion and to release herself by betraying me. So she fled to someone who was my opposite – someone cool, light and smooth. Although she had our child with her, I vowed never to see her again or even utter her name.

Once, quite by accident, she literally fell into my line of vision. It had been on my way to visit my tutor for the last time before I departed England and returned to Canada. I glimpsed her from the window of a bus. She was alone, walking along the river. We were stopped in traffic on a bridge. For longer than I wished, I sat there watching the size of her light figure diminish as she walked on. Although she was far away, there was no mistaking that it was Meg. It was a bright, spring morning and gulls were darting about. She got smaller and smaller, and then she was but a white dot indistinguishable from the white birds. Just as my bus jolted to a start, she vanished.

Hamilton had bought a place in a downtown Toronto neighborhood called the Annex. It was one of those late-nineteenth-century ghettos of red brick, painted mostly white inside, big maple trees and a Volvo in every other drive. Hamilton had little else to spend his money on. Until I got there, Hamilton led a kind of life he had fallen into, consisting of a bit of reading and maybe some writing in the evening, perhaps sports on TV, the gym twice a week and pick-up hockey on Thursday nights. There might be a movie on the weekends and a concert or a play about four times a year. Then there were the games at Maple Leaf Gardens. But without fail, no matter what had been on his agenda the night before, Hamilton was in the office every weekday at nine. No exceptions. His life was as regular as the clock.

And why was I back in Toronto? I had been given a temporary contract to teach American literature at Hamilton's university. As usual, my younger cousin had come through. Although it turned out that I would be teaching mostly basic grammar to freshman, I was pleased to get the job. I was slowly putting myself back together.

Hamilton never asked questions about mine and Meg's star-crossed relationship. I never even told him what Meg looked like. We had a deal: I wouldn't ask him anything about his painful marriage and he would ask me nothing about mine. Toronto, during those years, seemed to be a good place for both of us to mend.

Generally speaking, Hamilton went his way and I went mine. I seemed to provide just enough corruption to his placid and regular life to keep it interesting, and his stable influence gave some order to my chaotic soul. Well, it at least kept me working and sane. He gave me the top floor and took the bottom. We split the expenses.

Now this does not mean that Hamilton and I did not do things together. We did just as we had done as children during his visits to Altamaha and as young-adults during our weekends in London and Oxford and our many visits to Rye. We had many Saturday lunches at Toby's, a place down on Bloor Street that, at that time, had the best burgers in town. We spent many evenings at the Brunswick House, the place where I had washed glasses in the sixties and the place where the fat lady still sang "Okie from Muskogee" and the midget cried when he sang "Danny Boy" or crooned to "My Wild Irish Rose." We knew each other well enough that probing to see what stuff the other was made of was not necessary. We had no desire to change each other.

When I was not with Hamilton, I spent much time strolling around Toronto Island, where I would pick up girls and smoke joints with friends who lived in the aging hippie community that the city fathers were still trying to evict. Usually with one of a variety of female companions, I skied in an area north of the city called the Muskokas or canoed, camped and fished in Algonquin Park.

I spent many hours browsing in the second-hand and antique book shops down on College and Spadina looking for books about the War Between the States, but especially books that could tell me something about the covert activities of the Confederate Secret Service that had operated in Canada. I sought anything that might give me insight into the life and times of my Uncle Judah. Yes, I will confess it; I was becoming more and more obsessed with him.

It took exactly two years for me to become disenchanted with academe. Academics are not interested in writing poetry; they are instead interested in the poems others write or in the poet's lives and, especially, their misdeeds. Some of them are fond of setting up themselves and their own enlightened age as standards by which to judge the dead. They pride themselves in knowing the poet better than he knew himself. Often, if an academic writes poetry, he is considered indiscrete. In fact, most of them think that their criticism of art is more important than the works of art they write about. Since I was more interested in writing poetry than in writing about those who wrote it, I quit.

Well, I must admit that there were two other factors related to my unwillingness to continue with academe. First, I did not care to finish my dissertation on Conrad Aiken, for as great a poet as he was, I decided that my time could best be spent writing my own poetry and about the life and times of Uncle Judah. Besides – this is the second factor – I had to tend to my baseball team. At least, that is what Hamilton started calling them. He said that they loved to play because of the kink in my dick, the knot and twist that he said was caused by all those years it was balled up inside a jock strap when I was running the half-mile. But I knew better, I was born with the kink.

When playing my carnal ball game, I tried not to let anyone sit on the bench too long. It was my conviction that everyone should get to play – inclusiveness, they call it. In other words, I simply could not stay out of the undergraduates' uniforms. Hamilton and I even went so far as to call my team the "Savages."

But soon, just as I had grown tired of the university, and of Toronto, I tired of the game. Yes, the word had been tossed around, and some were calling foul. So when my second academic year was over, I took my jock strap and left.

Even before I could make up my mind as to how I was going to make a living, I got word from Uncle Durden that Aunt Vera Ola had died. Much to the surprise of everyone, she had left me some money. I had no idea how this could be since the last time I had seen her, way back when I returned from Vietnam, Aunt Vera had not even known who I was.

I left Canada and went to Georgia to collect what my Aunt Vera Ola had left me. I had not set foot in Altamaha for over half a decade and felt good about going back and seeing Uncle Durden. As the plane was landing in Savannah, I saw myself walking the streets of Altamaha, stopping and talking with people whose faces I had always known. I saw myself standing on the bridge, spanning the dark red river and gazing into the brightness reflecting off the distant flood coursing its way to the sea. I saw myself turn and look upstream, to the spot where the waters merged. I remembered myself there, perched in a deer stand snug between the forks of a live oak on a foggy morning. My hands were shaking; my finger searched for the trigger. Lowering my barrel and clicking the safety, I leaned back into the solidness of the tree, watching the doe chewing her acorns. With my scent reaching her on the change of the wind, I saw her leap and turn, dancing deep into the swamp.

At the airport I rented a dark green Mustang convertible. Yes, for once I would arrive in town in style. I threw back the top and thought about another glorious day, long ago, in another convertible in England with Hamilton and two girls. I avoided the new interstate and instead, drunk on the early-morning, November air and bright Georgian sun, took the old Savannah-Macon highway. I delighted as the long, straight stretch nearer the sea gave way to gentle curves, dips and rises. I gunned the car and, embarrassed by my attempt to render a tune I had learned in grammar school, switched on the radio. I hummed and shouted along with the choir of the African Baptist Church, who were singing live on a local station a song called "The Christian Automobile."

Soon I arrived in Altamaha and, as if on automatic pilot, found myself switching off the ignition at Uncle Durden's house. I noticed that the white clapboards needed painting, as I almost swooned at my surroundings. But now I wonder: Was it the actual place or my nostalgia, the memory of the place as it had once had been?

I knocked on the front door, and then I tried his office at the side. I noticed that there was no car under his shed and remembered The Southern Pine Café. Of course, that's where he would be at this hour of the morning.

The car took me to Malachi Street and down Main Street to the railroad tracks. When parked, I noticed that where the sign had always said "Southern Pine Café" it now read: "El Rio de Vida." I went inside and talked to a brown man behind the cash register, who knew who I was and who assumed that I knew him. Proudly, he reminded me that he used to be in charge of grading in the onion warehouse and his name was Juan, but now he was called Johnny.

"Your uncle, he comes in here. Sometimes. I think it's the chicken enchiladas with green sauce he likes best. But no, your uncle, he is not here now. Go to Wendy's, our new place, for hamburgers. He and his friends, they go there for coffee. You do not know Wendy's?"

I thanked Johnny and, indeed, found my uncle drinking coffee at Wendy's with his somewhat diminished coterie of friends. Among the coffee drinking crowd was Billy Strickland, the undertaker who was still in business, and Max Maxwell, who had sold his fish camp to one of the proliferating groups of the second born. They had erected a large, metal building there, put a prefab frontier-looking facade across the front, stuck a mail-order steeple on top and called it a church. "Foot washers" Max Maxwell had called them, laughing.

The "coffee club," as they referred to themselves, had been meeting at Wendy's since the closing of the Southern Pine Café. In fact, I learned that the Cootses had bought the Wendy's franchise when they closed their department store. Most of the other downtown businesses had relocated to the new strip that had built up around the Walmart and the new, twenty-four-hour Piggly Wiggly near the interstate.

Later, referring to the nearly closed downtown, I made the mistake of suggesting to my uncle that Altamaha no longer existed. When I teased him, asking him where exactly the town was located, he angrily told me that I had no right to say such things. He reminded me that the world changes, that there is progress and that, after all, it was I who had chosen to leave Altamaha. Consequently, I had no say in the matter.

I stayed with my uncle as long as I could, but he became more and more cross, telling me that I was wasting my life and would end up like Uncle Andy. He thought that it was high time I settled down, reminding me that I was his only heir.

"Lots of money to be made around here in real estate; and Juddy Boy, you now have money to invest. You could do much for our community. Come on, son, for once think of the future!" he pleaded.

I had thought of the future, I told myself; in fact, I had seen the future. The future was Altamaha, and that kind of future I did not care for. So, feeling like the desperate jerk that I was, I lied to my uncle: I told him that I would be back soon. Thinking myself a thief, I quietly took the inheritance my aunt had left me. I, like the other Benjamins who had left the First Benjamin Seaboard Bank without any Benjamins, made my deposit and left.

Months later, in Mexico City, I boarded a plane for Toronto. With my eyes floating in tequila and my weary and worried dick with many a new kink, I let my mind flash back to my erratic journey through Mexico: to the fortress-house of Trotsky in Coyoacán that Uncle Andy had told me about, where the guide with a hammer and sickle armband repeatedly assured me how much his Trotsky loved animals; to cantinas in a string of little towns in Oaxaca; to the highlands of Chiapas; to Belize; and finally, to the broken, vine-covered stones of a jungle graveyard on the edge of the town of Punta Gorda – the edge of the country, the edge of the world.

I had gone too far. Yet, I had returned. Alas, I had thrice returned. And when I stepped into the crunchy snow of the Canadian winter, I decided that I must live alone.

With his pen, Hamilton identified the fifth chapter, "Round Trip," on the label of the floppy and placed it in its clear plastic container.

The next morning at breakfast, Andy was both surprised and alarmed when he learned that Hamilton had attained a visa allowing him to travel into the Soviet Union. Hamilton had been able to get the visa only because the new reforms in the Soviet Union had created much confusion, and in this state of chaos and uncertainty, someone in the Soviet Embassy had not been paying attention.

This was neither what Andy expected nor wanted. He argued with Hamilton. He threatened that he would let Hamilton go alone. Andy did everything short of begging him, but Hamilton would not be moved. He planned to leave on the Trans-Siberian train in less than a week. If Andy did not get his own papers in order, and was not on that train, then Hamilton swore that he would leave without him. This, Andy could not allow.

It was Hamilton who suggested they visit the Ming Tombs and the Great Wall before departing. While Andy took this as a good sign, he worried that visiting a tomb would make Hamilton become preoccupied with Mo and, once again, slide back into the world of *Jud's Story*.

They took a bus to the tombs with several others from the Beijing Hotel and arrived at a place called Changping. From there, they walked along a road called "Spirit Way." After passing under an arch and then under a red gate, they were told that this was the spot where officials of the court dismounted before going further into the sacred burial grounds. They passed a great stone pillar and then walked past twelve life-size stone animals placed at intervals of several hundred yards. Every other animal – lions, tigers, bears, camels, wolves and even some mythological ones – were in a reclining position. Then there were statues of warriors, each with distinctive headgear. The guide knew absolutely nothing about anything. He reminded Hamilton and Andy of Xu, and as soon as they arrived at the tombs, Hamilton and Andy left the group.

They found the trip into the subterranean passages boring, and they were glad when they re-emerged into the sunlight and smelled spring air. The sun was warm, and they sat on a stone bench and opened their jackets. Across from them was a man selling bowls of soup. A cur wandered up and sniffed Andy's ankles and then pissed on a mugo pine.

"Don't see too many dogs around here do you? Wanna know why? They eat them. Yes, eat 'em! Can you imagine that?"

The woman who was speaking stood behind them. Turning around to look at her, they saw that she wore blue Nikes and a red tracksuit. Her parka was gray and looked like the kind of parka made by the Eskimos, but unlike most coats of that style, the hood was not trimmed in fur. She had blonde hair. On her back was a backpack, and in it was an Oriental child that was perhaps a year old.

"Did you know that in 1950 they rounded up dogs and either hanged them or clubbed them to death? Wanna know why? They did it because Mao had once tried to escape from a prison and a barking dog alerted his jailer. When he took power, he got the sparrows too. He said they ate grain. Sure they eat grain; they're sparrows, aren't they?"

They looked at her and then at each other.

"Well, you don't remember me, but I remember you. We saw you getting off the train in Canton. Where are the other two? That couple – the big black man and the woman who looks like a gypsy? You still don't remember, do you?"

Then, almost at the same time, Hamilton and Andy looked at each other and laughed. "Birdland!" they both said.

But they quickly realized the woman did not remember seeing them at Birdland. That day, she and her companion had been attending to the more pressing matter of "liberating the birds".

"My name's Jenny. Didn't you like the tombs? I find tombs real fascinating. Where all have you been? We've been everywhere. And guess where we are going? We're going all the way across Siberia. We're taking the Trans-Siberian Express! Aren't we Hera? Hera's our daughter. We got her in Singapore."

Then she looked at Hamilton. She was surprised by his surprise.

"I have heard that you are not a nice person."

They left the woman as quickly as they could, and to Andy's discredit, he used the woman's travel plans as a last ditch effort to persuade Hamilton to change his mind and fly to Vancouver. But that did not work with Hamilton, who merely laughed and said that he was amazed that, at his age, Andy would be intimidated by a woman.

They had been watching for their group from the Beijing Hotel and when they finally spotted them, followed them back to the van. Hamilton dozed or listened to the faint buzz of conversations around him. Soon, they were at the Great Wall.

The approach to the wall was from a curvy road with steep sides all around, and because of this, they did not see the wall until it loomed over them. It was still bright, but it was late in the day and had turned cold. They slowly followed the others to the steps and ascended. The steps were numerous and the small group stopped several times to rest. Finally, when they had reached the top, they stood marveling at the wall – the backbone of a giant stone serpent sprawling across the desert until it is swallowed up by the Earth's curvature.

"That's where we're going," Hamilton pointed.

Andy moved closer to him.

"Where?" he asked.

It was then that Andy noticed the durian ring pushed as far up as it would go on Hamilton's little finger, its points catching the light of the setting sun.

"There," Hamilton said. "The West."

# *FOLLOWING THE SUN*

Hamilton glanced at his watch; the numbers blipped 1:01 ... 1:02 ... 1:03. His thoughts wandered back to the night before, when they had reached the Mongolian border. He and Andy had cashed in all of their Chinese money for beer and were celebrating the ending of the first of seven days on the train. They were also excited because they would soon enter territory controlled by the Soviets.

They had sat in the station at the Mongolian frontier, drinking and watching the bodies of the railroad cars being lifted off their wheels by a crane and then placed upon wider axles that fit the Russia gauge track. Should Andy and Hamilton have any notion of pouring across the border, the Soviets were going to make sure they did not do it on train tracks.

At the border, Mongolian guards had come stomping into Hamilton and Andy's car. The guards looked at everyone's papers, grunted and disappeared. Then came the nurse. There was no mistaking this, for she wore a white uniform and a cap with a red cross on the front. She smiled and held out her open palm. For a moment, Hamilton felt like a naughty boy being forced to surrender a forbidden object. Then she said woodenly:

"Certificate du vaccination."

Hamilton was alarmed. Neither he nor Andy had health documents. Better act dumb, he told himself. So he answered in French that he did not understand what she was talking about, but that they both were as healthy as horses. As it turned out, it was the nurse who did not understand. The whole thing had been a masquerade, a harmless fraud. She smiled again, shrugged and walked on. Those three words were all the French she knew. And why French? This, they never figured out.

Hamilton glanced down at his watch again: 1:12 ... 1:13. The sun shined bright, and the air was a crisp cold. Hamilton rubbed his eyes. He was hung over. To lessen the glare, Andy adjusted the red velvet curtain, and they relaxed in the car of polished brass, dark inlaid wood and green leather. The dining car had been attached to the train when they changed the wheels, and although the train was Chinese, the dining car changed with each border crossing, along with the cuisine. The posh interior of the car made Hamilton think of a movie about the Orient Express, but, of course, this would be the Occident Express.

The waitress brought Andy a Carlsberg in a bottle and Hamilton a Diet Coke in a can. Andy took the napkin from his Champagne glass, shook it loose and tied it around his neck. He slowly poured the beer until the glass was full. Hamilton watched Andy, amused, but because he did not want to disturb his own exquisitely folded napkin, he drank from the can. Although they had ordered something Mongolian from the menu, what the waitress had been most keen about selling them was the Danish and American drinks along with Swiss chocolate, American, Canadian and Cuban tobacco, Clorets chewing gum and Russian tooth powder. With obvious pride, she had presented these items on an engraved silver tray and seemed disappointed that they chose only the drinks. But later, Andy did buy a pack of Winstons. Over the intercom, the Beach Boys sang of endless summer.

Again Hamilton glanced at his watch.

"We should be getting into Ulan Bator in a couple of hours."

There was a timetable posted in the car. It was in Russian, but with the help of his map and his rusty Russian, Hamilton could figure out place names and the approximate times of arrival. Outside, a dusting of white, powdery snow and tan steppe stretched to the treeless horizon. In that empty, bright cold they saw men on horseback herding furry, two-humped camels. Further away, where the earth met the sky, they could see a Soviet air base. They soon heard a squadron of fighters streaking overhead and then saw them in the distance, following them with their eyes as they made vapor trails in the clear, blue sky.

Along the way, they noted that the train stations looked as if they belonged on the Caspian or perhaps the Black Sea. They were of masonry construction, with neo-classical facades painted gay pastel colors. Every one of these stations had a larger-than-life-sized statue of Lenin out front. The statues were all gold and curiously uniform.

"She's on the train," Andy said. "I ran into her in the corridor."

"Who's on the train?"

"The Virgin Mary, that's who. You know, the woman from the conference in Jaipur. The woman who was so impressed with you."

"Yeah, sure, Unc."

"I'm not joking. I saw her. Was just a few minutes ago. She doesn't know I'm with you, so she started talking to me about China and then, out of nowhere, asked me if I knew there was a fascist on the train. Wanna guess who she was talking about? Boy, she's got your number!" Andy laughed, slapping Hamilton on the back.

"Well, what ..."

There was a commotion behind them in the rear of the car.

"Your hair! Now look what you've done! Jenny, I swear, sometimes you act like a child. You are worse than Hera! I can't take you anywhere!"

Yes, it was Jenny, the woman they had seen at the tombs and earlier at Birdland. And yes, Andy had been right, for with her was the Virgin Mary – Mary Aleo. As it turned out, Jenny had let a lock of her long hair fall into her bowl of beet soup, and the red liquid dripped great blotches on her yellow sweat shirt and stained the white tablecloth.

"Mary, please!" she begged, having no idea how loud she was whispering. "People can hear you. You're embarrassing me."

"Oh, here!" snapped Mary Aleo, handing the younger woman her napkin. "I just can't believe this! Why do you do these things to me? Server!" she cried, waving her hand in the air.

Hamilton and Andy listened. The child started to cry.

"Now, see what you've done!" Mary Aleo shrieked.

She got up, snatched up the child from its carrier and stomped from the car.

"They must be staying in first class," Hamilton said.

"Figures," Andy replied with a laugh. "Wonder if the Virgin is really the mother of what's her name – Jenny. Well, won't be long now."

Hamilton glanced at his watch.

"Another beer, Unc?"

As it happened, Hamilton's calculations were off by half an hour, but it was not long before they spotted the city. Ulan Bator had high-rise buildings, the kind one sees in Los Angeles, Milan or Teheran – "International style" as it is known in architectural parlance. But in Mongolia these buildings were painted a bright blue. There were mountains behind the city and trees, the first ones they had seen since leaving Beijing.

As the train pulled into the station, they looked into a square in the center of the city. Men on ladders were taking down a great portrait of the current Soviet leader and replaced it with a picture of a smiling, blonde-haired Oriental girl offering up a bottle of Pepsi.

The waitress came to the table, took a large Russian calculator from her pocket and began to poke numbers. Hamilton could tell that she was doing this randomly. She was not paying any attention to where her fingers landed. When some absurd, seven-figure number appeared, she took two pieces of paper from her pocket and wrote a "1" on each of them. Then she placed the slips of paper on the table and smiled.

"Dollar," she said.

They each gave her a dollar and then another for a tip, which she tried to give back to them.

As they stepped from the train, a Chinese man in a uniform called to them.

"American!" he said, holding out his wrist and tapping his watch with his finger. "Train go."

They eventually realized the man was trying to tell them that the train would be leaving in twenty minutes. He was the conductor. Apparently it was his business to see that no one was left behind.

Hamilton walked over to the gold statue of Lenin and rapped its head with his knuckle. It was hollow. Then he called Andy over and imparted to him his little revelation. At first, Andy was angry with Hamilton, but then he turned his anger toward the Soviets for their cheapening of Lenin's image. No wonder the statues were all alike; they were molded plastic. They both stood there laughing as they rapped on Lenin's bald dome. It was then that they saw the huge soldier. He wore black jackboots, a grayish-brown greatcoat and a dark-brown fur hat. Hamilton told Andy that he thought that perhaps the soldier had been following them. He did not appear happy with their knuckle drumming on Father Lenin's head. They immediately walked toward the square.

"Look! It's the Virgin, Jenny the Baptist and the baby Jesus," Andy laughed.

It was them alright. They were taking pictures of the men nailing up the new offering.

"Oh, hello," Mary Aleo said to Andy. Then she recognized Hamilton. "So, it is you!" she said, and then glancing back at Andy, continued: "Do you know who this is? He's the one I was telling you about ..."

"Oh, you mean Herr Doktor Goebbels?" Andy laughed.

"Very funny. Ronald Reagan would be more like it, but then, I know West's name. I've already written a letter about his misogynist behavior in India. I would advise you not to associate with him."

"And would you like to take my picture for your file?" Hamilton asked with a straight face.

Andy was trying not to laugh.

"When did you hurt your arm? Or were you born with a problem?" Jenny asked Andy, trying to change the subject.

"Was 1935 ..."

"Oh, gosh, that was a long time ago," Jenny said.

"Yeah, 1935 was a long time ago. I was pitching for the Tigers. It was during the series and we were playing the Cubs. One of my relief pitchers had come down with the mumps and the other had gone off with the Lincoln Brigade to fight the fascists in Spain. I had to pitch the whole series myself. Why, when the last game was over and we'd won the pennant, my arm was torn clear out of its socket. I got all these scars from the cleats of the first basemen and catcher. My arm was ruined for a good cause, mind you, but it's ruined. Nothing like winning."

"You lying ole cocksucker," Hamilton whispered to Andy, smiling.

"Hmm," Jenny hummed, looking at Andy. "Did you know that there are about two million people living in Mongolia? Half of them live here in Ulan Bator, and one million of them are Russians," Jenny announced.

Mary Aleo glared at her with disapproval.

The soldier reappeared, pointed to Mary Aleo's camera, and held out his hand. She was at first taken aback, but then she stepped to the side and stood with her hands on her hips in front of the Russian soldier.

"You have no right to do that. I am an American," she said, shaking her finger at him. "Who do you think you are? This is awful. And I thought I was on your side. So, like it or not, I'm reporting you to the authorities!"

Finally, she handed him the camera. He opened it and roughly pulled out the film, exposing it to the bright sunlight. His face was expressionless. Reaching across his chest with a gloved hand, he held the shoulder strap of his machine gun. He motioned them all toward the train with his other hand.

As best Hamilton could tell, they would be crossing into Siberia that morning around five. Determined to miss nothing, Hamilton decided to stay up until they got there. Not Andy, though. He had crossed too many borders to get that excited. So after they finished eating their dinner, Andy returned to their compartment to sleep.

Hamilton sat in the dining car reading a book that had belonged to Mo. It had "Margo Pangolin, Raffles Hotel, Singapore, 543-467" written inside. It was a story about a man who, on a long journey to strange and wonderful lands, falls in love with a beautiful woman who sacrifices herself for him. In this story, it is only after he becomes old and his journey is complete that the man realizes what the journey had been about. Hamilton wondered why the story did not make him sad. Perhaps it did not because it was a real story, a story about what can happen at the end.

He put the book away and took Jud's manuscript about Judah P. Benjamin from the blued metal box. He studied it. He remembered what Jud had once said about why he was so fascinated with the life of his ancestor. He had said that he wanted to know what kind of man Judah P. Benjamin was and how he came to be that way. After Hamilton read the manuscript, he glanced through the window into the blackness. It was then that he decided what to do with Jud's writing. He would continue just where Jud had left off and finish for him what Jud could not finish. His eyes refocused and he saw his own reflection in the window. His hair had grown back, as had his mustache. His hair was now less red and more white.

He sensed a presence behind him and at that moment heard a woman say:

"Coke please."

It was Jenny, and she was alone. Before long, she was sitting in the same booth across from Hamilton. She was laughing at Hamilton's story about how he and Andy had rapped on the plastic dome of Lenin with their knuckles.

"I guess the baby is asleep," Hamilton said.

"Yes. Hera is with Mary."

"Your mother has some definitive ideas about things – about the way things ought to be."

"Oh, no! You really got that wrong. Mary's not my mother. We're companions. You don't know her, but I can tell you that she is a very ... special person. By the way, what's a valley ... valleyocentric fascist anyway?"

"Damned if I know," Hamilton said. "So your baby is starting her travels early."

"We got her in Singapore. She's our baby – mine and Mary's. We couldn't get one at home and really she didn't cost much either."

"So, you bought her?"

"Well, we adopted her, but all we had to do was pay some money. It was easy."

"So when you get her back home, what are you and what's her name going to do with the baby?"

"Oh, you know, we are going to buy her lots of pretty clothes and toys and stuff. And we are going to train her."

As it turned out, Jenny was a dog groomer. She owned a shop in an Indianapolis suburb, and the name of her shop was the "K9 Korner." Mary set up her business. That night, Jenny was wearing a T-shirt that advertised her business. The name of the business was written on it with a picture of a poodle standing upright. The poodle's one "hand" was pointing to her spun-up hairdo tied in a pink bow, and the thumb and index finger of the other "hand" delicately held a long cigarette holder and smoking cigarette. The dog wore a pink miniskirt, which had a picture of a poodle just like her on it, thus issuing an infinity of poodles in miniskirt – a world without end. Amen. Jenny also wore a red baseball cap with a small picture of the green and blue Earth on the front with words above it that read: "One World." Despite the silly shirt, Hamilton thought Jenny was attractive.

Hamilton did not know how it happened, but soon he and Jenny were in the empty compartment at the end of their car. They had lowered the bed, pulled down the shade on the door and fastened the latch.

"Now Hamilton, we have to be quiet. Somebody might hear, and if Mary ever finds out, I'm toast."

Hamilton unfastened the metal button on the top of her jeans, pulled the zipper down and slid his hand into the rich fur. She rose up and pulled her jeans and underwear down. Hamilton pulled them from around her feet. She relaxed and parted her legs. Lying beside her, he opened his pants and Jenny placed her hand on his cock. But Hamilton was unable to concentrate; he kept thinking of Mo.

"Red Rider, you bastard!" Hamilton hissed, embarrassed. "I'm sorry, Jenny," he told her.

"Something I did wrong?"

"No, no. Jenny, you did nothing wrong. It's nothing you did. It's me. I have a problem."

"Oh Hamilton, I'm so sorry. Did you get shot in the war, or what? Something like in Vietnam, I mean? I saw it in a movie. This guy, he got shot there."

Hamilton told her that that war took place a long time ago and that because he was a Canadian, he was not in the war. Besides, neither she nor that had anything to do with his problem.

They both had fallen asleep and awoke to the train jerking to a stop. Hamilton instinctively held to Jenny to keep her from lurching from the bunk.

"What's that?"

Hamilton looked at his watch. The blue blip said 4:46. It was dark everywhere. They had even extinguished the lights on the train. Suddenly there was a flash of light, and then there was brightness everywhere. Squinting, Hamilton looked outside. Through the steam rising from the train they could see soldiers standing in the snow. Bellows of frost blew from their nostrils. Jenny turned away and held the blanket to her bare breast.

"Hamilton, the window!"

Hamilton slammed the shade down, enveloping them in dimness.

Someone began to rap on the door. "Jenny! Come out! Come out this minute. I know you're in there. And I know who you're with! You are with that fascist, that fascist rapist!"

"Go away Mary!" Jenny shrieked. Then she begged, "Mary, please. You are embarrassing me."

They must have come from either end of the car, for before another second had passed, the aisle was full of them.

"Return to compartment," the officer ordered.

"Now you just wait a minute. I ..."

"Return to compartment!"

"Well, I've never seen such fascist ..."

Her voice was lost as they heard her being shuttled down the corridor, muttering as she went.

There was a rap, then a banging on their door.

"Just a minute!" Hamilton shouted as they struggled to get their clothes on.

The man was wearing the green uniform of the KGB border patrol. He was tall, even handsome. A three-inch scar ran at an angle across the bridge of his nose and halfway across his cheek. Afghanistan? Hamilton wondered.

"Passport and visas," he said coldly from under his hat.

"Oh, Mary's got mine," Jenny said, stepping toward the door.

"You no leave compartment. Passport, visa," the officer ordered.

"Look. She just said that her friend has her papers. Her friend is in first class. If you ..."

"Passport!"

Hamilton fished in his pocket for his passport and visa, found them and handed them to the officer.

The officer looked at the picture and then, staring up at Hamilton, asked, "What your name is?"

Finally, the officer allowed Jenny to go to her compartment to get her papers.

"Produce to me all things for reading: books, magazines, maps." the officer told Hamilton.

"I don't have them here. They are down there. Down there, in my compartment."

"Ah, this is no your compartment?"

"No."

"What you do here?"

"I'm waiting for you to let me pass so I can show you what you have asked to see."

The officer did not detect the flippancy in Hamilton's remark, and soon he and another officer were sorting through all of his and Andy's reading material. They were especially puzzled by the contents of the blued metal box, but merely talked to each other and asked no questions. Hamilton concluded that they were merely killing time and amusing themselves.

Just as quickly as they had come, they left. The train jerked to a start. They passed into a darkness as deep and silent as Siberia herself. When there were lights again, they were the lights of a station. Hamilton saw the sign: "NAUSKI." There were three buildings, each made of logs. This looked like something straight out of a Solzhenitsyn novel, Hamilton thought.

A woman in uniform appeared before Hamilton and Andy in their compartment.

"I am from Intourist. My name is Comrade Olga Marchevski. Welcome to the Union of Soviet Socialist Republics. Everyone is required to change money."

"Change money? What the hell for? Do they know what time it is?" Andy asked while rubbing his eyes.

"It sounds like she has ordered us to comply. After all, we are in the U.S.S.R now. We better hand over the cash, unless, of course, you want to escape," Hamilton quipped, but Andy was not amused and shot Hamilton a bird.

Since there were only four westerners on the train, there was no way of avoiding Jenny and Mary. Hamilton had no desire for a further confrontation with Mary, and neither did Jenny. But that morning, as they all did what they were told and stood in line to exchange money in a log building, neither Jenny nor Mary looked at them. Jenny aggressively ignored Hamilton's presence, except once. When Mary was tending to the baby and had her back turned, Jenny smiled at him and blew him a kiss.

Around ten that morning, when Hamilton and Andy went into the dining car for breakfast, they found that everything had changed. The exquisite Mongolian carriage had been replaced with an old dining car that had been in service since the fifties. You could tell by the decor, for the car looked as if a committee of farmers on a collective had designed it as a composite of their ideas of what the future would look like. It was all circles, curves, chrome and dingy, pastel-colored plastic. Someone had tried to spruce-up the car with paint and soap, but neither the dirt nor the absurdity could be covered up or wiped away. It reminded Hamilton of the way many of the poor blacks in Altamaha had attempted to fix up old automobiles by covering them with useless accessories, scrubbing and polishing them and spot painting the rust. Hamilton felt embarrassed for the Russians.

Hamilton looked out the window at the vast, frozen waste. He was reminded of a train trip in winter across the Canadian prairies.

"It's Lake Baikal," Hamilton said, tapping his finger on the map to indicate the location to Andy. "We'll be in Irkutsk by mid-afternoon. That's what I've calculated."

Much to their surprise, they learned that the waiter spoke German, so Hamilton was able to ask him about the food on the menu. He also learned that the Chinese would not allow alcohol to be served once the train got into the Soviet Union. The waiter said that the ban had been imposed because of the many incidents of drunken Russians beating up Chinese visitors. Knowing that this would agitate Andy, Hamilton said with a shrug:

"After all, it is a Chinese train. Guess they can do as they like."

In addition to the Russian dining car, the waiter told them that they had picked up two Russian passenger cars. They were at the other end of the train near first class.

Taking the waiter's suggestion, they both had a glass of purple kefir, eggs, sausage, toast and tea. It was good. As they shot across Siberia, Andy sipped his tea, looked out the window and fumed about the alcohol ban. Hamilton spotted Jenny, Mary and the baby entering the car. To spare everyone the awkwardness, Hamilton got up and left.

"You get the breakfast; I'll pay for dinner," he told Andy, not waiting for a reply.

Hamilton thought Andy should at least pay for something. Ever since Andy had begrudgingly given Hamilton the ten crisp American fifty-dollar bills back in Beijing, Andy somehow managed to get Hamilton to foot the bill for everything.

"I'm off to our car," Hamilton said as he slid out of the booth. "I'm going to work on *Jud's Story*."

# CHAPTER VI

## THE INHERITANCE

Well, just as I said, I figured it was time I lived alone, but I didn't buy the cottage right away. I bought it after I met Ira Thompson.

For the two and a half months after I returned from Mexico, I stayed with Hamilton. Almost every day we would walk down to the university library. I was doing research on the activities of the Confederate Covert Operations in Canada, which I had begun calling, in late twentieth-century fashion, the CCOC. I noted that one of the references I was using had been donated to the library by a Mister Ira S. Thompson, who, according to the inscription, had a Toronto address – that is, he did if he was still alive. The book had been published in the thirties and donated in the forties. As it turned out, the head of the CCOC was none other than a Jacob S. Thompson. I wondered if this was just a coincidence. With a little searching, I found that, indeed, Mister Thompson was alive and that he was the great-grandson of the man who had been in charge of Confederate espionage and insurgency in Canada during the American Civil War.

The old gentleman was as active as an eighty-two year old could be. Each day he walked from his Rosedale residence to the newly fashionable district of Yorkville where he owned a well-known and exclusive establishment called Thompson and Sons Furriers, Ltd. It had been operating since 1863. It said so right on the sign. I soon learned that the company had been founded by Jacob S. Thompson himself.

Mister Thompson and I became friends. Often we met at the Royal Ontario Museum. There we would go to the exhibits together and, over long lunches, discuss every subject from the dinosaurs found in the tar sands of Alberta to the institution of dueling. I told him everything that I knew about Judah P. Benjamin. Mister Thompson had a particular interest in him because the Confederate Secret Service was an arm of the Department of State. Since Judah P. Benjamin had been the Secretary of State, he had been Jacob S. Thompson's superior.

One afternoon, as we were musing over the remains of a three-thousand-year-old Egyptian mummy surrounded by little clay statues of human bodies with dog heads, Mister Thompson invited me to his cottage up on the Ottawa River. We both liked to fish. With the help of a high-powered magnifying glass, Mister Thompson could still tie his own flies. Yes, his hands were still as steady and firm as his character.

Just about every weekend of July, and for most of the whole month of August, we were at his cottage fishing. During the last of August he told me that he had cancer and was expected to live no longer than two more months. He had known for some time, but had revealed this to no one and had refused the treatments.

He said he wanted me to have the cottage and that his lawyers had already prepared the papers. He told me that he believed in what I was doing and he regretted that he could not stay around long enough for me to write the book so that he could read it. I knew he meant it about the book, and he really didn't have any close relative to whom he could leave the cottage. But I just did not feel it proper to take the cottage like that, so we comprised: He sold it to me. Well, he sold it for a crisp, red two-dollar bill with its picture of Queen

Elizabeth on one side and on the other, two Robins pulling worms from the earth. Its value at that time was about eighty-nine U.S. cents.

The cottage sits on a rocky, two-acre hunk of land known to the locals as Jack Pine Isle. It is about three hours from Toronto and two from Ottawa. Because it is on an island, there are two ways to get there: in summer and early fall one must go by boat; in winter, you just walk over the ice. During late fall and early spring, the cottage is inaccessible altogether, for they are in-between seasons in which one would fall through thin ice. I always have at least two months during the year when I am absolutely isolated, or choose not to be there.

Originally, the cottage had been as a trapper's shanty. In those years, it was but one of many owned by the Thompson family and used by the trappers they employed in the Ottawa Valley. When timbering took over the Valley, most of the old trapper shanties were used by loggers, but mine never was. This was partly because it is on an island, but also because Mister Thompson's father, too, was a sport fisherman. He kept the old shanty for himself and even fixed it up a bit. This does not mean that my cottage is fancy. Actually, as you will see, it is quite plain and simple. But for me, it is just right.

There are only two rooms, and the larger room has a sleeping loft. I have an air-tight stove, and the place is well insulated. I cook and read by naphtha gas. There is an outhouse, and the river water is drinkable, if, of course, boiled beforehand. I am prone to laziness, though, and often bring in bottled water for cooking and drinking.

With the cottage came a chain saw, a twelve-gauge Remington pump shotgun, a World War I Ross rifle, pots, pans and dishes. I made an antenna for my portable radio, and I keep it hooked up to a twelve-volt, heavy-duty car battery – the best from Canadian Tire. I'm not hurting for fishing tackle, and there is a good Grumman canoe beached on the rocks in front of the cottage. There is even a bateau and a six-horse Mercury outboard. And if you look out about one-hundred yards across the water from my west-side window, you will see, there on the bluff, my 1986 Ford pickup.

I also have a number of books, a good but old typewriter, and always booze, some bought and some beer that I occasionally make and bottle myself. In a sunny clearing on the south side of the island, Mister Thompson had long ago planted an apple tree that never fails to offer more than enough of its fruit to last a winter, not to mention the blueberry and raspberry bushes he planted nearby. I, too, have my own little garden. Among my tomatoes, squash, asparagus, rhubarb and a plant or two of Mary Jane, I have a dozen hybrid tea rose bushes that bless me with blooms from June until late September. There's really not much else I need, except, occasionally, a good piece of ass, and I know where to get plenty of that.

So, in late October, Ira Thompson died. As specified in his will, two days later I took his ashes out into the middle of the river and slowly let them trail behind in the cold current. Then I cut the motor, drifted downstream and settled into my cottage. When the pines began to look black against the sky and the river became a prairie of ice and blowing snow, I realized that it was time to start writing about my great-great-uncle.

I did not want to just write about my ancestor's extraordinary yet mere life. Others had already done that. I wanted to explore those aspects of his sojourn that were unknown and uncontested. Simply put, I was interested in the part of Judah P. Benjamin's life that could have been otherwise – not his actual and factual life, but his possible life. After all, the possible is the true realm of the spirit. Yes, while we may know something of the meaning of man's life upon his death, we must appreciate that his life could not have happened in an infinite number of other ways. Like Ira Thompson's life, or any other man's, Judah P. Benjamin's life could have, and indeed might have, happened otherwise.

As if to divine something from them, I took the letters from the blued metal box – the letters Judah P. Benjamin had written to his brother Malachi while Malachi had been in British Honduras and Altamaha – and I carefully read each of them again and again. I must go backwards, I told myself, deeper, farther upstream. I thought of myself as sailing across a sea mad with waves and swells for the mouth and then toward the womb of that world. Yes, I saw myself sailing toward that great and ancient muddy stream called the Altamaha. Then I began.

**THE SECRET HISTORY OF**
**JUDAH PHILIP BENJAMIN**
by
Judah Anubis Benjamin III

This book is dedicated to the memory of
IRA SAMSON THOMPSON
Descendent of a patriot and
the best fisherman in the Valley

"The Sail ... hurl'd away both Knight and Horse along
with it."
Cervantes, DON QUIXOTE

## Chapter One
## ESCAPE FROM AMERICA

It was a sunny spring morning in early April of 1865. He raised the window and stood in the sunlight peering at the spectacle occurring in the capitol square. His hands were joined behind his back as he stood there in his shirtsleeves. The large gold ring on the third finger of his right hand caught a beam of light as he turned and paced.

Calling him "Falstaff" had been mere derision on the part of his enemies and a warm expression of affection by his friends; yet neither enemy nor friend would have dared use the epithet to his face. But had they done so, he likely would have smiled and chuckled, as he would have been please to be associated with the bard's rotund and roguish character. In fact, the second of Shakespeare's plays featuring Henry IV and that cast of colorful characters was his favorite. He was also like Sir John Falstaff in temperament, in that he was open, forgiving and cheerful, which all seem to go together. This round, happy man was Judah Philip Benjamin, Secretary of State for the Confederate States of America.

Like Falstaff, Mister Benjamin was exotic in that overtly occidental, Anglo-Saxon Protestant world of the American South, but there were differences quite apart from time and setting. First, although having been of similar physique and demeanor, Mister Benjamin was no rogue, but rather a gentleman from a line of gentlemen. And furthermore, Judah P. Benjamin did not look like a man whose descendents fared from the British Isles or any other clime in Northern Europe, as did so many white Southern males of that place and time. Mister Benjamin was the issue of a long line of Spanish Jews whose Sephardic blood was the same as that of other Jewish aristocrats, such as Baruch Spinoza and Benjamin Disraeli. Thus, the conditions that had lead to his being present on that particular day in Richmond, Virginia stretched back to the Spanish Inquisition and to Holland, Britain, Saint Croix – where he had been born – and then to Wilmington, North Carolina, the small town at the mouth of the Cape Fear River. So, while Mister Benjamin was not a son of the South, he had become a man of the South par excellence.

Mister Benjamin returned to his place at his third-story office window. Indeed, he thought, the turning point of the war had been exactly two years from this very day. It was the morning of the second day of April, 1863, that they had rioted in Richmond.

That morning he had placed his feet in the same spot and gazed from the same window. They had swarmed in like ants and then concentrated near the southeast corner of the square. Most of them had been women. Certainly scores of them, several hundred even, had been gathering since the early morning, and by noon they had stirred themselves up into a mad frenzy. Through his window he had heard gripes and curses. They had fought among themselves, groups shaking fists as they shouted at another. They had slung blame in all directions, but the most frequent targets of their derision had been King Davis and the Jew that lives on Madeira wine.

But the truth about the above is that when righteous causes turn into "Lost Causes," erstwhile heroes often are transformed into treacherous, villainous monsters. And a king for the American – whether he is Southerner or Northerner – is by their historically conditioned definition, a tyrant. And yes, just as Sir John Falstaff loved his Dry Sack, Mister Benjamin also loved his Madeira, the difference being that Mister Benjamin would never have been caught dead in a bawdy house like Falstaff's favored haunt, the Boar's Head, for he kept company only with other gentleman and he drank like a gentleman, which means that like any gentleman, "he could hold his liquor."

An hour after midday, the crowd had become feverous and throbbed with delirium. It was no longer a kaleidoscope made up of patterned change, but had become a series of liquid wholes that suddenly would run in any unpredictable direction. They had poured through the square's western gate, down 9th Street and then zigzagged across Main Street toward Cary Street. As the crown had sloshed along, many women had oozed from their houses to join the flow, building up the pressure as their ranks swelled, along with the increasing intensity of their chant: "FOOD! FOOD!"

Once they had reached Cary Street, they had emptied government warehouses of flour, cornmeal, dried and tinned meats and government-issue military clothing. One woman had carried a bale of gray long johns; another had been bent under the weight of two huge smoked hams; and then there had been the one rolling a barrel, which she was trying to push over a curb. "SALTED FISH DEPT. OF INTERIOR # 342678-C.S.A." was stenciled across its girth.

With their waves of swiftly accumulating booty, they had surged from Cary Street and neared the State Department.

## Disorderly Notions

They had thrown paving stones that had been miraculously liberated from the street. The stones had crashed into shop doors and windows and pelted both humans and animals within their trajectory. People, dogs and horses fled the stones. The crowd had then poured into the stores on Main Street, knocking over counters of merchandise as they withdrew with jewels, silk and other valuables, together with whatever flotsam had been caught up in the serge. A woman had run out into the street with several hats crammed on her head as she struggled to carry an armload of dresses. Another had come from a shop dragging something alive and fighting inside a gunny sack. It had been an angry Tom turkey that, upon its escape, had attacked the woman. There had been no evidence that the shopkeepers had protested. They had seemed stunned by the tide of angry women, and to Mister Benjamin they had appeared to have resigned to the situation.

Standing there and musing about the riot, a terrible thought occurred to him. He pictured the French Revolution and the "March of the Women" – that hoard of market hags and fishwives who had trudged the ten miles to Versailles and had frog-marched the royal family to Vendome and Bastille. They had taunted the family until they became bored and then had handed them over so they could be relieved of their heads. He thought of Edmund Burke's main argument in his "Reflections on the Revolution in France." Burke had said that revolutions, because they are built on abstract notions, enviably lead to anarchy and chaos. Neither the war of 1776, brought on by American succession from Britain, nor the 1861 succession of the South from the American Union, were revolutions. Rather both had been wars for independence and liberation from tyranny.

Then Mister Benjamin remembered seeing President Davis mounted on a small, dappled mare, sitting straight and as tall in his saddle as his small, gaunt frame would allow. He had tried to reason with the rioters.

"Forgo this, madam," Mister Benjamin remembered him saying.

He reflected that one could not reason with those who are incapable of such. Yet he noted that Davis had merely gestured with a raised hand and the members of the crowd nearest him had become responsible and free individuals again, dropping their booty and walking away. Well, perhaps they had known their own self-interest, which indeed is a form of reason. In fact, it is the most basic kind, he reminded himself. He concluded that Mister Davis must have persuaded the crowd that the source of their troubles had not been with him, but with Yankee aggression.

Yes, Mister Benjamin reflected, that day in Richmond had been a bad omen. It had foreshadowed the horrific decision he and Mister Davis had made to send Lee's Army of Northern Virginia into Pennsylvania. The few victories of the South after Gettysburg had meant nothing. The Confederacy had been reduced to a shattered country with a besieged capital city, a rump of a scattered, ill-supplied and demoralized military and a broken, bewildered cabinet.

In his role as Secretary of State, Mister Benjamin had made concerted efforts on the diplomatic front. He had sought recognition of the C.S.A. from a major power, such as Britain, France or Russia. Had one of the European powers recognized them, suing for an acceptable peace would have been likely. In 1864, the situation of the South had been so desperate that attempts had been made to frighten the Mexicans into recognizing the Confederacy. Mister Benjamin had argued that eventually the French-controlled puppet government would be attacked by the Union because of France's violation of the Monroe Doctrine, but Archduke Maximilian, the puppet emperor, would not budge.

Attributing to this desperation was the nearly eighty-thousand Irishman who had been lured by a five-hundred-dollar-enlistment bonus to immigrate and join the ranks of the armies of the Union. In late 1863, the South's troops had already been severely diminished in number and the addition of what had amounted to foreign mercenaries to the configuration had been a disaster. Not only had Mister Benjamin sent agents to Britain and Ireland as an attempt to avert this, but he even had gone so far as to send an envoy to Pope Pious IX asking for a pronouncement against what surely would become a mass slaughter of the green Irish Catholic troops. The pope had been sympathetic, but had seemed more interested in attempting to persuade the envoy to beseech their government to free the slaves. Mister Benjamin had tried to bolster the morale of Mister Davis and his cabinet by reminding them of the disdain Machiavelli had for the mercenary and arguing that even against larger numbers, the goddess Fortuna was always on the side of the citizen soldier fighting for his motherland.

Although there had frequently been the temptation to arm the slaves as a way of addressing the dwindling number of Southern troops, Mister Benjamin had always refused to bend. He had been more responsive to devising a plan of emancipating the slaves in exchange for loyal military service. This had been proposed to the British as an item to encourage recognition, but this had been near the war's end and Lord Palmerston, who knew that British public opinion had been swayed by the New England abolitionists and the novel *Uncle Tom's Cabin*.

With an ever-dwindling military and the lack of diplomatic success, the Confederacy had become disparate and on several occasions had resorted to innovative covert actions. As Secretary of State, Mister Benjamin had been the overseer of the Confederate Secret Service (CSC) and had often had a direct hand in their imaginative, if seldom successful, schemes. One had been the successful plan to sabotage shipping on the Mississippi after the river had fallen into Yankee hands in 1862. Indeed, many a riverboat did burn.

Jacob Thompson, who had been Secretary of the Interior under President Buchanan, became head of a clandestine organization called Confederate Covert Operations in Canada or, as it had been referred to by the cabinet, the CCOC. From across the northern border of the United States, Thompson had not only been able to exploit Confederate sympathy among the Canadians, but also mobilize Confederates in exile and antiwar Democrats within the Union itself, such as the Sons of Liberty and other Copperheads. Thompson's most daring exploit had been the raid on Saint Albins, Vermont, from Canadian soil. This attack on the small New England town by Confederate troops and Canadian sympathizers, though largely symbolic, had been a resounding, victorious insult.

By far the most distressing events experienced by Southerners had been the raids of "Butcher Butler" on civilians and military in Louisiana and the punishing war of Sheridan in the Shenandoah Valley, but the most horrendous event had been what Sherman had done to Georgia. The general had vowed to make Georgia howl. After he had literally burned Atlanta to the ground, he cut his own supply lines and turned his troops loose to live off the land. And so they had as they looted, pillaged, raped, tortured, scorched and burned everything in their great swath toward Savannah and the sea. Yes, Georgia had howled.

Mister Benjamin had surmised that the South needed a victory equally as spectacular as Sherman's burning of Atlanta, and so he and Thompson devised a plan to burn New York City. The fires were to be so much bigger! Thompson had organized a clandestine raid on carefully chosen buildings in the city – strategically selected for both their symbolic value and their location in what was hoped would become an inferno. In November of 1864, while Sherman was terrorizing Georgia, Barnum's American Museum and several hotels had been set ablaze. But in the end, either the arsonists had been quite inefficient or the New York fire department had really known how to put out fires. The raid had caused little damage, no terror and added dismay for the disintegrating Confederacy.

Standing there at the window and reflecting on those fateful two years, Mister Benjamin thoughts turned to the night he and his friend and fellow Louisianan, Jules, with whom he had leased a house on Main Street, had dined with Francis Lawley, the Richmond correspondent for the *London Times*. Mister Lawley had been the barer of the sad news that the last hope Mister Benjamin had for recognition by a major European power had evaporated. He had told Mister Benjamin that the Confederate sympathizer, Louis Napoleon, had failed to convene Britain to join France in not respecting the Yankee blockade, as it was terrible for trade, and then eventually recognizing the Confederacy. That night, they had finished Mister Benjamin's last bottle of Madeira and while it had not dispelled their sorrow completely, it had dispelled it enough for Mister Benjamin and Jules to recall a dinner in New Orleans in 1862 when the colored house servant had come to the table with the news that a Yankee was at the door.

"What did you say?" Mister Lawley had asked.

"What could I say? I am ruined, voilà tout. And alas, they will surely turn my house into a Yankee hospital."

Jules had gestured grandly with a sweep of an arm and laughed sardonically with his black Creole eyes. Yes, they all had known it was over.

Mister Benjamin continued to stare out of the window, but now he was staring blankly. He hardly noticed the troops and bureaucrats making piles of paper files in the middle of the square and setting them alight, destroying information that might be of some use to the Yankees. The trees were a light, spring green and the smell of honeysuckle hung on the air.

Earlier that morning, General Lee had sent a message to President Davis informing him that it had been necessary to abandon his position along the James River, which had, in effect, left Richmond open to attack. But the message had become even graver. Sherman, who had been severely punishing South Carolina for having led the secession, had

## Disorderly Notions

dispatched forward units into North Carolina. With the unavoidable retreat of Lee's army, the Confederate capitol would be gripped in a pincer.

Treasury, along with sensitive archives, had already been shipped south by rail. By the time General Lee's message had arrived, the president had ordered the capitol evacuated and for his cabinet to travel south with him by train.

The tracks had been in a poor state of repair and because of this the train had traveled slowly. Their slow pace meant they did not reach their destination – the little town of Danville in southern Virginia near the North Carolina border – that day. This remote place would become the first of three odd and short-lived capitals of the soon-to-be-defeated and defunct Confederate States of America.

This retreating party consisted of the president and his aide-de-camp, Mister Benjamin, his old friend Jules, Attorney General Mallory and, later, a Doctor Hodge, professor of classics at the University of Richmond. It had been a happy moment within a sad occasion for Mister Benjamin and Doctor Hodge, as they were old friends, having shared a room at Yale. Doctor Hodge, Mister Benjamin and Jules were billeted in the home of a local banker, to whom they were grateful.

That evening, they amused themselves with Doctor Hodge's recitations of Homer's *Odyssey* and Plato's "Apology," Mister Benjamin's recitation of passages from Cicero's "de legibus" and Jules provision of a scene from Molière's *Le Bourgeois gentilhomme*. Mister Benjamin and Doctor Hodge revisited an old, friendly disagreement that had gone as far back as the old Yale days about the merits of Tennyson's poetry. Mister Benjamin had loved it; Hodge thought it both sentimental and pedantic. Jules thought that it, along with all poetry not written in French, sounded barbaric.

Around noon on the ninth day of April, word came of Lee's surrender and the beginning of the occupation by Grant's army. They all gathered on the courthouse steps of the temporary capitol of the Confederacy while Mister Davis sadly but matter-of-factly told the crowd the grim news. As the disoriented crowd dispersed, Attorney General Mallory hung his head and muttered:

"May God help us. The honor of the Confederacy is lost!"

"No dear Mallory, it is the Confederacy that is lost," Mister Benjamin replied cheerfully.

Later in the afternoon, after much argument had been made by Mister Benjamin, Doctor Hodge was persuaded that his continual travel with a pack of war criminals with large bounties on their heads was not a good idea, and the professor left Danville on horseback. But Jules could not be persuaded to leave his friend, vowing to protect him with his life, if necessary. Next to the president, Mister Benjamin's face was the best known of the newly minted fugitives, and there would be a large price stamped to his forehead. Jules did not care.

The party of war criminals immediately fled farther south, well into North Carolina toward Greensboro. Upon their arrival, they discovered that Stoneman's cavalry had destroyed the railroad bridge over the river. They could have returned to Danville, but instead they elected to remain in Greensboro. However, fearing Yankee reprisals, the citizens of Greensboro did not make them feel welcome. So the leaky boxcar on the edge of town became the second-to-last Confederate capitol.

For nearly a week they remained there, never roaming far, and existed on jerky, hardtack and ersatz coffee made from chicory boiled in water from the river. During this time, generals Johnston and Beauregard arrived and made decisions based on the facts. The facts were that they had only 25,000 troops in the field and no one knew how many could or would fight, while the enemy had over 350,000. Despite these stark facts, Davis and Benjamin refused to capitulate, so the end was postponed for a few more days. During this brief period, the crates of gold coins that had been stored in the back of the boxcar were distributed to Johnson's army; the surrender of which was a certainty. The remaining treasure – about $35,000 in gold coins – would be disbursed to the rump of the Confederate cabinet. They would need it to escape from America.

On the fifteenth day of April, they began the rest of their odyssey south – deeper and deeper down into the heartland of Dixie. Most traveled on horseback, accompanied by two squads of cavalry. The president, the attorney general, Jules and Mister Benjamin brought up the rear in an ambulance.

On the road to Charlotte in the middle of a rainy night, the red glow of Mister Benjamin's cigar providing the only light inside the ambulance, Jules laughed:

"Gentleman, I find it ironic that it was Mister Benjamin's design for the new money that we adopted."

Everyone laughed at what had become an inside joke. Mister Benjamin struck a match with his thumbnail and held his hand under the light of the flame. There, on his finger, was a gold ring made from one of the several thousands of coins the Master of the Mint had made as prototypes. They fell silent as Mister Benjamin talked, and they looked at the gold ring in the blaze of the match:

"Gentleman, you will remember that the basic denomination was to be called a 'Cavalier,' and that the one-hundred-dollar version was to be a gold coin just like this one. The mounted horseman here shields his eyes from the rays of the rising sun. He peers at the horizon – the future. My idea was to have the legal tender of the South represent the opposite view of the world-despising Puritan with his venomous eye of resentment, whose new world exponent is the Yankee and his boring cult of the practical and useful.

"I envisaged him – the Cavalier, of course – as a gentleman. O Kaloskagathos," Mister Benjamin said as he imagined in his head Ο Καλοσκαγατηοσ. "He is the gentleman because he does that for which he is 'fitted,' to use Plato's term, because he knows who he is and what he ought to do. He is happy to be in this world, and is therefore at home in it.

"I figure him to be spontaneous and generous and, above all, a sportive man. This means he chooses risk over predictability, mystery over certainty, freedom over control, culture over cunning and technique. He is a man who embraces distinction and eschews vulgar sentimental notions of equality. He cares little for efficiency and strives after excellence. He lives by a code of honor that holds as a duty helping friends and harming enemies. When necessary, he can be cruel. While he has no pity for the weak and common, he has compassion for them, and he will defend them with his life, for this too he considers his duty. He is most at home sitting astride a spirited steed. He is a man who thrives on challenge, even on danger. He, gentleman, is the man I pictured as embodying the virtues of the South."

Then, to break up what had become a heavy silence that might engender among them a mood of melancholy, Mister Benjamin added:

"Yes, my friend Jules, you are right. It is ironic. I chose the mounted horseman as the image of our country, yet I would walk across Asia before I would sit astride one of those beasts."

They all laughed.

The streets of Charlotte surged with confusion; former troops from Lee's army staggered in the streets, and refugees who had come from Richmond milled about, lost. It was during the first days after arriving in Charlotte that they learned of Lincoln's assassination. Then there was the surrender. Mister Davis resisted it to the end, and he and this last band of die-hard Confederates entertained schemes of re-establishing the government in the southwest – beyond the Mississippi, in Texas, New Mexico and Arizona. But these were desperate and unworkable plans, they all finally admitted.

In the middle of the night, they fled farther south.

At Abbeville, South Carolina, Jefferson Davis made a final plea for them to accept yet another one of his plans, but this time even Mister Benjamin was politely silent. On the west bank of the Savannah River, across from Washington-Wilkes, Georgia, on the third of May, their party sadly disbanded. Mister Benjamin and his friend Jules crossed the river by ferry and departed southwest into Georgia. They were on horseback.

Considering the odd sojourn they were undertaking, Mister Benjamin began to amuse himself: He was Falstaff and Jules was Falstaff's page, Bardolph. Yet that did not quite fit, and it was an insult to his old friend Jules. Why not the Don of La Mancha? Yes, now that is fine, by Jove! I'm Quixote, he thought, and Jules is Sancho.

At that moment, Jules said, "My dear Benjamin, in that outfit you are the perfect picture of le bourgeois gentilhomme."

The experience had been painful for both Mister Benjamin and the horse, but about thirty miles from the Savannah River, near Washington-Wilkes, they had a grand stroke of luck that allowed them to change their form of transportation. The horse was shed of his great burden.

"Nice pair of horses you boys got there," said a huge, ugly man.

His body covered most of the seat of the buckboard parked in the shade of a chinaberry tree. His unhitched mule was drinking water from a muddy creek.

"Looks to me you got too much a load," he laughed, referring both to Mister Benjamin and to the load strapped behind Jules's saddle – a metal case with J.P.B. painted in script, strapped on top of their two suitcases and two C.S.A. field blankets. "You boys want'in ta swap?" he joked.

To his surprise, they agreed, and soon Mister Benjamin and Jules were riding in the buckboard.

They rode through Washington-Wilkes with Mister Benjamin driving. He wore goggles, a sweaty, brown derby and a long canvas teamster coat that they had pressed for in the bargain. Jules became a French journalist reporting on the Yankee victory. Mister Benjamin became Jules's French driver, who spoke not one word of English.

They went west. Macon, in the center of the state, was their destination. Mister Benjamin wanted to inquire about his brother Malachi, formerly a student of classics at Mercer University who became a captain in General Wayne's Dragoons. They talked about going from Macon to Mister Benjamin's aunt's house in LaGrange where his two sisters and his wife and daughter had relocated when New Orleans had fallen in 1862. Although his wife and daughter had long ago departed for Paris, Mister Benjamin's sisters were still there, so Mister Benjamin and Jules reasoned that LaGrange might be a good place to wait until Mister Benjamin could escape to England.

They had no map, but all along the way Jules – who was now Monsieur Pourier of the Paris Metiore – asked to be shown the direction to Macon, which he pronounced as if it were the city in France. This method brought much confusion, for the Georgians pronounced the name of their city in such a way as to have it rhyme with "bacon." Eventually, after passing through Georgia's main university town with the pretentious name of Athens, they crossed into the path made by Sherman's troops. This was at Monroe, some thirty miles to the southwest.

Green weeds were already growing through the blackened fields, and carcasses of starved cattle, horses and mules littered the sides of the road. The town seemed practically empty. No one even nodded as they passed through. These people were suspicious, and they had reason to be, for many strangers had been appearing there lately wanting to make deals and buy land.

Outside Monroe they were told by a friendly but sad farmer that they should take a back route to Macon, thereby avoiding the road that goes through Stone Mountain where the pickets around the rubble of Atlanta formed an outer ring. They did as he advised. On this long trip to Macon, Mister Benjamin lost ten pounds. They bought what food they could, but the food was worth more than even the gold money they carried in the metal box in their wagon. All in all, they took the trip cheerfully, and as they bumped along the dusty, red clay roads, Mister Benjamin recited Tennyson's "Ode on the Death of the Duke of Wellington." Jules listened politely only because he was a friend.

They arrived at a crossroads called Eatonton Factory, a charred settlement where Sherman's Fourteenth Corps had passed through four months before. There were no public or commercial buildings left standing. The factory, formally a farm implement company modified during the war to forge cannons, had been blown into the river. A score of shacks and peeling white-painted houses stood beside the road. Frightened faces, some white and some black, peered from the darkness behind cracked doors.

About ten miles from Milledgeville, in the valley of a small river, they looked down a lane of tall pines and saw the burned ruins of a great white house. They met a Negro on the road who told them the house had belonged to a Mister Howell Cobb.

"It wuz Massa Cobb's place, but it ain't his no mo'," the man said. "Wuz 'til the Lawd sent Gen'al Billy Shoman."

As they rounded a bend, they saw a foraging party of Yankee cavalry watering their horses in a sluggish stream. They had gunnysacks tied to the saddles, one containing corn and another containing sweet potato. In other sacks were glass bottles filled with blackstrap molasses.

Tethered behind one of the horses was a cow. Her bones at her shoulders and hips looked like poles under a tent of skin, and her ribs could be counted. When Mister Benjamin and Jules reached the creek, their mule snorted, but the soldiers ignored them; they were too busy passing around a bottle, joking and cursing. Suddenly, from a path along the river, a young man with pink skin and red hair wearing sergeant stripes arrived on a galloping, sweaty horse.

"You stupid louts!" he shouted. "That cow's worthless. Lame, she is! You'd be a draggin' her soon."

He pulled his .38 caliber service revolver from his holster, placed it behind the cow's left ear and fired. The cow seemed to leap into the air and, in a heap, splashed into the water at the edge of the stream. The man's pink face was rodent-like and his skin was blistered by exposure to the sun.

The sergeant noticed the wagon coming toward him.

"Halt! Identify yourselves!"

He held up a hand, ordering them to stop.

"Jules Pourier, reporter for the Paris Metiore, and here is my driver and secretary, Breton. Unfortunately, he does not speak English. I am reporting on the great military victory of General Sherman."

"You tell them people in France that our lads have whipped them Rebs. Do you have papers?"

## Disorderly Notions

His accent was Irish. He was from Boston or New York maybe, but he was Irish nonetheless.

Luckily for Jules and Mister Benjamin, everyone's attention was turned toward the dead cow. A woman appeared and was standing up to her ankles in water. With a butcher knife, she began skinning the flank of the animal. The soldiers looked on curiously as the haggard woman exposed the flesh under the peeled-away skin.

Occasionally she gave a glare of fury to the soldiers – a look that said she would rather use the knife on them. The blood oozing into the stream made the water around her bare ankles black. She tugged at a layer of hide, gouged out a hunk of flesh and shoved it toward a small girl. Under the child's eyes were purple circles; her belly was swollen. Her desire for the meat was so intense that those who were watching could feel it. She snatched the meat with a bony hand and vanished behind a clump of mulberry bushes. The soldiers said nothing, taking their horses by the reins and walking away. The sergeant spit; then he looked at Jules.

"Get yerself outta here! Go write to your damned French."

In Milledgeville, state government buildings were burned along with several blocks of stores and warehouses, and there was a smutty pile of bricks and rubble that had been the railroad depot. The Governor's Mansion had become the headquarters of General Slocum; the State House had been transformed into a garrison. There was a huge crater where the arsenal had been, and the explosion left no glass in any windows for blocks around. The gates of the Georgia State Asylum for the Insane stood open, and bug-eyed lunatics roamed the streets. "Ha, ha!" they could hear someone shouting. A great stained-glass window had been blown out of a brick church, and as they rolled past, they saw the shouting madman standing in the choir loft.

"Ha, ha! Jesus is a Jew! Ha, ha! God is a dead nigger! Ha, ha! This is the end of the world! Ha, ha!"

The man was wearing a black-and-white choir robe, but the robe had fallen open, revealing his nakedness. He was masturbating.

"Mon Dieu! What must Atlanta be like?" Jules sighed.

That night it rained, but it had been their good fortune to find an abandoned barn and, inside, corn and oats for the tired, old mule.

Late the next day, from the top of a hill, they saw the spires of Macon. As they came closer to the city, they spoke of the dread they had for what they might find. Yes,

Macon too would be ruined; of this, they were sure. But when they arrived at the bridge over the Ocmulgee River, they were amazed, for there was little evidence of invasion. They later learned that Sherman had been told that there was a terrible Confederate prison at Millen, and acting on this, he had diverted his main force away from the city of Macon.

The ploy had worked. Only two contingents of infantry and a company of cavalry had been sent to the city. First, they had fired a dozen cannon salvos into Macon in order to terrify the citizens, and then they had blown up the arsenal and a pistol factory. But that was all. Leaving behind only a small garrison of infantry, the other troops left the city and hurried to join the march to the sea.

Mister Benjamin wanted to locate a man named John Underwood. He had shared a suite of rooms with Mister Benjamin and Doctor Hodge at Yale and had been a classmate of Mister Benjamin's in law school. Since John Underwood was the dean of the law school at Mercer University, they searched for the campus. Mister Benjamin hoped that Mister Underwood might know something of his brother Malachi's whereabouts.

Their thin mule did not like the hard bricks on College Street. The poor beast had lost a shoe and had begun to limp. Mister Benjamin, feeling sorry for the mule, insisted that they unhitch the beast from the wagon and let it graze in the overgrown grass in the large square called Telfair Park across from the red-brick campus.

As they walked across the park and came to an empty fountain in the center, they saw that the Union flag had been attached to the top of the spire of the tallest building on the Mercer University campus. Then they saw the dark-blue uniforms; the Yankees were garrisoned there. Mister Benjamin and Jules reasoned that this was not where they would find John Underwood, unless he was being held prisoner there.

They devised a plan. Leaving the mule and wagon tied up in the park, they began to walk the streets of Macon, approaching those who appeared as if they could be helpful to them. Jules pretended to seek John Underwood for an interview for his newspaper, but everyone was so suspicious of strangers that they found it impossible to locate the address of John Underwood's house. In fact, those whom they encountered said that they had never heard of John Underwood.

Finally, they encountered an old Negro woman who was willing to take them there.

## Disorderly Notions

The house was on Orange Street, not far from the campus. John Underwood's sister, who kept house for him, met them at the door. At first she did not believe they were who they said. Although Mister Benjamin had removed the derby and goggles, exposing his famous face to her, she simply could not imagine that the elegant Secretary of State could ever look so disheveled and dirty. It was not until Mister Benjamin named all of her brothers and sisters, several of their slaves and her brother's boyhood dog that she finally believed him.

She prepared them tea and insisted that they stay for the night. That evening, after the first real meal that Mister Benjamin and Jules had eaten in almost three weeks, they sat on the porch and listened to John Underwood's sister tell them about her brother.

"They are offering a reward for his arrest. Only I know where he is. He is at an abandoned fishing camp at a place known as Seven Bridges. It is at the end of the Ocmulgee River, where it flows into the Altamaha. I will make you a map. You must memorize it and then destroy it. You can leave in the morning. I know he plans to escape, but to where I do not know. It is a possibility that he has already left."

Orange Street overlooked the city, and in the distance they could see the flicker of the picket's fires at the fairgrounds near the river where the Yankees had blown up the pistol factory. As they sat on the porch and looked out over the city, John Underwood's sister said how she and her brother both had admired Malachi, Mister Benjamin's younger brother. He was a fine young scholar. Sadly, the last anyone had heard of Malachi and Wayne's Dragoons was before the Yankees had closed down the newspaper. She knew he had fought at Milledgeville, and the battle had taken heavy casualties. Sherman took few prisoners. Maybe, they were still fighting; she heard that some were. Perhaps, though, he had gone down to Mexico with the many others who fled.

"The slaves should have been set free. Look at us, we all are slaves now," he said sadly as he poured the bourbon into their cups.

John Underwood was a tall, lean man. He had a large patrician nose and white hair. He needed a shave.

"No, I have no idea where Malachi has gone, but my feeling is that he's gone far away. I think you are right. It's the best thing for all of us. And, if you don't object, I'm going with you to England."

The following day, Jules kissed Mister Benjamin on both cheeks and left on foot for New Orleans. Meanwhile, John

Underwood arranged for a one-eyed cracker named Buster McNix to raft them downriver to where the Ocmulgee meets the Oconee River. At the confluence of these two rivers is the beginning of the Altamaha River. From there, it would be but a three-day journey on foot to Brunswick and the sea. Once they reached the sea, they could walk to Florida in perhaps a day.

Mister Benjamin, John Underwood, the frightened mule and Buster McNix floated down the red river. Mister Benjamin no longer wore the goggles and, because of the heat, had left the long teamster coat behind with the rickety buckboard. He kept only the derby.

Mister Benjamin assumed the role of a deaf-mute, yet they were not concerned about him being recognized, for the raft man seemed too stupid and the country where they were going was remote and sparsely populated.

Were it then written, Mister Benjamin might have made one of his fanciful literary comparisons between this river journey by raft to that of Huck Finn and Nigger Jim. It would have been necessary to decide who was which character - a difficult task to be sure - but an even larger problem would have arisen: Buster McNix, being an extra that spoiled the scene, would have to be eliminated, and how would one nix McNix? Then the reverse may be considered, too. Had Mister Clements - who had not yet become Mister Twain - known about this sojourn by barge on the Altamaha, it might well have inspired him to write about the adventure on the Mississippi. Granted, this is just fantasy; but alas, it could have happened an infinite number of ways.

It rained for two days. The three men and the mule huddled under an oily canvas. They ate fatback and biscuits. There was no conversation between John Underwood and Mister Benjamin because of the charade, but the cracker jabbered on unceasingly. The barge smelled of mule shit, stale tobacco and Buster McNix. McNix sung songs through his nose, which had a ghostly echo of a bagpipe.

At night, after they tied up alongside a peach-colored bluff or beach on a sand bar, McNix smoked his pipe and drank corn whiskey until he passed out. He mumbled, laughed and farted in his sleep, and he ceased to do so only when the sun woke the jungle and it began to sing.

They drifted with the current for three days. The land was no longer hilly, and the rolling woods of pine gave way to moss-covered oaks, cypress and tangles of palmetto palm. The river was deeper, and because of the tannin from the roots in the great swamps, the water was a dark brownish red or black. There were white, sand beaches, and the current was slower. They went ashore and, watching for cottonmouths, followed McNix into a swamp where they dug in the rich, black soil for worms. They took the worms back to the barge and, as they drifted along, they fished. Within an hour they had caught all they could eat.

The next morning, something large and swift struck a fish Mister Benjamin had hooked. In his excitement, he shouted:

"By Jove! It's an alligator!"

McNix tried to shoot the beast, but missed. John Underwood pretended it was he who shouted.

Later that day, McNix caught a cooter. He steered the barge to the shore, went into the swamp and soon returned with a handful of bay leaves and a load of firewood. He built a fire under the smutty black pot in the center of the barge. When the water began to boil, he dropped in the live turtle.

After the turtle cooked for half an hour, McNix fished it out with a spade and cracked open the shell with his machete. Then he removed the liver and eggs.

"Gotta mind out that ye don't bust the gall," he said to John Underwood.

McNix put the turtle back into the pot and stewed it again. After some time, he sliced up the meat and returned it to the pot along with three persimmons, six sweet potatoes and four onions. He crushed bay leaves and dropped them in, added a cup of corn whisky, salt and pepper and then motioned for Mister Benjamin to come over and stir. As a last gesture, he sliced another onion and dropped it in, and then he thickened the bubbling liquid with a cup of flour. Later, Mister Benjamin wished he had told Buster McNix just how good he thought the cooter stew had tasted.

At noon, on the eighth day after their departure, they arrived at a bluff and the village of Baxton. They were just ten miles upstream on the Ocmulgee from where the Ocmulgee meets the Oconee to form the Altamaha River.

"Well, boys, thought ya'd fooled ole Buster, didn't ya? Didn't take the likes o' me long ta figure out who ya were. No sir!"

He threw back his head and laughed, revealing his brown and black teeth. Then, pointing the shotgun into Mister Benjamin's face, he glared and said:

"I knowed 'zactly who ya were when ya slipped up and called the name of one of them there Jew gods. They got ya ugly picture up in the post office there on Cherry Street in Macon. Ya know how much money they gonna give me fo ya hide? Ha! I knowed a fat Jew boy anywheres."

With the shotgun, he gestured toward John Underwood.

"Ya get ya'r pretty arse over here and take that there rope and tie this here Christ killin' Jew boy up to that there post. Do it tight or I'll just have to have me an accident with ya, like stickin' this here barrel up ya'r arse and blowing ya'r guts all over this here river. Without this here fat boy, ya ain't worth much of nothing."

After John Underwood tied Mister Benjamin to the post and bound his own feet, Buster McNix preformed the tricky maneuver of getting John Underwood's hands tied while holding the barrel of the shotgun in Mister Benjamin's face.

"Tell you boys what I'm a gonna do. Just to be fair about it, so as to make sure you is who I know you is, I'm gonna check out your peter."

When McNix began to undo Mister Benjamin's belt, Mister Benjamin's eyes widened in astonishment.

"Mister McNix, this is not necessary. I confess that I not only am a Jew, but I am exactly who you so wisely surmise me to be, Judah P. Benjamin."

But McNix ignored him, grinned and proceeded to unbutton his trousers. With a big tug, he pulled them down to Mister Benjamin's huge thighs and began unbuttoning his long johns. He laughed as he had a look.

"Well, well. So, that's what one of them Jew peters looks like. He ain't got no hood, the baldheaded thing. Yeah, you is who you say you is, you and your Jew peter. Now, I see you boys ta reckly," McNix says leaving Mister Benjamin's trousers around his thighs and his underwear unbuttoned. "Them Yankees up in Baxton gonna be happy as two dick dogs when I tell 'em who I got down here on this ole barge. Boy! I'm gonna go drink all the liquor in Brunswick, and after that I might just go up to Savanner!" he said, laughing as he went scrambling up the bluff.

But Buster McNix was too impatient, and he did not take time to tie John Underwood's hands tightly. By the time Buster vanished over the top of the bluff, one hand was already loose. John Underwood had no trouble getting out of his ropes, but he found Mister Benjamin's knots troublesome. He found Buster's machete near the pot beside the hollowed cooter shell. The blade was dull, but he was finally able to cut Mister Benjamin's ropes.

They undid the barge from the stump holding it to the bank and moved out into the current. John Underwood took

Disorderly Notions

the long rudder, but because of his great weight, Mister Benjamin had more success with a pole. Although the barge went slight sideways, they did move downstream. Once they drifted around a bend and the bluff and the town of Baxton vanished, they finally felt relieved.

The river twisted and wound. They quickly realized that if they did not leave the barge, they were sure to be apprehended and captured farther downstream. They needed to get to the other side of the river. With difficulty, they finally moved the barge onto a sandbank on the opposite shore.

Mister Benjamin picked up his heavy, metal case and then the mule's pack saddle and heaved each of them to the sand. Then he shouted to John Underwood to grab the two C.S.A. field blankets and a bag of hardtack.

The mule became spooked, broke the tether and jumped off the barge. It shot across the sandbar and almost ran over John Underwood. Mister Benjamin, who had returned to the barge to get their suitcases and to look for a box of matches, jumped off and ran after the mule. He found the frightened animal several hundred yards away, drinking from a spring beside a well-worn path. When they return to the sandbar, they discovered that the barge had floated off. They spotted it down river, on the opposite side, lodged against a stump.

They hurried down the path for what they figured to be about a mile. Panting, and with a stabbing ache in his side, Mister Benjamin said that they should go away from the river in case Buster McNix and the Yankees should find the barge.

In places, the jungle was so thick that Mister Benjamin had to hack away the vines with the dull machete. In other places, the great pines and oaks had inhibited the growth of underbrush and they proceeded as if walking in a park. John Underwood had to yank and prod the mule to get its cooperation. In less than an hour, they saw a wide clearing, and much to their astonishment, they arrived at another river. Then John Underwood remembered: the other river is the Oconee and they were near the spot where it joins the Ocmulgee.

At first, they do not know which way to go. They couldn't get across; but they couldn't go back either. So they followed the river, and eventually walked into an even larger clearing. They had reached the place where the Altamaha River begins. And it was there on that spit of high clay bluff that an Indian village stood.

There were perhaps a dozen huts built on stilts. Their roofs were thatch from the fronds of palmetto palm. Women were cooking cornbread on a clay oven. They could smell roasting meat. Children were playing, and men were arguing, conferring and sleeping. Some of the men wore breach cloths, but others wore trousers. The women were dressed in brightly colored, long dresses, but some were bare breasted. They all stopped what they were doing and watched as Mister Benjamin and John Underwood approached, leading the mule.

Eventually, someone admitted to speaking English, but it was difficult to make him understand that they wanted to get across the river. Finally, the Indian smiled and opened his palms, indicating that he knew what they had been trying to tell him. They made a bargain.

The Indians blindfolded the mule, led it waist deep into the river and lashed it between two poles across two dugouts. While their other things were being put in another dugout, Mister Benjamin opened the heavy metal box. With a mixture of caution and curiosity, everyone crowded around. Inside were two smaller boxes that fit perfectly inside the larger box. Each was about twice the size of a shoe box, but not quite as deep. Mister Benjamin took the handle and lifted one of the two smaller boxes out of the larger box. Placing it on the bottom of an upturned dugout, he opened it with a brass key. There were gold coins inside. The box was half full of one-hundred-dollar Confederate States of America Cavaliers. The Indian accepted the box, giving it to an old man and calling for two younger men to help carry it. Following the old man, they vanished into the palmettos.

Mister Benjamin put the larger box into a dugout, and they, along with the mule, were paddled across to the other side of the river. When they neared the shore, the mule's feet came into contact with the riverbed. The animal began to run and dumped the two Indians into the shallow water. But the mule was easily caught, and the gear was again secured on its back. Two of the Indians returned to the village, and the third motioned for them to follow. As was part of the bargain, the Indian showed them the way to Florida. But just as they departed, they spotted a horseman on the bluff across the Altamaha.

"That's them! Over yonder! There 'cross the river with that gall darn mule!" they could hear Buster McNix shouting. He was with the Yankees. As shooting began and bullets zinged into the trees around them, they quickly followed the Indian into the jungle.

## Disorderly Notions

Within a few minutes, they again heard shots, but this time the reports were from pistols as well as from rifles. Then they heard screams and cries from women and children. There was an explosion and as they quickly looked back, they could see black smoke drifting over the canopy of the woods.

They followed the Indian as fast as they could, but they could not keep up. The Indian had to stop often and wait for them and the mule. They traveled through swamps with alligators sunning themselves on the banks of ponds, and they saw cottonmouths swimming in the dark waters. The air was rich with the smells of decaying vegetation and sometimes sweet with the perfumes of spring. When it was nearly dark, they stopped to drink from a creek and Mister Benjamin noticed the Indian's tear-streaked cheeks.

For two more days, they were led down the network of trails. In the afternoon of the third day, they came to a river with black water and white beaches. The river was small and fordable, and the Indian indicated that across the river lies Florida. They tried to thank him before he left, and Mister Benjamin tried to give him gold. But the Indian shook his head, indicating that he was not interested, and then he vanished into the jungle. They wonder if he was going back to the village where the massacre had taken place. He would likely be returning to bury the dead.

The next morning, Mister Benjamin awoke with the rising sun. He lay on his back looking at the sky and listening to the birds. They had camped on a white beach, and for the first time on the trail, have felt comfortable enough to build a small fire. He pulled his heavy form up on an elbow and looked over at John Underwood, who was still asleep under his C.S.A. field blanket. Suddenly, the mule began to whine. Across the narrow river was a mounted horseman.

Mister Benjamin went for the machete. He and John Underwood had vowed not to be taken alive. Yes, the man was in a cavalry uniform.

"Mornin' gentleman," he said. "Who might you be there across the Suwannee River?"

Mister Benjamin was on his feet.

"You better shoot now, sir, or be prepared to fight to the death."

"Whoa now, I have no interest in fightin' civilians. The fightin's over, or haven't ya'll heard? Guess the news travels slowly here in the Okefenokee Swamp. I'll just cross the river into Florida and be on my way."

As his horse stepped into the black water and the soldier was out of the glare of the sun, Mister Benjamin could see him more clearly. He wore a sweaty underwear top and his trousers were butternut and tan. His scuffed and worn boots were high, and, indeed, he was armed. A carbine and a saber were holstered on his saddlebags and there was a .38 stuck in his belt. Mister Benjamin tightened his grip on the machete.

"If you are a gentleman, sir, you will dismount and meet my challenge with the saber."

The soldier was on the beach. In his gray hat there is a blue plume, and he had a scarlet scarf around his neck. He was a Confederate.

"Clarence Cicero Fowler Jr., Lieutenant, Colonel Harry Wayne's Dragoons, Army of Georgia, is at your service, Mister Secretary."

He was a mere boy. The young officer told Mister Benjamin that they must not go along the trail on which they intended to travel. The trail would take them to the east coast, and the area is thick with Yankee patrols. They needed to go west. Being reasonable men, Mister Benjamin and John Underwood agreed and joined the young officer. At a remote spot on the Florida Panhandle, he planned to meet other members of his unit. From there they were to sail to British Honduras where General Beauregard's brother, a young captain in the Dragoons, had made arrangements with the British for them to start a colony. He told Mister Benjamin that his brother, Malachi, had been wounded at Milledgeville. Perhaps Malachi had been taken prisoner, but they both knew better than that.

The young man tried to persuade the two older men to come along with him to British Honduras, telling them with youthful optimism how they all could start life anew. But Mister Benjamin said that he and Mister Underwood were too old and weary for life in the wilds of Central America and that tamer, slower and more civilized Britain was a better place for two aging lawyers. As he said this, lines from *Henry IV* popped into his brain: "I am old, I am old" and "Jesu, Jesu, the mad days that I have spent!"

Before departing, the young man took the scarf from around his neck and, after washing it in the river, spread it out on a log on the beach. The scarlet square of tightly woven silk was a map conceived by Jacob Thompson and commissioned by Mister Benjamin himself. It was a detailed reproduction of the eastern half of North America that showed the cities, towns, military installations, roads, railroads, rivers and

Disorderly Notions

ports. It had been issued to all Calvary and reconnaissance units, and the detail was so fine it had to be read with a magnifying glass. The soldier insisted that they take the scarf and his glass and compass. Otherwise, they would have to go along with him, risk getting lost or maybe even captured by a Yankee patrol.

For the two days they traveled with the young officer, they agreed not to talk of the past. On the morning of the third day, when they were about twenty miles from the Gulf of Mexico, Lieutenant Fowler continued west and Mister Benjamin and John Underwood turned south.

Mister Benjamin had lost so much weight that his clothes were hanging on him and his feet were coming through the soles of his shoes. They figured themselves to be about a day's journey from Tampa Bay, where they hoped to find passage to Bimini - the nearest British possession. Two days before, their food had run out, and because it had been necessary to forge for berries, turtle and gull eggs, their progress had greatly slowed.

It was on one of those berry picking expeditions that John Underwood was bit in the chest by a six-foot Great Eastern Diamondback Rattler. Because of the location of the bite, nothing could be done, and within an hour, John Underwood was dead. There, with the view of the blue waters of the Gulf of Mexico, Mister Benjamin buried his friend in the sandy earth.

Several days later, Mister Benjamin awoke in a bed. He had been found wandering on the beach, delirious from the sun. Farther down the beach, lying on its side with the tide washing around it, still alive but already being devoured by crabs and birds, was the mule. Martin Lacey, Commander, C.S.N., had been driving his buckboard along the beach near his sawmill and had come upon the sorry circumstance. He shot the dying mule and somehow managed to get Mister Benjamin into the wagon, which, considering Mister Benjamin's still considerable weight and the fact that the Commander had lost an arm at Vicksburg, was quite a feat. The Commander took Mister Benjamin home, and he and his wife nursed him until he was able to travel.

After two months, dressed like a farmer, Mister Benjamin finally set sail for Bimini. Near the Florida Keys, they encountered a violent waterspout. The crew was rescued, but the boat sank. Luckily, Mister Benjamin was able to save his metal box, which he had painted to pass as a toolbox.

He next acquired passage on a boat that was visited by a Yankee boarding party. The captain, a former Confederate petty officer who knew Mister Benjamin's true identity, sent him below. When the galley was inspected, there was a large, greasy man stirring eggs in a frying pan. As the boarding party left the boat, one of the Yankee sailors said to another that this was the first time he had ever seen a Jew do common labor. Mister Benjamin was to become fond of telling this story, and when he told it, he was invariably asked how the man had known that he was Jewish. He would say that the answer was simple: To light-haired and blue-eyed Southerners, anyone who did not look like them was a Negro, an Indian, a Spaniard or a Jew. The chances had been one in four and the man had simply guessed correctly.

After a journey on rough seas, Mister Benjamin arrived in Nassau. From there he sailed to Havana, where he waited for four months for passage to England. His sail to Southampton was long and uneventful upon calm seas. He arrived to a new place – a new place for a new life.

After they left Novosibirsk, the temperature became warmer. For the past three days Hamilton had spent most of the time sitting in his and Andy's compartment looking out the window and writing. He was trying to be more accommodating to Andy, who had become irritable with the constant clicking of the computer keyboard. But really, if the truth be known, the real reason for Andy's grouchiness was the fact that, because of the vodka and beer ban, Andy had had to ration his Scotch.

But Andy was happier. There would be plenty to drink in Moscow, and he had rationed enough Scotch for him to make it until they arrived. He chattered on, and Hamilton listened and laughed at Andy's jokes. They commented that the streams and rivers were beginning to thaw and that the roads had become slushy. There was less distance between villages and towns, more industry and they seemed to be meeting other trains with greater frequency. After they rolled across the Tura River and rumbled through Sverdlovsk, their last Asian city, they began to climb into the Urals.

The next morning, Hamilton was awakened by a bar of bright sunlight that squeezed through the side of the window shade. He opened the shade, and Andy stirred and grunted. It was dawn. The birches and evergreens were washed golden as they stood against the blue sky. Hamilton continued to lie there and look out the window. The train cut through a mountain pass and then slowed. They were approaching the town of Bisert.

"Hey, you old red redneck, wake up. Look!"

Hamilton pointed to an obscure marker standing in a grove of fir trees about twenty yards from the tracks. It was an obelisk. The train was almost creeping, and Hamilton could see Cyrillic writing on the side of the stone shaft. As they

Disorderly Notions

passed by, he saw that the other side was carved in Latin letters. "EUROPA," it read.

"Big deal! Goddamn it, Ham, shut up and go back to sleep."

"Yes, Unc. It is a big deal. We've squared the circle. Well, almost," Hamilton said.

The next day, after pulling out of Gorky Station and crossing the half-frozen Volga at Nizhny Novgorod, they rolled west through Vladimir and then, already having pierced Moscow's outer ring of dacha country, on to Elektrostal. Except when the view was obscured by the ever-frequent eastbound trains, they saw dachas sitting slightly askew, yielding to the pressures of thawing, awakening earth. Some were just huts composed of this and that; others were more elaborate with brightly painted clapboard and fancy woodwork on the windows and doors. Most were mere log cabins standing darkly in contrast to the heavy, wet snow.

That evening, Hamilton talked to Jenny in the noisy passageway connecting the dining car and a passenger car. Jenny told Hamilton that it was impossible for her to talk with him again, but since she and Mary would not be stopping over in Moscow, and she will never see him again, she just had to take the chance and say goodbye.

"Please don't think Mary is a bad person. She just has to feel that she is in charge. She just wants everything to be right. She really is a caring person."

"Yes, I understand. Mary is really nice ... a nice person," he shouted over the rumble of the wheels.

"Yes, she really is," Jenny said, and then she kissed him.

The next afternoon, they saw the tip of the Ostankino Television Tower stabbing the gray sky on the northern horizon. They had reached the ring of apartment buildings on the outskirts of the metropolis. The suburbs seemed endless, and then there was the sweet, soiled smell of the city. They moved slowly but steadily past roads with vehicles creeping along and people walking in the slush. They passed commuter stations with people waiting on the platforms. It was rush hour in Moscow.

# *IDEAL WORLD*

Hamilton looked up at the rocket. Its base – a shiny titanium blast – held it three hundred feet into the air at an angle of forty-one degrees. The angle gave the viewer a sense of forward motion – of progress – commonly employed in socialist realism art. The rocket loomed over the "Exhibition of Economic Achievements," a large theme park from the Stalinist era, which Hamilton had entered through an arch of gleaming, white marble. When Hamilton had looked down from his window on the sixteenth floor of the Cosmos Hotel, he saw the park and a subway station marked with a big red "M" at the base of the soaring monument. He was supposed to meet Andy at Lenin's tomb at noon. They planned to view the famous corpse and then go to the Writers Union to look for Koldomasov.

Hamilton was still angry about what the woman from Intourist had done. For some reason, Hamilton and Andy had been booked into different hotels and she insisted, despite their strident protests, that the prearranged reservations on her computer printout could not be changed. She did not care if Hamilton and Andy were traveling companions; Hamilton had to stay at the new Cosmos Hotel on the edge of Moscow and Andy at the Metropol downtown. As far as she was concerned, that was that. Well, at least Andy got to stay at the Metropol.

Hamilton entered the glass doors and descended by escalator into the metro station. Earlier, at the hotel, he had exchanged his third-last American fifty dollar bill for rubles. Before stepping away from the front desk, he had asked for a map of the city. The woman at the front desk curtly said she had none. So when Hamilton spotted a subway map at the bottom of the escalator, he walked over to it and tried to figure out how to get to Red Square. He guessed from studying the map that he should take the orange line, but he grumbled to himself about how rusty his Russian had become.

Vapors from solvent and paint burned his eyes as the subway arrived. It was practically empty. He stepped into the car and the train lurched into the tunnel. Hamilton exited the train at Prospektmira Station and transferred to the circle line. His next destination was Belorusskaya Station. Upon arrival, he again needed to make a decision about train changes. Oh, what the hell, Hamilton told himself, and took the green line. He carefully noted the stops, and when he thought he had reached the right one, he stepped off the train at Mayakovskaya Station.

In the domed ceiling of the station was a great mosaic. The picture formed Red Square. Over the bright red star of Spasskaya Tower there was a dirigible, and behind and above it, a fleet of twelve biplanes. He found another map, came to the conclusion as to which train he should take and boarded that train when it arrived. After a few stops, Hamilton knew he had made a mistake and got off the train at the next station.

He looked at his watch. The blue blip had vanished. He unbuckled the band and held the watch to his ear, forgetting that digital watches have no tick. It must be the battery, he told himself, concluding that he had plenty of time anyway.

While looking for another subway map, Hamilton was again struck by the interior of the station. This one had great chandeliers hanging from the vaulted ceiling. They reminded him of the ones in the dining room in the Beijing Hotel – the part built by the Russians. It also made him think of the chandeliers in the Canadian Senate Chamber – the Red Chamber. They were a gift from the Soviet government to his own.

Hamilton found a map and discovered that he was at Kievskaya Station. How did he get there? Yes, he was lost.

"Mister, would you desire assistance?"

There were three young men standing behind him. The one who spoke was taller than Hamilton and had blond hair hiding under a fur cap. The other two were smaller and darker. As it turned out, the three young men were Estonian students on holiday. They accompanied Hamilton to Komsomolskaya Station, and the tall one practiced his English and told the others, who hung on every word, what Hamilton said.

"Do you like rock music?" the student asked.

Hamilton said yes, he liked some of it.

The student reported Hamilton's answer to the others, and then said, "They want you to name a musician that you like."

Hamilton tried to think of one they would know – somebody at least from that decade. "Stevie Wonder," he said.

Immediately one of the students began singing "I just called to say I love you." It was good Stevie Wonder-inflected English. Hearing the song made Hamilton think of the Filipino girls at The Roach Ranch, and it made him think of Mo. For some reason, he wanted to tell these young strangers everything that had happened and how he ached inside.

"We hate Moscow!" the student blurted as they stepped off the train.

"You hate it. Then why are you here?"

"No place else to go," he shrugged. "Do you know how many people Stalin used to build this metro?" the student asked with a sweep of his hand. "He used two million."

"Amazing."

"Yes. And he did it ... did it like this," he said, making a sweeping gesture with his arm. "He made it ... I do not know how to say it."

"He made it fine?"

"Yes, he made it fine to impress the peasants." He pointed to the ceiling. "We hate Russians! They steal our history."

On the ceiling was another mosaic. This one was of a mounted medieval warrior. Hamilton remembered that the Teutonic Knights had conquered and converted Estonia, and then the Estonians were conquered and transformed into Soviets.

Hamilton thanked the students, and began following the map that the blond one had drawn for him. He made his way along Prospekt Marksa and shortly found himself at Manezhnaya Square. He turned left and arrived at Red Square.

The slush was melting in the sun and the sky was clear. In the great open space, Hamilton felt overwhelmed and lost. Although he had not yet spotted Lenin's tomb, he recognized most of the buildings from pictures: the State Historical Museum, the GUM department store, St Basil's Cathedral and then, there along the bottom of the Kremlin wall, was the tomb. It was a squat block of red granite trimmed in black onyx, although its presence was obscured by the crowd.

"Damn it, Hambone! Where you been? It's almost one o'clock. Let's go."

"Sorry I'm late. My watch broke." Hamilton said, and then added while nodding toward the tomb, "I'm not going to stand in that line to see a dried-up corpse. Don't care if it is Lenin. You go and I'll wait."

Surprisingly, Andy said that the line was too long and it was not worth the wait. They stood around and stretched on tip toes to see over the heads of the crowd. Four guards wearing long greatcoats strutted from either side of the low square, their hats cocked down on their foreheads. The four of them were kicking their blackjack boots high into the air, and their bayonets were glittering in the sun.

"This is supposed to be the most sacred place in all of Russia – supposed to be the center of the country," Andy said.

Andy then suggested that they go, and soon they were on their way to the Writers Union. Andy's hotel had been more accommodating than Hamilton's. He was able to get a map.

The Writers Union was a gray building that covered a city block overlooking the Moskva River. Hamilton and Andy walked past the sleepy concierge at the door. The old, uniformed woman waved, blurted something and rushed from behind the counter. They tried to explain what they wanted, but she just shook her head and repeated: "Nyet, ne mozhno!"

Hamilton refused to give up and continued to say, as if she would eventually understand: "We want to see Comrade Nicholas Koldomasov. Does anybody around here speak English?"

"Angliskiy? Angliskiy!" she laughed.

"What do you want?" a man who came from behind them asked.

The man was short and fat. He wore thick spectacles that sat low on his red nose.

"We are looking for Nicholas Koldomasov, and I have reason to believe he lives here. I am Professor Hamilton West from Canada and I have corresponded with him."

"Wait here," the man said without so much as a smile. After several minutes he returned, handed Hamilton a piece of paper and a pencil and said, "Write Comrade Koldomasov letter."

"What did you write him?" Andy asked as they walked in the slush on the sidewalk along the riverbank.

"I asked that he call me at the Cosmos and gave my room number. He'll remember who I am; at least I think he will. I guess he'll call, and when he does, we will ask him out for dinner."

"Yeah, dinner at the Metropol. Great idea," Andy replied.

"Hey, speaking of that, let's go have lunch at your place. Then I have to get back to the Cosmos in case Koldomasov calls."

# CHAPTER VII
## THE HUNT

For many years, Hamilton and I had talked about going out to Cumberland House. I really wanted to see my aunt and uncle, and both Hamilton and I wanted to go duck hunting. We made the decision to finally visit one August afternoon while we were sunning ourselves on the rocks of Jack Pine Isle. We agreed to go during Hamilton's Thanksgiving break.

"Okay, I'll call my folks when I get back to Toronto and tell them we are coming. Then we can't back out," Hamilton said.

Two months later, we took a taxi to Union Station and walked the tunnel that led under the tracks and to our train. Within thirty minutes we were making a short sweep west, and later a turn due north to take the route of the Old Great Northern that, at one time, had run to Churchill on Hudson Bay. Before we got to Portage la Prairie, we were both nodding. When we skirted past Lake Manitoba, I was asleep and dreaming of Judah P. Benjamin. While I slept, the train rumbled through Dauphin and across into Saskatchewan. At the town of Burrows we were awakened by a disturbance. I did not move except to open my eyes.

"All you people. All you white people ..." a man ranted as he boarded the train.

He wore a red, open parka, a blue T-shirt, either greasy or wet jeans, loosely laced Kodiaks and a new tan Stetson that was pushed back on his head. Around his waist, under his gut, was a carpenter's belt that held pliers, a tape measurer, screw drivers and a hammer. He looked to be in his mid-thirties, but it was hard to tell. He wore glasses and had bad teeth.

"Hey, wanna drink?" he snorted, sticking a bottle in a brown paper bag toward an older couple near the door.

"What's wrong? You too good to drink with me?" Then he pulled the bottle from the bag and held it in front of them by the neck. It was sherry – nasty sherry.

"Look. Good stuff," he said as turned up the bottle.

Then he stumbled toward us. Stopping in the aisle and again turning up the bottle, he wiped his mouth with the back of his hand and looked squarely at me and Hamilton.

"What you looking at? You! I'm talking to you! I know who you are," he said pointing to Hamilton. "You with the red hair. Red hair! Ha, ha."

Hamilton ignored him, and then the man went on past us and out the door leading to another car.

"You know him?" I asked.

"No, but he's probably from the reserve. Maybe he knows me. I can't be sure, but he probably knows who I am."

The sun came up and the prairie gave way to what they call parkland in that part of the world. Stubby juniper trees and the odd lodgepole pine pierced the sky above the tan, grassy meadows, which, that morning, were dusted in snow. The train pulled into La Pas at 11:45. From the train we saw Hamilton's father standing beside the pickup, waving. In all these years, I had never met him. Hamilton had always come to Georgia – he even did sixth grade in Altamaha – but I had never gone to Cumberland House. When Hamilton engulfed his father in a hug, I was surprised. Somehow, I had expected him to be larger. Well perhaps his father had been larger, but with age had shrunk.

We drove along the gravel roads. Hamilton's father talked to us about life on the farm and reserve and about life in general. He did most of the talking. Around mid-afternoon, we pulled into Carrot River and stopped at a station because we needed gas.

"Mister West, is what we're hearing true about what's happening on the reserve? We heard they were holding him hostage – the teacher – the blond one, that is. The Mounties had the school surrounded and then the Christly fools, they shot themselves. And both of them are dead."

"No, I have not heard of this. I left early this morning. This is news to me. What about the teacher?" Mister West asked calmly.

"They shot him too, but he's okay. In hospital down in Prince Albert, I heard 'em say it was just a .22 to his rump. Me, I'm glad I don't live up there. No offence, Mister West. Just glad it's you who lives there and not me."

The small pocket of rich farmland around Carrot River soon gave out and we were driving through marsh, scrub and swamps. Strangely, it reminded me of South Georgia. Night came and we drove parallel to the Saskatchewan River. When the river made a sharp turn, our headlights would reflect into its muddy waters.

Around midnight, we stopped at the ferry dock beside a sign that read: "CUMBERLAND HOUSE RESERVE. BLOW HORN FOR SERVICE." After a dozen blasts, we saw the light flick on in the little house on the black barge across the river. Then we heard a door slam, dogs bark and a man curse. There was the knock of an outboard motor and the ferry slowly began to come toward us and cross the river. Finally, the ferry stopped and the rusty ramp slammed down on the concrete.

As Mister West gave the operator a dollar, the man nodded blankly and then glared at me and Hamilton. His old eyes with drooping lids were deep set and he had a wispy mustache. He wore a greasy, blue baseball cap, on the front of which was the letter "C" written in a red script resembling a flame – the logo of the Calgary Flames hockey team.

"Remember, they used to be the Atlanta Flames," Hamilton whispered, laughing.

I nodded, remembering and thinking that sometimes things burn up and become something else.

Below the ramp, and blocking our way, was a great, blue-eyed dog baring its teeth and snarling. The Indian kicked it, cursed and dragged it by its chain to the other end of the ferry. The engine reversed and the ramp banged down as we drove along it and on to the ferry.

Once we had passed over the river, Mister West thanked the man. He casually held up his hand – a gesture of a wave – as we drove up the ramp and off to the other shore. Dogs chased us, but when we reached the end of the dirt road and turned on the pavement, we left them barking in the darkness. In the distance, we could see a glow in the night. As we got closer, we saw that the brightness was coming from two bonfires in a cemetery beside the road on the edge of the village. There were a score of people milling around one of the fires – some standing in clusters and others dancing to the music played by a boom box that was being passed around by the dancing men.

"They are digging the graves for those two dead Indians. They melt the earth with the fires. They will go on all night," Hamilton's father said to me. He added, "Mother of God, have mercy on the poor buggers."

We drove past small, pre-fabricated houses nearly identical except for color and the items scattered around them: snowmobiles, canoes, motorcycles, discarded refrigerators and even animal bones. I noticed signs with burned letters in varnished pine over nearly every door: "THE RESIDENCE OF VERNON AND JULIA STARBLANKET," or "THE RESIDENCE OF JIMMY AND STELLA DOGRIB." Here and there, and on the side of the road, were abandoned vehicles rusting away where they had died. I smelled burning garbage.

Hamilton pointed out the Hudson's Bay General Store where his mother had managed for almost forty years. The windows were barred, as were those of Stella's Café and the Cumberland House Community Centere.

Our headlights caught a figure standing beside the road. He waved both arms and Hamilton's father stopped the truck. The man jumped in the back. His was named Terry Twisting Rope, and, as I learned, he had worked for the Wests for years. We drove on. Dogs howled.

I had not seen my aunt in over twenty years. The last time was when she visited Altamaha. Since then, she had become an old woman. I was astounded that she still spoke the way I did. We ate steak, talked, laughed and drank beer until she said:

"Boys, Terry will be gettin' you up soon. They'll be comin' in with the sun."

I looked at my watch. It was two o'clock in the morning.

Hamilton and I were in a double bed. He snored and took up so much room that I lay awake until Terry Twisting Rope cracked the door, telling us that it was time for breakfast. I smelled bacon and coffee.

My aunt and uncle, Hambone and I sat in the kitchen. Terry fried eggs and my aunt filled cups with black, steaming coffee. Hamilton's father told us about how a dog had got into the barn and the chicken coop and how he had to shoot it with his twelve-gauge.

"Blew 'em to kingdom come," my aunt laughed.

Terry said the owner of the dog was the boyfriend of Stella Starblanket's daughter. When Hamilton told them about the drunken Indian on the train, Terry said that it sounded like the man on the train was also the man who owned the dog. He worked in Burrows and was known around the reserve as a badass. Terry said that the word was that the man had vowed to get even with Mister West for shooting his dog, but my uncle said that he'd heard that before and wasn't worried.

Hamilton drove the pickup along the fence row. At a stubble field, he stopped. We grabbed our guns, got out and climbed over the fence. I followed the beam of Hamilton's flashlight into the field and then into a railroad tunnel that was full of liquor bottles. When we emerged on the other side, the sun was just about to rise. In the half-light, we made our way across a trestle that spanned the river. We went down a path into a ravine across from a point where two rivers flowed together and there, in a thicket of bare, tangled branches, we waited.

The birds came in high, circled, flew over us and landed across the river on a spit of beach jutting out into the water. But the birds were not ducks; they were buzzards. As we moved from the thicket and looked over the edge of the bluff, across the river, we saw that the birds were dining on the remains of a dead Indian baby. I shored my footing and started shooting, and Hamilton did the same. Greedily, reluctantly, the vultures scattered. Then, coming from behind, one bird flew directly over us and vomited, spewing us with filth.

When we returned to the house, we found that the situation on the reserve was grave. The funeral of the two dead men was to be held that afternoon and the atmosphere was tense. When we told my aunt what we had seen on the rocky beach, she called the RCMP Hamilton and I went to the RCMP station to give them details for their report.

"Yes," my aunt Becky said, "this could get ugly."

Apologizing for our ruined hunting trip, she told us that arrangements had been made for all of us to go to her sister's place at Carrot River.

For me the weekend in Carrot River was odd, to say the least. We went to the curling rink and I was forced to make a fool of myself as I tried to sling a stone down a path of ice, upon which I fell more than once. We went to a place where they played country music and many a local girl danced with me. Everyone was so nice. One might have guessed it would have been an ole home week for Hamilton, but Hambone was bored.

On Sunday, before we departed, Hamilton's aunt served us a dinner of potatoes, carrots, parsnips and roast moose. We talked about capital punishment, the weather in Georgia and the evils of Toronto. Of course, the problems with the Indians always lingered in the background.

As unusual as the particulars of my visit had been, I had felt very much at home. I remember thinking the next day, as we boarded the train and began the second turn of our round trip, that one day I would like to return.

Three days after arriving back in Toronto, we learned that Terry Twisting Rope had been right. The man we had seen on the train was the same man who had owned the dog that Hamilton's father had shot. He was also the boyfriend of Stella Starblanket's daughter, and he was the father of the dead baby on the beach. The RCMP arrested Stella Starblanket's daughter and charged her with the murder of her child. Her boyfriend had broken into the Hudson's Bay General Store, bludgeoned my aunt with a hammer, set the place ablaze and then blew his own brains out. When Hamilton's father learned of this, he fell dead of a heart attack.

So I got my wish. I returned to Cumberland House, but it was with Hamilton to bury his parents. I then stayed with him at his house in Toronto until that sad Christmas had passed. Finally in February, when I was convinced that Hamilton was better, I returned to Jack Pine Isle.

In the early spring, just before the ice on the river started to break up, I left for a different kind of hunt. Through my research, I had learned that in 1884 Judah P. Benjamin had been buried in a Paris cemetery called Père Lachaise. I set out to find his grave.

I got a room in a small hotel just off Boulevard de Ménilmontant, not far from the cemetery. My flight from Ottawa had been delayed by a snowstorm, and I arrived in Paris exhausted.

The next morning I got up late, but I was excited. I didn't even take time for coffee; I just dressed, left the hotel and started in the direction of the cemetery. It was drizzling and I had no umbrella. I tried to hold my *Michelin Guide* under the eve of a monument so I could read it, and at the same time, keep dry. I knew that although Judah P. Benjamin's grave was not there among the list of such notables as Chopin, David, Comte, Corot, Delacroix, Balzac and Murat, I could find it. I had the name of the street and, of course, the street would be on the map in the guidebook.

I stopped on the Avenue Transversal, across from the Victor Hugo family plot, and got my bearings. Then I found my way to Avenue Circulaire and walked past the weeping, white stone figures along the Mur des Federes that mark the spot where the Communards of 1871 had been buried after they were lined up against the wall and shot. Not far down a nearby lane, I found the plot for the Bousignac family – the family of Mister Benjamin's son-in-law – in which Judah P. Benjamin was buried.

A monument stood in wet, gray marble. It was of a cavalier leaning forward on his mount, one hand on the hilt of his sheathed saber, the other shielding his eyes as he looked into the distance. I discovered that until 1933, when the Paris chapter of the Daughters of the Confederacy had built the monument, Judah P. Benjamin's bones had lain lost among the splendor of the cemetery.

I returned to my room and slept. Early that evening I took a long walk in the area surrounding a street that was once called Avenue d'Iéna. It was the street on which Judah P. Benjamin's Paris residence had stood. A few years after Mister Benjamin had died, the house and street were demolished to make way for the Eiffel Tower and Place de la Concorde in celebration of the one hundredth anniversary of the French Revolution.

Disorderly Notions

The next day, I spent the day writing and compiling notes in the library at the École Boulle–Lycée Technologique. In the evening I silently drank at a bar, the name of which never even registered with me.

I flew to Gatwick the next morning and took the train to Rye. I planned to stay with Rodger for three weeks while I waited for the ice break on the river around Jack Pine Isle. Once in Rye, this is what I wrote:

### Chapter Two
### A COMMUNE IN FRANCE

"Mister Benjamin, it is not safe. You yourself know what the Prussians have done to Paris. The newspapers say ..."

"Ma cherie, ma Mlle Bakunin, laisse-moi te raconter une histoire," he said, laughing as he slowly turned his portly form away from the window and faced her. "You must remember that I have escaped the most persistent Yankees, the hungriest alligators and the vilest snakes, not to mention the most capricious of tempests and those whirlwinds on the sea. When it is I who has escaped that chaos and wilderness, how could you ever worry about my going to France? Many will tell you that France is the most civilized place on Earth – the very center of the world! Also, one cannot fail to appear at his own daughter's wedding."

"But the disorder! Paris! C'est revoltant!"

"My dear, this is not 1848, nor is it 1851. This, ma Liberté, is 1871. And I will not be in Paris, but in the provinces. There I will be safe, for sure. You always worry. Oh, we must do that telegram to Isbister. Will you take this down? And please, stop the worrying."

Dear Isbister/
Will arrive Rye Friday via Brighton and Hastings/ No time to go through London/ Meet at Mermaid Inn/ Will make arrangements/ Does Count K know English/ Should documents be done in French as well/ Advise/ Have received telegram from Sir J/ J expects us/ Tea on 26th/ Hope to have heard from Thompson before next week so as to proceed immediately/ Transatlantic cable under repair/
Sincerely/
Benjamin

"Thank you, my dear," Mister Benjamin said after reading the transcribed telegram. "What is the current situation with the transatlantic cable?"

"Well, it must have been repaired. This came from Canada today," she said, handing him a dispatch.

Mister Benjamin took the dispatch and began to read:

April 21, 1871
To: Judah P. Benjamin, Esq.
The Office XXX of Stone, Fletcher and Hull
42 Blackburn XXX St., Liverpool, England
From: J.B. Wilcox, Partner, Thompson XXX Furriers, Ltd.
32 York St., Toronto, Ontario, the Dominion of Canada

Dear Mr Benjamin:
Regret to say last Tuesday Mr Thompson disappearedxxx. Almost certain he was abducted by American bounty huntersxxx. This xxxnot xxxfirst attempt. XXXHave asked for intervention from ourxxx government. XXXOttawa awaiting advice from London. XXXDoes not look goodxxx. Sorry, know nothing of plan to sell Canadian furs through British firm to Russians. XXXThere are no records. XXXPlease advise with details and we will proceed as planned.
Sincerely
J.B. Wilcox

"My, this is indeed awful. Thompson has been abducted by the Yankees," he said, shaking his head and handing her the telegram.

Her name was Liberté Bakunin, and she was twenty-eight. Four years earlier, she had begun work at Stone, Fletcher and Hull, the Liverpool law firm where Mister Benjamin had been apprenticing for his admission to the Bar at Lincoln's Inn Court. Later, as a partner in the firm, Mister Benjamin had gained fame for the cases he had argued before the Privy Council and the House of Lords involving the formation of the new government of Canada and the Dominion of Canada's relations with Britain, which resulted in what became known as the British North America Act. Liberté had become his private secretary.

Liberté was the fruit of a passionate, though temporary, union between her mother, a labor activist in the Brussels textile mills, and her father, a Russian exile named Mikhail Bakunin. She never remembered seeing her mother, and had seen her father only when she could not avoid it. It had been said that he was a chronically discontent and foul-tempered man, who continually derailed his aunts, in whose charge he had placed his daughter, accusing them of raising her as a Parisian bourgeois. Indeed, this was true.

## Disorderly Notions

The aunts had been in Paris since the Decembrist Uprising of 1825 and had become established members of that society.

The aunts had seen to it that their niece acquired the manners and charms reflecting her family and, despite her sex, that she receive a liberal education. Liberté was grateful to her aunts, but in 1863, against their wishes, she went to London for the purpose of learning stenographic skills. The aunts, of course, were horrified. They considered their charge "la bas bleu." Liberté had remained in Britain because it was the only country where she would be allowed to practice her craft. And practice it she had, as the first and only female stenographic secretary in the British Isles or, for that matter, in all of Europe.

Thus their association had begun: she twenty-eight and the stateless daughter of a Belgian labor activist and an exiled Russian anarchist, and he fifty-six, a denaturalized cum defunct Confederate States of America refugee. Ah, what a pair they were.

It was Liberté who had persuaded Mister Benjamin to moderate his tendency to engage in zealous rhetoric before the bench and curtail his fondness for lecturing the court on the finer, but often unnecessary, details of international law. It was also she who reminded him to wear his wig and motioned to him when it was askew. She made his appointments and reminded him to keep them. She transcribed his words, and often pruned his flowery language, counselled him when he asked, listened to his plans and shared his frustrations and disappointments, not to mention his bed. But most of all, it was Liberté who had reminded him, in more ways than one, that he had a wife and daughter in Paris.

His wife, Natalie, and his daughter, Ninette, had been in Paris since fleeing the fall of New Orleans and taking a short detour to Mister Benjamin's aunt's home in Georgia. They had become so enamored with the life of the French city that they never thought of the world they had left behind. Through business connections with old Confederates of his, Mister Benjamin had bought them a house on Avenue d'Iéna, where his wife and daughter had received many guests and had retained a household of servants. Although this had been an expensive proposition for Mister Benjamin, it had allowed him, without their complaints, to live as he pleased.

The previous year, when the Prussians had invaded Paris and it became necessary for his wife and daughter to evacuate the city, Mister Benjamin had made arrangements for them to come to England and to repair to the estate of

Sir Joseph Hawley in Kent. But Mme. Benjamin – as she now insisted on being addressed, even when she was forced to speak English – had refused and took her daughter and servants to Montoire-sur-le-Loir. It was there in the provinces that she chose to live out the invasion of the Hun. She and her daughter stayed at the family estate of Henri de Bousignac, Captain of the 117th Regiment of the French Line and fiancé to Mister Benjamin's daughter, Ninette. Mister Benjamin had been relieved by her decision.

Mister Benjamin and his wife had a cooperative, though loveless, marriage and almost separate lives. She had her life in France and he had his in England. Mister Benjamin would not have given two pence to live in the palace at Versailles and would rather have high tea in hell than to spend one moment in a Paris salon. Mister Benjamin had his law practice and his long-standing friends, including British diplomats and Southern sympathizers from the Cotton Club in Liverpool, many whom he had known during his war years. He was in contact with the likes of Gladstone and even Tennyson; and, of course, he had Liberté.

Liberté stood and silently watched him as he peered out the window. His hands were clasped behind him. Liberté knew that he was worrying about the cable from Canada. This was Mister Benjamin's brooding position. Finally, she turned and walked toward the door. She was no longer concerned about his visit to France. Now the worry was about the Yankee bounty hunters. If they were able to capture Thompson, why could they not capture Mister Benjamin? And what a bigger catch her Mister Benjamin would be! As she left the room, she had to fight off tears.

Mister Benjamin did not hear her leave. The sky was full of dark clouds. The harbor, thick with masts and rigging, was inky. The ocean beyond raged, dipped and swelled. Thompson always had been extremely cautious. It must have been the Gideonites who captured him, Mister Benjamin thought. The name suited them: Fanatics. They were the former abolitionist and reformers revitalized in the name of revenge. The Gideonites had been successful in capturing Confederate fugitives and taking them back to stand before the bar of Yankee justice. Thompson must be their biggest catch yet, he had concluded. He thought of Thompson and of the humiliation he must be enduring.

His gloom over Thompson's fate hung over him for the rest of the day, but by early evening, when he kissed Liberté's hand at the train station, he had returned to his cheerful self.

## Disorderly Notions

Mister Benjamin finished his leg of lamb and glass of Madeira. He savored the taste of mint still in his mouth. He lit his cigar as the train rolled out of the terminal at Stoke-on-Kent and was in a deep sleep before they reached Birmingham. When the porter woke him at dawn, he sat over his tea, puffing his first cigar of the day and thinking about what an adventure life had turned out to be. Then the Gideonites appeared in his mind, but he just shrugged his round shoulders, smiled and forgot about it.

When they passed Cromley, he saw that the meadows were soggy and puddled by spring rain. At Brighton, he had a short wait and stood for a moment at the entrance of the station, looking down Queen Street. At the foot of the long hill, he saw the empty boardwalk and the angry, roaring sea.

An hour later he was back on the train, a local, and was crossing the downs toward the Channel. Between the sea and the downs was Hastings with its red-tiled roofs. The train strained up the cliffs and back into the downs, and the yellow heather on the hills blazed like the sun despite the gloomy weather. The rain had finally stopped, and the sky was clearing over the Channel. After a quick detour through Winchelsea, he looked across to the opposite hill, and there, surrounded by the Romney Marsh, was the town of Rye.

The sun was trying to shine when he took a carriage from the station and rode down cobbled streets and through the town gate. The driver stopped at the Mermaid Inn. Mister Benjamin stepped to the street and was handed his portmanteau. He thanked the driver and paid him double the fare. Inside the inn, he presented himself to the white-haired proprietor, who informed him that Mister Isbister had already arrived.

Mister Benjamin and Alexander Kennedy Isbister sat in red leather wingback chairs before the fire. Although the sun had finally turned bright, the air was still damp. The two men were about the same age, but in physical appearance, they were quite dissimilar. Whereas Mister Benjamin was short and stout, Isbister was tall and thin, though they both had prominent noses and dark complexions. Mister Benjamin's olive skin belied his Sephardic Jewish heritage, and Isbister's skin color, high cheekbones and slightly Oriental eyes were markers left by a long-forgotten Cree ancestor. These genes mixed with those of Isbister's voyager forebearers, who trapped around North America and settled in Cumberland House, a town in northern Saskatchewan established by the Hudson's Bay Company in 1774 as its first inland trading post.

He had come to know Isbister through Sir Joseph Hawley, his friend from Kent who they would visit the next day. Sir Joseph had known Isbister during the latter's long relation with the Hudson's Bay Company, from which the Hawley family had bought furs for over a century. The Hawley's family company, Imperial Furriers, Ltd. of London, kept Mister Benjamin's law firm on retainer. Mister Benjamin had become England's most eminent expert on the laws pertaining to international trade, after all. Also, Sir Joseph had a Virginia wife, whose family were friends of the Benjamin family.

At Sir Joseph's hunt in December, Isbister had told Mister Benjamin of a Count Kojevenekoff, who had expressed a desire to buy Canadian beaver and seal pelts. Russian fur production had become ruined when the serfs were freed a decade before. While the serfs had traditionally farmed in summer and trapped in winter, many of them had moved off the land and formed rings around the larger cities, such as Moscow. But the market was still there, and the Count claimed it to be more viable than ever; thus, his proposal:

Imperial Furriers could buy Canadian furs, and Count Kojevenekoff would make the arrangements with the Russians. Because of its years of experience and exclusive trade under a royal charter dating from the days of Charles II, the Hudson's Bay Company had advantages that small private firms did not have. There were many complicated rules and regulations of international trade to follow, making it expensive and even hazardous for these smaller private firms to deal on the international fur market. But, because of his previous employment with the Hudson's Bay Company, Isbister knew the rules, and Mister Benjamin both knew international law and was well acquainted with the owner of a large and reputable Canadian firm: Thompson's Furriers, Ltd. The idea was brilliant. All of them were bound to make a fortune.

"Yes, it is awful about your friend Thompson. I am very sorry for him, but I also hope that his abduction does not complicate our fur deal."

"I am hopeful, good Isbister. This Wilcox fellow has assured me that he will look into the matter, and I have written him the details. I am confident that it will work. I suggest we proceed with the legal work - the investigatory part, at least. By the time it is done, we will have heard from Wilcox."

"Will the Count be agreeable to this?"

"Oh, I should think so. He has nothing to lose, and I'm sure this small complication will matter not a wit to Sir Joseph."

## Disorderly Notions

"By the way," Isbister asked, "can you tell me more about the Count?"

"I know little about this Kojevenekoff," Mister Benjamin replied, "except that for reasons I suspect are both financial and political, he prefers Paris to Moscow. Sir Joseph says he is an astute fancier, but an odd sort of a chap."

"Odd?"

"Yes, the Count, so it seems, has odd politics."

"What do you mean?"

"I'm not sure. Just odd."

The waitress brought fried plaice for them both. The fish was golden brown, as were the potatoes, and both proved to be good with the bitter ale and early spring peas. The room had become noisy.

"This used to be a regular haunt for smugglers and pirates, so it is said," Mister Benjamin mumbled while lighting his cigar and looking across at Isbister's dark face.

"Yes, this is an old town. Much has happened here."

"And a beautiful place."

"Yes, indeed. And what has happened to your brother. British Honduras, I believe?"

"Yes, British Honduras. I am afraid the last news was not good. The organizer of the colony, a brother of General Beauregard, has died of the fever and the leadership of the colony has fallen into the hands of others – some latecomers who arrived there in considerable numbers. Religious fanatics, they are. The situation has caused my dear brother, Malachi, to leave the colony."

"Where has he gone?"

"Oh, he has not gone far. He's still in British Honduras. It seems he has been forced to take a job as a common laborer in a sawmill that processes tropical woods. Mostly mahogany, I should think."

"A lumber mill?"

"Yes, I'm afraid so. I have been encouraging him to leave and I will help him to do so, but he is pigheaded. He should come to England."

"But what happened at the Confederate colony? Who are these people? The 'new ones,' as you just spoke of them?"

"Well, it seems that these people, these zealots, are looking for someone to blame for their troubles, and I would assume they are those kind of people who generally despise the way the world is and seek to condemn and persecute those they think responsible. They've tried to turn the colony into their version of some New Zion. Many are members of some new organization – an organization of terror. Among them is a secret group known by the odd name of the Klu Klux Klan – spelled with all 'K's. My brother says they are very religious. Protestants, I would suspect, and I assume that they are altogether uneducated. Most of them are from Alabama. I think Malachi said the southern part. Anyway, they had some sort of trial and expelled him from the colony."

"Because he's a Jew?"

"Well, yes, I think so. Yes, surely that was part of it, but also he is my brother, so I'm biased. I just think there are many desperate people in the South these days who look for someone upon whom they can blame the loss of our country and the terrible troubles of Yankee occupation. I can't help but feel compassion for my countrymen. Look at me. I've escaped all that. Ah, they suffer an awful fate. I'm one of the fortunate."

"So these are the people who took over the colony?"

"Yes."

"I'm sorry."

"Thank you, but Malachi will survive. Now I must retire. Can we meet here at nine o'clock? We can walk about the town and have a look at the Martello Tower."

"Yes, of course. The train does not leave until eleven."

They walked in the direction of the chimes. It was all uphill, and several times they had to stop for Mister Benjamin to catch his breath. At the top sat the twelfth-century church of Saint Mary and its old graveyard with its crooked, worn stones. They stopped for a moment and look down upon the town, the marsh at Winchelsea Road and the two converging rivers – the Rother and the Tillingham – that flow into the Channel beyond. Rye had once been on the sea itself, but the sea had moved because of silting.

Without having passed so much as a word, they turned and followed the road downhill. Walking along the strand, they made their way toward the Tillingham River Bridge. There, on one side of the bridge, was a black-and-white windmill, and there was a shipyard in a basin beside the river on the opposite side. The shipyard was a relic from the days of wood and sail prior to the emerging age of larger ships with steel hulls driven by steam. Martello Tower was behind the rotting wood buildings of the shipyard near a gray stucco house.

Disorderly Notions

The tower was one of many that had been strung along the coast from Seaford to Folkston in anticipation of the invasion of Napoleon, which never came. It was a brick-built cylinder thirty feet high and about the same in diameter, and it was falling into ruin. At one time, a naval cannon had sat on its top and swung 180 degrees on a revolving platform, but from that height they could see that the cannon had been removed, probably for the purpose of making another cannon.

They stood beside the tower and looked at the window about halfway up. It, like the rest of the tower, was almost completely covered in vines. Mister Benjamin imagined Marines scrambling inside the six-foot thick walls to man their guns so as to blast the invading armies that never came.

"Who are you? And what in the duce are ye doing on my property?"

The man shouting was toothless, and one eye was clouded over by a cataract.

"We beg your pardon, sir," Mister Benjamin said. "We had no idea we were trespassing."

The man laughed and said that it did not matter. He had not been in the tower for thirty years, and it was just a good-for-nothing pile of brick.

"You want to buy it?" he laughed, as he cocked his brown-blotted head. "I'll sell it to you, the whole kit and caboodle. I'll even throw in the house and ruddy shipyard. I'll sell all the bloody lot of it for a quart of good whiskey and a night with a wench in the Mermaid Inn."

Mister Benjamin and Isbister laughed politely. Mister Benjamin even suggested that the tower could be put to use as a storage area. Then they wished the man a good day and left. They fetched their bags at the inn and took a carriage to the train station.

They stepped off the train in Paddock Wood well before teatime. Paddock Wood was a "higgledy-piggledy place," as Isbister called it. They were met by a landau and driven down a road bordered by bright meadows and orchards of blossoming Cox's Orange Pippin apple trees. It wasn't long before they stopped at the front of the half-timbered, fifteenth-century house called "Northian." It was the estate of Sir Joseph.

They were led through a garden of topiary with the shapes of birds cut to precision as if with a razor. Sir Joseph opened the gate and, after his usually energetic greeting, said:

"Gentleman, allow me to present the Count Alexandrovich Kojevenekoff."

"Call me Kojeve," he responded. "Everyone in Paris does."

The Count wore a cream-colored linen suit, shiny, black patent leather shoes and a yellow-and-blue silk cravat impaled with a diamond stickpin. Under his hawkish nose he wore a large dark mustache. He took his manicured hand and lifted a thick monocle to his eye. A quarter of his face was his blue iris. He was a small, bony man whom some might call elegant. Mister Benjamin thought he looked like a dandy or the men on the riverboats in New Orleans.

The maid wheeled out a tray of tea and scones. They sat under the tender blooms of a Doyenne du Comice pear tree, and the talk was easy and loose for a time. Eventually they got around to the subject of the fur deal. Mister Benjamin, in his thorough and clear fashion, explained the intricate aspects of the international trade laws, and Isbister talked of the regulations with which they will comply and the others that they will deftly circumnavigate. Then Mister Benjamin told them about Thompson's abduction and assured them that Thompson's partner, Wilcox, will follow his instructions. Neither Sir Joseph nor the Count revealed any concern.

"Ah, you English are so complicated," Kojevenekoff exclaimed in good but heavily accented English. "The French, they are simple. They have fewer rules. Business in France, it is easy."

"But the Prussians?" Isbister asked.

"Ah, no one knows."

"And the siege. What is Paris like now?" asked Mister Benjamin.

Kojevenekoff hesitated while Sir Joseph poured more tea.

"Ah, the siege, it was the worst. They ate not just cats and rats and ... how do you say?"

"Dogs?"

"Yes, dogs too, but also the animals in the zoological garden. This Bismarck, he is a very clever fellow."

"The papers talk of the international communists and the others," Isbister said.

"Yes, well," he smiled, "c'est très intéressant."

"And the collectivists?" Sir Joseph asked.

"Yes, the ones led by that Russian, Bakunin." Isbister added.

"Yes, Mikhail est très intéressant."

"Well, we don't have to worry," Sir Joseph said, smiling. "The communist Jew, the German one, has been living in

England and apparently has lost his wits. He spends every day locked away in the reading room of the British Museum. I have heard this from the Scotland Yard."

They strolled along the line of holly trees bordering the garden. Mister Benjamin told them that he had no worries of being apprehended by the Yankee bounty hunters. After all, he was now a British subject.

"And a most prominent one," Sir Joseph replied, adding, "The Americans do not want an international incident with the British. They have their scandals to keep them busy."

"And that drunk for a president," Isbister laughed as he looked back at Mister Benjamin. Again, Mister Benjamin smiled, but did not respond.

Later, when they returned to the house, Mister Benjamin agreed to meet the Count in Paris after his daughter's wedding. He decided that he needed to access whatever damage had been done to his property on the Avenue d'Iéna. Count Kojevenekoff had recently bought a factory near Paris in which he was producing cheese for importation for the gastronomically starved palates of the Russian nobility, who loved anything French. The Count had been looking for investors and Mister Benjamin was interested. This was another reason for him to go to Paris.

"It is a simple but high quality Port du Salut," the Count declared, looking at them through his fish eye. "I think we will see it on the table of the house of Romanov, for the Czar likes it to eat with his fruit from the Crimea."

Mister Benjamin awoke on a bench on the morning of the wedding and reflected groggily on his dream. It had been spring in New Orleans. He was lounging in the garden of what formally had been his house in the Vieux Carré, and his sisters had just been forced indoors by the bees swarming around the purple flowers dangling like clusters of grapes from the vines. Wisteria; wonderful, excessive, overflowing wisteria. For a moment he was homesick. No, I must not be, he told himself. That time has gone, and what was in the dream had never happened.

Bees had been in the dream because of the bees in the apple tree beside the bench upon which he sat. The tree was in the meadow behind a stone château in Dreux, which overlooked the Aure River. It was the ancestral home of the Bousignac family.

Two weeks before, when he arrived in Dieppe, Mister Benjamin had found that in order to get to Dreux it would be necessary to take a mad combination of trains. All the lines to Paris were still closed, and to get to Dreux he had to go by way of Le Mans. But after he had arrived at the house of his future relatives, he wished the detour had taken even longer.

His tardiness had not delayed the festivities. Natalie had been fluttering about like a free, happy bird, chirping in French to the guests and cooing to her future relatives.

Half of Paris was there, or so it seemed to Mister Benjamin, who had been treated as neither guest nor relative. Not being a member of Parisian society, no one deferred to him, and because his wife and daughter refused to speak English, even with him, Mister Benjamin had grown obstinate and would not speak French with them, thereby excluding himself from the family. Mostly, he was merely ignored, but he had found this space congenial. It was better to be left alone than to be expected to engage in the inane nattering and shameless preening going on about him.

This is why he spent so many hours under the apple tree. Earlier that morning, he had been snubbed by some prissy fellow who arrived in a flutter of pomp and fanfare. So he had taken to his bench, and with him he had brought along an old copy of Victor Hugo. He mused at the difference between the language he was reading and the cackling he could hear coming from the house. He shook the dream from his head, arose and straightened his waste coat. He stretched his shoulders and looked up into the blossoms. Ah, he said to himself, a beautiful spring.

He pulled a cluster of pink flowers toward him and sniffed the aroma, and it was then that a bee stung him below his left cheek, on the spot where the upper lip meets the nose. Although he quickly applied the old remedy of wet tobacco to the stings, the swelling had been immediate and profuse. His lip was already protruding by the time he entered the house, and his nose was swelling by the minute. He was beginning to look like a puffed-up adder. It was not long before his eye swelled completely shut.

Although Natalie appeared sympathetic, as soon as they were away from the guests, she clenched her teeth and shrieked: "Mon Dieu!"

"Speak English!" he muttered as firmly as possible.

By and large, the wedding went as planned. It had been a splendid affair - Captain de Bousignac in his grenadier's uniform, all braided and beribboned, his shiny black boots and his even shinier saber in its gilded scabbard, and then Ninette with her pearl-studded, flowing dress and sugary veil. The choir had sung a part of Gounod's Mass, and spring flowers made the church look like a blooming garden.

As is the custom, Mister Benjamin had been required to escort his daughter down the aisle. But because Mister Benjamin had looked like a blow fish and could hardly see, it had been she who had done the leading. After the wedding, his wife hissed at him:

"That was so humiliating! You looked liked a blind leper staggering along a gutter." Then she would speak neither English nor French with him.

Two days later, the swelling was almost gone. Captain de Bousignac had been recalled to duty due to renewed civil unrest in the capital, and Mister Benjamin was leaving for his appointment with Count Kojevenekoff and to assess the damage to his house at 26 Avenue d'Iéna. He was happy to leave and, my, how he missed his Liberté.

"Passeport!" the soldier muttered in his rough Breton accent. The man smelled of garlic and sweat, and he looked bored and tired.

Mister Benjamin said nothing and complied.

"Étranger!" the soldier shouts and an officer appeared.

"You are English?" the officer asked.

"Oui, Anglais," Mister Benjamin responded.

"What business have you in Paris?"

"I must inspect my house. My house is at 26 Avenue d'Iéna. I also have a meeting with a gentleman who ..."

"A meeting with whom?"

"A meeting with a count. Count Kojevenekoff."

"Ah, a Prussian!"

"No, a ..."

Mister Benjamin was taken from the train and was told to sit on a bench on a platform beside the station. In a few minutes, the officer returned and ordered the guard to accompany him to a tram waiting on the other side of the station. The tram was full, and the horse looked as if it might collapse from exhaustion as a soldier continually whipped it. On either end of the tram were two more soldiers with bayonets affixed to their rifles. It was not until they crossed Pont d'Austerlitz that Mister Benjamin knew where he was. Finally, after stopping at checkpoints every few blocks, they reached their destination. A sign over the door read: "ÉCOLE BOULLE-LYCÉE TECHNIQUE."

Inside, the place was as confused as a pest house. People were shouting orders; others shouted protests and some cried. Mister Benjamin was pushed into a lecture hall.

Several hours later, his name was called. He rose and was escorted into a large room full of machinery – hydraulic lifters, steam engines and strange looking water turbines. Behind a table was an officer.

"English?"

"Oui, Anglais."

Suddenly there were shots coming from outside. There were muffled cries and screams, more shots and then hundreds of them. Because of the disorder, the officer had been distracted.

"Monsieur, voilà pour vous," he said without expression. "Au revoir," he said, handing Mister Benjamin his papers and then walking toward a window.

Mister Benjamin was escorted into yet another lecture hall. By his watch, he already had been waiting for six hours. The room was half full. The men were given neither food nor drink and were relieving themselves in the back corners. The stench made Mister Benjamin gag.

"I am a commissioned officer, a lieutenant. I've been discharged, but I am an officer in la Grande Armée, nonetheless. Look what they have done to me. They are confused and frightened, and they do not listen. My name is Manet," the man said, smiling while making unusual clicking noises with his tongue. "Fools! They should be spending their efforts on the Communards!" he declared loudly.

The shooting started again, and then the building was rocked by an explosion. Shortly after this explosion, Mister Benjamin and the man called Manet were released.

It was dawn when Mister Benjamin and Manet walked down the Boulevard Diderot and turned right at the Place de la Nation. The streets were deserted, and while it was quiet, they could hear gunfire in the distance. The smell of gun powder was in the air. In an effort to avoid the fighting, which seemed to be in the direction of Place de la Bastille, they turned down Avenue Philippe in the direction of Père Lachaise Cemetery.

The sun was already up over the spires of Saint Ambrose. It was after seven. The day was bright and clear. Great black birds circled over the cemetery.

"Where did you say you wanted to go?" Manet asked Mister Benjamin as they passed along the cemetery wall at Boulevard de Ménilmontant.

"Well, I had wanted to go to a meeting, but that was for last night. I'd be quite happy to go to the place where that meeting was to have taken place."

"And where is that?" he asked, cocking his long head, amused.

"My house. 26 Avenue d'Iéna."

The street ahead was barricaded, forcing them to turn southwest on Boulevard des Italiens. They went around the Opera and eventually, after twisting and turning, arrived at the Place Vendôme. Manet stood before a barricade of broken carts, furniture and heaped paving stones and sketched a rat in the gutter along the street.

"Courbet. I have heard that he and the other fanatics did this," Manet declared, nodding toward the column lying across the open square. Its top was sliced into the facade of a building.

"Courbet?"

"Oh, Courbet – the overrated painter. It reminded him of Caesar," he said as he sketched with aristocratic indifference a man three-days dead.

"Bonaparte?" Mister Benjamin replied, his sleeve over his nose.

"Oui. Bonapartism, he would say. But I say imperialism. Oui, that's what he would say. That's how Courbet thinks." At the top of the column, there was a statue of Bonaparte. "But now he is in that butcher shop," he laughed, nodding to where the shaft had torn into the building.

Behind the ugly hole, in the interior of the building, was a lunatic sifting through the debris and muttering, "Le Allemand! Le Allemand! Sale Boche!" to a scruffy dog tugging at a cloth sack half submerged under plaster. Manet turned his tablet to a clean sheet and sketched the scene.

They walked on in a southerly direction. The dark vastness of the Louvre came into view. For some reason, Mister Benjamin thought of one of his most favored pictures in that gallery. It was of the Virgin standing on a crescent moon while holding the Earth and the heavens in her hands. The painting was inspired by an image from Revelation 12:1: "And there appeared a great wonder in heaven; a woman clothed with the sun ..." He wondered if the place had been looted. They walked on, and eventually they crossed the Seine at Pont d'Iéna.

The night was falling. Alone, Mister Benjamin stood before his house. He had invited Manet in, but Manet had declined, saying that he wanted to sketch life at the headquarters that had been set up at the École Militaire. I must find the Count, Mister Benjamin reminded himself. He will think I've forgotten. He reached in his vest pocket for his address book.

Mister Benjamin and Count Kojevenekoff had been sitting for some time in the Count's drawing room when a man servant opened the door and stepped aside, ushering in a large man. The Count and Mister Benjamin rose, and the Count put his monocle to his eye:

"Allow me to present Doctor Professor Vladimir Solovyov," he announced.

The man wore a coarse, soiled, gray smock tied at the waist with a length of rope and scuffed riding boots that had once been black. His light-brown hair hung matted under his lambs-wool hat. His unkempt beard was long and framed his face unevenly like the shaggy mane of a lion. Over the servant's arm hung his blue greatcoat. There was a hole at the elbow.

"Monsieur. Votre chapeau?" the servant said meekly.

"Non, merci, mon bon ami," Solovyov answered with a smile that showed his browned, ragged teeth.

Later, they sat at the table. Vladimir Solovyov, his hat still on his head, shoved sweetbreads into his mouth and washed them down with a goblet of wine. Then he held the glass out, grunting for the steward to pour another. The Count told Mister Benjamin about the public lecture Solovyov had made the year before in St. Petersburg when the Czar had been assassinated. It was a declaration that Alexander III should live up to the Christian ideal that Solovyov thought Russia to embody and forgive his father's assassins. Solovyov nodded in agreement, but said nothing. He picked up his carp with his hands and chewed it bones and all. His spoon was the only utensil he used. Again and again he grunted, holding out his glass for more wine.

"And that's how you got into trouble with the Czar's police and why you are in Paris, I suppose?" Mister Benjamin asked.

Solovyov grunted in agreement. Then he wiped his mouth on the loose sleeve of his smock and announced:

"Yes, but this is scientific."

"Scientific?" Mister Benjamin responded.

"He means that he has theories to support his statements," the Count replied for the Russian. "It is a theory he calls 'Godmanhood.'"

Mister Benjamin looked at the Count and wrinkled his brow. He was about to speak, but Solovyov replied:

"Yes, it is all scientific. The world should and will become one universal and homogeneous state. Everywhere, God will become man and man, God. The world will become ..."

"United?" Mister Benjamin asked.

"Yes, unite. All equal. All the same."

"How interesting," Mister Benjamin replied, touching the flame of a match to his cigar.

"It's a theory of history, a theory that this unification of the world is and all along has been the goal of history. The goal of history is this universal and homogenous state," the Count said, trying to help Solovyov explain as he lit a fat Russian cigarette.

"Yes. The gold. Gold of history," Solovyov mumbled, munching a stalk of celery.

"Ah, but Mister Benjamin knows all about unification," the Count replied devilishly. Mister Benjamin smiled back at him, nodding with a sparkle in his eye.

"Indeed. I'm afraid we fought a terrible war over just that – over our not wanting to be like those who wanted us to be like them."

"I've heard that if Britain or France had recognized the Confederacy, then you could have sued for peace. Is this so?" asked the Count.

"Yes, I thought so at the time. I still do. We had plans that I think might have worked."

"What plans?"

"Well, one was to abolish slavery in a way similar to the British in '32. Even from a purely economic perspective, the institution was fast becoming ineffectual. As an institution, it had value for us politically, but only when we were part of the United States. As a separate nation, slavery had already become a libel. Many alternatives were discussed."

"Africa?"

"Yes. And on a small scale, this was tried. But I'm sure you know about that. The Negroes had been in the South a long time. In many ways, even considering his status, he had become a Southerner. So we talked of giving Florida to the Negroes. We discussed reverting Florida back to a territory. It would later be returned to statehood; provided, of course, they wanted statehood in the Confederacy."

"They?"

"Oh, yes. Provided the Negroes wanted it. They would become citizens of Florida and later, if they wished, the C.S.A. They could also have gone their own way or immigrated to the North. You see, Florida is not heavily populated, and the whites who wanted to leave would have been compensated for their property. The land produces well, at least three growing seasons, and the climate would have been perfect for the Negroes. I envisaged great groves of citrus fruits that could be exported to the heavily populated cities of the North by rail. Florida would have flourished."

"Interesting. Please, tell me more."

Mister Benjamin looked at the Count. He knew the interest was genuine, and so he continued:

"The South always gazed in a different direction from the North. We perceived the founding of the American republic differently. Also, it was thought that Southern independence was in keeping with the original spirit of the American founding. In our breaking away from the Union, we were doing exactly what the colonies had done in respect to England. But what lies under these differences is deeper, even mythic."

"Mythic?"

"Yes, by Jove, mythic. In time, the Yankees came to associate the founding with his Puritan fathers, but our founding myth emerged out of the experience of the Jamestown colony. Our forebearers were not pure-blooded New Englanders. The origin of the Southerner, at least culturally, is part native."

"What do you mean?"

"I mean that our founding family is the Randolph family of Virginia. The archaic Southerner is half English, half Indian. The Yankee always accused us of being pseudo-aristocratic - pseudo-European. Yes, we did have a royal line, but we also had our own native one that goes back to an Indian Princess, Pocahontas. And this is why we always looked in a different direction. Culturally speaking, there is an Indian in every Southerner. This is why the South is always referred to by the feminine pronoun. As with our Indian ancestor, the land is our mother and the South, our motherland."

"Were their other plans?"

"Well, Mister Davis had many. Neither Cuba nor Mexico was happy with their European masters. In time, he felt they would join the Confederacy and, eventually, the Central American Republics too. Except for trade and a common defence, all states would be practically autonomous. We wouldn't have wanted to change any state, not basically anyway. It would have been a loose unification. Differences would not only have been encouraged, but protected."

"And how did Canada fit into this plan of yours and the president's?"

"It didn't, really. Although our cause had much sympathy in Canada, there was much opposition as well. Besides, we

## Disorderly Notions

never thought the Yankees would stand for it. And we had not wanted any trouble with the British. As it has turned out, the Dominion of Canada is now a confederation and will likely become more of one in the future," Mister Benjamin said, smiling.

"Yes," the Count laughed, "and I hear you are responsible for much of that."

"Ironic, isn't it. It was mostly two little cases I tried – a case called Potter v Rankin and another called Parson v Russel. Rather makes me one of the fathers of their Canadian confederation."

The Count allowed the steward to pour him a glass of wine and then he laughed.

"I can imagine it, the Caribbean and the Gulf of Mexico a Confederate lake!"

"Yes, I suppose," Mister Benjamin said with a smile. "It could have been interesting."

"Nyet! Impossible!" Solovyov blurted. "Never it could happen. History say 'nyet!'"

"I am sorry, sir," Mister Benjamin replied, "I don't understand."

Solovyov took the bottle from the steward and filled his glass to the brim. "Never it could happen. All worldly reality will become like Christian truth of Godmanhood!"

"Do you mean transformed right here on earth?"

"Yes! This will come to pass, as you say. World will become one organism. One organism like Europe becoming today. One universal organism. It is the ... the gold of man. Gold to unify mankind in history. To make universal mankind. No difference. All equal."

"Oh, you mean equal like in one big, happy family?" Mister Benjamin asked, smiling.

"Yes, like in family."

The Russian laughed and took a big gulp of his wine.

"God is energy inside all man. He works through every man to make His gold. He shows His gold in history – shows it through man."

"So, does this mean that everybody is good? Good as gold, as they say?" Mister Benjamin asked.

The Count smiled wryly at Mister Benjamin's question.

"Nyet! Nyet! There is evil. Evil is separation from God."

"Yes, I think I'm beginning to see. So, because there is God in everyone, then separation from each other is bad. And this is why disunity, or difference, is evil?"

"Ah! But you are clever man. I tell you, it is scientific!" Solovyov declared, slamming his goblet on the table. "Making history, it is man's duty and salvation. Society completed individual and the individual incomplete society. He is the complete man – God-Man. He is the citizen of the world state and the purpose of all history. Its ... its gold. But for solidarity there must be struggle and ... how do you say? Yes, sacrifice!" he almost shouted, as he gobbled a delicate piece of cake.

"Well, perhaps you are correct. I must admit that I would find all this unity and sameness boring," Mister Benjamin responded, puffing his cigar.

Solovyov filled his glass and quickly emptied it.

"Tell us about your trip to Egypt," the Count said to the Russian, thinking he is changing the subject.

"Well, it began as I was nine," he said, flicking crumbs from his beard. "I have visions then of Sophia – beautiful mother with shining eyes. The visions, they stopped. Then last year, visions returned. Vision told me to leave St. Petersburg. I go first to England. Am working on my theory in British Museum. I talk to rude Jew who always there writing in notebooks. He always there and always argue with me. He have crude material theory about Hegel. I go to Egyptian room to escape rude Jew. There the vision return. There beside statue of Anubis is wall hanging of Actaeon and Artemis, I see her just as before. She dark skin, dressed like Sahara queen. She say, pointing, 'Go to Egypt!'

"And I go to Egypt, to Misr Al Jadidah where Nile forks to make delta. And then, as sun burst over desert, I see Sophia again. She hold four corners of the world with wisdom. She hold all the world. I see now the world kingdom. Kingdom of Godmanhood is already here, and I make aesthetic life."

He swallowed the rest of his wine.

Mister Benjamin changed the subject to that of the cheese factory. They had planned to leave the next day and take Solovyov along for the ride. The civil unrest had calmed, and the Count did not expect difficulties leaving the city. Mister Benjamin and the Count talked on. Solovyov drank until he fell asleep.

Before retiring, Mister Benjamin and the steward took Solovyov up to his chamber. Mister Benjamin removed his hat, but neither he nor the steward dared to take off his boots. His snores could be heard throughout the house, and Mister Benjamin had a near sleepless night. He missed Liberté.

They arrived at the station at Dreux, where Croiset, a man who usually managed the factory, was waiting for them

## Disorderly Notions

with a driver and carriage. He was short, stout, bearded and wore a straw, broad-brimmed hat. Although he appeared to have a mild character, his diffident, peasant manner could not hide his consternation and panic. There had been a strike at the Count's cheese factory.

As it had turned out, the influence of the Brousse Party had been felt in much of provincial France, including the agricultural Plaine de Saint André. The day before, the municipality of Dreux had been taken over and the area was already being organized along socialist lines. They were keeping to what they thought to be the principles of the Paris Commune in that each cell, after being established, was allowed to go its own way. Eventually, as the communes transformed, all would gradually become socialist. The public service would replace government, eliminating hierarchy and authority, or so was the plan.

"They have made me a barn sweeper. Mon Dieu!" Croiset cried. "In my place as chief they have installed Jean Cavnot. You do not know him, monsieur," he told the Count, "but everyone knows it is really that awful woman, his wife, who directs. Mon Dieu! I was sent to tell you that you are welcome at the commune and that it is hoped that you will join them in fraternal solidarity. I am sorry, monsieur," he said as he hung his head.

"Très intéressant," the Count replied. "Perhaps it's not so bad. Don't worry. We'll see what they have done, and if what they've done is bad, it's not your fault, Croiset."

When they approached the cheese factory, the Count said that the black-and-white cows looked the same, as did the abandoned château and the barns. But then, high upon the roof of the three-story cheese factory, was a slender tree trunk stripped so as to make a high pole. On the pole flew a bright red banner. They stopped in front of the factory.

"Well, Well! Alexandrovich Kojevenekoff. Have you come to look, to complain or to work?" she asked, standing there with her hands on her hips and glaring inside the carriage.

"Madame Carnat, I presume?"

"Comrade Carnet!" she said with a smirk.

"This is my property and I..."

"This was your property, Alexandrovich Kojevenekoff. Now it is the Bakunin Commune, named in the honor of Mikhail, whose mistakes of 1870 we will not repeat. We have begun small, but soon we will be everywhere."

"What shall I do?" the Count whispered to Mister Benjamin. "You should have some advice for me. As a barrister, tell me a proper response to someone who claims to own your property."

"These lawless people are incapable of reasoning," he responded looking into the Count's fish eye.

"Do not get out of the carriage. In other instances, where property has been taken, troops have been sent in to evict the past owners. I suggest we leave immediately, and do so without another word."

At that moment, Vladimir Solovyov opened the door and stepped from the carriage. He walked around to where the woman stood. A large crowd gathered behind her. The Count and Mister Benjamin looked on in silent wonder and horror.

"You are instruments of the Lord, the Lord God!" He shouted, throwing up his arms. "Children of the soil; the one soil of the earth ..."

At first the crowd laughed nervously, but the laughter grew when the woman shouted:

"Dieu! Ha! Dieu est mort! Le Prêtre! Le Prêtre!"

Some doubled over laughing. Children had begun to run around Solovyov.

"Dieu est mort. Dieu est mort," they chanted.

Solovyov put his hands over his ears; his face reddened and he collapsed in a mound of cow dung. Finally, and with much difficulty, Mister Benjamin and the Count dragged him into the carriage. The driver cracked the whip and they drove away. When the carriage reached the top of the hill, they could still hear the shouts: "Viva la Petite Republic! Viva La Commune de Paris! Viva la Commune de Bakunin!"

They returned to Paris as fast as they could. The Count filed a complete report at police headquarters. Three days later, the cheese factory was cleared by three squads of provincial militia and the commune was destroyed. Jean Carnat was sent to Guyana and his wife to New Caladonia.

The phone rang three times during the night, just like it had for the past three nights. Each time, Hamilton stumbled from the bed, crossed the dark room and picked it up. And each time, no matter what Hamilton said, the only sounds that came from the telephone were moans and breathing. He knew that whoever was calling did not understand him when he told them to "fuck off." He was sleepy and angry and did not care. To make matters worse, that damned Stevie Wonder telephone song started running through his head.

The next morning, it took him over an hour to get to the Metropol Hotel. He was still sleepy, and he expected Andy to continue to berate him because he had refused to go to the Bolshoi Theater with him the night before. He decided that he would put up with no more of Andy's foolishness. If he wanted to spend the evening at the Cosmos Hotel writing for Jud about Judah P. Benjamin, then that was his business. Maybe Andy made the phone calls. No, that's stupid, he told himself, further saying to himself that he needed more coffee.

Later, Hamilton and Andy sat in the café at the Metropol. Hamilton got his coffee. Andy was puffing on the tube of a fat Russian cigarette and drinking orange juice and mineral water. It was near noon, the usual time for Andy to have his first drink. But Hamilton knew that Andy was trying to wean himself off, for Andy had done this many times before. Andy must be cold sober when he arrives at Seven Bridges. His hand shook.

It was their last day in Moscow. Andy had decided that he would not continue on the train through Germany. The year minus twenty days he spent in a German prisoner of war camp was all the Germany Andy ever wanted to see. His plane would leave for Helsinki that evening, and Hamilton planned to take the ten o'clock train to Berlin the next day.

"Come on! Germany has changed. It's very different from what you remember. You seem down right paranoid about the Germans."

"Don't you try to lecture me on the Germans, professor! You don't know Jack Shit about 'em!"

"Have you read Goethe, Schiller and Hegel?"

"Have you read Marx?"

"Of course, but I gave him up for Hegel. He is redundant, you know."

"I'll bet you've read Hitler too."

"No, I don't read him for the same reason that I don't bother to read Marx. That's the whole point. The old Germany is as dead as Hitler. And by the way, why did you call me in the middle to the night and practically blow your nose in the phone?"

"What the hell are you talking about?"

"Seriously Andy, you didn't call?"

"No! Why in hell would I want to do that?"

"I don't know why. I'm sorry, Andy. It's happened a couple of times. My sleep has been terrible. Yes, the calls were just two among my many bad dreams. I'm really sorry."

"It's okay, Hambone. The bad dreams are understandable."

Since they would not be dining with Koldomasov until five thirty, most of the day was free. Hamilton had looked forward to a long walk, for the sun was shining and the snow was almost gone, but to his displeasure, he learned that Andy had made arrangements for them to take a bus tour of the city. Andy thought Hamilton had not seen enough, that he had wasted too much time in his room at the Cosmos Hotel writing about his nephew Jud and their ancestor, the crypto-fascist Judah P. Benjamin. Also, he didn't want him up there in that hotel room grieving over Mo.

Hamilton was annoyed at not being consulted about the city tour, and he decided to go along with Andy's plans for one reason only. After all the arguing,

Andy had failed to get a ticket to the Bolshoi. At the box office he was told that to get a ticket, he must be with a group.

"Go see Intourist," the woman had said.

"Oh, don't you tell me," Hamilton had said, "that it would have mattered if I had gone along. Two doesn't make a group. Your wonderful socialists are just like us capitalists; they are in it for the money. They're in it for our money because socialism makes only worthless money!"

He and Andy had been together for a long time and for long enough.

Although there was plenty of room on the bus with a group of American dentists, for some unexplained reason, Hamilton and Andy were put on a bus alone, with the exception of the driver and an Intourist guide. The guide had a spiel from which she did not swerve, and both Andy and Hamilton were frustrated before they even arrived at Red Square.

When they stood beside Lenin's tomb, almost in the exact spot where they had stood four days before, Andy asked our guide:

"Say, comrade, did you know that a man named Bogdanov prepared Lenin for eternity?"

She ignored him, but Andy would not let it rest.

"Embalmed him. A man Bogdanov embalmed him."

"Oh, come on Andy. Let it go!"

"I do not know this Bogdanov," she replied curtly as she turned to face him.

The GUM department store was full of old ladies and babies. The old ladies wore babushkas; the babies rode in strollers. Looking at the glass arching everywhere over them, Hamilton imagined himself to be in a palace of ice. The crumbling building was a brittle testament to some dead man's utopian imagination.

"Hey, comrade, don't we get to see the Kremlin?" Andy asked, but the guide did not answer.

They returned to the bus and drove along the Moskva River to the outskirts of the city. The guide rambled on, ignoring their questions.

"This is Gorky Park ... and this is the Olympic Stadium ..."

When they saw Moscow University, looking like a great, corroded wedding cake, Hamilton asked:

"Hey, look Andy, the university. Can't we stop there?"

The guide glanced back at him and said:

"We have no time. Now we must go to Novodevichy," she said, and she turned away.

As it turned out, Novodevichy was a sixteenth-century monastery that they were looking at as they stood on a gravel walk under a naked tree. The tree reached up toward the onion domes of a church.

"Excuse me," Hamilton said to the guide. "Where is the washroom? The toilet?"

She pointed to a building in a corner of the courtyard beside a wall. Hamilton and Andy walked over to the building and did their business. Minutes later, they stood at a gate and Hamilton stood on his toes to look over it.

"Andy, Come over here," he said.

The gate was unlocked. Inside was a vast graveyard. They walked along a path beside marble slabs – grave stones – many with photographs of the deceased. The marble slabs made Hamilton think of the apartment blocks in Moscow decorated with their huge pictures of politicians. When they came to a life-size statue of a dreamy figure carved in stone, Hamilton read the inscripted nomenclature:

"Nadezhda Alliluyeva Stalina."

"Stalin's wife?" Andy asked.

Hamilton said that it just might be, and Andy said that he thought that he remembered that she had committed suicide. On a flat surface of the monument someone had left a rose. It was thawing and wilting.

"Hey, look at this!" Hamilton shouted.

It was a six-foot statue of a tank, its long cannon protruding into the thicket of an evergreen. There was a photograph of a man in military uniform under it. Near it was a larger-than-life statue of a cosmonaut. His name, "Pavel Belyayev," was carved into the black onyx, and encircling his marble likeness was a great, stainless steel whorl, undoubtedly representing the cosmonaut's orbit in space. Hamilton commented that the monuments seemed to be mere abstractions from lives – from life. Andy told Hamilton that he was full of shit.

"You are not supposed to be in here! We must leave immediately!"

It was the Intourist guide, and she was angry. On the ride back to Moscow, she scowled and said nothing.

They entered the Metropol dining room around five. The decor was black marble, burled wood and stainless steel. Geometrically, its lines were a blend of the square and the circle – art deco.

In a back corner table, a lone man sat straight as a statue. Hamilton stepped toward the maître d' and nodded toward the man. Before he could speak, the maître d' motioned and said:

"Comrade Koldomasov."

The skin on the man's dome was stretched as tight as the head of a drum. He was as lean as a tall pole, and Hamilton was struck by his youthful appearance. They followed the maître d' to the table, and as they sat down and began to talk, Hamilton was astounded by his almost flawless command of English.

"I beg that you will accept my humble apology for not being able to meet you sooner, but arrangements had to be made at my place of employment and for my traveling to Moscow. These arrangements take time. This, you understand?"

They learned that he was employed in an office of the Department of Translation for the Institute of Canada and the United States. The Institute had a branch in Gorky – the city from which he had traveled.

"Yes, I was once at the Institute here in Moscow as a researcher, but that was years ago when you, Professor West, and I corresponded on the works of Alexander Bogdanov, the man to whom I owe my life. I lived at the Writers Union then, but my superiors decided that my usefulness would be greater served at the translation branch in Gorky. I'm afraid someone did not like some of the conclusions I had drawn from my research. Ah, but things may be changing with the new government."

He was a cheerful, optimistic man.

They learn that his complete baldness was the result of a high fever caused from typhoid and malaria, which he was stricken with in 1928 while still a student. Bogdanov saved his life by pumping his own healthy blood into him. As a result, Bogdanov himself succumbed to the diseases. Koldomasov not only attributed his life but also his remarkable youthfulness to Bogdanov's healthy blood. He could still run five miles each day, and he was at least as old as Andy, Hamilton had guessed. Koldomasov smiled at him, baring his shiny steel teeth – a gift from Soviet dentistry.

The meal had begun with what tasted like a Tilsit cheese, a bowl of Volga caviar, black bread, a bottle of sweet Crimean wine and sardines from the Black Sea. Koldomasov had ordered for them. Andy managed to stay away from the wine. The conversation was loose and friendly. As they were finishing the second course, a dish called shashlik, or shish kebab, Andy asked a question:

"Comrade Koldomasov, how did Bogdanov embalm Lenin?"

The Russian took the leg of pig from his mouth, and gesturing with it towards Andy, cleared his throat and answered:

"Well, to be exact, although he had been a participant in that process, if the truth be known, Bogdanov was a prominent member of a group arguing to have Lenin's body cryonically preserved.

"You mean freezing him?" Andy asked.

"Oh yes, Mister Benjamin, freezing, but at a very low temperature."

"And when the technology became sufficiently advanced, they could thaw him out, repair and resurrect him," Hamilton chimed in, smiling.

"Yes, but, of course, the embalmers won the argument. At first Comrade Bogdanov reluctantly went along with the plan, but in the end could no longer approve of the direction the process had taken. Either he quietly just resigned or was pushed out."

"Well!" Hamilton exclaimed, "I had no idea that ..."

"You had no idea, my dear Professor West, because until recently it was kept secret. But now many know of this, along with many other things that for so long remained hidden. But now no one cares about such matters, not even the KGB."

"What else was hidden exactly?" Hamilton asked.

"I would say that Bogdanov's experiments concerning the prolongation of life were the most sensitive and guarded. He had been experimenting with hormones extracted from the testes of monkeys."

"Monkey sperm?" Andy gasped.

"Yes, Mister Benjamin, this was the basic substance from which he synthesized it. And there were, like all else in modern science, unexpected consequences: spin-offs, I think we say. This particular substance proved to preserve dead human tissue. But, of course, Comrade Bogdanov, who had been championing the preservation and prolongation of human life, was appalled that his own scientific findings were used for the preservation and prolongation of a dead human. While the cryonics plan he had embraced might have lead to a kind of life after death through technology, this hijacking of his work lead to nothing but the preservation and prolongation of a semblance of life in death, and he wanted nothing to do with it."

"Do you mean that Lenin was pumped full of monkey ..."

"Yes, Mister Benjamin, this is correct. Synthetic monkey sperm. But, of course, the process was much more complicated than that. Yet, that is the basic idea."

"Well, I'll be dogged!"

"Yes," the Russian said with no expression in his voice, but with the hint of a smile on his face.

"Did Bogdanov's experiments on the prolongation of life have anything to do with his interest in blood?" Hamilton asked.

"Yes. Blood itself was very important to him. He considered it the basic substance of life – a kind of common denominator for everything else. It was his work on the circulatory system that convinced him that we could build a social system that, if managed properly, could function in complete equilibrium, like a healthy body."

"Thus, his invention of cybernetics!" Hamilton interjected excitedly.

"Yes. Everything he did was connected. He wanted to make the dream of Marx scientific. You see, he was much influenced by one of Marx's contemporaries, a man named Vladimir Solovyov, who conceived of a kind of universal society that would function like a single body with all parts in harmony – a world family. His idea was crude, but ..."

"One family. There's blood again," Andy said, now excited.

"True. But for Bogdanov, in terms of a world society, it was only symbolically true. While the blood is the common denominator of the body, efficiency is the blood of this new world of ours – efficiency is its common denominator. Our technology is like the heart in that it pumps the blood efficiently throughout the system. The system is like a servo mechanism in that it is self-adjusting. If the system is functioning correctly, the system adjusts itself by its own feedback, much like the immune system of a complex biological organism.

"Inefficiency is equivalent to a disease or virus. The tendency of efficiency is to develop to ever greater levels of efficiency and, eventually, to reach perfect equilibrium. The closer the congruence of cause to effect, the greater the efficiency, hence control. But, since the system is self-adjusting, all it needs is tuning. The system of complete efficiency, or complete equilibrium, is what Solovyov had meant by his world society. Bogdanov was developing Solovyov's and Marx's crude ideas into an all-embracing science. Well, basically, this is its foundation."

"He called it 'Tectology.'" Hamilton said to Andy.

"Okay, so, what were you up to when they nailed you? Tell us exactly what you were researching that pissed them off so much," Andy asked.

"Oh, you mean when I was at the Institute here in Moscow? Well, I was doing scientific and political research. I was trying to corroborate the ideas of Bogdanov."

"Did you?" Andy leaned toward him, asking.

"Yes, and that is what they did not like."

Hamilton took the coffee cup from his mouth and sat on the edge of his seat, cocking his ear toward Koldomasov.

"I concluded that for all the apparent differences between the Soviet Union and the United States, they have a common dominator – efficiency. This translates into two organisms built of similar tissue, materialism and secular humanism – a kind of religion of man. Since the protoplasm of technology is efficiency, and since efficiency strives toward a kind of harmony or equilibrium, the two societies are not only built of similar tissue, but they are tending toward equilibrium with each other and ever so swiftly bringing the rest of the world into their orbit."

"One big, happy family. The world society, eh?" Hamilton asked.

"Exactly. It is precisely what efficiency demands."

Andy did not like what he was hearing.

"Don't you think this place might be bugged? Don't you worry that somebody might hear you?"

"It is not a worry. They already know what I think. Anyway, we have a new government. A reforming one, I am told."

"I told you," Hamilton gloated to Andy. "Americans are just rich Russians, and Russians are just poor Americans."

"Well, that is a rather impolite way of putting it, don't you think? You should think of it this way: think of it as just a matter of genes. How do you say ... genetics? Yes, social genetics. And this common gene – efficiency – translates into a radical secular religion of man. It is a code that is just as common to Marx and Lenin as to Jefferson, Lincoln, Roosevelt and your Ronald Reagan."

"I'm sorry, but that's just bullshit!" Andy blurted.

"Russo-American way of life, I call it!" Hamilton laughed.

"Yeah, and I've heard that crap from you before. Both of you are full of shit. I have to go up to my room and pack. My plane leaves in two hours. You pay, Hambone."

Andy turned to the Russian, pointed to him with a tobacco-stained finger and said:

"And you, sir, are a fucking Stalinist."

When Andy returned with his bag, Koldomasov had gone. Hamilton saw Andy off at the curb in front of the Metropol.

"Goddamn, Hambone, I always thought my nephew Jud was crazy, but now I have decided that it's really you who's nuts. I want you to tell Jud I said that, and tell Rodger the Dodger that I'll be waiting for that painting of the parrot. Collect my money from those suckers, and tell them I said for them to come on down to Georgia to see me. So, I guess you've decided to stay in Russia, since you like it here so much."

"Yeah, I'm staying until tomorrow. I'll remember to give Starman your address, and I'll collect our bet. And maybe we will all go to Georgia."

"Listen," Andy said, looking at Hamilton as the taxi pulled to the curb. "This is what Mister Whitman would have said about all of this bullshit: Roaming in thought over the universe, I saw the little that is Good steadily hastening towards immortality. / And the vast all that is call'd Evil I saw hastening to merge itself and become lost and dead." He stepped into the car. "To the train station comrade," he told the driver. When the driver looked puzzled, he extended his arms as if wings. "I'm leaving on a jet plane, you fucking commie."

Andy then showed the driver his plane ticket, and the driver understood. As the car pulled away, Andy smiled at Hamilton.

"One of these days, boy, somebody's gonna lock up your royal Canadian ass."

Hamilton returned Andy's grin, and as Andy shot Hamilton the bird, the car shot down the street.

During the night, in Hamilton's room at the Cosmos Hotel, the phone seemed to ring in the distance. Hamilton stumbled across the floor in the dark and picked up the receiver. Silence.

"You son of a bitch," Hamilton said through his teeth.

"Hammy."

"What the ...?"

"Hammy?"

"Oh, my God! Mamma? Mo?"

Silence.

# *REAL WORLD*

Hamilton sat in a smoky dining car. He had been joined by two Poles who had been to Moscow as representatives of their factory, which manufactured electric sausage makers. Although both Poles were fat, one was dark and the other fair. They wore identical brown suits with wide lapels, yet their ties were different: Tweedledee and Tweedledum.

Hamilton remained there for at least an hour conversing in German with the Poles, which in itself was tiring. Finally, when he had enough of the cigarette smoke, the German and the Poles, he decided it was time to return to his compartment. He asked for the bill, and when the waitress brought it, he realized that he had forgotten to exchange his money before boarding the train. All he had in his pocket were a few kopecks and the last of the crisp American fifty-dollar bills. He glanced at the picture of Ulysses S. Grant, but the Poles were looking keenly at the bill and asked to examine it. The waitress was quite happy to take the American bill and in exchange handed Hamilton a wad of red-and-white rubles.

The train was identical to the Chinese one, except that there was a little booth and a porter in every car. The porter in Hamilton's car was a middle-aged woman who spoke German and wore glasses spangled with shiny stones. Her German was no surprise, for Germany was where the train was going – East Germany, to be exact. She had told Hamilton that they would be crossing the Polish border around six thirty that evening, but they would first stop in the town of Brist and have the axles and wheels changed to fit the gauge of the standard European track.

Hamilton stopped in the aisle and looked at his watch, but he had forgotten that it was dead. After two nights of interrupted sleep, he was weary. He tried not to think about the nightmare he had had the night before, but he couldn't help thinking about it, or about Mo.

Although his compartment was equipped for four, there were only three people inside, including Hamilton. The other two bunks were being occupied by a young Polish man and his Russian wife. Well, that is what Hamilton assumed, and he guessed that they were newlyweds. She had two brown imitation-leather suitcases.

Although Hamilton could not converse with them, he tried. Yes, they were newly married, and they showed Hamilton their new rings. When Hamilton was finally able to communicate that he was from Canada, the young woman said:

"Ah, Canada ... hockey."

Her husband repeated, "Hockey ... Canada."

Hamilton smiled and said, "Yes, hockey-Canada-hockey."

The lights were out and all was quiet except for the rumbling and bumping of the wheels on the tracks. There were no phone calls with ghostly voices calling in variations of Hamilton's name and, mercifully, all Hamilton heard was the sound of the train and the Russian bride breathing lightly. For a while, Hamilton breathed with her and then he slept, but he did not dream.

Hamilton was awakened by someone tugging at his foot. Someone was pulling at the toe of his sock and saying "Raus! Raus!"

"What do you want? What in hell's going on?"

It was the porter and with her was a woman in a green uniform.

"Was ist los? Was ist los?" Hamilton grumbled while looking at the porter, who still held him by the sock.

"Die officer," she replied, nodding at the blonde woman in the Russian uniform.

She proceeded to tell him that the officer wanted him to get his things and follow her. He rubbed his eyes, got up and did as he was told. The train had stopped. It was dawn. Was this just another bad dream?

As they stepped on the platform, the officer barked some orders to a young soldier lounging beside a cart of wooden crates. In one motion, he grabbed the shoulder strap of his Kalashnikov, stepped on the butt of his cigarette and saluted.

Soon Hamilton found himself standing beside a gray military vehicle with numbers on its side. The officer had neither spoken a word to nor looked at Hamilton. The young soldier opened the trunk, took Hamilton's bag and then opened the back door for Hamilton and the front door for the officer. The trunk and door slammed shut, and they drove away.

Within minutes they were out of the town and in the countryside. They made a sharp turn and drove beside a river. Hamilton could see a black-and-white striped guardhouse ahead. It had high fences topped with coils of barbed wire – a military base. The barricade rose, and as they passed, guards saluted. They drove past gray stucco barracks that looked like something the Nazis might have built, likely with Polish slave labor, Hamilton thought while still wondering if he was dreaming. Hamilton felt as if he were in a movie.

The car stopped at one of the gray stucco buildings. Before he knew it, Hamilton was standing in a large room beside a long table. The woman officer had disappeared. Except for Hamilton and a helmeted, submachine-gun-carrying soldier, the room was empty. Then a voice came from behind.

"Mister West, please empty the contents of your bag and all your pockets on the table."

Hamilton turned and looked into the face of a tall man, who was perhaps forty. The stubble on his head was brown and his eyes were green like his uniform. Hamilton did as he was told, and the man quickly shuffled through the items Hamilton had deposited on the table. The soldier picked up what he had been looking for: Hamilton's passport and visa, his laptop and the blued metal box.

"Please, come with me," he said, motioning in the direction of a corridor. "After you," he added politely, and Hamilton walked until he heard the man say: "Here, Mister West. Please, come into my office. Sit here."

The chair was red molded plastic and had a stainless steel frame. When Hamilton sat, it gave under Hamilton's weight. The officer sat behind a gray metal desk and shuffled some papers around. He looked up at Hamilton and opened Hamilton's passport. He thumbed through it, as if he had done this many times, and then he stopped. Hamilton could tell that the officer was looking at his picture. Again the officer glanced through passport and said:

"England, Singapore, India, China, Mongolia and then, of course, the Union of Soviet Socialist Republics. You have been to many countries in such a short time, yes?"

His accent was Oxbridge.

"Could I ask why you have brought me here? What do you want from me? I'm sure my train has already left."

"We need to talk, so I will ask you to wait. I will make sure that you are comfortable and that you have something to eat."

Hamilton leaned toward him, for a question was forming in his brain, but before he could gather his thoughts, the man spoke.

"Yes. You must leave now. He will show you where to go."

Hamilton turned around and saw the door opening and a large soldier step inside. Hamilton rose, glanced back at the officer and then turned and followed the soldier down a hall. They stopped at a door, which the soldier opened. He gestured for Hamilton to enter. The soldier closed the door and the lock clicked. Hamilton tried to turn the knob, but it would not budge. He looked around: white stucco walls, iron bed and a bare mattress with a pattern of orange sunflowers with green leaves. There was a sink and a light high on the ceiling. Hamilton smelled disinfectant. The room had no windows.

Oh, shit! He told himself as he sat on the bed and tried to think. His mind was racing and he was breathing fast. He could feel his heart pounding: blood, blood, blood – the common denominator. Again he wondered if he was dreaming. He noticed a Styrofoam cup on the sink and got up and turned on the tap. Water rushed from the faucet. He filled the cup and drank, but he could hear water splashing beside his feet. The sink drained into a metal bucket sitting directly under it. Hamilton stood up and tightened the knob, and the drip stopped.

As he stood at the sink, the door opened and a woman in a white smock and white pants entered. She was holding a white piece of folded cloth and a roll of tan toilet paper. She placed the toilet paper on the sink and began to speak a Russian that Hamilton could not understand. Hamilton thought the white cloth was a sheet, but when she unfolded, he could see that it was a white gown. She pointed to Hamilton and continued talking and gesturing until she was satisfied that Hamilton understood. She wanted him to put on the gown. She draped it across the bed frame and left.

For a few minutes, Hamilton just sat on the mattress. Finally, he began to undress and put on the gown. Almost immediately, the door opened and the woman returned. He stood and watched as she gathered his clothes and then, carefully, folded each item. She pointed to his feet. He looked down at his red running shoes. She said something in Russian and handed him a pair of paper slippers. He took off his shoes and handed them to her one at a time. She tapped her wrist, and Hamilton, knowing what she wanted, surrendered his watch. It doesn't matter, he told himself, it doesn't work anyway, and he smiled at the small victory. Then she pointed to his socks.

Hamilton walked about the room, taking many, varied routes. Okay, I'll just admit it, Hamilton thought. Then he put his hands to his face, pressing his temples with his fingers, trying to gather and still his randomly scattered thoughts. He stumbled into the center of the square room and, craning his neck, stared up at the light and the white ceiling. Yes, that's what I'll do, I'll just admit it. After all, Koldomasov did get permission for us to meet. Yes, he got permission. The mission! I am a commissioned officer in Le Grande Armee. Yes, just like Manet and Mister Benjamin, I've been arrested! And then Hamilton told himself that this was crazy, that he was the one who sent Mister Benjamin on his mission to Paris and got him arrested. Yes, it was he who had concocted the whole story. Am I making this up too? He asked himself.

Then Hamilton turned around, stepped to the bed and sat back down. Oh my God, Hamilton thought, panicking. They will read what is on the laptop and they will destroy the computer and the floppies. What will I tell Jud? And then another terrible thought crowded into his head: What if that wasn't really Koldomasov? What if the whole thing were a setup? This can't be happening. Have I gone nuts?

The door opened. It was the woman again. Immediately, she began to talk. Hamilton noticed that her face was pocked and scared. She must have had pimples, he thought. She extended her hand toward Hamilton and in it was a Styrofoam cup. Hamilton took it and looked inside at the thick, purple liquid. It was grape-flavored kafur, just like he had had on the train. Ah, breakfast. The officer had said that there would be something to eat. She waited and watched while Hamilton drank. After taking the last swallow, Hamilton had a chalky aftertaste left in his mouth. The woman held out her hand for the cup, which Hamilton gave it to her, and she left.

He returned to the bed and lay back, his mind racing. The metal box with everything in it, he remembered. What if they take Jud's box? *Jud's Story* in the computer and also Jud's box! But why would they want to do that? There was nothing of interest to them in either the computer or box.

Hamilton looked at the ceiling. They have put my ass in a box. Man, *animal pyxis*, he thought. Man, the box creature. The creature that is born in a box, lives in a box. Man, the creature that travels around in boxes – flies in boxes and goes upon and under the seas in boxes. When he goes after his food, he goes to a box and often finds it in boxes. He reads history from an open box, for history has become an open box – boxed history. The world is boxed. Everything is boxed. *Animal pyxis* has put the world in a box. The creature that puts everything in boxes dies and is buried in a box. Man: boxed in.

I need sleep, Hamilton told himself. He looked around for a light switch, but found none. He became desperate and ran his hand over the wall. The stucco felt rough like sandpaper. There was no switch, but somehow he had known it all along. I'll throw something at the light bulb and knock it out, he thought; but there was nothing to throw. He remembered the bucket; no, that's crazy, Hamilton told himself.

Soon he felt a slight pain in his lower abdomen. Then it got sharper and his stomach rumbled, growled and cramped. He stumbled from the bed toward the bucket, whipping off his gown. He barely made it. Finally, thinking that he had lost his insides to the bucket, holding the sink with both hands to steady himself, he staggered back to the bed. He had thought that he might have to take another visit to the bucket, but this did not happen and soon it was over. He put the gown on, lay back and fell asleep.

When he awoke, the woman in the white smock was standing beside the bed. At her hand-signaled request, he followed her down the corridor and into another room. There was a green, stainless steel machine in the center of the room.

The woman motioned for Hamilton to stand on a steel platform. She gently placed her hand on his chest, pushing him back so that his weight rested on the slightly inclined sheet of steel behind him. Then she walked away and disappeared behind a screen. There was a purring noise and Hamilton began to recline with the platform. It was an X-ray table. The woman continued to talk calmly in Russian. Hamilton heard the machine klunking over her soothing words, only twenty percent of which Hamilton could understand. Those bastards, there is nothing in there for them to see. KLUNK. The woman came around and turned him over on his side. KLUNK. Then she turned him on his stomach. KLUNK. Then she turned him to the other side. KLUNK. Finally, she lowered the table and escorted Hamilton back to the room.

There was a Styrofoam container on the bed, and on the floor was a stainless steel samovar. He smelled tea garlic. Inside the container was a roasted half chicken, cucumbers in yogurt and a thick slice of brown bread. He picked up the chicken, smelled it and bit into the browned skin. It was not thoroughly cooked, and blood oozed from the flesh close to the bone. I'm not that hungry, Hamilton told himself, yet he ate some of it anyway. The metal bucket was gone from under the sink and in its place there was a yellow plastic one with green numbers stenciled on its side. He walked over and dropped the chicken into the bucket; then he took the plastic spoon and ate the cucumbers. He chomped down the bread and drank all the tea. Suddenly, he felt relaxed, perhaps even resigned.

He laid back and wondered how much time had passed, and as he was asking himself if he would ever get out of there, he fell asleep. He awoke several times, but only twice did he move from the bed, and this was to pee in the bucket. The bed seemed the only safe place in the room.

The door opened and a soldier entered. He was a different soldier from the one Hamilton had encountered before. The soldier was holding a tan paper package that turned out to be Hamilton's clothes. He put the package on the bed and Hamilton's shoes on the floor. The clothes had been washed and everything had been folded neatly. Hamilton's shirts had been starched and ironed. Without a word, the soldier left.

Hamilton removed the gown and dressed. Soon, another soldier entered and motioned for Hamilton to follow. In the hall, he saw the female officer who had taken him from the train, but she did not look at him. He continued down a set of stairs and into the office where he had been taken before. He wondered how much time has passed since then. The sun was rising. A day, perhaps? Yes, a day had passed.

"Please sit, Mister West. We must talk."

Hamilton sat. What now? Hamilton wondered. I'll tell him about Koldomasov, he said to himself. I'll just volunteer the information. But then the officer spoke.

"Tell me, who is this Kojevenekoff?"

"Kojevenekoff? You must be joking. Kojevenekoff doesn't exist. He doesn't exist except in my mind and in the computer that you obviously looked into. So, you read the story?"

"I am sorry, but we must follow procedure. Mister West, tell me, what were you doing in China?"

"I went there on a trip. I was just looking around. I know you want to know about my meeting with Koldomasov, and I am willing to tell you whatever ..."

"Oh, we know all about Comrade Koldomasov. He's not a bad fellow."

"Look, I'm a university professor on sabbatical – just that and nothing more."

"Yes, we know that, but I want you to tell me what you were doing in China."

"Okay. I went to China to get married. To Hong Kong, that is ..."

Hamilton continued to tell him the whole story. He got so caught up in what he was saying that, for moments, he forgot where he was and to whom he was speaking.

"Well, that's all of it. I've told you all there is to tell."

"Mind if I smoke?" the officer said.

"No, of course not. It's your office."

He lit a king-sized Camel from a box and held it vertically between his first finger and thumb. "Are you sure she is dead, this ... Mo?"

"Mo, dead? Of course I'm sure. Why would you ask me such ..."

"You yourself said she had just vanished from the room. I've read your notes Mister West."

"I don't know what you're suggesting, but whatever it is, it's not true. You have misinterpreted what I wrote."

"The Chinese. They are very sly. They have always lived by their cunning."

"Well, I suspect that you are right about the Chinese, but you are wrong about Mo. She had never even been to China before."

"Did she tell you that she had been associated with a Maoist organization?"

"No. Exactly when and where?"

The offer smiled but did not answer.

"When and where?"

"Does it really matter? If she is dead, as you say, then it surely doesn't matter; if she is alive then she will be with her comrades."

"She's dead!"

"Fine, have it your way; but now we must turn our attention to another matter. Mister West, one would assume that you would have known better than to have lied on official forms."

"What are you talking about?"

"I'm talking about your checking the block on the visa application indicating that you had never been denied entry to the Soviet Union. The application you made for your travel permit at our embassy in Beijing. We have records showing that you had been denied a visa just last year."

"Did I do that? It must have been a slip of the pen."

"Yes, perhaps it was, but whatever it was it has resulted in considerable inconvenience for you."

"You are telling me!"

The officer exhaled smoke and smiled.

"Okay, I give up. What are you going to do with me, send me to Siberia? I've been there. It didn't look so bad, not from the train anyway."

"Siberia?" He smiled "Oh, no, you may go. In fact, your train will be arriving soon."

"What about my belongings."

"That is your property. Except for your film, nothing has been harmed. We had to expose it to the sunlight, and for this I am sorry."

Hamilton slumped in his chair. The film in Mo's camera contained the only photographs he had of her. Now they were gone – vanished just like her.

"Mister West, are you feeling well?"

"Yes. When can I go?"

"You can go in just a moment, but first there is another matter."

"Another matter?"

"Yes. You owe us the equivalent of two thousand Singapore dollars for the plane tickets for you and your friend – the old fellow with the afflicted arm. The Aeroflot tickets from India to Singapore. I'm sure you must remember."

"Yes, I do remember, but I have no money. None except a few rubles. I can send you a check when I get back home. If you want me to sign something, I can do that."

"This is no problem," he said as he opened his drawer. "I have here your VISA card, Mister West. I regret that I must charge you forty percent interest."

"Whatever," Hamilton said, recognizing his well-used card. The officer ran it through the machine, filled it out and Hamilton signed the slip. Then he took his card and his bill fold.

"The car is waiting."

"I may go then?"

"Yes. You must or you will miss your train." He handed Hamilton a piece of paper. "Please sign here. It is about your things. Everything will be there, except the film, of course.

"Thanks," Hamilton said as he signed the slip.

"Your copy. Tell me one more thing before you go."

"What?"

"Whatever happened to this Mister Benjamin?"

"Mister Benjamin? Actually, I have no idea. Anything could have happened," Hamilton laughed.

# *Dawn*

The other disembarking passengers had vanished like specters, leaving Hamilton alone on the platform. He pulled up the sleeve of his parka to look at his watch; remembering that it was dead, he felt foolish. He glanced up and saw a big black-and-white clock hanging from the ceiling inside the station. The sign under the clock told anyone who wanted to know that this was Alexander Platz; the clock told them that it was almost five in the morning in East Berlin.

Hamilton had been on and off trains and waiting in train stations for almost twenty-four hours. Hamilton had to backtrack from Brest, the town on the Polish border where he had been arrested, to Warsaw in order to get to Berlin. Halfway between Brest and Warsaw, his train had suddenly slowed to a crawl and had proceeded in that fashion for over two hours. They had eventually come to a complete stop and had sat there for another two hours.

Hamilton had not known what was happening until he heard someone say in German that there had been a flood. Well, after all, it was spring. Eventually, all the passengers had been bused to another train station in the town of Wyszków, where they had taken another train on to Warsaw. There Hamilton had waited for almost five hours for another train to Berlin. He had gone to a restaurant in the station and had ordered a big plate of cabbage rolls and fried potatoes, which he had washed down with a couple of beers.

An old lady appeared on the platform. Hamilton watched her as she moved toward him, pushing a broom along the top of the dirty, cracked concrete.

"Entschuldigen sie mich bitte. Wie komme ich nach Westberlin?"

She looked at him and, for a moment, gave him a vacant stare. Then she rudely informed Hamilton that he should go in the opposite direction to get to West Berlin. She jabbed her crooked finger toward the door and grunted:

"Da! Karl Marx Platz."

"Danke. Thanks," he said and started for the door.

"Excuse me, mister, but why not take the train? The West is too far to walk."

Hamilton turned and looked at the stout man standing under a green wool hat with a small plume of hair affixed to its band by a pen made of pewter and deer antler. He held two plastic, mesh bags full of groceries.

"Go down those stairs and under the tracks; you will come up over there," he said, pointing across to the opposite platform. "The train comes every half hour. It will take you to Leipziger Strasse – Checkpoint Charlie."

The man spoke English with a slight German accent.

Hamilton told the man that he did not have German money and had only rubles. They would not even accept the Soviet money for tea on the train.

The man nodded sympathetically, reached into his pocket and handed Hamilton two coins. He told Hamilton not to worry about a loan from a stranger. He said that while the coins would get him out of East Berlin, they too were worth nothing. As it happened, the man was from West Berlin and had come to visit his aunt.

Soon Hamilton was in Leipziger Strasse. In the station, he saw a sign and under it a line of people that was short and moved steadily. He picked up his bag, walked to the back of the line and followed it into a tunnel.

I must be under the Berlin Wall, he gathered. He stepped to the counter at the first checkpoint and presented his papers. The East German soldier smacked a stamp on it without looking up. It was an East German again at the next check point. The soldier glanced at his papers and sleepily nodded for him to go on. Next there was a Soviet check point.

"Oh, shit!" Hamilton muttered under his breath.

He placed his passport and visa on the counter in front of the helmeted soldier. The soldier looked up at him, then down at the picture on the passport and back again at Hamilton. The soldier's face was without expression. WHAP. He stamped the passport. Hamilton sighed and walked on.

The next counter was West German.

"Wellkommen zu Berlin," the soldier said, returning his passport.

At what turned out to be the last stop, there was a black military police corporal sitting behind a thick sheet of glass.

"How long you been gone, Mister West? Oh, here it is, right here. You left England last year on the twenty-sixth of December. So was it business or just a holiday?"

"A ... holiday," Hamilton answered with a smile.

He stamped the passport. "Thanks. Welcome home. And you have a good day now."

Hamilton walked through the remaining twenty feet of tunnel and stepped into the street: "Friedrichstrasse." The sun was rising. He went down the sidewalk. When he reached the end of the block, he turned and looked back at the wall. He saw a woman standing not fifty paces from him. Her hair was dark and silky. She was tall, tanned and athletic looking. The sun was in his eyes and her back was to him, but through his squint he could discern silver earrings and something shiny on her finger. No. No, it can't be. I'm seeing things, he told himself. Hamilton quickly moved toward her. The sun was still in his eyes and he brought his hand up to shield them. No, he said to himself, this is impossible.

"Mo? Mo!"

She turned. He looked at her black miniskirt and her black boots, a bad match for her heavily shoulder-padded, orange, artificial fur coat. She did not look a day over twenty.

"Ich entschuldigen ... Ich ..." Hamilton said.

"Kennen wir uns von irgendwoher? Haven't we met before?" she asked.

Hamilton told her that no, they had never met.

She asked Hamilton if he wanted to do something, but before he could answer she had gone on to say: "Wir können zu meinem Platz gehen. Ein gutes zimmer. Wir können partei."

She offered for Hamilton to go to her place. It was a nice room and they could party. Then she added that she knew what Americans liked. Hamilton began to tell her that he was not an American, but she interrupted.

"Nicht sie mögen mich?" she asked. The girl told him that they could do anything he liked, but that he must use a condom.

Hamilton replied that he thought she was very pretty, adding that she was too young for him and he never liked doing anything like this before breakfast. But then Hamilton had second thoughts and reached into his pocket, producing a wad of red-and-white rubles.

"Was kostet das?" he asked, with a sheepish smile.

"Ha! Russische scheiss! Ha!" She turned and crossed the street, laughing.

Hamilton was hungry. He walked on, looking for a place to eat, but he soon found that everything was still closed. He had no idea where he was and began taking streets randomly. The traffic thickened – first with buses and trucks and then with cars. The streets had a smell of spring mixed with the sweet fumes of diesel. The city was waking. At Kurfurstendamm, on the facade of a building with a gaudy sign covering up one of the few remaining vestiges of monumental Prussia, he saw a restaurant with a fat man wearing an apron and carrying a boom stepping from the door. As he moved closer, Hamilton could see the VISA sign on the window. The "Alt-Berliner" – ah, nice name – looked just fine. He could already taste sausage, eggs and coffee. He had not had coffee since Singapore.

Hamilton had sausage and eggs, and with them he had rye bread with butter and black currant jam and lots and lots of coffee. When he finished, he presented his VISA card to the waiter, but the waiter returned with the man Hamilton had seen with the broom, who turned out to be the proprietor. Hamilton was told that the card was no longer valid; it had expired the last day of January 1989. When Hamilton told him why he had no other money except the rubles, both the proprietor and the waiter thought the story was funny and believed that Hamilton had not known about the expiration date. The proprietor told Hamilton that he would take one of the rubles for his little nephew, but that Hamilton should keep the rest as a souvenir. He said that Hamilton could forget about paying for breakfast.

Then he showed Hamilton the pictures on the walls – old photographs of Imperial Germany. There was one from the heart of darkest Africa. "Kongo," the proprietor said, pointing at the picture of pith-helmeted Germans standing beside a sea plane tied to a dock on a great river. At the margins of the proud Germans were Africans – pygmies holding spears and their little bodies decorated with swirls of white paint. The proprietor tapped his finger on the glass and laughed: "Der barbar, savages."

Hamilton waited for the German bank to open. He had chosen it when he noticed the VISA logo on the glass door. By noon he had been issued a temporary card and a one-thousand-dollar cash advance. He had feared that, with all the charges on the card, he had exceeded his credit limit, but the blue-suited manager said that the computer showed that the last valid use of the card was from a place called "Lucky Plaza Jewels." This was the place in Singapore where Hamilton had bought the durian ring for Mo – the ring on his little finger.

Hamilton left the bank. He would find an inexpensive hotel or maybe a pension, soak in hot, soapy water, sleep and spend the next few days finishing *Jud's Story*. He wanted to have it done when he arrived in Rye. Won't Jud be surprised? He'll laugh his ass off.

# CHAPTER VIII
## THE WORLD TURNED UPSIDE DOWN

When I arrived in Rye, Rodger had just returned from Frankfurt where he had held a one-man show for the first time in that city. He had sold three paintings and to celebrate his success and my arrival, he took me to the Mermaid Inn.

I did not want to spoil the evening, so I waited until later to tell him about what had happened to Hamilton's parents and how hard Hamilton had taken it. Just as I had predicted, when I did tell him, he was upset. Rodger is the kind of man who is capable of hurting for everyone. Perhaps this explains the reason why his paintings are often humorous and ironic and why he treats the pain of the world with the unguent of comedy and the balm of fantasy.

It had been Rodger's suggestion that I bring Hamilton to Rye later that year. After all, he had not been there for over a decade, since the sabbatical when he did research for his Bogdanov book at an institute at the University of London. More importantly, it would be a good place for him to spend Christmas. Also, Rodger said Uncle Andy had written saying he would be coming at Christmas as well.

The golden heather on the downs had just begun to bloom and the sheep-dotted meadow behind Rye's Benjamin House was the color of jade. After two good months in Rye, I decided that the ice should be breaking up on the Ottawa River and that I was ready to get back to

Jack Pine Isle. That day I bought a used copy of The History of Tom Jones from the bookseller on Mermaid Street. It would entertain me on the plane and I looked forward to reading it in the solitude of my cottage. I said farewell to Rodger, and as my train pulled out of the station, I promised to consider returning to Rye for Christmas.

When I arrived in Canada I found, much to my dismay, that because it had been an unusually severe winter, the spring was late and it was still not possible to get to my island by walking on the ice or canoeing in the open water. I needed a place to stay for at least a week, so I went to a pay phone at the county store where I usually bought provisions and called Hamilton in Toronto. I didn't feel like I'd be imposing because he had plenty of room and, besides, I wanted to see how he was. He sounded different. I couldn't quite figure out why, but he was different.

"Sure you can come," he said. "We'll go to Brunswick House and get wasted and you can get up and sing "Dixie." Come. We'll be glad to have you."

I paid no attention to his use of "we." I had taken it to be a mere manner of speech.

As I stood there on Hamilton's porch, wiping the slush from my boots, he opened the door.

"Well, there you are, Juddy Boy. Come on in and we'll fix you a Jack Daniel's."

Never before had he called me by that name, and never before had I seen him with a shaved head and a mustache. And this wasn't just a mustache – not any ole garden of whiskers growing under a man's nose – there bloomed the biggest, thickest and rustiest red patch of mustache hairs that I had ever seen.

"My horn, I call it. Like it? I wax the ends."

"Well ... Sure," I answered as he hugged the breath out of me.

"Come on in, ole Jud. Come in and meet Daniella."

Now, who was this Daniella? I almost asked, but before I got myself past the hall cloak closet, she was there pressing my hand.

"Oh, Jud! Hamilton has told me so much about you. He's told me all about when you and he were boys and all the things the two of you did in Georgia, the bad things you did too."

She spoke with the trace of a French accent.

"I'm from Montreal. I study architecture."

She would not shut up.

"Yeah, but Daniella's really an artist. Come on in and you'll see."

The place looked like a gallery. Paintings of a single, amateur painter hung everywhere. "Private showing," I said, laughing.

I was looking at what is called Horror Vaccui – Daniella's attempt to do something about what must have been her fear of unoccupied space. Her paintings were in Hamilton's living room, dining room and even his kitchen. When I went into the bathroom and stood over the toilet, there, on the wall facing me, was a dancer. Her arms, which to me didn't quite match her body, were held high into the air. Under her feet was a bed of what I took to be burning coals.

"Yes, you are right. They are burning coals," she said when I asked her about it. "I got the idea from a picture I saw. You know in India they really do that? I hear you are a poet. I love poetry."

She must have been almost twenty years younger than Hamilton, who I decided had gone completely mad.

That night Daniella cooked especially bad lasagna. She said it was her grandmother's recipe, which let me know right away that her grandmother was certainly not Italian. I thought that, had the grandmother been a sensible woman, she would have prepared the dish only once and, after tasting it, burned the recipe and given what remained to the dog.

But I was beginning to feel bad for Daniella. She was falling all over herself to please Hamilton and trying her best to impress me. She talked on and on about art and architecture and about what was going on in France – always France. "Diarrhea theoria," I called it. She would sit at the table, the diamond stud in her nose reflecting the light, smiling and chirping like a little bird, peering at Hamilton through her wire-rimmed glasses and tossing back her reddish-brown hair. Her every sentence contained "Hamilton and I," "our house," "we think" or "we like." To hear her, you might get the impression that they had been together for decades. Of course, that could only have been possible had Hamilton shared responsibility for her birth. I later learned she had just moved in a month before. Only four months before that she had gone to hear Hamilton lecture on that Russian guy, Bogdanov. That's how it all had started.

At dinner, Hamilton told me that he had come to a conclusion. Oh God, I thought, to what conclusion had this new Hamilton West come to?

"Well. You know that I've been reading the Germans a lot lately," he said.

He looked at me slyly and paused to let the suspense build.

I nodded. I knew what German philosophers he was going to mention. This much I had heard before.

"Mostly Hegel and Nietzsche. My conclusion is that history is over. That it's dead, dead as a door nail."

I wasn't sure that I had heard him right, but if I had, I was sure he had gone completely bonkers.

"What? Whose history is over?" I asked.

I thought he might just be talking about himself – a reference, perhaps, to himself and this new life he had adopted as some bazaar remedy for his grief over the death of his parents.

"Nobody's history in particular, but everybody's in general," he laughed.

Then Hamilton went on to explain this theory in detail. Everything everywhere, he explained, was becoming more and more alike, and it was now impossible to act or to create anything new. The only real change left, he said, was the development of the world through the use of technology. It sounded like bullshit to me, but I sat, listened and asked a few polite questions.

The night before I was supposed to leave for Jack Pine Isle, we went to the Brunswick House. The place looked just like it had when I was washing beer glasses there back in the sixties. Not only did it look the same, but I swear to you that the same fat woman got up and sang "Okie from Muskogee" and the same midget treated us to "Danny Boy."

As I sat there with Hamilton and Daniella, Hamilton told me how he had, as he put it, "really stirred them up over at the university." He had written an article entitled "The End of History and the Russo-American Way of Life." When we got back to the house, he brought the article out and showed it to me. Yes, you bet he had stirred them up! I could imagine. After all, I too had worked there and knew what academics were like. If I didn't know what was going on with my erstwhile steady, dependable, ex-hockey playing cousin, then surely those characters at the university didn't know either. They must really think he's nuts. But then, this just might give them reason to ignore him for not writing about the trends of the day in the latest academic style.

The next morning, Hamilton insisted on accompanying me to the bus station. As we walked down Dundas Street, I asked:

"Hambone, now that history is over, exactly what is one supposed to do."

"Live dangerously!" he replied, laughing and looking surprised, as if I had asked a dumb question.

We went into the station. I did not ask him what he meant, for I thought I had a pretty good idea.

Later, while reading as the bus was winding through the Haliburton Highlands, a line from Fielding's book struck me as altogether appropriate to what I had seen over the past few days:

"... life most exactly resembles the stage, since it is often the same person who represents the villain and the hero; and he who engages your admiration today, will probably attract your contempt tomorrow."

Over the next two months I tried to call Hamilton twice, but there was no answer. After that, I sort of forgot about it. Finally, I wrote him a note asking that he pick a time to come to Jack Pine Isle. I had to make myself tell him to bring Daniella along, for I feared if I did not, he might not come. I told him to call the store and leave a message telling me when to phone him. He didn't call. Later on, when I bought myself a good used truck, I thought about driving to Toronto to see what was going on, but again, as time passed, I forgot about it.

Soon it was June. This meant black fly season in the Ottawa Valley, but it also meant that, if you know what you are doing, it is one of the best times of the year to fish. I arose before first light, covered myself in musk oil to ward off the flies and canoed a couple of miles upstream to a good spot I knew. I tied a fly to resemble one of the marauding, dive-bombing blood suckers that had invaded my world, and even soaked the hairs and feathers hiding the hook in a goo that I had made from captured and executed black flies. I caught two nice-looking pickerel and a two-foot muskie, but I threw the muskie back.

Around noon, after letting the canoe drift in the current, I went back to my cottage and cleaned the fish. I soon realized that I was low on naphtha gas and made my way to the county store. Once there I reminded myself to try, once again, to call Hamilton. I called, but again received no answer.

Late that afternoon, as I was looking out the west window of the cottage that faced the Ontario shore, I saw a dirty, blue Volkswagen pull up beside my truck. It was Hamilton, and he was alone. Swatting flies, I went to the rocks and shouted.

"Hey Hambone, what the hell are you doing?"

"Standing here listening to you ask me a dumb question. Don't just stand there, get your redneck arse in the canoe and come get me. I'm being eaten alive."

Before I got to the shore, I realized – as my Uncle Durden would say – that Hamilton was as high as a Georgia pine. He was also smoking a fat cigar. Hamilton never smoked. He held up the cigar for me to see it.

"Cigar's for the bugs," he shouted. "Goddamn flies! Can see how they drove the voyagers crazy," he yelled from a cloud of smoke, as I was half way between him and the shore.

I noticed for the first time that, despite his accent, he sounded a little bit like me. I guessed what I was hearing was simply a choice of words here and there and a common idiom now and then, both undoubtedly the result of his having had a mother from Georgia.

Swatting flies, we raced inside the cottage. Once safely inside, he produced a bottle of Jack Daniel's.

"Here, I thought you might need the Black Jack."

At sundown, as we sat over the table eating the pickerel, he finally agreed to tell me where Daniella was. Picking up the bottle of sour mash whiskey, he said:

"Guess I swapped one Daniella for another. I decided to sell my house, so she had to move out."

"Move out? Where to?"

"Hell, I don't know. Doesn't matter. It's all over between us."

"But what about your house? You've lived there for well over a decade."

"Yeah. Got a damn good price for it too."

"So where are you living?"

"Well, the way I figured it, I have this nice big office with a chesterfield and all. I got myself a hot plate and a little fridge. Of course, you've seen it. You've seen my office. Why not?"

"Hambone, you are not living in that office? Where do you bathe?"

"Sure I am, and why not? Oh, I bathe at the gym. Been working out with those machines too. Wanna arm wrestle?"

Hamilton rolled up his sleeve and showed me a bulging bicep.

"Don't get so worked up, Juddy Boy. Not going to be there much longer. I'm leaving. And soon."

"Where are you going?"

"Sabbatical."

"You're not due for another sabbatical for at least two years. I remember. I was there. There at the university. Don't forget."

"Well, I worked this thing out with the dean."

"The dean?"

"Yep. Good ole Bland – Bland the Bald. I'm going to Russia."

He leaned his chair back and put a foot on the table. Behind his running shoe, I could see that he was twirling an end of his mustache.

"An Exchange. September."

"Hey. That's great. Moscow?"

"Yep, Moscow," he confirmed as he reached over for the bottle of Black Jack and poured a drink in my coffee cup.

"To Moscow!" I said, holding up my cup.

He touched my cup with his and the tin made a click.

"Moscow!" he repeated.

The next day, I made Hamilton go fishing with me. As we sat in my boat, I admitted to him that the biography of Judah P. Benjamin was not going well, stating that it is difficult for a poet to change to prose. That was the only excuse I had. Throughout the morning, Hamilton sat in the boat puffing cigars, listening to me and bringing up his business about the end of history. We didn't catch a single fish.

That evening Hamilton pulled off his shirt and showed me the tattoo on his left shoulder blade. When I asked him why he had done such a thing, he said he'd done it just for the hell of it, because it was something different, and that he had had some cockeyed dream about the Virgin standing on the moon.

On a day in August, I went to the county store and the lady there told me that I had received a telephone message. I was supposed to return the call. I recognized the number right away; it was from Toronto, with the university prefix. Yes, it was the number of Hamilton's office, or home.

He was there alright. He told me to expect him at Jack Pine Isle around the first week of September and that he wanted me to help him execute what he referred to as his "random plan." It was a plan that he said must be carried out during the first few days of classes and before he left. I had no clue as to what he was talking about. He was so mysterious about it. I decided his plan was probably something else about his hair-brained theory and soon forgot about it.

On a Saturday at the beginning of the first week of September, he arrived. I heard him blowing his horn on the river bank. This time he was sober and had no cigar. He stood beside the blue Volkswagen, waving.

That night, after we had finished the steaks and bottle of Bordeaux he brought, we started in on the bottle of Black Jack that, this time, I had bought in anticipation of his visit.

"Not going to Russia after all. Plan's been changed. The Soviets, they're pissed. Don't like that stuff about the Russo-American way of life. The Yanks are pissed too, I hear. But I didn't want to go to Washington, so that doesn't matter," he said covering with forced laughter what I knew was disappointment.

"And what are you going to do?"

"What am I going to do? I'm going to Britain. The dean insists upon it. Damn Russians."

"Why can't you go to Russia?"

"Hell, I don't know. They won't give me a visa. Damn Ruskies. Fuck 'em. Shouldn't complain, I guess. I've been given a grant by the university. I'm leaving for the U.K. next week. The Warburg Institute at the University of London again. Just like last time."

"Hey, a grant, that's good! Look. When I was in Rye during the winter, Rodger was real anxious that I get you to come over and spend Christmas there. Uncle Andy's going to be there. I'm leaving in late December, as soon as the ice starts to form on the river. What do you say? Will you come to Rye? You'll be in England anyway."

"You can count on it. I'm not looking forward to London. Too familiar. It's become like every other place. Rye will be a change. And last I saw Andy was quite awhile ago. Yes, it was one of his trips up here on communist business."

"Great! Here's to Rye."

I let the Black Jack slowly trickle into our cups, and then we picked them up and clicked them together.

"It will be like old times," I said.

"So," Hamilton said, as I made some coffee, "it's time we talked about the random plan that will be executed tomorrow – Monday – at 11:00 in the morning sharp. And I hope your truck is running, because we'll need it."

What was Hamilton's plan? And why did I agree to it? Well, what was executed went as follows:

Monday morning we got up at three and, after coffee, paddled over to the shore where Hamilton's Volkswagen and my pickup were parked. I followed Hamilton's taillights down the gravel road and out onto the highway as we drove toward Toronto. Five hours later and forty miles north of the city, we stopped at a stockyard on the edge of the town of Stouffville. They were just opening up. Hamilton rolled down his window and tapped his watch.

"Eight o'clock. We're right on time," he said, pulled into a parking space.

He shut off his engine and hopped out of the car.

"Let's go, Juddy boy."

"We need some chickens," Hamilton told the man – a scrawny fellow with a long, skinny neck like Uncle Andy's.

He pushed his baseball cap back on his head. "Well, we got 'em. What kind and how many you want? And you want 'em dead or alive?"

"About two dozen of the quickest ones you have," Hamilton answered, smiling.

"What kind? We got layers, fryers. We got Reds. We got Rock Islands. And we got some real nice Cornish Rocks. We got roosters, even the fighting kind, but we have to keep that quiet."

"Give us a dozen of the cheapest, liveliest hens you have, and your meanest fighting rooster. And we want you to divide them up and put them in gunny sacks."

"Gunny sacks?"

"Yep, gunny sacks."

"Well, they'll be your chickens and we'll do what you want, but you better put the ole rooster in a sack by hisself."

"Good, we're in a rush," Hamilton said as he tapped his watch.

Soon we were back on the road and the bags of chickens were in the back of my covered pickup. When we got to the city, it was just after nine. I followed Hamilton to a parking lot on a back corner of the university campus. He parked his car and got into the truck.

"MacDabb Hall," he said, pointing to the stone, neo-gothic building that dominates the campus. "Go to the back at the service entrance," Hambone ordered, smiling. He nodded in the direction of a brown paper bag he had with him, laughed and gave his mustache a twirl. "They're expecting us at ten, so we're a little early," he laughed again as he gave his mustache another twirl.

At the loading dock behind the building, Hamilton hopped out and went into a back door. Soon he returned with two guys from the maintenance staff. You could tell by their brown uniforms and because one of them was pushing a large, blue, plastic container on wheels. Hamilton opened the back of the truck, reached into the paper bag and took out two bottles of Jack Daniel's – black label – and handed them to the men.

"This stuff as good as you say, Doc?"

"Yep. You'll see. The birds are here in the back. Let's get 'em. Come on, Jud. The plan is in operation. I'll get the ole rooster."

We put the six bags of birds into the container. Hamilton took the bag containing the rooster and we hurried down a hall, through some double doors and into some storeroom crowded with crates, old chairs, tables, lecterns, tools and cleaning equipment. The two men led us into another storeroom full of boxes of toilet paper and paper towels, napkins and cups.

"We have twenty minutes," Hamilton said, glancing at his watch.

"Yep, we got plenty of time to sample this stuff," one of the guys said matter-of-factly, fishing into his pocket as he did. He brought out a Swiss Army Knife and, slicing open one of the boxes, produced four cups. They had a dartboard and for twenty minutes we sipped the Black Jack and threw darts. It was awfully early and I had difficulty getting down even a sip, but the two grateful recipients of Hamilton's gift drank greedily. The guys kept calling Hamilton "Doc" and one could tell that they knew him. Well, after all, he did live in the building where they worked. Meanwhile, the chickens were clucking. I guess they were getting restless, anticipating their mission.

"Okay, you guys. It's time to coordinate our watches. I have three minutes to eleven. Jud, you get the girls and I'll get their bad ole boyfriend. Okay guys, you know the plan."

Hamilton and I followed the two guys out of the storeroom and down a maze of corridors. At an elevator door we stopped.

"Well, here she is," one of the guys said.

He took a key from his key ring, placed it in a slot and turned it. With his other hand he gave Hamilton his Swiss Army Knife. Then he pressed the button and the doors slid open.

"Now, Jud and I are going to take the chickens out of the cart to put them in here. Then we're gonna have to close the door just for a minute – just long enough to set 'em free. Don't let the elevator go anywhere."

"No problem. It's not going nowhere 'til you say, Doc," one of the guys said, sounding tipsy.

We got into the elevator and closed the door.

"Okay, Juddy Boy, let 'em lose."

We cut the binder twine and dumped the squawking birds on the floor. The rooster immediately began chasing the hens and feathers were beginning to fly. From top to bottom, the space was full of chickens. I covered my eyes and batted.

"When I open the door, you go first."

Hambone opened the door.

"Now! Go!"

Several hens got off the elevator with me, but one of the guys caught one of them and threw her back in. Then, as Hamilton jumped out – kicking, swatting and pushing the storm of birds away from the door – the door closed. We could hear them clucking, squawking, flapping and hitting the sides of the elevator.

"Okay guys. Combat stations. We have exactly one minute to go. Let her up at exactly eleven. Come on Jud, follow me."

We dashed up the stairs and stood beside a bank of elevators in the main hall of the building. In front of the doors was a large crowd of students and professors about to attend eleven o'clock classes. It was the busiest time of day on the busiest day of the week during the busiest month of the academic year. I saw Dean Bland's bald dome showing itself off like a celery root.

"Look!" Hamilton said, pointing to the back of the throng. There was a large yellow dog on a leash held by a small, blind, female student.

"This will be even better than I dreamed," Hamilton whispered gleefully.

The doors slid open and the bad ole rooster led the way. With feathers flying, the chickens fluttered into the crowd. Chickens were in the air, on the floor, jumping, squawking and clucking. People screeched and laughed. For a moment, it was difficult to tell the people from the chickens. It was a great swirl of arms, legs, wings, feathers and chicken shit. The dog had gone wild and broken loose from his leash. He bounded into the vortex. There were barks, laughter, screams, cries and, of course, feathers. Chaos, wonderful chaos!

After fending off the terrified birds, the crowd began to loosen and scatter. The dog chased a hen down the hall and his mistress cried out at him. Then the rooster attacked the dog. By this time we are bursting with laughter and so was most everyone else – even the blind student.

"West! I could have guessed. But ... you're not supposed to be here! And you ... Benjamin, I thought we'd seen the last of you!"

It was the dean.

"Hamilton West, you'll pay for this."

"Pay for what?" Hamilton answered, laughing.

"You'll pay for pulling this outrageous stunt!"

"Now, that's strange. Here we were standing in this crowd and these chickens fly out of the elevator. We've been here all the time. I'm sure we can produce witnesses. Looks like the chickens just randomly wandered into the elevator. Perhaps they got lost. I hear chickens are not too smart. Not too smart like ... well, I won't say it. Look, this kinda thing happens, you know. I guess, when time is up, everything is random."

The dean gritted his teeth and blushed. Then he stomped his foot, turned and left.

When Hamilton and I said our goodbye in the parking lot, we were still laughing.

"Okay, Hambone. Christmas in Rye? Be sure to send me your number in London. I'll call when I arrive."

"Righto. When we tell Andy and Rodger about the chickens, they'll laugh their arses off! That dog went after those chickens, eh?"

"Fuckin' eh, he did! And did you see that rooster go after that dog?"

Again, we bent over laughing. Hamilton was slapping my shoulder and then he pulled me to him, engulfing me in a hug – a big, bearish, Hamilton hug. Finally, he got into his dirty, blue Volkswagen and drove away, still laughing.

Now, why did I do it? Why did I agree to the plan? I did it because it was Hambone's plan and I knew it was important to him. Hamilton needed to leave with a good laugh. And Hambone, well, he got his laugh. We did something new and wonderful, and something people might just remember and marvel at. They might laugh about it and try to figure it all out long after this generation of students is gone to mirthless jobs, mortgages, ungrateful children, baldness, betrayals and bankruptcy – and even later, to wrinkles, fat bellies and limp dicks, dying parents and disease.

Yes, indeed, long after those professors have pontificated on the definitive theory of how often King Henry VIII changed his socks, excreted the last deconstruction of a work of art – revealing the last misogynist, homophobic or racist artist – and flunked or promoted their last student; long after they have established for eternity the last politically correct program, together with the most efficient strategy for transforming the world into a likeness of themselves; and when everyone has finally offended everybody, all of this will be forgotten. But what will be remembered is the freeing of the chickens.

So now it must be said: Hamilton is wrong about history. For that day we made history. But it is okay for Hamilton to be wrong. He is my cousin and Hamilton is – and always has been – my best friend.

In late December, when it became difficult for the bow of my canoe to cut through the ice on the river, I decided it was about time for me to leave Jack Pine Isle. Besides, I was ready to go to Rye. The biography had not been going well. I thought just being in Rye in Benjamin House, around that world that had been Judah P. Benjamin's, might stimulate me.

I decided to stay in England until the end of spring. I knew that Rodger would not mind, and I needed the time to go through the material in the library at the University of Sussex, where the archives of that region are kept. I hate historical research, but it had to be done. And, yes, I was lonely. I couldn't wait to see Hamilton, Rodger and, of course, Uncle Andy. So, on the eighteenth day of December, I wired both Rodger and Hamilton and told them to expect me in two days.

When my train pulled up at the little gray station, there was Rodger, grinning and waving. Hambone was there too, sticking up his middle finger, shooting me a bird. His mustache was even bigger and curved like the lethal forks on the head of a bull.

"We're walking up to the Mermaid to celebrate," Hamilton said, taking my bag.

"Fried plaice, mash and peas – sound good?" Rodger said.

"That sounds great, but first a glass of bitter. Where's Uncle Andy?"

"Andy had a problem at Seven Bridges. Something about the heat in a barn. Oh, I don't know the details. Anyway, something happened during the night and all those birds he always talks about froze. He was awfully upset. We'll fetch him at Gatwick tomorrow around noon."

When Rodger told me this, I imagined the blue metal building behind the white farm house at Seven Bridges. I knew how much those exotic birds meant to all those guys, and that the birds were their main source of cash. But I also knew that the birds were special in other ways to Andy. After all, it was he who had come up with the idea of raising them as a project that would produce profit. Ironic for an old Marxist, I thought. But he really loved the birds. He thought they were beautiful, and by naming them as he did, he vested them with special powers, as words have the tendency of going their own way. Well, tomorrow we would hear all about it, I said to myself as we stepped inside the Mermaid Inn.

When we were finished with our supper of fried plaice, I asked Hamilton about London.

Boring," he replied. "Boring just like I said it would be. I can understand why that ole crotchety Marx spent so much time in the reading room of the British Museum. He did it so he could imagine how life was in other places, like life in the satanic mills of Manchester. At least that place's not as boring as London. But, anyway, I have a plan."

"A plan?" I smiled as I wondered if this time he was going to let hundreds – no thousands – of chickens loose on the University of London or in the British Museum, or maybe in Westminster or Buckingham Palace itself.

"Yep, a plan."

"Oh God, not another plan ..."

"Yes, and you'll like it even better than the last one. I have to wait until Andy arrives to tell you. I shouldn't have to tell it twice, should I?"

"God, Hambone, what have you come up with now?" I said.

The next afternoon, after meeting Andy at Gatwick, we drove along the M1 toward Rye. Andy told us that because he had forgotten to pay the oil bill, the oil company had not delivered it and the oil had run out. Without oil, the furnace had stopped and the tropical birds froze.

"I'm always forgetting that when you get away from the coast, Georgia can get cold. But those sorry bastards at the oil company! They only think of the money. Oh, how I loved those birds. Yes, it was time for me to leave," Andy said.

We all tried to make him feel better. "Here's a bottle of Johnnie Walker. Got it for you from Duty Free," I said. "Got it just for you, Ole Unc."

"Well I'm glad you still got some money to buy your po' old uncle something 'cause he damned sure ain't got no more money. Finally, boys, all our Benjamin money is done run out!"

"Damn it, Andy! Hard to believe it's been so long since we've seen each other," Hamilton said.

"Yeah. And they say you've changed," Andy growled. "Well, you do look different. You look like the sword swallower in the sideshow that used to come with the fair to Altamaha. Ever see him? Whiskers like yours and shaved head too."

Hamilton smiled at Andy's statement, nodded and replied:

"Actually I do remember him. But Andy you haven't changed. You know the earliest memory I have of you is when you were covered in cow shit."

"And as long as I can remember, Hambone, you've always been full of cow shit. But I must say that I like your new look better. Like it better than when you used to look like the stodgy professor. Besides, the way you look now will keep people from looking at people like me."

"Guess I just ran out of tweeds."

"Hey. There it is! Turn here. Turn at the Ripe exit!" Andy said to Rodger. "I know what we gotta do with this bottle of Johnnie Walker."

"No. No," I said. "This is not the turn! I remember."

"Don't give me any of your shit, Juddy Boy, or I'll tell Hambone and Rodger the Dodger about how you used to dress up in your Aunt Vera Ola's clothes. Rodger, go to the old Norman church. You know the one."

We drove through the town of Ripe. The town is not as old as Rye, yet some of its houses are listed in the Doomsday Book. Soon, we were standing in the graveyard of the Church of Saint John the Baptist beside a grave on the edge of the cemetery in unkempt grass. It was a grave in unconsecrated ground. The writing on the headstone was moss covered and almost lost: "MALCOLM LOWRY 1907 - 1957."

The ladies of the altar guild were just leaving the church and they stopped on the steps for a moment and watched us. Then scurried away like squawking hens.

"You know, Malcolm was quite specific about what he wanted on the stone. But they just wouldn't have it. Shame, shame," my uncle said.

Then he pulled a book from the pocket of his tan trench coat.

"Here it is," he said ironically, holding up a recent biography of Lowry.

He opened the book and tapped a page with his thick, nicotine-stained nail and pushed up his glasses.

"Read here," he ordered me.

As I read, Andy poured the bottle of Johnnie Walker over the damp earth and the eroding stone:

"Malcolm Lowry
Late of the Bowery
His prose was flowery
And often glowery
He lived, nightly, and drank, daily
And died playing the ukulele"

"Bet he's laughing his ass off," Andy muttered as the last drop fell on the ground. "Let's go. I'm hungry and thirsty. Stop at the next pub. You know, I discovered Lowry. Good drinker. Good writer. Bad politics. Now a dead, drunk writer with bad politics. Good man, that Lowry."

We already knew about Andy having "discovered" Lowry. He had told us many times, and he had made Rodger bring him there before. We, of course, had told Hamilton. My uncle always claimed that it had been during a wild winter in Mexico, but we suspected that it had occurred on an ordinary day at Mister Jonathan Capes' publishing house in New York where my uncle had worked for a short stint as a junior editor. But maybe he had known him in Mexico. Hell, I don't know. It could have happened any number of ways.

That night, after we finished the Chinese food that we had ordered in and moved into the studio for port, fruit and Stilton cheese (Rodger is so bloody English), I popped the question.

"Okay, Hambone, that plan ... what is it? You said you would tell us when Andy got here. Now he's here, so let's hear it."

Hamilton sat back in the green wingback chair and twirled his mustache. Eventually, he leaned forward and looked at me and Rodger earnestly.

"I'm going to Asia."

"Asia?" I asked, surprised.

"Yep, Asia. And Andy's going with me. We talked about it just this afternoon. Yep, Asia. You wanna come?"

"No. No, I don't. Why Asia?" Rodger asked.

"Because that's where it all began. I have a grant to do research. I have to produce something. It's always about producing. You remember that, eh Jud? I think my project could use a bit of "field research." And it's better than rummaging around in the Warburg Institute and being in boring ole London. History began in Asia. It ended here. I want to see if there is really anything different on this planet – and by different, I mean, really different."

"When are you leaving?" I asked.

"As soon as possible," my uncle replied.

"Well," I said, "I'd tell you what I know about Asia, but it's not good. I've been there. I know. And you'd never catch my ass in that part of the world again. I'm going to bed."

I wanted to read over the last notes I had compiled on the life of Judah P. Benjamin – all bullshit I had put together in iambic pentameter, blank verse. Hell, I was so desperate that I'd even tried heroic couplets. None of it was working out, especially just plain ole English. I needed to be alone, but it was still early and the buggers were getting pissed.

I went to the third-story bedroom, where, on the wall, hung Rodger's painting of Cockaigne scenes from the medieval world. I looked over my mess about Judah P. Benjamin, shut the box that contained it and for perhaps an hour, fitfully, slept.

When I awoke, I heard them going at it. I needed a drink of water and, in the dark, made my way down the stairs to the kitchen. Rodger heard me and came in.

"Tell me. Did you see old Judah P. wandering about the upper reaches of the house? He's here, you know," Rodger teased as I stood at the sink.

It had become a familiar joke. Rodger swore that, from time to time, you could hear a billiard ball bouncing down the stairs.

"If I do see him, I'll ask him to do something about our nutty relatives. Uncle Andy and Hamilton won't listen to us, maybe they ought to talk to the dead," I said.

Rodger grinned and then Uncle Andy and Hamilton appeared at the door.

"Jud doesn't believe in ghosts, eh?" Hamilton asked.

"He damned sure used too. I can tell you that," Andy said. "You remember hearing that story, Jud, about ole Cora being stuffed into the ice box? You always used to swear that you could hear her banging the pots and pans in the kitchen, and you refused to go to sleep? So, Juddy Boy, when did you quit believing in ghosts?" Andy asked, smiling, but serious.

"Guess it was when I quit believing in God. No God, no ghosts," I said.

I went up stairs, fell into the bed and slept. I dreamed about Judah P. When I awoke, finally the words came.

### Chapter Three
### SUNSET

"Yes, my brother Malachi snared it in his barn. He caught him during the night. They are all like Minerva's owl in that they only fly after dusk, you know. Malachi said this beast is about as big as they come. Malachi's done well. He has quite an operation there now, and he's making a fortune in timber. Perhaps, someday he will visit. More tea, my dear Isbister?"

Mister Benjamin was referring to the stuffed great-horned owl under the glass bell - a gift that he had recently received from his brother in Georgia.

"Exactly where is this place? I'm afraid my knowledge of North American geography has slipped. I've been in England for so long now."

"Come over here, if you please - over to this map."

Mister Benjamin pointed with his cigar to the scarlet silk map in the gilded frame hanging over the mantel. He walked across the room; Isbister joined him.

"Here, just down from this spot where these two smaller rivers meet to form this large river. Here is the location of my brother's town, Altamaha - the town being named after the Altamaha River that you see there on the map. But, of course, the town is not on the map. The map was made before the town ever existed."

"An unusual map, indeed. I've often thought to ask you about it."

"Ah, it is a long story, Isbister. I promise to tell you about it sometime."

Mister Benjamin and Alexander Kennedy Isbister were in Rye. They were waiting for Count Kojevenekoff. The three were to have their annual meeting to discuss the operations of the cheese factory in France. All three had heavily

## Disorderly Notions

invested in the factory and it proved to be a successful venture. The fur deal had failed.

Thirteen years earlier, back in 1871 when Mister Benjamin had returned to London from his trip to France, he found a seriously ill Liberté Bakunin. It had been consumption, and a chronic case it was. The doctor had told her that she would not live long unless she moved to a warmer, dryer climate, away from the London fog. That was when Mister Benjamin had bought the house in Rye. Although it had cost him considerably more than the pint of whisky and a night with a whore for whom the previous owner had originally bargained, he had acquired it for a reasonable sum. Along with the house had come the abandoned shipyard, its dock and old, wooden warehouses and, yes, the Martello Tower.

Just as the doctor had said, the new location allowed Liberté to live, and the move even improved her health. Liberté was not allowed to exert herself, so they hired a housekeeper, a Scottish lady by the name of Cross, whose duty was not only to care for the house, but to look after Liberté and Mister Benjamin's son, Michael, who was eleven.

The three of them lived a happy, quiet life there in Rye. Liberté spent much of her time tending to her garden and playing the piano. Michael was attending school at Saint Andrew's in Rye. When Mister Benjamin was not in Rye, he was in London where he lived like a bachelor, frequenting the dining and billiard rooms of the Junior Athenaeum Club. Next to Liberté's and Michael's company, Mister Benjamin preferred the company he kept in the billiard room. He still needed male companionship.

Infrequently, Mister Benjamin would try a case, but then only as a favor for an old friend. For some years now, he had been working on a revised version of his text on the laws of international trade and at times would sit up late in the parlor writing. Mister Benjamin traveled to Paris as seldom as he could. His wife and daughter knew nothing of his life in Rye. Were someone to tell them, they would not have believed it anyway.

The Count arrived. Missus Cross, who did not like the Count, or any other foreigner for that matter, showed him in. She was not rude, though she revealed her resentment when she served him tea. The Count had grown old, but hadn't they all? Yet, while the Count and Isbister were frail, Mister Benjamin, though gray and a bit stooped, remained robust.

"So, happy to hear about your friend Thompson – to hear he's doing so well," the Count said.

"Yes, his health has improved and his business flourishes."

Thompson had been released along with other political prisoners. Time had passed since the War Between the States, and Thompson had gained his freedom as a result of the American government's Amnesty Act.

"Yes, but his release and the release of the others have not stopped the Gideonites. They are as bad as ever," Mister Benjamin added, shaking his head sadly.

"The name, Gideonites, from where does it come?" Isbister asked.

"It comes from Jeroboam Gideon, the former abolitionist senator who has made it his aim to force former Confederates to taste Yankee justice. Since the Amnesty Act, they spend their time conjuring up outlandish charges that former Confederates are conspiring with each and all enemies of the Yankee Union. Thompson informs me that somehow they have got it into their heads that I am behind a plot to sabotage the imperial designs of their government on the western frontier. They have even published a pamphlet called "American Destiny," in which they allege that I have conspired with Mister Macdonald, the Canadian prime minister, claiming it was I who first advised Macdonald to build a Transcontinental Railroad for the purpose of inhibiting American expansion into British Columbia. Utterly preposterous! As if Macdonald needs advice from the likes of me! I've never laid eyes on the man. I've never even been to Canada, and I have no plans to ever visit the frigid place."

"Yes. It is also bad in my former homeland," said the Count. "In Russia, there are rumors of conspiracies and there have been many arrests. You do remember Solovyov?" the Count asked as he put his monocle to his eye and looked at Mister Benjamin. "He dined with us at my house. It was back in '71, I believe."

"Oh, Solovyov. Yes, of course, how could one forget such a fellow as Solovyov?"

"Well, the Czar's secret police have remembered him too, so it seems. They are pursuing him. But he is harmless, and has done nothing ... nothing except making himself a nuisance. Alas, it is sad, the poor chap. His health has failed and he has lost touch with reality. Although I have no idea where he is hiding, I'm sure that he has left Paris."

As they talked, Mister Benjamin heard Liberté come in from the garden. It was autumn, and she had been clearing away the dead flowers and tending to her succulents and herbs in the rockery. Her health had worsened. She had become very slight and her color was not good, but she was still beautiful. Mister Benjamin heard her open the piano bench, pull the bench out and slide it under her. She began to play and the music filled the house. The piece was Edvard Grieg's Opus 71: "Remembrance."

Mister Benjamin waited on the River Tillingham Bridge for his son to return from school. He looked at the time on his pocket watch and thought about how short the days were becoming. Soon he tired of waiting and proceeded along the road beside the river in the direction of the school. Just past the black-and-white windmill, he saw little Michael near the water's edge. With a long stick, the boy was pushing a folded paper boat into the current. Michael put a bare knee on the soggy bank and leaned out further, giving the boat a final prod. The edges of his black scholar's gown dipped into the river. The boy sensed his father's presence and turned.

"Oh, Father," he said matter-of-factly, as if his father was perpetually watching over him. "Isn't it grand? I learned it from a chum. Do you think it will sail into the Channel? Perhaps it will make it to France?"

"Ah, Michael, perhaps it will sail to Africa or even to America; it has happened before and will happen again. Chance is a wonderful thing. We should have included a note, asking your uncle in America to visit."

Mister Benjamin picked up the bag containing his son's books and with some effort, cheerfully exclaimed, "Now that the rain has stopped, we should take a stroll along the strand. There is something I need to tell you."

The boy took his father's arm and they walked along the base of the hill below the town. Following the river, they turned at the Strand, which runs alongside the marsh. The boy glanced back.

"Look, Father, my boat has gone toward the sea."

They stopped and looked at the boat as it passed the spot where the rivers converge.

"We have great tides in winter. There is probably a storm in the Channel," Mister Benjamin said to his son.

For a while they walked on, silently.

"Michael, I must tell you that your mother is very ill."

"Yes, but God will make Mummy well. This is what Missus Cross says. She says that if I pray very hard, God will make her better."

"I am afraid that Mummy will not get better."

"But I prayed. So God will make her ..."

"So, you did pray; but not even God can make her better."

It had started to rain and Mister Benjamin told Michael that they must turn back, as he had forgotten to bring along his umbrella. As they crossed River Tillingham Bridge, Mister Benjamin told his son that the doctor was expected to come to the house.

Upon their arrival home, Mister Benjamin removed his wet coat and Missus Cross informed him that the doctor had already arrived. He was in the bedroom with Liberté.

"Now come young Mikey, I have made for ye a wee gingerbread man. And there's warm buttermilk, there is."

The boy looked up at his father and then followed the housekeeper down the hall and into the kitchen. The boy had forgotten to remove his black student's gown, but no one had even noticed.

Mister Benjamin hastily draped his coat at the spot where the banister and newel met, making a convenient crevice for grasping whatever was deposited there. In having done so, he violated one of his few strict rules.

He ascended the stairs, but paused as he reached the bedroom door. As he moved to grasp the knob, the door opened and the doctor stepped out.

"She is resting. I have given her a sedative, but I don't believe she will sleep long, for the next attack will wake her," he said, pulling at his gray whiskers and looking Mister Benjamin straight in the eyes.

"She suffers badly, yes?"

"Yes - terribly. The right lung is filling fast and the left one is useless. It will get worse. I am sorry, my dear Mister Benjamin. There is nothing else I can do." He shook his head sadly. "But send for me, if you wish - whatever the hour. I will ..."

"Yes I know, Doctor, and I am grateful. When will she ..."

"If God is merciful, it will be soon - tonight, tomorrow? It will be no later, I should think."

Soon after sunset, Liberté awoke in a fit of coughing. Masses of phlegm blew from deep inside her. She was drowning. When she collapsed from exhaustion, falling back into Mister Benjamin's arms, he lowered her gently to the pillows. For a short time, she was still.

"Liberté, mon Chere, mon Chere," he repeated over and over as he stood looking down at her, unable to do anything except wipe the mucus from her mouth and gown and smooth her matted hair.

## Disorderly Notions

She wheezed and occasionally panted. Finally, she was quiet and he moved to a chair beside the bed. Numbed, he looked at her and for a moment felt as if he was hovering – watching himself watching his Liberté. Everything was in sharp focus, as if it were a world seen for the first time; but it was a world that had been turned inside out. Her color was almost white – white with a purplish-green tint – and her breathing was short. From time to time, she gasped for air. For a moment, he looked not at her, but at his Liberté laughing in the garden, along the strand in Rye, in Regency Park and then at Coventry Gardens in London. Then he looked at the wilted flowers beside her bed as she gasped for air – for breath: "To take into the air my quiet breath ... upon the midnight with no pain ... Thou wast not born for death ..." He closed his eyes, slumped in his chair and sighed.

Again, she coughed and gasped; then she began to kick the covers. Mister Benjamin reached for her and she locked herself to him, gripping him as would a drowning swimmer. In an attempt to raise her so that air could more easily flow into her flooding lungs, he attempted to free himself; but as he tried, she loosened her grip and began to thrash, gasping for air. Suddenly, her hands loosened and she began to kick and turn. The covers wound about her and this went on for a moment. Then she stopped. Her body quaked and she fell limp. There was a last, weak cough.

He winced looking at the terror in her dead, fixed, open eyes. For a moment he dropped his head and buried it in his hands. Then he reached over and wiped her face with a cotton ball. He put his hand on her forehead and brought it down gently, closing Liberté's startled eyes.

Missus Cross was the only person in Rye who knew that Liberté was not really Mister Benjamin's widowed niece, and that Michael was not a fatherless child. No questions were asked when arrangements were made for the burial. No one had ever thought it odd that Michael had always referred to Mister Benjamin as "Father." They considered it normal for a nephew to think of a loving uncle who had assumed a fatherly role to call him such.

The interment – as it was called – had been held in unconsecrated ground in the cemetery beside Saint Mary's Church, since Liberté had never attended their church. Except for the mandatory graveside rites, there had been no ceremony – none other than the private one held by Missus Cross and God when she had pleaded with Him to have mercy on Liberté's soul. Missus Cross often prayed for the family. While she always had known that something about them was amiss, she had gone along with the couple's charade. After all, despite the illegitimate coupling, her employers had always provided Missus Cross with her scones and butter. What Missus Cross had never suspected was that Mister Benjamin was a Jew, the only Jew to whom she had ever spoken being the green grocer on Mermaid Street from whom she begrudgingly bought shallots and potatoes. Had she known, she would have quit on the spot. In general, Missus Cross was pleased with her employment. She was paid well, most of which went to the evangelical church down the street. And besides, God would figure it all out.

The crowd that had assembled in the church yard had been small. Isbister had come from London and Sir Joseph from Kent. There had been the doctor, the undertaker and the green grocer. Little Michael had stood lost between Mister Benjamin and Missus Cross. There were also a few others lurking about the shadows of the burial – people who seem to show up at every funeral. Mister Benjamin had known none of these people and had hardly noticed them, except for a man standing among them. The man had rodent-like features, which Mister Benjamin could see beneath the man's black hat. The vicar had stood at the head of the wet hole and read from the prayer book:

"For we brought nothing into this world, and it is certain we can carry nothing out ... For a thousand years in thy sight are but as yesterday when it is past ... Thou carriest them away as with a flood ... Teach us to number our days ..."

That day, water had fallen from the sky. It had fallen on the gravestones, the spire of the church and the walls of the ancient town. The rain had fallen on the bare trees and the lacy evergreen hedges, and it had darkened the gray stucco of Benjamin House. It had wet the brown garden and had fallen on the fallow meadow behind. It had seeped into the red brick of the Martello Tower and had blown into the hole on its side where there was a window once. It had fallen on the windmill and the Tillingham and Rother bridges, had leaked through the rotting roofs and had seeped into the old boards of the warehouses at the abandoned shipyard. The rain had fallen on their black umbrellas, had splattered the mourners' shoes and had fallen into the muddy grave, bouncing on the brown board of the casket. It had poured down the cobbled stones of Mermaid Street and the hill upon which sat the town of Rye.

## Disorderly Notions

It had rained on the strand beside the marsh and on the rivers. With the tide – quick and high – the rain had been carried out into the boundless sea.

For many nights, Mister Benjamin had been unable to sleep and wandered about the house like a ghost. Time after time, he thought he could bear neither to look at Liberté's piano in the hall nor to walk in the garden behind the house. But late at night, as he stumbled about in his dressing gown, trying to refrain from the cigars the doctor had told him to quit smoking, he had found himself opening the mahogany top of the piano and looking at the ivory keys that still revealed the prints of Liberté's fingers and then stepping into the dark along the stones where she had stepped in the rockery.

Little Michael had returned to school, but in a few days his Christmas holiday began. Whenever his father tried to talk with him, he merely answered in a monotone, "Yes, Father," and otherwise remained silent.

Missus Cross was unusually quiet too. Mister Benjamin decided that she had been talking with God. But then, for Mister Benjamin, the whole house – the whole world rather – had become silent.

On a bright morning, after a telegram had arrived, Mister Benjamin went into the kitchen. Missus Cross was singing a hymn about Zion and scrubbing a pot. He asked her to come into the parlor.

"Please, do sit, my dear Missus Cross. Our plans have changed. First, I will not be going with you and Michael to Sir Joseph's for Christmas; but the two of you will go just as planned. I have business here to which I must attend. Next, I want you to deliver a letter to Mister Isbister in London. This, of course, will give you the opportunity to visit your brother there. Here is Mister Isbister's card. Please, when you arrive at Victoria station, give this card to the driver and he will take you to Balfour Street. You need not return until next week. Mister Isbister will be expecting the letter, for I will telegram ahead. Can you leave immediately?"

"Well ... yes. Yes, sir."

"Here is some money. This will cover all your expenses. A train leaves around noon. You will return next Thursday and immediately leave for Kent with Michael."

When the housekeeper left, Mister Benjamin composed the letter.

December 17, 1884
Rye, East Sussex

My dear Isbister,
    Count Kojevenekoff has written. The letter was posted Geneva, but it is doubtful he is actually there. I am sorry to say that there is bad news. He is being pursued by the Czar's secret police. It seems someone has sabotaged our cheese factory. The last large shipment to Russia was poisoned, and I am afraid some people have died. I presume the anarchists are again up to their old tricks, but it is we who have been blamed, along with the Count. Considering the gravity of this situation, Kojevenekoff warns us that we should take every precaution. He suggests we go into hiding; however, I think I have a better plan. I refuse to further disrupt my son's life or to live as a fugitive. The latter I have done before and will never do so again. The plan I suggest is for us to hire a bodyguard. If you agree, then you should be able to find adequate protection for us. There are several agencies in London. Sir Joseph is, at this moment, in his London offices. He will direct you to the proper people at Scotland Yard. There you can procure references.
    Please advise me by telegram, but be sure the message is sufficiently cryptic. I urge you to act with haste and caution. These people are fanatics.
    I know you will reward Missus Cross for her trouble.
    I remain yours sincerely,
    Benjamin

As he signed and sealed the letter, he heard Missus Cross in the hall. He opened the door and saw her standing there with her bag.
    "I am ready, sir," she said from under her black hat.
    "Good! And thank you ever so much, Missus Cross. Here is the letter."

Four days later, as Mister Benjamin sat in the parlor trying with little success to write his text on international trade law, he heard a rap on the door. He rose, walked into the hall and opened it.
    "Beg your pardon, sir, but might you be Mister Judah P. Benjamin?"
    The man had fair, reddish skin and looked to be in his fifties. He wore a brown wool suit under a black-and-white, herring-boned top coat. In a humble pose, he held a derby in his hands.

## Disorderly Notions

"I am Lawrence O'Dougal from the Clawson Security Agency. A Mister A.K. Isbister ..." His accent was Irish.

"Oh yes, Mister O'Dougal, I have received Mister Isbister's telegram. I have been expecting you. Please do come in. Let me take your coat."

They went into the parlor and closed the door. Mister Benjamin did not want Michael to overhear. He sat across from the agent and read his resume.

"So you were in India?"

"Yes, sir. A sergeant, I was, in The Queen's Own Hussars. There for eight years, as you can see. Arrived there in '58."

"So, you were there during the Mutiny then - the Indian Mutiny ... 1858?"

"Yes, sir. Those Indians are savages."

Carefully, Mister Benjamin explained to the agent the complexities of international intrigue and the gravity of his situation. When he was satisfied that the man understood, he asked:

"Alright then, now that my protection is your responsibility, what shall we do? I want you to explain this to me and then it will be I who shall take the orders."

O'Dougal told Mister Benjamin that he was to remain with him at all times. Since the house will contain only himself and Mister Benjamin by the following day, it will be more easily secured. Then he asked to inspect the premises.

Mister Benjamin went into the kitchen and, without explanation, asked Missus Cross to walk to town and arrange for a carriage to come to the house and drive her and Michael to the station. He told her to take the boy to town with her. After they had left, he escorted the agent through the house and through the abandoned shipyard. When they were standing in the garden, the agent told Mister Benjamin that he would nail all of the windows shut and that the curtains must remain drawn at all times. The doors were to remain locked.

"What is this, sir - this tower here?"

"The old Martello Tower - built during the days of Napoleon. They thought he would invade, you know; but thanks to Lord Wellington, and the grace of Fortuna, it never happened."

"Lord ..."

"Lord Wellington."

"Oh. For a minute there I thought you were speakin' of the Lord himself. The Lord God in heaven, I mean - Jesus."

"No. I'm speaking of the hero of the battle of Waterloo."

"Waterloo?" The agent asked, but before the astounded Mister Benjamin could reply, the agent continued. "I've heard of that, but I'm afraid, sir, that I don't know so much about the olden times."

Mister Benjamin marveled at the man's ignorance, but let it pass.

The carriage arrived. Mister Benjamin kissed his son and gave Missus Cross a bag containing three wrapped gifts: a scarf for her, a silver goblet for Sir and Lady Hawley and a wooden sailboat for Michael. As the carriage crossed the River Tillingham Bridge and went up the hill, around the bend and out of sight, Mister Benjamin felt emptiness creep into him.

Later that day, Mister Benjamin and the agent walked to town. Mister Benjamin had been instructed that they were to buy enough provisions to last a week. When they arrived at the tobacconist's on Mermaid Street, Mister Benjamin purchased a box of cigars and O'Dougal bought three editions of the Police Gazette. Just the kind of rubbish I would expect him to read, Mister Benjamin thought. They had to hire a carriage to get the bags of provisions to the house.

Night fell and the agent cooked beef, potatoes and cabbage. They sat at the kitchen table and ate silently. Mister Benjamin offered Madeira wine, but the man refused, saying that his agency forbids it while on duty and that he does not drink anyway.

After they finished, Mister Benjamin insisted on washing the pots and dishes; he smiled to himself as he recalled a day long ago when he had been mistaken for a sailboat's scullion. Meanwhile, O'Dougal was given a hammer to nail the windows shut.

The days passed. Although they had little to say to one another, Mister Benjamin tried to remain cheerful and cordial. However banal O'Dougal may be as a man, Mister Benjamin told himself, he is now in my house and therefore a guest, employed or otherwise. They spent what was for Mister Benjamin sad holidays, as his heart was heavy because his Liberté has flown away and he knew that little Michael was so unhappy.

On the evening of Boxing Day – the day after Christmas – Mister Benjamin and the agent sat at the table across from each other in the studio. Mister Benjamin was reading a book written by Defoe about the smuggling that takes place around Rye and the Romney Marsh. O'Dougal leafed through a

Police Gazette. Mister Benjamin was in his dressing gown; O'Dougal was in his shirt sleeves.

"Tell me, Agent O'Dougal, what was it like during the Indian Mutiny?"

"Excuse me, sir?"

"The Mutiny in India."

"Oh that, sir. Well, it was bad. Bad for them at least. We had to lay waste the land. We taught the rebels a lesson. Really licked 'em, we did."

O'Dougal returned to his magazine. Mister Benjamin rose and excused himself. After a few minutes, Mister Benjamin returned and sat in his chair facing the agent.

"Tell me, Agent O'Dougal, for I cannot remember, who was the Queen's viceroy during that time - during the time of the Mutiny in 1858?"

"Roy who, sir? I am afraid I don't know the man."

Mister Benjamin reached inside his dressing gown and from his vest pulled out his C.S.A. service revolver. He cocked it and rested his hand on the table, pointing it at O'Dougal's rodent nose.

"You blackguard. Ah ha, you are but Sergeant O'Dougal, if that is your name. But I do know that you were a sergeant - a sergeant with the invading army of William T. Sherman in 1865. We met in Georgia at a muddy creek near Milledgeville."

"What is this, sir? I know nothing ..."

"Let me help you. Your drunken men had stolen a skinny, lame cow, about which you were quite unhappy. You took your pistol and placed it behind the cow's left ear and fired. The animal fell into the creek and a woman appeared with her starving daughter and butchered the cow, which they proceeded to eat raw."

"But ..."

"Quiet or I'll make a dead cow of you. If you deny it, that denial will be the last words you ever utter. I will do it, but I would prefer not. Do you remember two men in a buckboard pulled by a mule?"

"Uh, yes. Yes, sir."

"So, do you admit it then?"

"Yes, but that was so long ago and ..."

"For whom do you work?"

"I am an agent for the Gideons, sir."

"And what could they possibly want from me. As you were saying, it has been such a long time. You can't arrest me. The Amnesty - remember?"

"Oh, not arrest, sir. A confession, that's all they want."

"A confession?"

"Yes, sir. I'll show you. Can I get my case there?"

"O'Dougal, or whatever your name might be, why don't you rise and bring the case to me. And do it slowly"

He brought the leather case over and Mister Benjamin instructed him to place it on the table and return to his chair. Keeping the pistol trained between O'Dougal's eyes, Mister Benjamin opened the case. Inside were four items: a sealed envelope, the man's phony resume, an open ticket for a steamer from Holyhead to New York and a Confederate service revolver just like the one Mister Benjamin was pointing at the agent.

"Where did you get the pistol?"

"Georgia, sir. Took it as a souvenir, but it's the best pistol I ever did shoot. And in the envelope is the confession, sir."

Mister Benjamin handed the envelope to him. "Read it."

O'Dougal shakily stumbled through the words:

"I, Judah Philip Benjamin, hereby do confess to conspiring against the national interests of the United States of America and her people. Specifically, I hereby acknowledge my role in engaging in activities pertaining to the construction of the Transcontinental Railroad across British North America, an activity that has inhibited the God-given destiny of the United States of America to expand her principles of life, liberty and the pursuit of happiness throughout the world. Signed Judah Philip Benjamin, formally Secretary of State of the Rebel Republic of 1861-1865."

"You people always have had a way of attending to the business of others, a desire to turn everyone into a likeness of yourselves and an uncanny inability to forget, much less to forgive. But it is I who gives the orders now. After all, this is my house. When I tell you to do so, I want you to rise and pick up that lamp. Disobey my orders and I shall not hesitate to kill you."

With one hand, Mister Benjamin opened the chamber of O'Dougal's pistol and removed the cartridges. Carefully and slowly, he replaced two of them to its chamber. Keeping the agent's pistol trained on his face, he emptied his own pistol of all but two cartridges. O'Dougal shook and looked on silently.

"What are you going to do, sir?" he finally asked.

"We, O'Dougal, are going to play a gentleman's game. A game guided not by the rules of calculation, but by the caprice of the goddess Fortuna."

"Sorry, sir, but I don't understand."

## Disorderly Notions

"Of course you don't. Tell me one thing, how did you manage to get yourself into my house?"

"Well, sir, I had help. Your housekeeper; I talked with her about you and she helped me."

"I'm sure you told her that confession was good for the soul, and then she was happy to oblige."

"She is a very righteous woman. Yes, she cooperated for what she said was your own good."

"Yes, I see."

Mister Benjamin chuckled, rising and keeping the pistol trained on O'Dougal's nose. He walked to the south side of the room, pushed aside the table on which the stuffed owl sat and bumped the wall with his knee. A portion of the wall moved and he stood before an opening in which there was a dark hole.

"Now pick up that lamp and come here. SLOWLY!"

When the beams of light shined into the hole, O'Dougal saw a few stairs and then a passage way. It was a tunnel.

"Go down," Mister Benjamin had ordered him. "Do exactly as I say or you'll end up like that cow. The pistol is trained on the spot behind your left ear."

After they walked for perhaps a hundred paces, the tunnel intersected with another tunnel and then it became larger and higher and they could easily stand up without bending. Finally, there was a metal door.

"Give me the lamp. SLOWLY! Open the door widely."

The rusty door creaked and O'Dougal had to use the force of his body to open it.

"Wider. Now, go in and do it slowly."

They were inside a cavern, it seemed, but then the light settled and O'Dougal could see that they were standing in a large, dusty and empty wooden building.

"What are you doing?"

"Quiet! I am going to place the lamp between us and then you will walk until I tell you to stop. Go, or I'll blow off the front of your head."

Mister Benjamin placed the lamp on the floor and O'Dougal did just what he was told.

"Stop! I'm going to throw the pistol you stole across the floor. There are two rounds in the chamber and there are two in mine. We are going to have a duel. When I slide the pistol towards you, you may pick it up and fire at will. If you wound me and I miss you, then you must kill me. If such should occur but you are gravely wounded and wish to die honorably by your own hand, then you shall discover two bullets in the pocket of my waistcoat."

"And what if ... what if we both miss?"

"Ah, in that unlikelihood, I shall sign your confession."

They both took aim. Mister Benjamin had the sight right between O'Dougal's beady eyes, but Mister Benjamin was determined not to fire first. Then O'Dougal shot out the lamp.

Three days later, when the heap of charred timbers and twice-baked brick had been cool enough, they found Mister Benjamin's remains in the rubble. They were able to identify him by his C.S.A. pistol. Mister Isbister notified Mister Benjamin's family in France of the unfortunate accident and arranged for Mister Benjamin's remains to be shipped to Paris. Isbister then told his own bodyguard that his services were no longer needed, and he left for a lengthy visit with his relatives in Canada. Little Michael was adopted by Sir Joseph. Because Lady Hawley could not tolerate Missus Cross's sourness, she was paid well and dismissed.

# *ARRIVAL*

As he sprang from the train, he glanced at the sign hanging from the canopy at the station; as usual, it read "Rye." He put the strap of Mo's laptop case on his shoulder, picked up his bag and bounded up the hill toward Mermaid Street. You've done it, Hambone! You've squared the circle, he told himself. Hamilton smiled at the thought and at the bright morning. Reaching the top of the hill, he turned down Mermaid Street toward the river and without breaking his stride, crossed it.

As he walked beside the yacht basin along Winchelsea Road, he could hear the blued metal box bouncing in his bag to the quick time of his pace. He passed between the green hedges and stood at the ancient black door. Yes, he had arrived at Benjamin House.

Hamilton started to knock, but then hesitated. He wondered if they were up yet and instinctively extended his arm to look at his watch. His wrist was bare; the memory of hurling the watch into the sea on the ferry somewhere between Calais and Dover made him laugh. He imagined the ugly piece of plastic with its hidden, dead chip floating among other filth and flotsam in the Channel. What the hell, he told himself, so what if I wake them. He knocked, knocked again and then shouted:

"Hey! Rodger, Rodger the Dodger! You and my cousin get your lazy arses up. It's late!"

He knocked again. Finally, he heard someone coming down the stairs. The door opened and there, in half-zipped jeans and his old, green wool sweater was Rodger.

"Well, if it isn't the Red Rider! Thought you would have turned into a yogi by now. Perhaps you have. My God, ole boy, your hair is almost white. And where are your whiskers? We tried to locate you, but we couldn't find you. Why didn't you write? And where's Andy?"

"Oh, the ole rooster decided to go on back to Seven Bridges after all – flew from Moscow."

"Moscow?"

"Yeah, Moscow – long story. I'll tell you later."

They moved through the hall and stood in Rodger's cluttered studio.

"So, Moscow?"

"Yeah. Andy didn't want to go to Krautland with me, so he flew from Moscow to Helsinki and then on back to the States. Go tell Jud to get his lazy arse up."

"Hamilton, sit down," Rodger said.

His look told Hamilton that he should do as Rodger had ordered. He plopped down in one of the green wingbacks beside the fireplace.

"Something wrong, Rodger?"

"Yes, Hamilton, I am afraid so. Hamilton, Jud is dead."

"What? Jud ... is dead?"

"Yes. He died in the Channel. He's presumed drowned. They never found him."

Hamilton, put his hands to his face and leaned back, allowing the chair to engulf him. In a moment, he sat up straight, lifted his head and wiped a wet cheek with the back of his hand.

"When?"

"The first of January – in a storm. He took the dingy out on the quick tide."

"And was swept into the Channel?"

"Yes, well, yes and no. Hamilton, Jud did sail into the Channel and out into a storm. The French coast guard found the boat washed up on a beach near Dieppe."

"So, if they didn't find him, there's still a ..."

"No, Hamilton, there is no chance. I went over there myself. All the sails were ripped off. No trace of anything except shredded sailcloth, broken lines and a battered hull." Then Rodger gave a little laugh. "The crazy bugger was using a spinnaker. Under those conditions, it was suicide. Normally, he would have known better. Spinnakers were never made for those little boats. You remember that we always did it just for the hell of it, but always in calm seas. My God! These were twelve to fifteen foot swells, and the wind was up to fifty knots! The sheets probably blew off before he even got into the Channel. It was crazy – just crazy."

"Why didn't somebody stop him?"

"Stop him? I was asleep when he left. Nobody, including the police, has been able to figure out how he got into the yacht basin. It was thoroughly locked, and you've seen that nine-foot fence with the barbed wire. There's an inside fence too, and it's electrified at night. How he got in is a mystery to everyone."

"Jesus! Why would he want to do a thing like that – yes, it's plainly suicide."

"No, not really. That's not how I see it at least. He was drunk on his Black Jack – New Year's Eve – and Colin from the yacht basin was over. Ole Calvin, the mayor and others dropped by too. We had spent most of the afternoon at the Mermaid.

"I get the picture," Hamilton said, wiping his eyes.

"Well, you get some of it. The day after you and Andy left, Jud borrowed the Rover and drove to Brighton to do research in the archives at the university. Yes, I know, he often did that, but that night, when he returned, he was quiet – preoccupied. He was often like that, but this was different. I could tell that something was wrong."

Hamilton looked up at him. "The book he was trying to write on Judah P. was not going well. By the way, that's what was in my package," Hamilton choked.

"Your what?"

"Oh, you remember. You and Jud gave us gifts wrapped in Christmas paper. You gave us the red Reebok shoes. Remember?" Hamilton stuck out his now well-worn shoe. "These," he said.

"Yes, of course I remember," Rodger answered.

"Well, my present from Jud was his Judah P. manuscript – if one could call it that. A lot of it was in poetry, but it was mostly notes and scribble. It was a real mess. He had put it in that metal box of his with some other stuff. I thought he wanted me to try and straighten the manuscript out. There was a note to that effect. And I tried."

"No. I doubt that had anything to do with whatever had come over him. A few days after he had returned so bloody depressed from Brighton – this would have been the thirtieth of December – I thought he might need some time alone, and I had some things to see about down in Winchelsea, so I left for the day. When I returned, his behavior was even more bazaar. He acted manic, his eyes looked funny, and he was as drunk as a lord. He kept saying to me, 'Look, ole Dodger, it's in the "V"; the answer is in the "V" – the "V."' Was he talking about the female sex organ, the genitalia?"

"Well, maybe."

"He just kept telling me that there was gold at this 'V.'"

"Well, some think that it's gold. He could have been talking about the forks of the two rivers that flow together to make the Altamaha in Georgia. I remember him referring to that river as 'the pussy of the world,' so you could be right about that part. But that was long ago, when we were teenagers, and that kind of thing was always on our minds," Hamilton said.

"God! Was he ever pickled. And when I would ask him to explain, he just kept laughing and saying he'd show me soon enough – when he had figured out the question to the answer. He kept on talking in riddles like that. Finally, he passed out and I put him there on the sofa. The next afternoon, he got up and we went to the Mermaid, joined our party, and the next day he was gone. And that's all there is to tell."

"We'll have to phone Andy," Hamilton said. "Oh, do I dread that."

"Yes, I know. He will be devastated. Everyone else was contacted, though there are only a few. I called that place in Georgia. The ..."

"The Seven Bridges near Macon."

"Yes. I called several times, but they were no bloody help. They were rude. Said they had no idea where Andy was. They even told me not to call them anymore. If you like, you can try for yourself later. There's lots of time; he's dead. For now, you just need to get used to the fact that he's gone."

"I'll never get used to that," Hamilton said, tears streaming from his eyes. "He was my cousin and my best and oldest friend. I really loved him."

A week passed. Hamilton had told Rodger all about the journey, about how he had met the Dikshits – and, yes, how Dikshit was an old Brahman name – and about Starman. They decided to call Oxford and invite Starman down to Rye. Finally, with a quaking soul, Hamilton told Rodger about Mo: how he had loved her and how she had vanished with their baby in the sky lands of Tibet. Because Rodger was the kind of man who must suffer for everyone, Hamilton could feel Rodger's pain as he told the story. By then, they both were beyond tears.

Hamilton telephoned Starman at Oxford and two days later, Starman arrived. He was wearing the same blue seersucker suit he had been wearing when Hamilton had first met him at the New Year's Eve party in Singapore. One afternoon, when Starman was jogging in the meadow behind the house, Rodger told Hamilton:

"Yes, I see what you meant. He is one of the most elegant men I have ever met. He is like a god; he shines."

The three of them took it easy. They went about the town, ate at the Mermaid, walked the paths around Rye, hiked up to Winchelsea, and even did some fishing. Rye was in bloom. It was May and then June. They spoke about all that had happened since Hamilton and Andy's departure just before the astonishing year of 1989. Along with the many events of their long journey, so much else had happened that year. The last Soviet troops had fled Afghanistan; the Solidarity Movement had swept Poland; Salman Rushdie was still in hiding, but Khomeini had just died and his zealous followers had inadvertently dumped his naked body with its hideously huge schlong from his coffin for millions to see on television sets across the planet. Starman told Hamilton about an article he had read about in *The National Interest*, which was published in America about the end of history. Hamilton knew nothing about it and did not seem to care.

"Who wrote it?" Hamilton asked.

"The name is Japanese, I believe: Fukuyama, or something like that. Yes, that's it, Francis Fukuyama."

"Never heard of her," Hamilton replied.

One evening, before dark, Rodger, Hamilton and Starman sat in the studio watching the BBC news on television.

"My God!" Rodger said, leaning forward in his chair and pointing to the screen. "Look at that statue! I can't believe it."

"The Statue of Liberty? This can't be!" Starman replied, almost whispering. "Those young people ... those students parading around right in the middle of

Beijing! We were there, weren't we, Hamilton?" Starman said, turning to the window where Hamilton stood preoccupied.

Hamilton was gazing out into the evening light and through a gap in the holly hedge. He was looking at the yacht basin across Winchelsea Road, trying to figure out how Jud could have managed to get inside.

"Look at it, Hamilton!" Starman continued. "And now there's a tank with a guy in front of it! Look Hamilton! What on earth does this mean?"

"It means that we've won. That's what it means," Rodger replied.

"Well, it might mean that it's over," Hamilton said, turning from the window and walking closer to the television. "Yes, it does mean that it's over, but it damned sure does not mean that we've won. Not like you mean it, ole Dodger."

"And what in bloody hell are you saying? You're talking in riddles like Jud," Rodger said, annoyed.

"Okay, Rodger, yes, we've won; but then, yes and no. Yes because this communism business may really be dead, but its ghost in other forms may be resurrected. I think what will be called our victory will piss a lot of people off. Yeah, to speak about it in this way – to say 'we've won' – is going to make people angry because they know it's true. Our victory will be seen as a threat," Hamilton said, and yawned.

"Okay, I get it," Rodger replied.

"Starman do you remember seeing all those useless Chinese fans?" Hamilton asked. "Well, they may be put to good use."

"Yes, I remember, but I don't get your point."

"Actually, it was Andy who pointed this out to me. We were at the Forbidden City looking at all these fans. Andy said that he had no idea when or how it would happen, but that there were just too many contradictions and that shit was going to hit the fan. Maybe what we're watching is just the beginning. Tomorrow, life will be different."

For a moment they were silent as they continued to watch the unfolding drama on the TV screen.

"Well, I'm making a big change," Starman said, in an attempt to change the subject. "I'm going home."

"Yes, you told us, you'll be finished at Oxford in a few weeks," Hamilton replied, not interested.

"No, that is not my point. I'm not returning to Virginia. I'm going home to Alabama. There are some things I need to find out, and besides, I've decided that's where I belong. Think I have a job teaching English and coaching football – a high school in Opelika."

"Really – football? Oh, you mean that ghastly American football?" Rodger joked.

"Yes, that is what I mean and it is my sport, thank you very much."

"This sure is a surprise. I guess you know what you're doing," Hamilton said, distracted.

Rodger told Starman the story about the two items in the house remaining from the days of Judah P. Benjamin – the scarlet silk map in its gilded frame and the stuffed owl under the glass bell. The subject drifted to other parts of the room and Rodger told Starman all about the mock-Vemeer – the seventeenth-century Flemish painter whose costume Rodger wore in the picture hanging over the mantel. Then Rodger asked Starman about the thesis he was writing about Henry Fielding, and Starman confessed that the thesis was not going well. He had decided that he was not really interested in somebody who wrote about the sexual exploits of roguish, white gentleman after all.

Hamilton, who had been sitting on the sofa reading the short story "October Ferry" by Malcolm Lowry, returned to the window and stared at the yacht basin through the hole in the holly hedge. Again he was wondering how Jud could have got into that yacht basin.

"Starman, do you remember Dicky telling us about a tunnel that used to be under Benjamin House. He said it led from the house to the river and was once used for smuggling? No, of course, you wouldn't. He was telling me and Andy when we first met him in the airport in Moscow. We had not met you then."

"Well," Rodger replied, "there once was a tunnel. But it was filled in long ago. Funny, Hambone, I would have thought you'd known about it. Guess the subject just never came up. Look," he said.

Rodger walked over to the mantle, removed the large painting from the wall and placed it on the sofa. He returned to the mantle and pushed the wall above it with the flat of both hands. Then he backed up and pushed again, this time using his weight. A panel on the left side of the fireplace rose, revealing a large opening.

"Have to get a torch," Rodger said, heading toward the kitchen.

He returned with a flashlight. They all peered into the gloom, and then Rodger flicked on the light and directed the beam into the dark hole. It was filled with garbage: cans, shoes, metal pipes, broken furniture and what seemed like hundreds of bottles. There was a coating of dust and a lace of cobwebs over everything. At the top on the heap, with its nose stuck into the air, was a rat.

"You see all those bottles? The story is that they are from my grandfather, Michael; he drank himself to death. You can see where the tunnel is caved in." Rodger pointed the beam of light to the back of the hole where there was a pile of rock. "After my grandfather died, my grandmother had the tunnel destroyed; but it had been sealed at the other end before that. Think grandmother still worried that someone somehow might be able to come underground and harm her. Well, that's it. So much for the tunnel," Rodger announced.

He pushed the top of the panel behind the mantel, and the other panel – the one on the left wall – began to close.

"So, are you sure that's it? Because if the tunnel was usable, it might explain how Jud got in the yacht basin. Look. I'm going to call Dicky. He knows about such things. Do you mind?" Hamilton asked Rodger.

"No, of course not; but I'm sure about the tunnel. Call him anyway and invite him over. We'll go to the Mermaid for dinner. I want to meet him. Tell him that I would be pleased to meet him."

Hamilton called Brighton and the old professor answered. Yes, he did have some vague recollection as to where he ran across the information about the tunnel.

"Yes," he said, "I think it's in an article about the smuggling during the wool excise. Oh, perhaps it was later. Anyway, it seems there was a map. I will go to the library and dig it up."

Hamilton told him about Mo's death and the old man was shaken. He was so upset that he had to pause and catch his breath. He said to expect him the next day around noon. Jeri will not be with him; she was in California attending her sister's wedding, or so he said. Dicky did not want to talk about Jeri.

The next day, Doctor Dikshit did not show up until after six. When his old Vauxhall pulled between the hedges and into the yard, they were relieved. They had all been concerned that there might have been an accident.

"I am so sorry to be late, but these motorways! I took the wrong turn and found myself in Canterbury, and then, when I finally got to Rye, I couldn't find the house. But this nice chap at the yacht basin helped me."

He stepped from the car. He wore his dark-blue pinstriped suit and his blue polka-dotted bow tie. There was a sad smile on his brown face. It seemed strange for Hamilton to see him there in Rye and not in Singapore or India. Having thought that, Hamilton had an odd sensation that there had been no Dicky in those places; Dicky really belonged to England.

Hamilton introduced him to Rodger and they all talked for a moment in the yard. Then Hamilton took Dicky's bag and briefcase, and they went inside.

"I have the article about the tunnels, and yes, there is a map."

"We'll look at all of it later after we've eaten. First, professor, I'll show you your bedroom. You'll want to wash up before dinner," Rodger said.

"Do call me Dicky; everyone does," he told Rodger as they mounted the stairs.

At the Mermaid Inn, they explained to Dicky why they wanted to know about the tunnel.

"Oh my, another terrible tragedy," Dicky said as Rodger told him about Jud.

He appeared to have difficulty understanding, but he never knew Jud and, besides, nobody understood.

"Now, what did you say the name of this chap was?" Dicky asked as they finished their meal.

"His name was Jud – Judah, Judah Anubis Benjamin," Hamilton answered.

"Oh yes, named after that famous ancestor Judah P. Benjamin. But that other name – Anubis. I know that ..." Dicky replied.

"Wait a minute, Anubis, that's Andy's name too. Andy is short for Anubis," Rodger said.

"And would you want to be called Anubis?" Hamilton interrupted, laughing.

"No, but I am called 'Dikshit.'"

They all laughed.

"Anubis is a family name. There was a classicist in the family – Judah P.'s brother." Hamilton told them. "He gave his son the middle name Anubis, and the name just made its way through the generations, the way things do."

"Yes," Dicky said, "now I remember. Anubis was an Egyptian god. He was mediator between the upper and lower worlds and had a dog's head. He was like the Greek god Hermes in that he guided people to the underworld. Funny, if I'm not mistaken, this was the name that appeared on the list in the East Sussex archives that one must sign upon receipt of documents. Yes, I'm sure of it. I wrote my own name just below it," Dicky said. Then he added, "I was thinking about it again when I was photocopying the article. Anubis III – how strange."

"That's it!" Hamilton announced, getting up. "Let's go," he ordered, motioning for the waiter to come.

They quickly paid the waiter, left and caught a taxi back to Benjamin House. They were too excited to take the time to walk.

When they were in the studio, Dickey took the pages from his case and spread them out on the table.

"Here is the map," Dicky said, pointing with his little, well-kept brown finger.

The copy was good and the map was clear. Above the map was the following writing:

STRATEGIC TUNNEL
COASTAL BATTERY
MARTELLO TOWER 35
RYE, EAST SUSSEX
31st ROYAL ENGINEERS
Commanding Officer P.C. Hawley

The map showed a tunnel running from the river toward the house. The tunnel began near the present site of the yacht basin, and then it split: the smaller branch went to Benjamin House, and a larger one continued to the Martello Tower. They noticed a line drawn across the smaller, older tunnel leading to the house, indicating that it was of no use to the Royal Marines and showing that they had erected some sort of barrier blocking it. They could read the small script when Rodger held a magnifying glass over the map; it read, "STEEL DOOR."

"That's it. That's how he did it. That's how Jud got into the yacht basin," Hamilton announced.

"Well, maybe," Starman replied, "if the tunnel is still there."

"There's only one way to find out," Rodger said. He was holding the flashlight. "Come with me. I think I know what to do."

Rodger shined the light against the side of the house as they crossed the garden.

"Hamilton, can you and Starman fetch the ladder? We'll need it to get into the window of the Martello Tower."

Starman and Hamilton brought the ladder to the tower and placed it among the vines under the window fifteen feet above them.

"Sure you want to do this Dicky?" Starman asked.

"Wouldn't miss it for the world," he replied.

"Well, if you're sure; but why don't you let me go up behind you," Starman, in his subtle way, demanded.

When they were all in the tower, Rodger moved the beam of light about the round room. He was looking for a door.

"There it is," he said, "under Starman's feet."

There was a rusted, metal trapdoor in the beam of light. Starman reached down, took the handle and lifted the creaky door. There were stone steps that led to the tunnel. They had no trouble standing, and the passage was wide enough for them to shuffle along two abreast. The air was damp, stale and cold. They followed the beam until Rodger suddenly stopped. The light had fallen on something on the floor of the tunnel, and Rodger steadied the light. It was a white, grinning skull. What looked like a bullet hole was about where the left ear would have been.

"Jesus, a bloody skeleton!"

Rodger stepped closer and the others followed.

"Hardly bloody," Starman said, proposing that it was probably the remains of a smuggler.

"No. They were here long before the marines and their tunnel, but the skeleton has been here for a long time. You can tell," Dicky answered.

At the feet were the remnants of shoe leather, and there was a belt buckle where the waist would have been. A ring was on the third finger of the left hand, and then they saw the rusty pistol. Hamilton bent down and picked it up.

"Shine it here, Dodge," he said. "My God, look at this."

Engraved across the top of the pistol was: "C.S.A. Macon 1864: 13245." Hamilton could hardly believe the thought that came into his head.

"Jud's notes – his wacky poetry. I thought he had made most of it up. There really was a duel down here. This is the man that Judah P. Benjamin shot!"

"I don't understand," Dicky said.

"I'm not sure I do either, but I'll explain later. Shine the light on the ring," Hamilton told Rodger. They squatted down and looked at the ring. It was corroded, but its detail could be recognized. It was made from a coin embossed with the picture of a mounted horseman, the initials C.S.A. and the date 1865.

"My God! Gentlemen, what you are actually looking upon are the remains of Judah P. Benjamin. The man with whom Judah P. had a duel lies in a grave at Père Lachaise in Paris. At that site is a gray stone monument – a statue of the mounted horseman, which is a copy of what you see here on this ring. Cut into the stone on the monument is the name "Judah Philip Benjamin." I'm guessing that they mistook the other man's remains for those of our Mister Benjamin. Yes, that's it! The other man was burned in the warehouse fire – the man who Judah P. shot."

"Who?" Rodger asked.

"The man Judah P. shot in the duel. Judah P. must have escaped to the tunnel. He either died of a shot from the other man's pistol or knew that he was going to suffocate from the fire and shot himself. Who knows?"

"Hamilton, whatever are you talking about?" Rodger laughed, nervously.

"Look. Rodger, pick up the belt buckle. I can see the initials from here."

"By Jove! Hamilton, you must be right. It says 'J.P.B.' right here."

"Yes, Rodger, and this is what Jud knew about. This is what Jud discovered. The skeleton lies precisely where the tunnels split. That's what he meant about the answer lying at the 'V.' Let's follow the tunnel and see how he got into the yacht basin," Hamilton replied.

At the end of the tunnel was a rusty metal door. Starman pulled at it and it stubbornly creaked open. Among the debris and charred rubble they could see through a small opening. The boats, docks and sheds that comprise the yacht basin were not a hundred yards away.

"We are under that pile of rubble on the south end of the basin," Rodger said. "You're right, Hamilton. This is how Jud got in."

As they were returning to the Martello Tower and passed the skeleton of Judah P. Benjamin, Dicky's foot hit an object on the floor next to the wall of the tunnel.

"Ah, wait. Stop. What is this? The torch, please, Rodger," Dickey said.

Rodger shined the flashlight. It was a box. Through the grime and corrosion, Hamilton imagined its original surface to have once been gun metal blue. He squatted down and opened it. One side was empty and the other contained a smaller box identical to the one Hamilton had in the house containing *Jud's Story*. Hamilton opened the smaller box and they saw neat rows of corroded gold coins – Confederate Cavaliers. They left the skeleton where it lay, but Hamilton lifted the heavy box and handed it over to Starman, who carried it under his arm as if it were a large, fat telephone book.

They sat in the studio. Rodger had brought out a bottle of Scotch and they were trying to sort out all that had just happened. Hamilton had brought out the box containing *Jud's Story* and, yes, it fit perfectly inside the larger box containing its twin. Hamilton opened the twin box, placed his manuscript on the table and began to read the part in *Jud's Story* about Judah P. Benjamin's duel with the agent. Dicky became so confused that he had to go to bed. But it was late, and Starman retired as well. The sun would soon rise. Rodger and Hamilton poured what they said would be their last drink.

"Rodger, the conjunction where those tunnels meet is not the only 'V,' and it is not the only 'V' where gold was found either. Similar gold coins also lay at the 'V' made by the confluence of two rivers that form the Altamaha. That's where Jud was going. Ole Jud was sailing home."

"Hamilton, now you have me confused; but you can explain tomorrow. Let's sit on the sofa, Hambone. We'll be more comfortable there," Rodger said.

Rodger got up and removed the painting from the sofa so that they could sit. Hamilton glanced at the painting and said to Rodger:

"Ole Dodger, that painting just reminds me of what a beautiful woman your Marti was."

"Hambone – ah, Hambone, she's in shadow, so you're not meant to identify her. And that's not Marti; that's Meg."

"Meg? Jud's Meg? I always thought that her hair was blonde."

"I can't imagine where you got that from. No, Meg's dark."

"I guess I thought she was blonde because I knew that Jud like blonde women," Hamilton said.

"Come on Hambone, blondes, brunettes, red heads, he liked all women – provided, of course, they had that soft spot between their legs, which is the qualification for belonging to the female version of *homo erectus*."

"Yeah, that spot – the 'V.' That's where the gold is buried."

"What?"

"Nothing."

"Come on, Hamilton, surely Jud told you all about Meg."

"No, he didn't. We had agreed not to talk about the women we had been married to. It was too painful and best left in the past."

After a long pause, Rodger said: "She is ... ah, was a great girl. You know she was not yet twenty-one when she and Jud got together. She really was a girl – not just young but also a bit flakey, if you know what I mean. She had been something of a student radical back in America. Styled herself a Maoist, I think. Jud quickly put an end to that nonsense. She couldn't handle him, but did he ever handle her. He loved her with a tyrannical intensity, and she would even anticipate his desires and follow them slavishly. But she was a wreck when the baby came, and Jud showed her no sympathy when she didn't want to give the baby up."

"What do you mean?"

"Oh, of course, you don't know. The baby was badly deformed. Not only was he terribly mentally deficient but physically deformed as well. He had a kind of dog-like face. Jud was adamant, and the child was put in a home in Kent."

"A home?"

"You know ... an institution."

"Against Meg's wishes?"

"Yes. Jud behaved badly, I have to say. In fact, the truth was that he was quite cruel."

"What do you mean?"

"He showed her no mercy. When she became very depressed, he became angry and abusive. But things really took a turn when, shortly thereafter, Meg turned twenty-one and the trust her deceased parents had left her became available."

"How much?"

"I don't know, but it must have been a gracious sum. Along with the trust, she also inherited documents before unknown to her. Meg had been adopted by an attorney – a Mister Pangolin and his wife. They were originally from Savannah, Jud said, but moved to somewhere in the north – a place called Providence, I think. It was where Meg was raised."

"Providence, Rhode Island?" Hamilton asked, puzzled.

"Yes, that's it. I think Jud said there had been newspaper articles about some murder trial involving both her biological parents. It seemed her natural father had committed a murder. The father went to the electric chair, and I don't remember what he said about her mother. I remember something about the welfare folks taking her away from her mother. They must have been the ones who arranged the adoption. It seems that these kind of repressed memories came back to haunt her when she read the documents."

"Oh God! Jud's notes – the clippings and the court records. Was this what she kept trying to tell me?" Hamilton muttered to himself. He dropped his head down into his hands.

"Hamilton. Are you alright?"

"Yes, please go on," Hamilton replied, composing himself.

"She had a complete breakdown and had to be hospitalized for almost a year. When she was released, she was a different person. She let Jud have exactly what he deserved – she divorced him. Meg never looked back. She married some bloke who worked for that museum in Oxford, but he later went into the family business – spice merchants. They moved to the Far East, I think."

"Yes, to Singapore."

"You are right! Oh, it's all so confusing."

"Are you telling me?"

"I actually met him – her husband. It was when he came with her on one of her trips to Kent to see the boy. They dropped by and we had tea. Nice chap. This was quite awhile ago. Jud was long gone by then. He would have already been in Canada with you."

"Tell me, did Jud ever visit the boy?"

"No, he washed his hands of the whole thing. He told me he didn't want to talk about him or about her ever again."

Hamilton slowly shook his head in disapproval. Then he walked closer to the painting, peering sharply at one particular area of its surface.

"Dodger, tell me what this is on the small canvas – the canvas that the painter is painting."

"Oh, it's just one of my little jokes. It gives us what one sees from the opposite side – a kind of mirror image. It is much clearer than the larger image in the shadow. It's difficult to notice at first, but in the miniature image you can actually make out her face. I can get us a magnifying glass, if you like."

"No, no, that's not necessary," Hamilton said. He picked up the canvas and held it in a ray of light beaming through the window.

"Here, take the glass," Rodger said, taking the picture and holding it for Hamilton.

Hamilton took the magnifying glass and held it close, peering at her face. He stopped for a moment, rubbed his eyes and then continued to stare. Hamilton's eyes were welling up with tears. He put the magnifying glass on the arm of the sofa and wiped his eyes with his sleeve. Turning and looking at Rodger, he said:

"I have no photos of her and was even wondering if I had dreamed it all up – if it all was just ... a bad dream. But now I have evidence, and it's her alright."

"Who?" Rodger asked.

"Mo ... Meg ... Margaret Rose. Mo is Meg. Meg is Mo."

"Hambone, you are talking in riddles again. Go to bed and try to sleep. Things will be different tomorrow."

"It already is tomorrow, and things are already different," Hamilton said, picking up the magnifying glass and peering again at the face in the painting. Like a small boy awaking from a long sleep, he rubbed his eyes with his fists.

"Yes, that's her," Hamilton said, looking at Rodger with a resigned yet uncanny near-smile on his face.

"Hamilton?"

"Clothed with the sun, and the moon under her feet ..."

"What does that mean?"

"Everything, ole Dodger."

"Everything?"

"Yes, everything – everything and nothing. We've squared the circle. And now we're all in the same box."

# Iguana Books
*iguanabooks.com*

**If you enjoyed *Disorderly Notions*...**
Look for other books coming soon from Iguana Books! Subscribe to our blog for updates as they happen.

iguanabooks.com/blog/

You can also learn more about Tom Darby and his upcoming work on his blog.

tomdarby.iguanabooks.com/blog/

**If you're a writer ...**
Iguana Books is always looking for great new writers, in every genre. We produce primarily ebooks but, as you can see, we do the occasional print book as well. Visit us at iguanabooks.com to see what Iguana Books has to offer both emerging and established authors.

iguanabooks.com/publishing-with-iguana/

**If you're looking for another good book ...**
All Iguana Books books are available on our website. We pride ourselves on making sure that every Iguana book is a great read.

iguanabooks.com/bookstore/

**Visit our bookstore today and support your favourite author.**

CPSIA information can be obtained
at www.ICGtesting.com
Printed in the USA
LVOW04s0929271116
514626LV00008B/413/P